HE WITHOUT YOU

Cooper's Ridge Series

Book 2

JJ Harper

JJ Harper

© J J Harper 2021

Second edition

All rights reserved. No part of this book may be reproduced or transmitted in any form or by any means, electronic or mechanical, including photocopying, recording, or by any information storage and retrieval system, without permission in writing.

This is a work of fiction. Names, characters, places or incidents are the product of the author's imagination and are used factiously, and any resemblance to any actual persons living or dead, events or locals are entirely coincidental.

The author acknowledges the trademark status and trademark owners of various products referenced in this work of fiction, which have been used without permission. The publication/ Use of these trademarks is not authorized, associated with, or sponsored by the trademark owner.

The author acknowledges all songs and lyrics are the ownership of the original artists.

All rights reserved.

Cover design by Jay Aheer at Simply Defined Art

Edited by Tanja Ongkiehong

Formatted by Brenda Wright @ Formatting Done Wright

Cover model: Ben Selleck by Wander Aguiar

Here Without You

Mallory

You never believe when someone says good-bye to you, it might actually be good-bye, as in never see, never speak to, never hear, touch, and taste again. But it happens; it happens more times than you'll ever realize. I know this because it happened to me.

"I'm off to work, Mal," Archer called to me from the hallway.

"Hold up, mister. Not so fast. I want kisses before you leave me alone." I mock-pouted at him, then pursed my lips expectantly.

"Oh, sugar, I'll always give you kisses. Come here, hot lips." He laughed and dragged me into his arms. Holding my face in his palms, he kissed me soundly. "There you go. Now I love you, and I'll see you later."

"I love you too. Be careful, Arch."

"Always." He gave me another soft kiss. "Good-bye, Mallory."

Two hours later, my life shattered around me, and I was left alone.

JJ Harper

Eighteen months earlier.

"Hey, hey! Hold up. What's the hurry?" A deep, rich, dark-brown voice called to me as I tried to dodge past the owner, clipping his shoulder. He caught my arm.

"What? Shit, I'm sorry. I'm running late, and I can't be late today." I went to move off again when he dropped his hand.

"Where are you going?" Mr. Sounds-sexy-as-fuck asked me.

"Work, and I'll lose it if I'm late," I shouted over my shoulder and darted off again down the sidewalk.

I sneaked into the kitchen of the coffee shop I worked at and dumped my bag and jacket into my locker. Phew. Just in time. I washed my hands, snatched my apron, and tying it behind my back, hurried toward the front. The line was out the door already, and I slid up to the counter to take my first order of probably hundreds today.

Eight hours making and serving coffee wasn't really what I'd had planned for my life, but when my folks had cut me off and stopped paying my tuition, I'd needed to earn enough to stay in college. My student loans helped, but it still wasn't enough to live on. I needed to keep this job. Situated in an affluent area, it was one of *the* places to get coffee. Lots of rich city kids and wealthy business people were more than happy to wait an extra few minutes to be served by the cute staff who worked here. Not that I'd put myself in that bracket. I was just happy to get what I could, like the large tips the patrons had no trouble leaving us.

The next couple of hours were crazy busy, and I served customer after customer, hardly having time to look at anything other than the espresso machine, the coffee cups, and the shaker with chocolate powder.

"Welcome to The Perfect Blend. Can I take your order?"

Instead of an answer, I got silence, followed by a chuckle. Startled, I looked up. Straight in two bright-green eyes that sparkled with mischief. Damn. It was the gorgeous guy from this morning.

"Hello again. Good to see you made it"—he peeked at my name badge—"Mallory."

I shot a glance at my boss to see if he'd heard the comment, but he was too busy gawking at the table of cute college girls to be paying attention to what went on at the counter.

"Oops, sorry." He swiped his fingers over his lips, pretending to zip his mouth shut.

"What can I get you?" I asked, trying not to stare at him. God, he was hot. I took his order—a large cappuccino, don't hold back on the foam, and two Americanos—and he moved down to pay at the cash register. My hands trembled, but I managed not to burn myself on the steaming milk. I chanced a peek around, and my heart skipped a beat. He leaned against the wall, watching me intently with eyes that hadn't lost their gleeful gleam. His blond, carefully styled hair was just the right length to grab and tug. Everything about him exuded wealth and privilege; his suit alone must've cost more than I made in a month. As I held up his coffee holder with the three cups, he sauntered back to me with a confident smirk.

"Thank you, Mallory. I'll see you around." He gave me a shit-eating grin.

"I would've thought an important guy like you would have minions to fetch your coffee for you." I laughed as hot coffee guy, as I now called him, stepped up to the counter.

"I could, but then I wouldn't have gotten to speak to you, now would I?" He winked. "Too bad you weren't here yesterday. I didn't get anywhere nearly as much foam on my cappuccino from the sullen girl."

"I don't work here every day. I'm in college, and my shifts fit around my schoolwork." Heat flooded my cheeks. I hadn't expected him to notice whether I was here.

"What time do you finish today?" he asked.

"Why?" I carried on making his order, knowing full well he wouldn't move off until it was finished.

"I wondered if you'd like to grab a drink or maybe something to eat with me." I stared at him, my mouth open like a goldfish. "You're old enough to drink, aren't you?"

"Um, yeah, I am. But why do you want to have a drink with me? You don't even know me." Admittedly, I'd seen him every day I'd been here, *and* he did wait for me to serve him, letting others past until I got to him.

He laughed, and it sent shivers through my body. "I guess that's why I'd like to have a drink, to get to know you. So what do you say?" His tongue darted out and dampened his bottom lip, and I followed the motion, unable to tear my eyes away.

"I can't tonight. I have a study group. I go straight from here." I handed him his drinks.

"Tomorrow then?" He leaned forward and whispered, "I really would like to get to know you, Mallory." His voice was husky in my ear.

"I don't think it's a good idea. I'm sorry." I was already kicking myself for turning him down.

"That's okay. I'll ask again tomorrow and the day after. And every day until you say yes." He winked and paid for his coffee.

And he did just that, the next day, and the one after that, and every time I said no. Oh, I wanted to say yes, so badly, but we would never work. He was miles away from me. He was some hotshot businessman who earned a shit ton of money, and here I was—a student busting his ass off at a coffee shop because his study loan wasn't enough to keep him afloat.

Then I had two days off, and when I got back to work, I looked forward to seeing him again, but he didn't show up. Not that I was surprised. I'd been just someone to flirt with, and when he'd accepted that I was adamant in my denying him, he'd gone to greener pastures. It was what I'd wanted. Still, disappointment flowed through me. I had no time to dwell on it, though. Customers came in, in a steady flow, for which I was glad. They were a good distraction, but they were also difficult as hell. Summer had arrived, but it seemed that the more the temperatures had rocketed, the worse the mood of the customers had become. Why did they change their mind three times and then walked away with an Americano? And not even a muffin with it. Hell, we were all in a bad mood. The day dragged on, but finally, it was time for me to leave. I couldn't get out of here fast enough.

I rushed out the kitchen door and straight into a furnace as the heat hit me in the face. Dragging my T-shirt over my head and tucking it into my back pocket, I rounded the corner. Someone whistled and called out my name. Hot coffee guy stood outside the shop front. My heart galloped behind my ribcage. He'd come after all.

"Mallory." He sounded breathless as his eyes roamed over my bare chest. "What a pleasant surprise. I was just thinking about you."

"Really? It can hardly be a surprise, considering I work here." I tipped my head and gave him the once-over. He wasn't all dressed up in one of his fancy suits today. Instead, he wore a pair of pale-blue shorts and a white polo shirt. He'd shoved his sunglasses on the top of his head, pushing his blond hair away from his forehead, which gave him a much more approachable and younger look. And an even sexier one, if that were possible.

"Okay, you're right. I hoped to find you leaving and persuade you to come for a drink." He looked at me with puppy dog eyes, and I burst out laughing.

"Fine, but on one condition."

"Anything you want." He took a step closer to me. Damn if he didn't smell amazing. So not like me. The scent of roasted beans wafted off me.

"Well, you could tell me your name."

"You're kidding? Haven't I told you? No wonder you wouldn't go out with me." He thumped his hand against his forehead theatrically. "It's Archer, Archer Hawkins."

"Okay then, Archer, Archer Hawkins. We can go for a drink."

We walked to a bar not far from the coffee shop and found a table away from the bright sunlight pouring in through the large windows. I shrugged my shirt back on as he headed over to the bar. He really was incredibly good looking and didn't seem aware of the admiring glances he received from both men and women.

He turned back halfway over and asked if I wanted a beer. I gave him a thumbs-up. His smile floored me. I groaned. What the hell had I gotten myself into?

Two

"Can I see you again, Mallory?" Archer asked as we stood at the intersection, waiting for the WALK signal to light up. "And I don't mean just when I buy my coffee."

"I'd like that." I smiled shyly. We'd had a great evening. Archer was interesting and funny and wanted to know about me. I kept trying to deflect his questions, but he was very good at asking things in just the right way to get me to open up. Not enough to talk about all this recent shitstorm with my parents but enough to make him laugh.

"When?" Archer touched the back of my hand, sliding his fingers over my knuckles, making little sparks shoot up my arm.

"I'm not sure. I've got exams starting in a couple of weeks and need to cram. I'm going to be busy a lot of nights with my study group and then in the library. I need to work hard, or I won't get my finance..." My words dried up when he frowned.

"Don't you get help from home? Or a scholarship? Is this why you're working every spare hour in the coffee shop?" Archer sounded annoyed. No, not annoyed. Shocked.

I bristled, and he must've sensed it because he apologized. "Shit, Mallory, I'm sorry. That was rude and out of place of me."

"Yeah, well, shit happens, and life doesn't always go the way it was supposed to. Look, I've gotta go. I've had a nice time, Archer. I'll see you around." I hurried to the bus stop, hoping to be back on campus quickly. Maybe I could put all this out of my head. I knew it was too good to be true.

"Mallory. Mallory, please wait," Archer called out, but I didn't stop.

The next day, I worked a late shift, which allowed me to study in the morning. I just sat and stared at the same page in the book, though, and thought about Archer Hawkins and how he was perfect for me. We liked the same music, the same baseball team, the same books. It was just unfortunate we didn't have the same choices in life available to us. We would've six months ago, but not now. Not now that my family had cut all ties with me because of my "lifestyle choice," which was how my stuck-up asshole father had put it. Our last conversation was still vivid in my mind as if it had happened yesterday.

"Being gay isn't a choice, Dad. It's who I am. I was born this way. I didn't wake up and think 'Hey, gay looks fun. I'll give it a go.' For fuck's sake."

"Language, Mallory!" my mother barked at me from the other side of the table.

"What's it you're saying, then, Dad?" I cringed at the sneer on his face.

"I'm saying that unless you quit this ridiculousness, I'll stop paying your allowances, your tuition fees, and your apartment. I won't have you bring my name into disrepute. You'll make me a laughingstock. I can't believe that after all the privileges you've had, you still act like some sort of lowlife." He pointed his knife at me. "You won't be welcome here again. I don't want your type near your siblings."

"Unbelievable. You really are a shit. Fine, do that then because I won't lie. I have more self-respect than that. And I think the real lowlife here is you, turning your child away because of who he is and who he chooses to love." I yanked my napkin off my lap and dropped it on my plate.

"Self-respect? You think being queer makes you have self-respect. I don't know how you can look at yourself in the mirror." He grabbed his glass of expensive red wine and gulped it down, then slammed the glass on the table with such force the stem fractured.

"I do, actually. You just carry on sleeping with your secretary as long as we all pretend we don't know about it, and you, Mother, can keep the bottle of vodka in the back of the pantry, and we can turn a blind eye. But I'm not allowed to choose the gender of the person I want to sleep with? You don't know the meaning of self-respect." My chair scraped back over the floor, making my mother wince; it just made me laugh even more.

I sent my dumbstruck brother and sister a smile. "Sorry, you two. Not for who I am, but for who they are. I hope you get out of here as soon as you can."

I walked out the door and out of the house.

Ten days later, I had a letter from my dad's lawyer, telling me to leave my apartment and return my car. I'd preempted his callousness and had already spoken to the finance office and the housing office and had arranged a dorm room and a grant for my fees. Luckily, I was at the top of all my classes, and I only had one more year to go. So fuck him.

The next step had been getting a job. One of my buddies had heard about the job in the coffee shop, so had I hot-footed it down there and grabbed an application.

My phone rang, startling me out of my reverie. I didn't recognize the number and let it go to voicemail. I got my head back into my book, and this time I focused enough to make some decent notes before having to go into work.

As soon as I walked inside, Carlos beckoned me over, a strange look on his face. "What's up, dude?" I asked as I tied my apron around my waist.

"Your man over there has been waiting all morning for you." Carlos nudged his head over to the corner. Archer sat with his back to the wall, shoulders slumped, rolling his coffee cup between his hands.

"What the hell?"

He straightened when I stood in front of him, my hands in the pockets of my apron. "What's going on, Archer? Carlos told me you've been here all morning. Why?"

"I wanted to see you. I needed to see you and apologize again." He reddened as he reached out a hand to me, but I stepped back.

"You didn't need to do that. You said you were sorry last night." A throat cleared behind me, and I glanced over my shoulder. My boss was shooting daggers at me. "Look, I need to get to work. Don't worry, Archer. It's okay."

"Can I see you again? Tonight? Please, Mallory, give me another chance." He smiled softly, and my traitorous heart skipped a beat.

"I can't do tonight. I'm here until ten." Another throat clearing. "I've got to get to work. I'm sorry, Archer. Maybe another day." I scurried back to the counter, avoiding eye contact with my boss, and served the next customer.

"I'll be here at ten, Mallory," Archer called after me as he walked out of the coffee shop.

"This isn't a pickup joint, Halston. Get to work," Mr. Kowolski muttered to me, then stomped back to his office.

Carlos patted me on the shoulder. "He's a hot guy, rich too. You should go for him." He winked.

The day didn't seem to end, and I was hot and sweaty by the time I finished. All I wanted to do was go back to my room and get under a cold shower. The night had cooled down, but even in the darkness, the heat was suffocating. I closed the kitchen door behind me and stopped in my tracks. Archer, his long legs clad in denim and a tight-fitting short-sleeved shirt showing off his broad chest, pushed off from the wall. I swallowed hard. He was too damn sexy for his own good.

"You shouldn't have come here again, Archer. I'm tired and in desperate need of a shower and my bed. Can we take a rain check?" I asked quietly.

He stepped into my space. "I'm here now, and I can offer you both of those options if you'd like to come back to my place." His voice was deep and husky.

"Huh? I don't think that's a good idea. We don't know each other." I struggled to speak as the crisp citrus scent of his cologne wafted into my nose.

"What better way to find out more." His mouth was so close to mine his warm breath washed over my dry lips. I slid my tongue over my lower lip, dampening it or maybe trying to capture his flavor. He brushed his mouth over mine, a touch so light I could've almost believed I'd imagined it until he sighed.

"Shit," I muttered under my breath. My heart beat frantically in my chest.

"Come back with me, Mallory." His words resonated in my chest. How could I refuse this man? I nodded and let him take my hand. "Thank you," he whispered.

We ambled toward a tall and impressive apartment building. Even more exclusive than my parents' home, and that took some beating.

I chuckled. "Nice address."

"Yeah, it's not bad."

A doorman man held the door open for us and greeted Archer by name. With my hand in his, he strode to the concierge desk.

"Good evening, Winter. I'd like to introduce Mallory Halston. He has access to my home at any time."

I gaped at him, but he ignored me.

"Of course, Mr. Hawkins. Good evening, Mr. Halston."

"This way. Come on." Archer led me toward an elevator and pressed the Call button. The door silently slid open, and we stepped inside. Archer opened a keypad and entered a code.

"It's 47531. You'll need to remember that, Mallory." He smirked.

"I'm not sure that's necessary right now," I muttered, making him laugh.

"Oh, Mallory, I'm not letting you go that easily. I want you. I've made that perfectly clear." He stroked his thumb over the back of my hand the whole time.

"Do you always get what you want?" I felt...not nervous but apprehensive, maybe?

"Yes." His eyes darkened.

"Have I made this too easy for you? Should I turn around and go back home?" I joked.

"Easy? I've asked you every day for a couple of weeks, and then after one date, you bolt off into the night. Hell, Mallory, you're anything but easy. And please don't leave yet."

As the elevator swooshed open again, Archer pulled me out onto a hallway with only one door. Wow, he had to have the whole floor to himself. He dropped my hand, only to open the door for me. He fumbled to get the key into the lock. Maybe he was more nervous than he'd let on. That thought calmed me a little. As the gentleman he was, Archer let me enter first. A large open-plan room opened up before me, expensively decorated but stylish. It was like Archer. It showed money but was also lived in. Candid photographs hung on the pale blue walls. No stiff, posed, and forced family pictures here. The cream-leather sofas were soft and squishy, inviting you to cuddle up with a good book and a cup of hot chocolate, or better yet, with your loved one. So different from the couches in my old family home that always left me sitting rigid as if perching on an unexploded bomb. The paperbacks and magazines scattered on the coffee table I wanted to investigate further. What did Archer read for pleasure? A small smile broke out. I liked it here.

"Let me show you where my shower is. Would you like me to get you something to eat? I can order pizza?"

I followed Archer to his room, which had the biggest bed I'd ever seen. And comfy. The crisp white-and-navy bedding and cushions were an invitation to plop down, snuggle in, and never leave. The light polished wood floor gave an airiness to the room, but the floor-to-ceiling window was the real showpiece.

"Wow, Archer, that's some view." The city was laid out before me, blanketed in darkness, the lights glittering like stars. A fairy tale come to life. And my prince charming stood right behind me, his reflection drawing me in more than the landscape below. He was so beautiful. I might be making a mistake, but in that moment, I wanted him. I wanted him as much as the lust in his eyes said he wanted me.

Three

Time seemed to come to a stop as we stared at each other, neither making a move.

"Where's this shower, then, hotshot?" I tried to lighten the mood, but I didn't think it was working, as he swallowed hard.

"This way. Can I lend you some shorts and a T-shirt? I'm guessing you don't want to put the clothes you're wearing back on."

"That would be great, thank you." I followed him to the bathroom, which was more a wet room than an enclosed shower.

"There are towels and everything you'll need already in there. Take your time, Mallory. I'll order some food." I waited until Archer had walked out. Then I stripped out of my clothes and turned on the shower. The water powered out. This was heaven. I was never going to want to shower anywhere else ever again. Definitely not in the weak version my dorm had to offer. I scrubbed the sweat and coffee from my body and washed my hair, enjoying the products I could no longer afford but used to have. Then I just stood with my head tipped back and my eyes closed, letting the water hit my chest.

Eventually, I turned off the water and ran my hands through my hair and then down my body, shucking the water away. Stepping out, I reached for the towel. A movement caught my eye. Archer stood in the doorway, squeezing his dick through his jeans. Eyes blazing with lust, he strode toward me and took the towel from my hand.

"Let me." His voice was rough and hard, but his hand soft and gentle as he wiped the towel down my neck and over my chest. My breathing got quicker as he circled my pecs, slowly, lazily as if it were his hand, not the fabric, caressing me. "I've never wanted anyone the way I want you."

He moved his hand lower, and I grasped his wrist, stopping him from going any farther. His eyes widened in surprise.

"Why?"

"I don't know. I just know I can't leave you alone." He leaned closer, letting his forehead rest on my own—a touch I'd always found very sensual.

He brushed his mouth over mine and stilled, waiting for me to agree. I nodded. I was lost to this man. As he pressed his lips firmly against mine, I knew this was going to be like no kiss I'd ever experienced before. Still, the softness of his lips surprised me as his tongue slid over the seam, seeking entry. This was a take-no-prisoners kiss. He was in total control as his tongue delved into my mouth. He explored every part, stroking against my tongue, then pulling back out to suck on it.

I let go of his wrist and grabbed his hips, pushing my naked and aroused body against his. His erection poked against mine through the rough fabric of his jeans. I wished it wasn't between us. Archer's hands were in my hair now as he continued to fuck my mouth with his tongue. He tightened his fingers as he slowed down his kisses, and we broke apart, panting as we drew heaving gulps of air into our lungs. He kissed me again, softer this time but still so controlling. I never wanted it to stop.

"I need you, Mallory. I need to taste you," he whispered, then let go of my hair and dropped down to his knees. "Fuck, look at you. So hard, weeping for me, your cock aches for me."

I groaned as his hot breath washed over the sensitive, swollen head of my dick. My head lolled back as he ran his nose up and down my length, breathing in deeply as he reached the juncture of my groin and thigh. My hands gripped his hair, which was even softer than I'd imagined. I stroked my fingers lazily over his scalp as he licked back up the crease to the base of my dick. Long flat strokes of his tongue traveled up my length until I couldn't bear it anymore.

Then he closed his mouth over my crown and sucked. The tip of his tongue flicked over the slit, and more precum burst out. Archer moaned and then sank down, taking my whole length deep inside the warm, wet cavern of his mouth. My cockhead bumped the back of his throat, but he kept going, and I slipped deep inside as he swallowed around me.

"Fuck! You need to stop. I'm gonna come if you do that again." I pulled on his hair, but he was relentless, sucking my dick as one hand played with my balls and the other skimmed up and down my ass crack, just teasing as he got close to my hole. He pulled hard and tugged on my balls, then released them so they drew up inside my body. As my knees shook, my orgasm fired through me, and I poured my load into his mouth and throat. Eagerly, he took every drop of me. As I finished and softened, he licked me clean and scraped his teeth over the tip of my cock, making me flinch at the sensitivity.

"Wow, Mallory." Archer stood and cupped my face. His lips were red and swollen but still so fucking sexy. I licked across his bottom lip, making him moan as I dragged it between my teeth, then released it to dive into his mouth. I tasted myself and sucked on his tongue. Growling, he increased his grip on my ass.

"I need you to fuck me," I panted into his mouth.

Archer's groan, filled with need, sent shivers through my body.

"Oh, thank god. Get on my bed. Fuck, Mallory, I want you so much."

We rushed to his room, and I clambered up onto his mammoth bed, pushing cushions to the floor and kicking down the duvet with my feet. Then I settled back and watched as Archer took off his clothes. His shirt slipped from his body and down to the floor. Then he popped the button on his fly before dragging down the zipper. I slid my hand down my stomach over my tight muscles and back onto my now, once again, hard dick.

"God, you look stunning."

"Open the drawer, sugar. Get the lube and condoms out, then bend your knees, open your legs," Archer ordered. I complied, loving the instructions. I never thought of myself as a submissive lover, but the growl in Archer's voice showed how much he needed me, and all I wanted to do was obey.

I stretched across the bed and rummaged in the drawer. I glanced over my shoulder at him just as he stepped out of his pants. "Condoms? Plural?" I raised an eyebrow.

"Hell, yeah, plural. We've got all night, Mallory." He stalked over to me, his hand wrapped around the impressive length of his dick. "It's Friday night, and you have no college, and you aren't working tomorrow. Now lie back down. I want to explore your body."

Archer mapped my body with his fingers and his tongue, sending me higher and higher. "You taste divine, Mallory. Your skin is so soft, and it loves my touch."

He was right too. My skin felt alive as he traced every line and contour. Goose bumps broke out as he scraped his teeth over my nipple. I couldn't hold back my moan as I arched my back into him.

"Oh, honey, I can't wait to feel you clamped tight around me. You're so receptive to my touch. I knew we'd be perfect together," he murmured as his mouth covered my other nipple.

"Then do it, Archer. I need you inside me. Take me. Please god, take me." I puffed out the words as he pushed my legs back, folding them over my chest.

"Christ, you're perfect." He slid his tongue over my hole and up over my taint, then down again. "Hold your legs, Mal. Don't move them." His breath was warm over my skin. He circled my pucker with his finger, then sucked the digit into his mouth, wetting it, and pressed it down on my hole. "Let me in. I'll make you feel so good."

Slowly, he pushed inside me, and hell, yeah, it felt good, but it wasn't enough. I needed more.

"Archer, give me more. I need you inside me." The grip on my thighs was punishing as I held on tight, not wanting him to stop. As his finger slipped out, a moan escaped me, but soon he added another finger and pumped in and out of me, stretching me. "Enough. I'm ready."

The condom wrapper ripped, and then his hands were gone. Opening my eyes, I watched, mesmerized, as he rolled the thin latex down his rock-hard dick. He squeezed the lube bottle, coated his dick, and dripped some over my hole. The tip of his cock pressed against my pucker and slid slowly inside.

"Fuck, you're so damn hot. You ready for more?" Archer moaned.

"Yes, god, yes." I bore down, and he slipped through the tight ring of muscles, then stilled again. "Don't stop," I begged.

Pulling back just slightly, Archer looked at me, then pushed inside me completely. "Mine," he groaned. "I need to know you're mine, Mallory Halston."

I'd never felt so full not just with him inside me but also in my head and my heart. Everything about him consumed me. "Yes, yours," I cried out as he withdrew and plunged back deep inside me.

Leaning over my body, he kissed me, his tongue mimicking his movements. Pulling his mouth away, Archer gripped my ankles and pounded inside me. It wasn't enough.

"More. Harder. Give it to me." I wrapped my hand around my dick and tugged hard, working myself at the same punishing pace as he was.

"Christ, I'm not going to last. I want you to come. Come for me, Mallory."

"Fuck. Archer." I screamed out his name as I came. Ropes of cum pelted my stomach and chest. I didn't know how I could produce so much after I'd come already. Archer stiffened further and, roaring out my name, poured his load inside me. Even through the condom, the heat of his orgasm was intense.

He collapsed on top of me, squishing my cum between us, but I didn't care. I wanted his skin on mine. Slowly the haze cleared from his eyes, and he gave me a shit-eating grin. He dipped his head down and kissed me tenderly, almost reverently.

"Damn, Mallory, I knew you'd be good, but I hadn't imagined just how good. I'm never going to let you go. You get that, right?" He kissed me again before I could answer. As he lifted his weight off me, he slipped out of me. He dragged the condom off his now flaccid dick, tied it, and threw it into the trash. "I'll get a washcloth, honey. Stay still."

Just moments later, Archer came back from the bathroom, kneeled back on the bed, and wiped the sticky residue off my stomach, then cleaned between my legs. Throwing the cloth back in the direction of the bathroom, he flopped next to me, and I chuckled. He caught my eye, and soon we were both laughing hard.

"Shit, Archer, you sure don't hold back."

"No, no, I don't. Are you okay with that? I meant every word of it. You're mine, and I won't let go of you." He faced me, the honesty glimmering in his gaze. Surprisingly, I found myself nodding, agreeing with him.

We lay quietly until my stomach growled, embarrassing me. "I guess I'd better order that pizza now." Archer laughed and slid off the bed again. "Anything you don't like on your pizza?"

"Nope, I'm happy to take whatever you want."

Archer's eyes twinkled. "Good to know, sugar. That's good to know."

When I woke, it was still dark outside, but I wasn't sure what time it was. Archer was still fast asleep. He really was beautiful, but this was all too much for me. I couldn't let this move on this quickly. I needed to keep my head down and my grades up, or I'd lose my college grants. We'd both said some heady stuff to each other, but surely that had been in the heat of the moment. He couldn't be really that into me, claiming me as his. He couldn't mean that. We were too different. He was a lawyer, a man who'd accomplished things, and I was…maybe not nothing, but it wasn't too far off.

Carefully, I slipped out of the bed, grabbed my clothes, and quickly pulled them on. I felt around on the floor for my Converse and tiptoed out of the room.

A glance at my phone told me it was three thirty. After shoving my feet into my shoes, I headed out of the apartment and hurried to the elevator. Panic flashed through me that Archer might wake up and notice me gone.

He really was an amazing man, and damn, he knew how to fuck, but I couldn't get involved with him. Before long, he'd get bored with the college kid, and I'd be the one ending up with a broken heart.

The doorman nodded at me, but I didn't say anything. As soon as I was outside, I broke out into a jog back to my dorm.

I collapsed into my lumpy, uncomfortable bed, closed my eyes, and let sleep capture me again.

Four

As I woke up slowly, my brain confused yet again, I tried to work out why I was here. I remembered bolting from Archer's apartment. I didn't have to work today, but I did have a study group this afternoon and an essay to write. I dragged myself out of bed and into the bathroom. As I peed, my phone rang, but I ignored it. Washing my hands, I caught my reflection in the mirror. What did he see in me? My shaggy black hair could use a cut, and my dark blue eyes were not that special, so similar to my father's and brother's but now so different, burdened from what I'd seen in a simpler life. On the outside, I looked the same as always, but inside, I felt different. Changed by one night with an amazing man who could never really be mine.

Last night with Archer had been so real, so life altering. Was that why I'd bolted? I didn't believe in love at first sight, but the tug in my heart when I thought of him waking up alone this morning contradicted my head. Would he be angry or relieved that he was spared the embarrassment of getting me out of his apartment? Under the hot water from the shower, I washed the remnants of last night's sex away. My ass still ached pleasantly; he had been that good. Maybe I'd been wrong to have left. If so, it was too late to change anything now.

I was sure he'd understand why I'd had to leave, or maybe he'd gotten what he wanted and wouldn't be back again. That thought bothered me more than it should. I could always try to reach out to him again and explain.

As I switched off the shower, my phone rang again. Who would call me? Unless it was the coffee shop, but I didn't want to go in, so I ignored it again. After I pulled on some clothes, I grabbed my bag with my laptop and all my notes and headed out to the library. It was busy in here today. Exams were coming up, and everyone was cramming. I found a table in the corner and sat with my back to the window. The sun was warm on my back, and I ditched my hoodie before I melted in a puddle. I flicked my laptop open and pulled out my notes and textbook. I loved this course, and doing this instead of the business degree my father expected from me had been my first act of rebellion.

The second had been admitting who I was, but that one hadn't worked out too well for me. I was happy now, though, happier than when I was living a lie. I might not have the luxuries I was used to, but this felt more real. I was working hard at school, and I had a job that paid me well enough to eat.

The phone buzzing again pulled me out of my concentration. I was ready to throw it out the window. I needed to get this essay finished before study group. Tomorrow, I'd be in the coffee shop all day, working a double shift.

An hour later, I was finished. I'd checked and double-checked it, and all I needed to do was email it to my professor, and I was done. When I stood, all the muscles in my back flexed and contracted. Ouch. I'd been sitting in the same position too long again. It was easy to lose track of time when I was immersed in my work. With my arms over my head, I stretched the kinks out, the satisfying *pops* giving me instant relief. My stomach rumbled, and I wandered down to the cafeteria to grab something to eat.

By the time I turned in for the night, my head was spinning. I'd had so much to think about today. The guys in my study group were awesome and so bright. We'd bounced ideas and answers off each other. It just wasn't the best thing to do before bed. My head was so full of information I knew I wouldn't sleep. I dug my earbuds out for my phone and switched on some music.

I tuned out everything and relaxed. As I drifted off to sleep, thoughts of Archer popped into my mind. Would I ever see him again? I doubted he'd come back into the coffee shop. I'd never talk to him and hear his laugh or see the flare of heat in his eyes when he spotted me. Perhaps I had made a mistake. But it was too late now.

The next morning brought the joys of ten hours of serving coffee to every kind of person there was. The orders would be a yard long with ridiculous ideas, such as venti-iced skinny hazelnut macchiato, sugar-free syrup, extra shot, light ice, no whip or grande chai tea latte, three pumps, skim milk, no foam, extra hot, lite water. What the hell was lite water? These people really needed to get a grasp of what was important in life. Would they make that shit at home for themselves? Of course not.

So with that in mind, I headed to work. In the kitchen, I stripped off my hoodie and tied my apron around my waist, then joined Carlos at the counter. The place was already swamped.

"Hey, bud, you okay?" I asked as he looked up.

"Yeah, it's been crazy since we opened. You here all day?" He grinned, the bastard, as if he didn't already know the answer.

"Fucker," I muttered under my breath.

With a smile, I turned to the next customer and made the lady her tall, nonfat latte with caramel drizzle. No idea how she could drink the stuff. The line didn't dwindle, and I was rushed off my damn feet for the next few hours. Thank god we had a lull around eleven, and we could catch our breath before the crazy lunchtime crowd came in. I leaned back against the counter behind me and rolled my shoulders, closing my eyes for a second. Carlos had finished his shift and said a quick good-bye as Jessie took over.

"Mallory, there's a man asking for you." Jessie nudged me. In front of the counter, looking so stunningly handsome but also so incredibly pissed, stood Archer Hawkins. At the sight of him, my heart beat faster, something I hadn't expected. His grim face soon turned any happy feeling off.

"Archer, it's good to see you. What can I get you? Your usual?" I was talking shit, but his eyes bored into me.

"Forget the coffee. I'd like a moment of your time. Please." His words were pleasant enough, but anger was radiating from him. Hadn't he ever gotten up and left in the middle of the night? I'd bet he had.

"I can't, Archer. I'm on a double shift. I haven't got time today." I looked as apologetic as I could. Sure, I could take a break. It was quiet, but he was too intense for me to deal with right now.

"You owe me, Mallory. You owe me an explanation. Why didn't you answer your phone yesterday?"

"That was you? How did you get my number? Never mind. I'm sorry, Archer, but I'm busy here today. I can't talk now."

"What time do you finish?"

"Uh, nine," I answered reluctantly. I knew he wasn't going to leave until I told him.

"Then I'll see you at nine." With that, he strode out the door, his back ramrod straight.

"Wow. That was intense. What did you do? Kick his puppy?" Jessie asked.

"I left him in the middle of the night," I muttered.

"Ouch. No wonder he's pissed. He's hot. Why did you leave, then?"

"It seemed like a good idea at the time. You know, the whole walk of shame the next morning? I didn't want to do that."

"Not so much now, though, right?"

"What do you reckon?" I got back to work and got through the crazy-busy two hours that was lunchtime and then again through the evening post-day coffee to get them home. Some of these people were in here three times a day, and at six or seven bucks a cup, they threw their money away. Idiots.

At last, I could take off my apron and hand it over to the night staff. I said a general good-bye and headed out through the kitchen to the staff entrance. My heart beat a little faster. Did I want Archer to be there or not? I wanted him to want me enough to fight for me, but I dreaded his anger. Leaving him had been a shitty thing to do, but at the time, I'd thought it was best. I grabbed my hoodie from the clothes hook and pulled it over my head.

As soon as I pushed the door open, I got my answer. Archer was leaning against the wall, tension pouring from his body. Every tendon and sinew seemed tightly strung, ready to snap.

"Archer," I greeted him as he pushed away from the wall.

"Really? That's all you've got to say? You left our bed, Mallory. In the middle of the night, according to the night porter. Is that your usual MO? I thought we were on the same page, that you felt the same as I did.

When I closed my eyes that night, I felt so complete. So happy I'd found the one, the man who would change my life. Was I just a hookup to you?"

Wow, I hadn't expected his passion and hurt. I'd never taken his words that seriously. I'd thought he was acting with the whole "here's my code to my floor" and all that shit. So what should I say? Should I apologize? No, that didn't sit comfortably. The truth would be the only way forward.

"When I woke up, it suddenly felt too much, too overpowering. You told me I was yours. You kept saying, 'you're mine.' No one had ever said that to me. When I lay there in the dark, it all scared the crap out of me. I didn't know how much of it was true or how much of it was a way for you to tap my ass. Archer, I don't know. It was all too intense."

"So you thought it was better to leave than to wake me and talk to me? Mallory, how could you've dismissed everything we shared so easily, so callously? I woke up feeling so damn good until I saw the empty side of the bed. You hurt me, Mallory."

"Hey, hold on. How come this is all about you? Have you never woken and sneaked out?" A shimmer of guilt slid over his face. "Yeah, you have. I'm guessing you just thought I'd better get outta here because you may have to have the awkward conversation in the morning. The one where both of you pretend to have something important going on. Of course, you have, so think of this from my point of view for a moment, will you?"

He sagged back against the wall and shook his head. "Don't you feel anything for me, Mallory? Didn't you mean it?"

"Archer, I meant everything I said. I just needed a breather, time and space, to collect my thoughts. This could go one of two ways. You would either ignore me and never see me again, and I'd put the night down to us being horny and willing. Or you'd come back and fight me over it."

"Which one did you expect? Which one did you want?" he asked me quietly.

"Honestly, Archer, I expected never to see you again, but that's very different from what I want." He tensed again. "I want you to mean what you said because I meant it. I want you to want me for me, for who I am." I fell back against the wall, exhausted, not just from standing on my feet for ten hours but also from deciphering my feelings and how I would react to seeing him.

"Oh, honey, I meant every fucking word of it. I've never felt anything like the way you make me feel. I want you, Mallory, but more importantly, I want you to want me the same way. I won't do this if we're not both in this for real."

"Then I'm with you. I'm in this with you for the whole nine yards." I smiled shyly at him, but it soon turned into a gasp as he stalked toward me, predator-like.

"I want to kiss you, Mallory, but only if you mean it. Only if you're prepared to stay the night, the whole night."

"I won't leave again, Archer, not until you tell me." I squirmed as he leaned into my body, melding his to mine.

"That's good to know. I'm never going to tell you to leave." His emerald-green eyes had darkened as he lowered his head to mine. The moment his lips touched mine, his eyelids flickered shut. As he pressed harder against my lips, I closed my eyes, lost in his kiss. The sweet slip of his tongue over the seam of my lips had my blood pressure rising and my heart pounding. I grabbed his hips and clutched him to me. A deep groan shattered the silence, but I didn't know if it was from him or me. The bulge in his jeans swelled and hardened as he pushed into me.

The clatter of a dumpster lid being slammed shut brought us both back into the present. "We need to get out of here. Where do you want to go, Mallory?"

"Your place," I mumbled against his neck.

"Our place," he countered me.

"Not yet, Archer. Don't push me."

"Okay, I won't. Much." His lips curling in a smile tickled my neck. "Let's go." He clasped my hand in his. "Are you with me, Mallory?"

"I'm with you," I answered confidently.

"Hey, sugar, what time do you want me to come over?" Archer's deep voice sent shivers through my body. Even over the phone, he affected me. We'd been together for three months now, seeing each other every spare moment. His work was crazy hectic at times, especially in the run-up to him going to court. Right now, he was working his regular hours, and he'd been pestering me to move in with him at every opportunity.

"Anytime, baby. I'm all packed up and ready for you." Okay, so I'd caved. I wanted to be with him just as much but had thought we were moving too fast, and I'd held off until now. Now I was ready to be with him.

"Awesome, I'm on my way. See you in twenty." He blew a kiss down the phone and ended the call.

I scanned around my room one last time. Everything important to me was packed. When I'd left the apartment my father had paid for, I'd taken what was personal to me. The only reminders of my family were the photos of my brother and sister. I missed them but hadn't been able to reach out to them. My parents had severed all ties. They could've moved away for all I knew. I wished I could say I didn't care, but that wasn't true. It still killed me to know they'd turned me away because of my sexuality. Something as simple as who I chose to love had wrecked a family, all for appearances.

A knock sounded on the door, and I opened it to the most gorgeous sight—Archer. I softly sighed as he leaned in to capture my mouth with his.

"Have you missed me?" He gripped my hips as he walked me backward into my room.

"Actually, you've caught me at a bad time. I've got a hookup from Grindr on his way. Sorry, we'll have to do this another time." I bit my lip to hold back my smile.

"Really? I'm sure I'll be better than him. I bet he can't make you come as quickly as I can. Or torture you slowly until you beg for release. Choose wisely, Mallory."

"Fuck, you've got me so damn hard," I moaned.

"Good." He winked and stepped away.

"What? No...wait, you've gotta do something about it. I can't carry heavy boxes with a stiffy. I could damage it."

"Hmm, maybe you shouldn't have teased me." Archer grinned but closed the distance again. He snaked his hand down my body and cupped the bulge in my pants. "Would be a shame to waste this, I suppose," he murmured in my ear, then bit down sharply on the lobe.

Archer was on his knees and had me out and in his mouth so quickly I stumbled back in surprise. I was engulfed in his throat in seconds. I fisted his hair as he worked me frantically with his hand and mouth, and he'd been right. I was going to explode so damn quickly.

"Fuck, yes. Yes, don't stop, baby. Take me deep," I groaned as his hand left my dick and grabbed my ass cheeks, separating them so he could push his finger inside me. I knew that the moment he did that, he'd go for my prostate, and then it would be game over.

I threw my head back and roared out my orgasm as he sucked and stroked me through the aftershocks. He pulled my pants up and zipped me closed, then gave me a wink and picked up the first box.

"You're welcome." He chuckled as I stood still, my mind in a daze. "You gonna help me?"

I shook my head and dragged myself back into the present and then followed his lead and lifted up a box.

"Are you sure that's all?" Archer frowned at me. He seemed surprised by my meager belongings. Ten boxes weren't much to sum up over twenty-two years of my life.

"Nah, most of it is shit anyway. You've got my vinyls out, and that's good enough for me." We'd flopped down on his sofa and had a pizza order on its way.

"Don't just think of this as my place, Mal. It's yours too. Do what you want with your stuff. It'll be nice to see someone else's things all over the place." He grinned. The buzzer at the door went off. "That'll be dinner. You want to grab a couple of beers?"

I wandered down to the kitchen as he opened the door. Muffled voices drifted toward me, but it didn't sound like a conversation going on between a delivery guy and a paying customer. I pushed the door of the fridge shut and walked back to the living room, uncapping both bottles.

"Look, it's just not a good time. No, nothing is wrong. In fact, everything is most definitely very right." Archer sounded strained, but I smiled at "the everything's right" comment. "Okay, yeah, fine. Sunday brunch is doable. We'll be there. Yes, both of us. I'm not messing around anymore."

I couldn't hear anymore, and the door closed, only for the buzzer to go again. At least this time, it had got to be our dinner.

We chatted comfortably about nothing much, but I could tell Archer was mad at something, and it had to be at whoever had been at the door. I wasn't having that ruin our first night living together. Wiping my fingers on a napkin, I swung my leg over both of his so I was straddling him and cupped his face. His tongue swiped his lip as if in anticipation of a kiss.

"You wanna tell me what got you so mad, babe? Or am I gonna have to fuck your bad mood away?" I pitched my hips forward, grinding against him. His eyes darkened when I rolled my hips. He gripped my ass hard, holding me against him. His erection pressed up against mine.

"Hmm, I'd like you to fuck it away," he murmured.

"Yeah? You're gonna let me top?" I'd taken him a few times before, but I loved him in my ass so much I tended to bottom more. And Archer preferred to top.

"Yeah, I want that fat cock of yours in my ass." He bit down on his lip as I ran my hands through his hair.

"I want you bent over this sofa," I whispered.

"Fuck, yeah."

I clambered off him and reached in the drawer of the coffee table. We'd worked out early on that we needed supplies in every room. I grabbed the lube and a condom, then shucked out of my sweat shorts and T-shirt. Archer was the fastest stripper and was naked by the time I turned back to him.

"Get in position, baby. I want it hard and fast." I ran my hand softly down his back as he leaned on the sofa, his muscles bunching under my fingers as he writhed. With his knees on the cushions, resting his elbows on the leather, he shot me a smoldering glance over his shoulder. His pupils were so dark the vibrant green I loved so much was all but gone.

"Spread your legs, Archer. I wanna see that hole." I was desperate to be inside him.

Widening his stance, he leaned his chest on the couch and pulled his cheeks apart. His tight hole clenched and quivered, and I fucking loved it.

"Ready, baby?" I tipped the bottle of lube and let it stream down his crack to his ring over his twitching pucker. I followed the liquid with my finger and pushed inside him, making him groan loudly. Pumping the digit in and out a couple of times, I added a second.

"I'm ready, Mallory. Fuck me now," Archer growled. I pulled out my fingers and grabbed the condom, but Archer shook his head. "No condom. We've been tested. I want to feel you, all of you."

"You sure? I don't mind carrying on using them." I was shocked he wanted to go bareback.

"Just fuck me, Mallory. Get that gorgeous dick in my ass now."

I wasn't going to argue. I squeezed more lube into my hand and stroked it over my dick, then lined the head up to his hole and pushed in. "Oh, god, I've never felt anything this good. Archer, you're so hot and tight."

"God, yes, yes," Archer cried out as I thrust all the way inside him. This felt so damn good.

Picking up speed, I clutched his hips and pistoned in and out of his ass. I licked at the sweat beading on his neck, then scraped my teeth over the tender spot behind his ear, knowing this would tip him over. I sucked hard, bruising his skin. He shuddered as his orgasm built. I slid one hand from his hip, grasped his dick, and stroked him hard and fast, matching it to my thrusts.

As Archer shouted out, he filled my hand with his cum, and his ass tightened around me, clenching me hard. I exploded inside him, the heat of my release flooding him as he trembled and flexed.

His arms and legs gave way, and I collapsed on top of him so that we slid down, lying half on, half off the sofa. My dick slipped out as I tumbled to the floor, and he fell into my lap. I held him tight to my chest, kissing his face and hair as I wiped the sweat from his forehead.

"I fucking love you, Archer Hawkins." I poured all my feelings into my kiss.

When Archer pulled away from me, his voice was shaky. "Not as much as I love you."

"More," I whispered. "Forever and always."

We scrambled up on wobbly legs and stumbled to the bedroom, where we flopped down onto the bed. "We should shower. I'm all sweaty, and so are you."

"You like me sweaty." Archer laughed.

"I do, but I'm sure you'd like to wash the cum off your body." I nudged him. "C'mon, I'll help with all the hard-to-reach places."

It didn't take us long, too tired to do anything more than wash and rinse off. As we got back into bed, I lay with my head on Archer's chest, our legs entwined. He was quiet, no doubt back to brooding about his visitor.

"Talk to me, baby. What's going on?" I tipped my head up.

He sighed. "It was my mother at the door. She bugs me at the best of times, and she knows I hate it when she turns up unannounced. I'll have to remind the desk to let me know if she's on her way up."

"What did she want? Does she know about me?" Have I made his life more complicated? I didn't know his mother, but from everything I'd read and seen, she was a difficult woman, a woman of power. As a supreme court judge, she was important, and she knew it, thrived on it. Just like my father—a passive-aggressive bully.

"She knows, but my mother doesn't like to admit I'm gay. She thinks if she doesn't acknowledge it, it'll just go away. I've never hidden it, and I'm not ashamed of it. I won't hide you, and I'm sure as fuck not ashamed of you." Archer dipped his head and kissed my hair.

"At least she didn't disown you like mine did. One minute, I was the pride of the family. The next, I was out on my ass. No apartment, no car, and no college fund." I let out a deep sigh. "But I got you, and you make it all worth it. If I hadn't had to get a job, I'd never have met you."

"I've agreed to go to brunch on Sunday, so be ready to be subjected to her interrogation."

"What? Why am I going? Shit, Arch. I don't want to make it worse. I can stay here."

"No way. If I've got to put up with her, so do you. You can't leave me alone with her." Archer wrapped his arm around my neck, laughing. "We're a team, sugar."

"What's your dad like? Is he cool with who you are? You don't talk about him much."

"My dad is okay, but my mother is in charge in their house." He snorted. "Please come."

"Fine, but only because I love you."

His breathing evened out as he fell asleep, but I was too wired to sleep. My head was full of a woman I had yet to meet but, I was sure, was going to dislike me. Would she know who I was or, more interestingly, who my father was? Hell, they probably knew each other.

Six

"You ready for this?" Archer held my hand, a frown on his beautiful face. He wasn't happy about doing this. He'd said we could walk out at any time if she got to be too much.

"Nope, not one bit, so let's do it." I let out a shaky laugh.

Archer rang the doorbell on the large impressive oak door, then stepped back. I looked at him quizzically.

"You don't have a key?"

"Oh, I do, but she prefers it if I ring. Just don't ask." He smiled, but it was strained.

As the door swung open, I came face-to-face with Archer's mother. They looked alike. They shared the same green eyes, but whereas Archer's sparkled bright with glee and mischief most of the time, his mother's were cold and sharp as she gave me a once-over. The color of their hair was the same: blond like buttercream. Archer's hair was soft and messy, and I loved running my fingers through it. Hers was stiff and lacquered in a rigid knot at the base of her neck, making her skin look too tight, but I was pretty sure she'd some major help from Botox as well. I doubted she could crack a smile. Her tailored linen cream pants and silk lilac blouse were so smart and wrinkle-free there was no way she'd made brunch.

"Archer, you're late." She sneered.

"Good morning to you too, Mother. And no, I'm not. I'm on time." He tapped his watch. "You said eleven, and it's ten fifty-nine."

"Then you should've been here five minutes ago." She stepped back and opened the door farther. "You didn't say you were bringing a friend, Archer. How typical of you."

"Yes, I did, but you just chose to ignore it. This is Mallory Halston, my boyfriend, not just my friend." Archer's hand still held on firmly to mine. I wasn't sure if it was to stop me from bolting or him.

"Halston, as in Martin Halston's son?" Her sharp eyes fixed on mine.

"Yes." Then muttered, "unfortunately" under my breath.

"Hmm, I thought I recognized the name. You're not much like him, are you?" It was more a statement than a question.

"I try not to be. My father is a difficult man, Mrs. Hawkins."

"Are we actually going to get some brunch, Mother? Or just have twenty questions here?" Archer stood rigid, his shoulders taut as a bowstring. I squeezed his hand, and he clenched back so tightly I had to swallow my cry of pain.

"Of course, this way." The infamous supreme court judge Valerie Hawkins led the way through the kitchen and out into the immaculate garden. A large wooden table was laden down with every kind of breakfast product known to man.

As soon as we stepped out onto the patio, a tall but rail-thin man hurried toward Archer and pulled him into a tight hug. This had to be his father. His dark brown hair was peppered with gray. His eyes were brown, but unlike Archer's mother, they sparkled with delight at seeing his son. And his mouth, which was exactly like Archer's, split into a wide smile. "Good to see you, Archer. It's been too long." He slapped Archer on the back, then turned to me. "Hello, young man. Who's this, Archie?"

"Dad, this is Mallory, my boyfriend." Archer tugged me forward with a proud smile.

"Very nice to meet you, sir." I offered my hand, which he shook firmly.

"Welcome, Mallory. Please call me Lawrence. Come now, let's eat."

We took our seats, and Archer loaded my plate with pancakes and bacon. He knew what I liked, and we were all soon eating in uncomfortable silence.

"So, Mallory, do you intend to follow in your father's footsteps and take up a place next to him in commerce?" Valerie asked.

"No, I'm in my final year in college, majoring in engineering."

"Really? How disappointing for your father. Always so sad when a child doesn't want to emulate his father." Oh, great. She was back to sneering again.

"Unfortunately, I disappoint my father in more ways than not joining his firm." I shot Archer a sideways glance as he gripped my hand in support.

"Yes, I can imagine."

"Mother, stop this now. You invited us here, so at least have the decency to be polite, or we'll leave," Archer snapped.

"For goodness sake, Archer, stop making such a drama. I'm just asking," she bit back. Their expressions turned into a glaring competition.

"Valerie, that's enough," Lawrence Hawkins spoke for the first time, and she broke her eyes away from her son.

We continued eating, but the atmosphere was awkward and painful. I wanted to whisk Archer away back to his apartment and wrap my arms around him. Finally, Archer put his knife and fork down, lifted his napkin from his lap, and placed it on the table.

"Thank you for a delicious brunch, Mother. We really need to be going." He stood, and I followed suit as quickly as I could, swallowing my bite of pancake. "Dad, I'll speak to you later in the week."

"Yes, I expect you have things to do. I'm sure you can see yourselves out." Valerie waved her hand derisively.

"Lawrence, it's been a pleasure to meet you, and Mrs. Hawkins, thank you for your hospitality." I offered my hand to Archer's father, and we shook again.

"I'll walk with you," he said as we strolled back into the house. "Mallory, thank you for coming with Archer today. You both look very happy together. I hope you and your family reconnect soon."

"Oh, you all know what happened?" My cheeks heated with embarrassment.

"Don't be embarrassed, Mallory. I know how difficult your father is. I wish you and Archer both happiness together."

"Thanks, Dad. I'll call you in the week," Archer replied for me.

As soon as we were outside, Archer heaved a huge sigh of relief. "C'mon, sugar, let's get out of here."

"Jesus, Archer. How do you cope with her?" I pulled him into a hug, and we stood together for a few minutes, just enjoying each other.

We settled into a routine quickly. I'd finished this year in college and picked up some extra daytime shifts at the coffee shop. I was saving as much as I could so I wasn't living off Archer's salary, even if it was a huge one. In fact, our first argument was over me paying my way. Archer was more than happy to let me keep all my own money and he'd carry on with all the utility bills and grocery shopping.

"I've done it for so long now, sugar. It doesn't matter. It's only food. I'd rather you saved your money. That way you can pay off your student loans." Archer gave me a tender smile.

"That's ridiculous, Archer. I need to pay my way. I'm not living off you. We're a partnership. Please let me do this." I stared at him, not smiling.

"Fine, you can buy the groceries one week, and I'll do it the next. But once you're back in college, you don't pay. Your hours at the coffee shop will go down again, and your final year will be hard enough without you busting a gut at work."

"Okay, now come here and kiss me."

"Now you're talking." Archer stepped into my arms and kissed me hard.

Seven

"No. I've told you at least three times. Don't do this, Mother. It'll only make you look stupid. Stop trying to pretend it isn't happening." Archer paced the room, scowling, his phone up to his ear. "You'll look like a fool, Mother. The Urquharts know exactly who I am. Marcus is in my firm, for fuck's sake."

He continued to listen to what his mother was saying. He must've sensed me looking at him, as he lifted his eyes from the floor and met mine. He grimaced and shook his head at me.

"Mallory will be attending the gala with me. Whatever you choose to do will only make you look foolish. Don't do it. I mean that."

Archer threw his cell phone onto the sofa, where it bounced off and hit the floor.

"You wanna talk about it?" I asked quietly.

"No, it's not important. My mother is being her usual overbearing self. There's nothing we need to worry about, I promise." He popped a kiss on my mouth.

"Okay, but I'm guessing this has something to do with the date you need to bring with you on Saturday night. Am I right?" I asked.

"You got that, did you?" He pinched the bridge of his nose. "She's arranged a date for me with Cecily Urquhart. The sad thing is I've been her beard, as it were, in the past, but we both realized that, at thirty, we needed to man up to our parents and move past our sexuality."

"Yeah, because that always works out well." I gave a dry chuckle, thinking back to my parents' rationalization of what *their* truth was.

"Honey, there's no way I'm going to go to this incredibly stuffy, boring night without you holding my hand. I can't wait to get you in a tuxedo." His eyes darkened as he scanned my body. "Then out of it at the end of the night."

"Is that so? I'd better rent one, then. You can practice if you'd like." I bit my lip, knowing it would drive him crazy.

"We'll have plenty of nights out when you'll need to wear a tux. We might as well buy one. Let's go now."

"I'm not sure I can afford to buy one, Arch." I knew what he was going to say. Any arguments we had, which weren't many, were over money.

"I'm buying it, Mal. It's because of me that you need one, which means it's up to me to buy it. Don't argue with me. It's not worth it."

"Fine."

Of course it was a stunningly tailor-made suit that fit like a dream. I smoothed the fabric down over my chest as I took a final check in the mirror.

Archer walked up behind me. Wrapping his arms around my waist, he dropped a kiss on my neck and breathed in deeply. "You look and smell divine. Let's not go. We can stay here and fuck all night."

When he scraped his teeth over my heated skin, it was my turn to moan. "No, but we don't need to stay too long. We don't, do we?" Our eyes met in the mirror.

"Mallory, we can leave straight after dinner."

"Let's go, then."

Archer drove and soon pulled up outside the Hilton, where he handed the car over to the valet. "Don't bury it in the middle, please. We're not staying too long," he informed the young lad, pressing a fifty-dollar bill in his hand.

"I'm sure you didn't need to tip him that much, Arch," I grumbled at his extravagance.

"I know that, but he'll do as I asked because of it. Come on, I really want this night over with."

The minute we walked in, I knew this was a mistake. Valerie Hawkins was waiting in the foyer with Lawrence, another equally uptight couple, and two stunning women.

"I knew you'd do this, Archer. Why do you have to be so defiant?" she snarled, ignoring me completely.

"It's not defiance, Mother. It's me bringing the man I love, just as I said I would." Archer walked up to his father and shook his hand, then turned to the younger woman I assumed was Cecily. "It's lovely to see you, Cecily, and you too, Miranda." He kissed both of their cheeks and then tugged me gently forward.

"This must be Mallory." Cecily smiled at me warmly. "I've heard so much about you." She pecked my cheek. "Don't let the witch get to you," she whispered, and I coughed out a nervous laugh.

"Well, I suppose this dreadful situation can be salvaged. Archer, your date can go in with the other women. Then you can follow with Cecily." Valerie sneered.

"No, Mother. I will walk in with Mallory holding my hand. I'm not hiding him. Most of the people there know I'm gay and have a boyfriend. It's just you making a scene about it. Get over it. I mean it. It stops now."

Her face turned the most hideous puce color, and she looked ready to explode as they glowered at each other.

"It's good to see you again, Mallory." Lawrence shook my hand, then gave his wife a glare. He was obviously not pleased with her. "Valerie, let's go inside now. Everyone is here."

The night turned out to be surprisingly fun. Cecily and Miranda were a brilliantly funny couple who were so in love it was beautiful to see. We ignored Valerie just as much as she ignored us. Dancing with Archer's arms around me was an amazing feeling. Very different from his usual grinding when we were in clubs.

"What are you smiling about?" he asked as he twirled me around.

"I was thinking this is a very different way of dancing for us, not our usual hot and sweaty routine." I pulled him closer. "Just as fucking sexy, though." I let him feel my arousal as I pressed our hips together.

"Maybe it's time for us to leave, then?" he murmured and licked the shell of my ear.

"Fuck, yes." I sighed.

We said a brief good-night to Cecily, promising to have dinner together soon. Archer didn't even bother to seek his parents out. Lawrence was watching us with a minute smile on his face. I mouthed "good night" to him, and he nodded.

When we got home, Archer did everything he'd promised me—stripping me slowly out of my tuxedo and kissing every patch of bare skin as he revealed it. My dick was painfully hard, and precum dampened my underwear.

"Oh, my ever-loving Lord," he moaned as he slid my pants down my legs, leaving me standing in a black satin jockstrap. "Thank god I didn't see this before, or we'd never have left the house."

Kneeling in front of me, he sucked on the head of my dick through the damp fabric. His hands were tight on my ass, kneading the tight globes. He traced down my crack with his finger, then back up again, teasing me as he never quite reached my needy hole.

"Archer, I need you inside me. I need it hard tonight, need you to own me." I whimpered as he tugged the fabric down with his teeth, exposing my dark red weeping cock.

"You got it, my love." He scraped his teeth over the mushroom head, then lapped at the slit and sucked on the precum beading there.

I stepped away, clambered up onto our bed, and stripped off my underwear as I waited for him. With no regard for the expensive clothes, Archer undressed so quickly he climbed up between my legs seconds later.

"Turn over then, on your hands and knees."

As soon as I was in position, his mouth was on me. I loved him rimming me; he was a master at it and could keep me on the brink of orgasm with just his tongue.

I shamelessly ground onto his tongue, but too soon, he pulled away, and I cried out for more. His hand came down hard on my ass cheek, making me yelp, begging for more rather than for him to stop. The coldness of the lube he poured slid down my crack to my hole as he spanked me again and again.

"Get inside me, Archer," I growled over my shoulder.

"I haven't stretched you yet, lover."

"No, rough and hard. Get inside me and pound," I barked at him.

The head of his cock nudged at my entrance, and I shuddered in anticipation. He slammed inside me, balls deep with the first thrust. My back dipped as I arched my ass up to him. Yes, this was what I wanted.

"I'm good. Go, baby. Fuck me." I gave him the green light.

And he did exactly that. Plunging hard and fast, his hips like pistons, he fucked me. Sweat poured over my body as he slapped my ass again. This set off my orgasm.

"Oh, god, Archer. So good, so, so good. I'm gonna come, baby. You ready?" I panted as my arms gave way, leaving my ass in the air and my head on the sheet.

"You're so fucking hot. Squeeze me tight, Mallory." He sounded like he was gritting his teeth as he powered into me.

As I clenched around him, he hit my prostate, and I groaned loudly. Without even touching my dick, my orgasm shot from me. Archer stiffened, and the white heat of his release filled my channel as he pumped more and more inside me.

Collapsing on top of me, he trailed his lips over my neck and kissed, sucked, and bit me. His dick finally stopped twitching inside me, and he tenderly pulled out of me. I'd feel this for days. Giddiness flurried through me.

He rolled off me and lay next to me, and I turned my head. His eyes were glazed, and he had a sex-drunk grin on his face.

"You're one fucking hot piece of ass, Mallory, my love." He snickered, and I joined in.

"We need to shower, babe. We're all sweaty." I raised one hand and cupped his cheek.

"I like you sweaty." He turned his face in my palm and peppered it with kisses.

Eight

At last, I had a day off. I'd worked seven days straight after Carlos got sick. Today I planned to do absolutely nothing. Archer was at work and had given me strict instructions to rest, so who was I to argue?

Dressed in just sweatpants, I lounged on the sofa, watching Netflix when the buzzer on the door sounded. I wasn't expecting anyone or any deliveries and was tempted to ignore it. It went off again.

"Fuck it." I paused the program, strode over to the door, and yanked it open. Shit. Valerie Hawkins stood there with her permanent sneer on her Botox-frozen face.

"Mrs. Hawkins, Archer isn't here. He's at work." I wanted her gone as soon as possible.

"I know that, Mallory. It was you I wanted to talk to." She stepped past me, even though I hadn't invited her in.

"So what do you want?" I shut the door behind her.

"You. I want you out of here and out of my son's life. You're not good enough for him." She scanned around the room, which luckily was clean and tidy, but the glint in her eyes told me she was looking for something to criticize.

"Excuse me?" My mouth dropped open. "Archer is a grown man, an intelligent and successful man. He's capable of making his own decisions. Archer loves me as much as I love him. You have no say in this. I want you to leave." I crossed my arms over my chest as she looked me up and down.

"Don't be ridiculous. Archer has a hugely successful career ahead of him, and he needs to snap out of the gay stupidity and get real. He needs a wife and family. Do you really think he'll make it to being a judge with you hanging around? You made a complete spectacle of yourself, embarrassing Archer and all his friends and superiors at the gala last month. I've spoken to his bosses to assure them it won't happen again. You're not the one for him, so this is what I'm prepared to do."

She rifled in her bag and pulled out an envelope, which she offered me with a smirk.

"In here is a check for twenty-five thousand dollars. Take it and leave him. I don't care where you go. Just leave this city and never see my son again. If you don't accept this, I will be speaking to your college professors, and I'm sure I can persuade them to fail you in your final exams. Don't mess with me, boy. You're not big enough to play my games. Take the money, Halston, and leave."

I stared at her as she held out the envelope. Her hand was steady, and she locked her eyes on me. Without saying another word, I turned on my heels and opened the front door again.

"Get out," I growled. "You're an evil bitch. You get out of here."

"Fine, fifty thousand. I'm sure that will be enough for you to forget about him." She pulled out another envelope.

"I told you to leave." I shook my head at her.

She took a step closer and hissed, "You won't win this, Halston. I will ruin you." Dropping the second envelope on the table by the door, she strutted past me.

"I'll tell your son all about your visit. Expect a call from him later. Get out of here now and don't come back."

The moment she was out the door, I slammed the door as hard as I could. "Fuck!" I stormed back to the sofa, swiped my phone open, and hit my contacts list. My fingers shook as they hovered over Archer's number. I was desperate to call him, but I knew he was busy. A text would have to do.

Hey baby,
Please come straight home.
We need to talk.
ILY
Xxx

I immediately got a message back
What's happened?
Have I done something wrong?
I love you, honey.
Xxx
I didn't want him to think that.
No, baby.
It's not you.
It could never be you.
I need you.
Xxx

I'm on my way now.
Xxx

Damn, I didn't want to scare him, but I needed him. I needed him to hold me and tell me it was going to be all right. It would only take him ten minutes or so to get here, and I paced the floor, ignoring the ominous envelope that was taunting me.

The door swung open wide, and Archer stormed in, his face red and his hair messy. He must've sprinted home. Without a word, he dragged me into his arms. As I ducked my head into his neck, I broke down.

Our relationship had been full on from the start. I'd given myself totally to him. My heart lived for him, and I knew he felt the same way. He'd loved me from the beginning, as he told me every day. Even when we were fucking hard and dirty, his love for me poured into me. He was my forever. I couldn't imagine not having him with me for the rest of my life.

"Tell me what happened, Mallory. What has you so upset? You're scaring me, my love." Archer held me close, rocking me as if I were a little boy.

"Archer"—I lifted my head up—"am I holding you back? Is you being with me going to damage your career?"

The shocked expression on his face flashed to anger. "What the fuck has gone on? Of course, you're not holding me back. I love you. We're a team, you and me." His eyes skimmed around the room and fixed on the envelope with his mother's handwriting on the front. "What's that, Mallory?"

"That's a check for fifty*K*," I answered, my voice shaking.

"Let's sit down, and you start from the beginning." He dropped his head and kissed me softly.

I sat next to him, but he pulled me onto his lap with his arms wrapped around my waist, keeping me close and centered.

"Your mother paid me a visit. She said I'd embarrassed you and your friends. That she had spoken to your bosses." I continued to run through our conversation. He tightened his hand around me to the edge of pain.

"That blasted woman. God, she has gone too far this time." Archer let go of me, and I slid off him. He paced the room, dragging his hand through his hair. He pulled his phone out of his pocket and swiped it open.

He held my gaze as he waited for it to be answered. "Mother, how fucking dare you? You have no idea what's right for me. You need to back the fuck off out of my life. I know you haven't spoken to my boss because he told me how happy I looked with Mallory."

I cringed at the rift I'd caused in his family.

"You do this every time I meet someone, but this time you've gone too far. I'm gay, Mom. Nothing is going to change that. Mallory is the most important man in my life. I'd marry him today if I could. He's my future. Not some blond empty-headed woman you approve of. I am gay. I like men. I like fucking men. You can get out of my life. I'm done with you. Don't call and don't come any-fucking-where close to Mallory." Archer ended the call and strode back to me, then pulled me up and against him.

"I love you, Mallory. She can't change that, I promise."

The next call Archer made was to his best friend. I hadn't met him because he lived a couple of states away, but they talked all the time. This time Archer moved away and spoke quietly to his friend, preventing me from hearing what he said, but I didn't care. I trusted him completely.

Later, when we were lying in bed and I was curled over him in my usual position, Archer ran his fingers through my hair.

"I meant it, you know." His voice was low. "About marrying you."

"Is this a proposal?" I chuckled. "Because it was crap." Chuckling, I kissed his chest. His laughter bubbled up.

"Yeah, I guess it was. I'll think about how to do it properly. I want you to say yes."

"Baby, I promise you I'll say yes however you do it." I kissed him again.

"Even after everything my mother has said?"

"Your mother scares the shit out of me. The thought of her wrecking my exam results and thus my future just to stop us from being together baffles me. Why is she so against us being in a relationship?"

"My mother hates me for being gay. She ignores it most of the time and still thinks I should hide back in the closet. She says it's okay to fuck whoever I want as long as I go home to a wife afterward." Archer's chuckle was dry and painful.

"Oh, Archer, I don't know what to say." I pushed myself up and stared into his eyes. The hurt and disappointment in his gaze pierced my heart. I cradled his head against my chest, letting all my love flow into him

"Just love me, Mallory. Make love to me," he whispered back.

"Always and anytime." So even though he'd come home to soothe me, Archer was suffering the most.

We made love all night, pouring everything we had into each kiss, each caress, each sigh. In the morning, we were exhausted but peaceful. Archer called into the office and canceled all his appointments, which allowed us to stay together.

We didn't have any further contact from Valerie Hawkins. Archer had spoken to his father, but I didn't think that had gone down too well. He was stomping around the apartment, muttering under his breath.

Would we get through this?

Nine

It was my graduation day. Valerie's threats had been unfounded. Whether the professors had ignored her, or she hadn't attempted to sabotage my life, I guessed I'd never know.

Archer was still wonderful. I'd never been so happy. I scanned around the auditorium for him, and my heart did a happy dance when I spotted him. His face lit up, and he gave me two thumbs-ups. I kept my eyes on him through the whole ceremony until someone nudged me, and it was my turn to collect my degree. I managed to get up onto the stage without falling on my ass, my gaze locked on my man, who whooped and hollered at me.

As I stepped past all the other graduates, weaving in and around them, I sought out Archer, then stopped dead in my tracks. He was leaning against a motorcycle, a huge red bow wrapped around the handlebars.

"What's this?" With a smile, I stepped into his arms.

"Congratulations, Mallory. It's a graduation gift. I've seen you eyeing it in the bike shop for months. I love you, sugar, and I wanted to give you something special." Archer gave me his thousand-watt smile, then in front of everyone, dropped to his knee.

"Mallory Carter Halston, will you please do me the absolute honor of becoming my husband? I love you and promise to keep loving you for the rest of our lives," he pronounced proudly.

It was as if the world had stopped turning. Nobody and nothing moved as Archer held out his hand and offered me a light blue box. Tears were burning in my eyes as I nodded.

"Yes. Oh, my god, yes." My hand shook as I reached out for the box. Archer stood and lifted the lid. Inside was a platinum ring with an onyx band in the middle. It was elegantly perfect and timeless in its beauty.

As Archer slid the ring down my finger, the crowd around us cheered and clapped. People held up phones and filmed or photographed us. I bet this would get onto social media within seconds, but I didn't care. In fact, I was grateful for it. I wanted to see this moment over and over again.

"I love you, Archer. I seriously fucking love you," I whispered against his lips.

"Yeah? I reckon I love you more." He pressed his mouth on mine, and his kiss was pure ownership. Archer claimed me in front of my friends and peers.

Breaking apart, I turned my attention to the bike. "You ready to get out of here?" I ran my hand down the sleek black paintwork and leather seat.

"Hell, yeah." Archer stepped around to the other side of the bike, picked up two helmets, and offered one to me.

In minutes, we were away and racing down the wide campus roads and onto the highway. Archer had his hands on my waist, but he wasn't clutching at me; he felt comfortable and at ease with me riding away. Twisting and turning through the city streets, I brought us back to our apartment building. I waited at the barrier for the underground parking to lift, then drove us down to the space next to Archer's BMW.

Letting Archer climb off the bike first, I lifted my helmet off and swung my leg over the bike. "Wow. That was awesome. Dammit, Archer, you're about to get so lucky." I grinned and wrapped my hand around the back of his neck, tugging him up to my body. "I can't wait to see you in leathers."

His laughter filled me with so much happiness. The twinkle in his bright-green eyes so full of promise sent shivers over my body.

"We need to get inside and get naked. I think we've got some celebrating to do." Archer grabbed my hand and dragged me to the elevator.

As the door slid shut behind us, Archer pushed me against the cool steel wall and tangled his hands in my hair. "You've made me the happiest man alive. Not just because you said yes but every minute of every day."

As he leaned in to kiss me, I felt so complete. He slipped his tongue between my lips, dueling and dancing with my own. My helmet hit the floor with a clunk, and I dragged him against my body. His erection rubbed my own. The ping of the elevator arriving at our floor broke us apart. The door opened, and I rushed forward to our door. Archer crowded me from behind as I fumbled with my key.

"Open the door, Mallory, unless you want me to fuck you out here? I will, you know. I want to be inside you so damn much."

The key slipped into the lock, and I pushed the door open. We stumbled inside and pulled our clothes off.

"When do you want to get married?" I asked as we lay together in the huge tub, my back to his chest. The warm water flowed over me as Archer ran his hands over my abs and down to my junk.

"Anytime. The sooner, the better. I want you to have my name. I want to show the world you're mine and I'm yours," Archer whispered into my ear.

"Then we need to go to city hall and get a license. I'm happy to marry you tomorrow or as soon as we can."

"Me too." His mouth was so close his breath was hot on my damp skin.

"What about your mother? Will you tell her?" I hated bringing her up. Archer hadn't seen or spoken to her since her visit to me. He still spoke to his father, so I guessed Valerie knew we were still very much together.

"My mother is nothing to me. I won't let her anywhere near us. Us being together is what's important to me. That's all that matters." Archer leaned down and kissed my neck.

Ten

We had a lazy breakfast today. I'd been tasked with getting the marriage license, since Archer needed to be across town and I wasn't working. I'd finally given in and handed in my notice. Now that I'd gotten my degree, I needed to look for engineering positions. Something I should've done before now, but the threat of not passing my finals had put me off searching. An honors degree should be enough to get my foot in the door somewhere good.

"I'm off to work, Mal," Archer called to me from the hallway.

"Hold up, mister. Not so fast. I want kisses before you leave me alone." I mock-pouted at him, making him laugh.

"Oh, sugar. I'll always give you kisses. Come here, hot lips." He dragged me into his arms. Holding my face in his palms, he kissed me soundly. "There you go. Now I love you, and I'll see you later."

"I love you too. Be careful, Arch."

"Always." He kissed me softly. "Good-bye, Mallory."

He walked out the door, and I still couldn't believe my luck. This amazing, beautiful man wanted me. Sighing at the closed door, I headed back to the bedroom to shower. My head was filled with promises of a good life to come.

When I got back from getting the license, I made myself some sandwiches and searched through the job sites on the Internet. A knock on the door startled me out of my concentration. My first thought was of

Valerie Hawkins, but two cops stood in front of me, a grim expression on their faces.

"Can I help you?" What were they doing here?

"Mallory Halston?" the taller of the two men asked.

I nodded.

"Can we come in?" The taller, dark-haired cop took a small step closer, encouraging me to open the door.

"Of course." My stomach clenched.

When they stepped inside, I closed the door behind them. I led them through to the living room and offered them a seat.

"What can I do for you?" I sat opposite them. The taller man shared a look with his partner I couldn't decipher.

"Mr. Halston, unfortunately we have bad news for you. Mr. Archer Hawkins was involved in a traffic accident this morning. A semi ran a red light and hit Mr. Hawkins's vehicle."

I jumped up. "No, no way. He only had a short drive. Where is he? What hospital was he taken to?"

"I'm sorry, Mr. Halston, but Mr. Hawkins passed away at the scene. I'm very sorry to have to tell you this." He carried on talking, but I couldn't comprehend what he was telling me.

"Mallory?" His partner walked toward me, but I backed away.

"No, no! We're getting married. I got the license this morning. He can't be. He loves me. He wouldn't leave me."

"Is there someone we can call?" he asked, but I shook my head.

"I need to go to him. Please take me to him." My body shut down as my brain tried to make sense out of all this.

"We can do that. Let's go." The man didn't look happy about it, though.

After a tension-filled silent ride to the hospital, which seemed to take forever, the cop finally pulled up in front of the ER.

I didn't wait for the car to come to a complete halt but jumped out and raced inside. A huge man stepped before me and blocked my way.

"Let me through. I have to get in. I need to see him." I pushed against this wall of a man, but he shook his head.

"I'm sorry, Mr. Halston. You aren't allowed in here. Mr. and Mrs. Hawkins have asked for you to be refused entry here. This is for family only. You aren't family."

"But we're engaged. We're going to get married. I need to see him. I need him. He'll want me here," I begged with tears pouring down my face as I clawed at his chest.

The two policemen walked past me and talked to Archer's parents. Lawrence wouldn't meet my eyes, but Valerie marched up to me with her usual sneer.

"Get out of here. Get away. I warned you." She slapped my face.

Stunned, I clutched my cheek and stumbled backward, then collapsed to the floor. I dropped my head in my hands and cried as I'd never cried before.

Hands lifted me up and led me to the exit. "I can't leave. I don't want to leave. Nooooooo."

I was back alone in the apartment, with no idea how I'd gotten here.

Lying on our bed, Archer's pillow in my arms, I rocked. The scent of him was all over it. I couldn't let it go.

It was dark now, only the moonlight streaming through the huge window. How long had I been here?

The door opened, and I sat up. Archer's mother stood in the doorway.

"Get out, Halston. I'm giving you fifteen minutes before I call the cops and have you arrested for trespassing."

Archer might look like his mother, but he was nothing like her. How could her son, her own flesh and blood, be so amazing while she was so evil.

"What did I ever do to you to make you hate me so much? Why couldn't you be happy that your son had found someone to love, someone who made him so happy?" She narrowed her eyes at me. "Are you jealous? Is that it? Have you never had someone who loves you so much it makes your heart sing?"

"I want you out right now. You have no right to talk to me like that. You're despicable. You stole him away. This gay idea he had would've gone away if you hadn't come into his life."

"You really are fucking crazy." I slid from the bed and strode up to her. "You have no idea how to be a decent human being. The man I love with my whole heart is your son, and he has just died. He's been taken away from me. Everything we planned for, every dream we had, has been stolen from us, and all *you* can think about is hate."

She didn't say anything, just stood there, tapping her foot.

I knew I'd never win from a supreme court judge and had no other choice than to do as she'd ordered me. I spun away to the closet, grabbed a duffel bag, and shoved clothes into it. Tears blinded my vision, and I had no idea what clothes I was taking.

I wiped at my cheeks and looked at her cruel face again. "The only joy I have is knowing he loved me. He loved me more than anyone else in the world, and you have to live with that. You have to live with the fact that he never wanted you. He never wanted to see you again. The last thing he said to me was that he loved me. The last thing he said to you was that he never wanted to see you again. And you're right. I want to be out of here. I hope never to see you again."

Storming around the room, I collected some photographs and a few of the special mementos of our life. Unable to bring myself to look at her again, I walked out of the room that had brought me so much joy and happiness. After shrugging on my leather jacket, I grabbed my helmet as well as Archer's—I had to have it with me—and stepped out of the apartment, leaving everything behind. The pain in my heart cleaved me in two, but here wasn't the place to fall apart. The place where every day up till now had been filled with nothing but love, laughter, and joy, something I hadn't expected to find again. I'd had my chance and lost it.

Starting Over

Eleven

Mallory

As I wandered up the high street, I got a good vibe about this town. It was quiet enough to keep my head straight and to ease some of the pain and sadness that had been wrenching my heart and soul. A place for a new start, maybe. I stopped outside a bar, where a vacancy for a bartender hung in the window. Would they be interested in a new face in town? Would they trust someone who looked like me? I had nowhere to live, no possessions. I was too thin, and my hair was too long. I didn't look like the best person for the job, but I hoped they'd see past all that. I'd give it my all if they gave me a chance.

I tried the door, but it was closed. I didn't see a sign with their opening hours. What should I do?

"Hey, you okay?" a voice behind me asked. I spun around. Wow, the man was incredibly good looking.

"Um, yeah, I guess. I was just looking for the owner," I stammered.

"I'm the owner. I'm Kes. What can I do for you?" Kes hooked his thumb over his shoulder to a shining new pickup truck parked several feet away. "I was just driving past and saw you. Are you interested in the position here?"

"Yeah, I am. I haven't done bar work before, but I've worked as a barista." Working in a coffee shop couldn't be that different from bar work, could it? I forced myself to stand straight. Losing Archer had made me shrink into myself. I'd stayed away from people and busy places, finding quiet motels to lock myself away to grieve. The pain of losing him was still raw and painful, but for him, I needed to straighten myself out. He wouldn't want me to be this way.

"Okay, are you local? I don't think I've seen you around." Kes sounded kind, but I still flinched at his question.

"No, I've just moved here. I'm Mal...I mean, my name is Carter." I really needed to stop stuttering.

"Okay, Carter. We open at twelve, but I won't be here till three. Can you come back then?" He seemed to be taking me seriously.

"Yeah, sure. Thanks, Kes. I'll see you then."

With a nod, he walked back to the pickup, hopped in, and drove away.

Okay, that was the first hurdle taken, but now I had to wait until three. I wandered down the street, enjoying the quiet and fresh air until the sign of a coffee shop caught my eye.

I sat quietly in the window of the cozy coffee shop. My first thought, as always, was to call Archer and tell him. My heart wrenched again, making my stomach twist in knots and my breath hitch in my throat. Would I ever feel any better?

The last four weeks had been excruciating, the pain and emptiness inside me unbearable. Maybe here was the chance to start again, to be a different me. That was why I'd given the bar owner my middle name. I could be alone with my grief. Leaving the man I had been with Archer behind me wouldn't be easy, but what choice did I have? I needed to start over.

Not knowing where to go or what to do, I'd just ridden, putting miles and miles behind me, stopping only to crash in a cheap motel. The first time I'd stopped, I'd stayed for four days, consumed with pain and loss. Even in sleep, I grieved for him, calling out, searching for him. I sprinted down corridors and through doors, never reaching him. He was always just out of my grasp.

At just before three, I made my way down to the bar again. Nerves raced through me as I got closer. Taking a deep breath, I opened the door. Inside, another gorgeous man greeted me.

"You here to see Kes?"

"Um, yeah. Is he here?"

The man gestured at Kes walking out from a door at the rear of the bar.

"Hi, Carter, thanks for coming back. Let's go to my office." I followed him to the back, where he stopped halfway a dimly lit corridor. He let me step through the door, then closed it behind us.

He was about the same age as Archer but so very different. His shoulder-length hair was tied back at his nape. His eyes sparkled as he told me about the position and hours available. The pride as he talked about the bar rang through in his voice. I couldn't believe my luck. This guy seemed so nice and genuine.

"What do you think, Carter? Do you think you would fit in here?" Kes asked. I was still waiting for him to ask me why I was here, but he didn't ask. Okay then. I could let him know a little bit about me.

"Yes, I think I'd like it here. Like I said, I'm new to the town and am looking to settle somewhere quieter than the city. I've been through a rough time, and I'm trying to find myself again. This looks like a good place for that." Would this be enough, or would he ask me anything else?

"I can tell you've had a hard time, but as long as you're clean and sober, I'm happy to give you a chance."

"I promise it's nothing like that. Just my personal life took a heavy blow, and I had to get away. I'm not much of a drinker, and I've never done drugs. I can take tests if you'd like."

"No, that's not necessary. I trust you. You don't look like a bad guy, Carter." Kes lowered his gaze, then looked back up at me. "Do you have anywhere to stay?"

His question surprised me. Why would he care where I was staying? I was a stranger.

"N-no, I'm going to see if I can get a motel and then find an apartment or just a room. I hadn't expected to find a place to stay, let alone a job," I stammered again, not sure why I'd suddenly become nervous again. He wouldn't turn me down until I found a place, would he?

"Okay, there's a small apartment upstairs. It's nothing fancy, but it has a living space, bedroom, kitchen, and of course a bathroom. It's furnished, but again, don't expect too much. It's yours if you want."

Wow. I hadn't been expecting that. My chest expanded as it filled with unexpected emotions. I bit down on my cheek to stop myself from crying at the kindness of this stranger. I nodded and tried to find my voice to thank him.

"I'd like that very much. Thank you, Kes. You're being very kind to me." I smiled, something I hadn't done for a while.

"Okay then, that's settled. Come on, let me introduce you to the guys, and you can have a look around. I'll get Denver to show you the ropes. You'll be replacing him. I'm sure we'll find more hours if you want them too."

"What about rent for the apartment? I can give you a deposit if you'd like?" I still had money in the bank. Valerie hadn't been able to get her hands on any of the accounts.

"Don't worry about it. It comes with the job. Trust me, Carter. I'll find you living on the premises very useful on early delivery days." Kes laughed and moved around his cluttered desk. "Let's go."

In the bar, the guy who'd spoken to me first was kissing another man. I tensed, and a quiet gasp escaped me. What would Kes think of his staff kissing at work? But he chuckled, walked behind the bar, and kissed the guys with just as much tenderness. I clapped my hand over my mouth.

Kes let go of the men, a smile lifting the corner of his mouth. "Carter, these are my boyfriends, Denver and East."

"B-b-both of them are your boyfriends?" I stuttered, my cheeks burning.

Kes narrowed his eyes. "Do you have a problem with that?"

"No, no, not at all. I'm sorry." I ducked my head.

"Don't worry about it. Both of them are all bark and no bite." Denver eased the tension. "Come on, let me show you around."

The man exuded a calmness that comforted me. Although I was sure he was interested in knowing more about me, he kept his

Here Without You

conversation light and talked me through the typical sort of day I could expect here. I relaxed a little and even asked a few questions.

Twelve

Carter

Life had become more bearable, and at times, I was even happy. I didn't feel like I was still one nudge away from falling apart, but then the dreams came back and dragged me back under. Cooper's Ridge was a good place to be. The people were so friendly and welcoming. Kes, East, and Denver were amazing men, and they'd let me be. They hadn't pried but listened when I let a piece of my past slip out.

I'd been here for over six months now and had witnessed the three men learn and develop their relationship. I'd watched as Denver bared his soul and was pulled back together by the men who loved him the most. I'd never even thought of a trio. I wasn't naïve, but it wasn't something I'd expected to find in such a small town. But the acceptance of the townsfolk to these men made me happy. The headcount of gay men in this town was larger than I would've imagined. Maybe it was the acceptance of these three individuals that encouraged people to be themselves. I wasn't talking pride marches or the likes, but a man holding another man's hand in the street wasn't unusual. The bar was so open to everyone that it made its mark not just here but in the surrounding towns too.

I even made new friends here. East and Denver. And Kes, who had become more than my boss. Shelley, who worked with me and kept everyone from me, especially on rowdy nights where I seemed to be fair game. I'd told her where I came from, and she knew I'd lost the love of my life. And yet she'd never asked me about my sexual orientation. And I'd never divulged it.

Archer still owned my heart, and until I was at peace, I couldn't imagine being with another man, or anyone else making me feel anything.

But last night's dream had been different. It started the same, with me sprinting through the corridors, but this time I found him. He was standing tall and strong and so heartbreakingly beautiful. His blond hair stirred as if in a breeze, but I couldn't feel it. All I could feel was him reaching out to me. I stumbled forward into his arms, his embrace familiar, the rightness of it oozing through to my core. As his lips met mine, we both moaned softly.

"I miss you, Archer. I miss you every day. I didn't get to say goodbye. Your mother..." My words faded away as a look of deep pain flashed over his face.

"My mother will get what she deserves," Archer spoke bitterly. "That's not why we're here, baby." His voice and his eyes softened again.

"What do you mean?" I got the feeling I wasn't going to like the answer.

"I'm looking for you, Mallory. I never want to let you go. I'll find you again, I promise. I love you, sugar. I'll always love you. Just look after yourself until we're together again."

The pain in my chest burned through me. "I don't understand. I need you. I need to remember you. What if you're wrong? What if you never find me? That you were it for me? I need to keep you in my heart and my head." My chest heaved as I dragged air into my lungs.

"Baby, I've seen it. I've seen us happy. Just promise me you'll wait." Archer's eyes twinkled as he gave me a mischievous smile.

Then he became more serious. "Mallory, I need to go. I love you. I'll always want you. I just need more time. Wait for me."

He pressed his mouth against mine, and I could taste him on my tongue. I could feel his hands in my hair as I deepened the kiss. With a sweet smile, he was gone.

My eyes flew open, and I was panting. I still smelled his cologne, felt his touch. I licked over my lower lip, and I tasted him, but for the first time, I wasn't crying. I felt peaceful, rested. The tear in my heart wasn't ripping me apart. Being called Mallory again, by him, only him.

"Oh, look, your fan club has arrived." Shelley nudged me in the ribs.

I'd been at work about three hours, and I was closing tonight. I had a long way to go yet. I wasn't in the mood for Shelley's games, but I looked up, nonetheless. Dan Mortimer and Conn Martinez sauntered toward the bar. They were good friends of Kes and came in often. Shelley was messing with me, but the way Dan looked at me still made me uncomfortable.

His amber-colored eyes sparkled with humor. "Good evening, Carter. You're looking good tonight."

"Thank you." Giving him a shy smile, I placed my hands on the pumps of the draught beer. "What can I get for you?"

"It's good to see a smile on your face, Carter. It suits you." Daniel shook his head at his friend, who studied me not too subtly. I waited patiently for their silent conversation to finish. "Sorry, can we have a bottle of merlot, please? We'd like to eat too, but I'll sort that out with your server when we're ready." He gave me a wink.

"Er, okay, shall I bring it over to you?" What was going on here? He didn't usually act like this, and I ignored it.

"That would be good. Thank you, Carter." With that, he walked over to his friend, who had taken a seat at a table at the back.

"Well, that was weird." Shelley dried her hands on a towel.

"Oh good, I thought it was just me. What's going on there, do you reckon?" I asked as I opened the door of the climate-controlled wine cabinet. I pulled the red wine out and grabbed two wine glasses from a shelf at the left.

I chanced a look at their table and met Conn's eyes, which seemed to be studying me. Then he nodded as if he'd come to a decision.

Again weird. Again I ignored it, instead uncorking the bottle and placing it and the glasses on a tray with a dish of nuts. Holding it in one hand, I carried it over.

"Gentlemen, would you like me to pour?" They both swallowed hard, then looked at each other.

"No, thank you, Carter. We'll take it from here." Conn was the first to speak.

"Okay, then. Let the server know when you're ready to order. Enjoy." I hurried back behind the bar. What the hell was going on with these two? I had a feeling it had to do with me.

But they left me alone for the rest of the evening. Kes and East showed up and sat with them for most of it.

Thirteen

Carter

The garden was crowded with people I now considered my friends. As I stood at the gate, taking in the laughing faces, Kes spied me and called out my name. I strolled over to him and handed over my contribution to the barbecue.

"You didn't need to bring anything, Carter," Kes said but accepted the bag. The invitation for a cookout had come as a surprise. I didn't usually have a Saturday off work, but Kes insisted I get out from behind the bar and arranged coverage for me.

"I can't turn up and not bring anything. That would be rude. It's only some ribs. I marinated them in my secret sauce." It was only recently that I'd started cooking for myself again. Since Archer died, I hadn't bothered to prepare anything. I'd lived on takeout and frozen TV dinners. Cooking was making me feel more of my old self. I hadn't dreamed of Archer again and slept through the night deeply and peacefully.

"I can't wait to try it, then. Come on, let's grab a beer and join the others." Kes walked over to a large plastic tub filled with ice and beer bottles. Following him, I scanned the garden. Dan was joking around with East, but when his eyes met mine, he gave me a blinding smile. Whenever I was around him, I got an unsettled feeling in my stomach. He said something to East, then headed in my direction. Yep, knots—or were they butterflies?

"Carter, it's great to see you outside the bar." Dan's eyes roamed over my face, lingering on my mouth. I swallowed hard and licked my bottom lip. His pupils dilated. "You're looking good."

"Um, yeah, thanks. It's good to see you too." I darted my eyes around the group of people, looking for anyone else to talk to but him. When my gaze fell on him again, he was watching me so intently a bolt of heat burned through me.

"Yeah, the place is packed with friends." Dan winked at me. "Here comes one of them now."

Conn walked up to us. As he reached us, he slung his arm over my shoulder and let it hang loosely there. I froze, but he didn't seem to notice. "How come you always get the best-looking man to talk to?" he asked Dan.

Dan chuckled. "I'm lucky that way."

Conn grinned and kept his arm around my shoulders. "It's good to see you here, Carter."

"Thanks. Kes was keen for me to get out of the bar for a while." I took a small step forward, trying to get out from under Conn's arm, which seemed to grow heavier the longer it lay there.

"Let go of him, Conn." Dan nudged Conn away from me.

"Excuse me," I muttered and scurried away to Denver.

"Hey, Carter. You okay?" Denver gave me a welcoming hug and clinked his beer bottle against mine. "Cheers, it's good to see you. What's going on with Dan? You looked uncomfortable there."

"I don't know. Dan seems to be flirting with me all the time, and I don't understand why or what he wants. Last week, he asked me to have dinner with him, but I'm not sure. It's confusing me, though. Are he and Conn an item? Sometimes they look like they are, but at other times, they seem to be just friends." I glanced over my shoulder. The men stood close together, their attention on me.

"They're not an item if that's what you mean. I think they've messed around a bit, but no, they aren't together," Denver answered matter-of-factly. "I think Dan likes you, Carter. He's a good guy. He was a geeky guy at school but always friendly, someone good. He's looking at you again."

"What, like he wants to eat me? Because it seems that way to me."

Denver barked out a laugh. "Yeah, I guess that's one way to describe it. The question is, do *you* want him? I know you've been through hell, but recently you've looked lighter and happier. I wondered if you might be looking for someone."

"I don't know. I'm not sure if I'm ready." I swallowed away the lump in my throat as grief washed over me. "My fiancé died. His mother hated me and forbade me to see him. I never got a chance to say goodbye. I'm not sure my heart can take any more hurt. If I let him, Dan could do me a whole load of damage."

"Oh, Carter, I had no idea. I mean, I guessed something bad had happened. You were so lost when you got here, but I would never have guessed that." Denver rested his hand on my shoulder as I shuddered at the pain I'd just unleashed.

"I haven't spoken to anyone about it, but I'm beginning to feel human again. Whether I'm ready to be with someone else is hard to work out." I ran my hand through my hair.

"That's only something you can figure out, but if you find it too much when he flirts with you, maybe you're not ready yet. There's no set time for grief, Carter. You will go through some very tough times. Maybe you could talk to someone about it. Have you thought about counseling?"

"I don't think I am. Ready, I mean. He's a bit too intense. I'm not comfortable with that. Thanks, though, Den. I appreciate your thoughts." Around me, everyone was having a good time, but my heart just wasn't in it yet. I was not as ready as I'd thought I was. "I'm gonna head off. I'm sorry, but I can't do this."

"Yeah, okay. Take it easy, Carter. Don't let yourself forget what it's like to be happy." Denver gave me a sad smile, his eyes clouding over as if he knew all too well what it was to lose someone.

I walked through to the kitchen and made my way down the hall to the front door, where I'd left my helmet and jacket on a table just inside the door. I hurried out, but I had a feeling my admirer would notice I'd gone soon enough.

I'd just thrown my leg over my bike when Dan rushed out of the house. By his moving lips, he must've called out to me, but I pretended

Here Without You

not to notice. I needed to be away from him and the confusion he caused me. I knocked the visor down, revved the engine, and raced away.

Fourteen

Carter

I kept quiet at work in the weeks since Kes's cookout. Kes had been watching me. What was he expecting me to do? I just wanted an easy life. Dan hadn't been in much lately. Had Denver talked to him? Not seeing him had been good for me to gather my thoughts and analyze my feelings. I missed his flirting and easy smiles. Maybe a dinner date with him wouldn't be such a bad thing to do. It didn't have to go any further than being friends, but perhaps I could take a small step forward.

I hadn't been able to stop thinking about what Denver had said. Archer had been my whole life, just as I had been his. The pain of his loss weighed me down again. Tension crept into my shoulders and face. It was as if I could see my frown cross my forehead, which wasn't good when the bar was full of tourists. They wanted to have a good time, not a scowling bartender. Just as I pulled myself together and stopped thinking, the door opened, and Dan walked in. What was I going to do now? I looked around for Shelley or Kes. I could let them serve him; I was due a break anyway. Or I could man the fuck up and say hello to him.

His smile was tentative, but when I met his gaze head on, his eyes lit up, and a genuine smile broke through. He was a beautiful man. Tall, with strong legs and a broad chest. His amber eyes sparkled with laughter and mischief. I didn't get the massive buzz of excitement flooding my stomach I'd always had with Archer, but I felt some attraction to him. The butterflies were fluttering.

"Good evening, Dan. What can I tempt you with tonight?" I asked, a joking tone to my voice. His eyes widened.

"I was coming in to see you and maybe get you to agree to dinner with me. C'mon, Carter, it's only dinner. I'm a nice guy, I promise." He gave me a wink.

"I'm free on Thursday. Would that suit you?" I chuckled at the surprised look on his face. "What? Were you expecting me to turn you down?"

"I *am* surprised, Carter, but it's a happy surprise. Thursday night is perfect for me. Thank you." His smile was contagious, and we kept staring at each other. A cough behind me broke our connection. Kes and Shelley stood there with their eyebrows virtually disappearing into their hairline but grinning like loons.

"Cut it out, you two, and leave me alone." I laughed, but heat rose up my neck and cheeks.

Kes slung his arm over my shoulder. "You'd better behave, Dan. I'd hate to have to take you down if you hurt my man here."

"I promise I'll be the perfect gentleman. I'm a well-respected man around here, I'll have you know." Dan mock-punched Kes on his arm.

"Yeah, yeah. I'm sure you are." Kes laughed, then strode away back into the office.

"Okay, now that I've been embarrassed by my friends here, what would you like to drink, Dan?" Time to get back to work.

"A beer would be good tonight, Carter." Dan took a seat at the bar. "You mind if I keep you company?"

"As long as you're drinking or eating, you're more than welcome to stay." I smirked and gave him a wink that had him blushing this time.

It wasn't too busy tonight, and I managed to to talk to Dan more than I'd thought. He was a nice guy. Our conversation was easygoing and more of a fact-finding mission. I was surprised just how much we had in common. He was the same age as Archer at thirty-one, but he didn't seem to care about the nearly seven-year age gap. It certainly didn't bother me.

Dan left at around ten thirty with a sweet smile and a squeeze of my hand. "I'll see you on Thursday, Carter. Is seven thirty good for you?"

"That's great. Shall I meet you here?"

Dan nodded, then strolled out into the night. Shelley nudged my arm. "He's a nice guy, Carter. I wouldn't have encouraged you if I didn't like him."

"I know, Shell, but I've had such a tough time lately. It's difficult to look forward. I'm trying, though, and I like him. I'm just not sure if I'm ready to take it any further than friendship."

"Don't overthink this, Carter. I think it's exactly what he said, just a dinner."

The rest of the evening passed quickly, and even though it had been a relatively easy night, I was ready to go upstairs and to my bed.

After seeing Shelley to her car, I went back inside, locked up, and took the internal stairs to my apartment. I liked living here. It was small, but I'd put my mark on it. I'd bought some extra furniture and put out the few pictures and mementos I'd managed to snatch up as I'd left. It was enough for me.

I stripped off my clothes, dumped them into the hamper, and stepped into the shower. As the hot water pounded over my head, memories of Archer flooded my head again. The tug in my chest as my heart hurt hadn't lessened, but I was feeling something else now, something a bit like hope. I wasn't over Archer and nowhere near ready to tempt my heart with someone else. But I was so tired of being sad. I needed some respite. I didn't know how to get over him, but maybe I didn't have to get over him. Maybe I simply needed to accept a new chapter of my life.

I scrubbed my body as I contemplated what to do next. No, I wouldn't be cheating on Archer if I went on a date with Dan. It might turn out to be a disaster anyway. I chuckled. Somehow I doubted Dan would let anything go wrong.

I got into bed and cleared my mind, which was surprisingly easy to do tonight. It only took moments until the heavy blanket of sleep came over me.

Fifteen

Archer

My head felt so heavy, and my eyelids were like cement as I tried to open them. I had to cough, but something in my throat made it too painful. My breath hitched. I thrashed my head, trying to swallow, but it hurt. What was in my throat? Panic clawed its way into my chest. Then a cool cloth wiped over my forehead, and through the fog in my head, my name being called registered.

"Archer, Archer. Can you open your eyes for me?" a quiet female voice asked.

I tried to lift my arm to my mouth, but it was like lead. It was as if I was choking, and I coughed again, trying to dislodge whatever was in my mouth and throat.

"Okay, steady. I'm going to take the tube out of your throat. Try to relax, Archer. It'll just take a moment."

A hand touched my face. "Take a deep breath, then exhale." The hand tugged gently, and the tube slid out of my throat. I coughed heavily, a thousand pins pricking into my throat, which felt like the roughest sandpaper, and my mouth was too dry to make any lubrication for it.

"Thirsty," I croaked as I tried to lift my hand again, but nothing moved. "Where am I? What happened?" I finally found the strength to open my eyes, and I blinked in the bright light, wincing in pain.

"Archer, relax. You're in the hospital. You were in a car accident. Let me get the doctor. I'll tell your family you're awake."

"Mallory, where's Mallory?" I scanned around me and didn't see him.

"I don't know about a Mallory, but your mother is here. I'll let her know you're awake," the nurse said.

I hurt everywhere. I could hardly move, and if I did, every movement felt like torture. What had happened? My eyes fluttered shut again as pain shot through my body.

"Archer," a male voice spoke my name, and I forced my gritty eyelids open again.

"I hurt." I grimaced as my voice scratched through my throat.

"Archer, my name is Dr. Cavanaugh. I'm the chief trauma surgeon here. We can sort your pain out for you. If you're up to it, I want to run through your injuries and the treatment you've received so far."

The same nurse came back and handed me a controller. "This is for your pain relief, Archer. Just press the button. It'll only administer the correct dose. You can't overdose on it, but it gives you more control."

I pressed the button and turned my attention back to the doctor. "What happened?"

"You were hit by a truck on your way to work. The driver had been drinking the night before and was still over the limit when he ran a red light and crashed into you. I'll start at the top. You've sustained cuts and lacerations on your face, neck, and scalp caused by the glass breaking and the airbag, so you needed sutures. Your wrist and both your ulna and radius are broken. We had to pin both bones. Also, you have a hairline fracture in your left collarbone. How are you doing so far?" he asked.

"I'm okay. The meds are kicking in. Please carry on." I wanted to get this over with. I needed to see Mallory. He had to be going out of his mind, which raised the question...how long had I been here? "When did this happen? When can I see my fiancé?"

"Please let me finish, and we can talk about your visitors. You suffered a pneumothorax, and the paramedic had to insert a chest drain as you were being transported here. Scans show that your spine is intact, but you have bruises all over your back. Scans also showed a ruptured spleen, so we had to remove it."

"Damn." I wasn't sure I could deal with much more. The quicker it was over, the sooner I got to see Mallory. "Go on. What else?"

"I'm sorry, Archer. You're very lucky to be alive. If you'd been in a smaller car, I don't think you would've made it. Because you were hit from the side, the protection bars in the door shielded you, but the impact still snapped your femur and only just missed your femoral artery. If it had been nicked, you would've bled out before we reached you. Unfortunately, the bone had to be pinned and plated, and we've fitted an external fixator to hold everything in place. Your ankle was also broken. The right side of your body isn't as badly injured, but your ankle shattered, and our orthopedic guys had to do some serious repair work. Do you have any questions?"

"You haven't told me how long I've been here. When did this happen?" How long had Mallory been waiting? He had to be out of his mind.

"Five days ago. We kept you heavily sedated and intubated when you went into breathing difficulties. We reduced the level of sedation, allowing you to wake up when you were ready. Your mother is here. Would you like her to come in?"

"I don't give a shit about my mother, but I want to see Mallory, my fiancé."

"I don't think anyone of that name has been here. You'll have to ask your mother."

"When can I go home?" I just wanted Mallory. He should be here holding my hand, listening to this, helping me understand what had happened. Why wasn't he here? Somebody must've told him I was in the hospital. According to the doctor, I was here five days already.

"You're going to be here for a long while yet. I'll go into more details later. Right now, you need to rest."

I closed my eyes, giving in to the sedative effects of the pain meds.

I dreamed of Mallory calling me, shouting my name. I tried to yell back, but no words came out. I followed his voice through a maze of corridors, but instead of gaining in on him, I got farther and farther behind until his voice faded away. The walls came down, leaving me alone in an empty space, devoid of color or sound. I was alone, the weight of my sadness crushing me into darkness.

A different voice dragged me from my sleep, one I recognized but didn't want to hear or see. My mother.

"Archer. Archer, can you hear me?" Her loud whine bored through my skull like a hammer drill.

"I think the hounds of hell can hear you, Mother. Shut the fuck up." I pried my heavy eyes open. She was standing with her arms folded across her scrawny chest with her usual scowl on her spiteful face. "What are you doing here? Where's Mallory?"

"I'm here because I'm your mother. And as for that lowlife, who knows where he is? Good riddance to him."

"What do you mean, you don't know where he is? Did you see him? Have you told him what happened to me?" My heart beat wildly. What if she hadn't bothered to tell him?

"Of course he knows. I sent someone over to your apartment to tell him. I haven't seen or heard from him since. He obviously doesn't have any feelings for you. He was just after your money, darling. Everyone could see that."

"Get out. Go and find him. I don't care what you think about him. What we have is real. We're going to get married. I don't want or need you here. Find him." I tried to move, but the pain was too bad, and I cried out, reaching for the button to administer more pain relief.

"Well, he already seems to have failed on the 'in sickness and in health' part of the vows, don't you think?" Her sneer made me shudder.

"Just get out and don't come back until you have him with you." I closed my eyes as the tears burned. I wouldn't cry in front of her. I wouldn't give her the satisfaction of seeing how devastated I was.

Sixteen

Archer

"This is it. Are you ready?" Mason Reynolds, my boss and friend, was here along with his brother, Austin, to take me home.

"I've been here for three months. Damn sure I'm ready. Hell, I was ready three months ago." I laughed and grabbed my crutches.

Austin picked up my bags and handed a couple over to his brother as I pushed myself up to stand. When we walked out of my room, cheers and applause erupted. My doctors, physical therapists, and nurses were standing under a good-bye banner. Tears prickled my eyes as I looked at the people who had helped me walk again, who had listened to me rant and cry as I struggled through the pain. The pain of my broken and battered body had been nothing compared to the ache of my broken and shattered heart.

The nurses would let me talk all night if I wanted to. They listened and never judged me or told me to move on. They knew never to let my mother in my room again. Even when she'd tried to show up with my dad, they'd turned her away. I didn't know what, but she had done or said something to Mallory to make him leave me. When I allowed a visit from my father, I didn't believe him when he backed up my mother's story. He wouldn't quite meet my eye, constantly smoothing my sheets or looking around the room. "Why do you put up with her? You know something, and you're too chicken shit to tell me," I shouted. My anger issues weren't completely under control yet, and I didn't give a damn. "Get out and don't come back until you're prepared to man up and tell me what she did. Because that bitch doesn't have a decent bone in her body."

He hadn't returned, and I didn't care, not for them, not anymore.

Now it was time to go home and get my life back on track. I still had a long way to go to be healthy again with many more hours of physical therapy to get the strength back in my legs. But I was determined to get the old me back. I'd go back to work, and I would move forward.

"You shouldn't have done this." I slowly made my way to the nurses' station, where cards and gifts were waiting for me.

"We love you, Archer. How could we let you go without a send-off?" Malik, my favorite physical therapist, hugged me.

"Yeah, yeah. I've been a pain in your butt for the last twelve weeks. You can't wait to get me out of here."

It took another thirty minutes of hugs and good-byes before we made it out to Mason's SUV. It felt strange to be going home. What was I going to do there by myself? I'd had the locks changed after I'd banned my mother from visiting me. Her poisonous vitriol had been too much to bear. I hadn't spoken to her for nearly five months. My recovery had been long and painful. I developed an infection in my thigh from the pins, and they had to operate again to clean it and replace them on the fixator. Then my lung collapsed again, and that really hurt. More tubes and more drains, which had led to more heavy painkillers and the loss of time as the days floated into each other.

Mason had handled the case against the driver of the semi that had hit me. He'd run a red light and had been over the legal limit for alcohol. He'd already had previous DUIs, and the last had expired only a few weeks before. The CCTV had caught the moment he hit me, and hell, I didn't know how I'd survived. He got a lifetime driving ban and four years in jail. He also had to pay damages to me, but the money was unimportant. I just wanted that asshole off the road.

"Are you okay back there?" Mason asked as I tried to sit comfortably while still keeping my leg straight. The fucker grinned at me through the rearview mirror.

"Yeah, fucking awesome. I'm covered in dog hair, and I'm sure the seats are drenched in spit or juice." Although he had kids and a huge dog, his car was immaculate. "You been letting your lovely wife use your pride and joy again?"

"My wife and kids are my pride and joy," he growled back, "but if she's messed it up, she'll get her ass spanked."

Austin burst out laughing. "That's why she's messed it up, bro."

Minutes later, we pulled up at my apartment building. When I'd lain in the hospital, I hadn't been able to wait to go back home, but now dread filled me to enter the tall steel-and-glass structure. I didn't want to see the empty spaces where Mallory had cleared all his stuff out. I was going to sell it and find somewhere else to live. I might even move away. I needed a few more weeks of work on my legs, but I was going to the rehab center in a local gym. They mainly dealt with veterans with amputations, but Mason had sorted it with the guys who owned it that I could continue my exercises there.

"Are you sure you want to go in, Arch? I've told you we've still got our apartment in the city you can have." Mason swiveled in his chair to face me.

"No, maybe after I've been inside, but I've got to get my shit together. Everything I own is in there. I need to look around and see with my own eyes. He may have left a note or a forwarding address, or maybe he's cleared out everything. I have no fucking clue what happened."

"Come on, then. Let's do it. After, we take you out and get you drunk." Austin clapped his hands, then opened his door and stepped out of the car.

I shuffled closer to the door, wrenched the handle open, and tried to get out. My main problem was not having a dominant leg. The ankle on the right was still so weak, and any heavy pressure on my left made my thigh throb. It took a couple of minutes, with both of them helping me, but I got out and upright and hobbled on my crutches to the entrance.

The doorman held the door open for me. "It's good to see you again, Mr. Hawkins. Welcome home."

"Thank you," I answered, but it didn't feel right. I really didn't want to be here.

Mason took the key from me and opened the door. I stepped inside my home, a place I used to love. It looked just like the last time I was in here. The magazine I'd been reading was still on the sofa. On the sideboard stood a vase with the flowers I'd bought for Mallory before he graduated, the leaves and flowers now withered and brown.

As I walked farther inside, the musty smell of an unlived-in space hit my nose. A stab of pain pierced my heart, and I could hardly breathe, but I kept moving, desperately looking for any evidence of him. I found plenty: shoes on the rack in the hallway, a sweater on the sofa, his favorite mug on the coffee table. Why would he leave his belongings if he'd walked out on me? It didn't make any sense at all.

At the door to our bedroom, I staggered. Mason's hands kept me from falling. Our bed was unmade, but on the top lay a marriage license. He got it. Confusion flooded me as I hobbled farther into the room. His clothes were still in the closet, his toiletries still in the bathroom. Why hadn't he packed his stuff? But wait. Things were missing. The photographs of us, the box in which he kept something from every date we'd had. Silly mementos I'd laugh at, but he'd never cared. *I love them. We will always remember everything we do together.* His words came back to me loud and clear.

"Something's wrong. This doesn't make sense." I turned to my friends. "Why would he leave his clothes but take our pictures and trinkets?"

"I gotta agree. A guy leaving you wouldn't give a shit about his photos of you, but he'd want at least a couple of sets of clothes." Mason gazed around the room, shaking his head.

"Why don't you get Lucas to look for him?" Austin asked. "You know he'll find him."

"I don't know. I'll think about it. I could be wrong, and he really did just walk out of my life. Do I really want to be faced with that again? Thanks, Austin."

"What do you want to do? Do you want to stay or come back with us?" Mason placed his hand on my shoulder and gave it a squeeze.

"Yeah, there's nothing for me here. I'll decide what to do with it another time." I picked up the piece of paper that would've meant so much to us and put it in my pocket. I pulled open a drawer, took out a small photo album, and handed it to Mason. "Can you put that in my bag?"

With one last glance around my happy place, I turned and hobbled out the front door, away from my past life.

Seventeen

Carter

Butterflies stirred and rose in my belly, swirling in nervous circles, as Dan walked toward me. He looked mighty fine. This was our fifth date, and tonight, we were going to a club. Dan had called me earlier with the change of plan, saying he was in the mood for dancing. I hadn't danced in what seemed like a lifetime, but I was ready for it tonight.

"Hey, babe, you look amazing." Dan's eyes roamed over my tight black T-shirt and skinny black jeans. He cupped my face and leaned in for a kiss. As his lips touched mine, the need for me poured out of him. We hadn't done too much touching and only shared a few kisses. I liked the boldness of his action tonight, though; it set the scene for a night of hot bodies moving to the same beat.

"So do you. I like the fitted shirt." I slowly perused his midnight-blue tailored shirt tucked neatly into a pair of gray slacks. I trailed my fingertips from his collarbone to his waist, reveling in the tiny tremors that ran over his skin.

"We need to go. Otherwise I'll be dragging you back to my place," he growled and grasped my hand.

"Shall we grab something to eat before we hit the club? I haven't eaten much today," I asked him as the cab drove us into Denton.

"Good idea. What do you want?" Dan was still holding my hand, his fingers entwined with mine, as he stroked his thumb up and down my own.

"Pizza will do. I don't need fancy, just something easy."

Twenty minutes later, we were in a pizzeria, digging into a everything-added pizza. "What made you think about dancing tonight?" I wiped my hands on a napkin and leaned back in the chair. I picked up my beer and waited for him to finish chewing.

"I dunno. I was at work, and I've had a really tough case lately. So I just thought what could be a better way of letting off some steam than having a hot guy grind against me while the music pounds. That would be you, by the way." He winked and sipped his beer. "The thought of you rubbing up to me as you get lost in the beat has had me hard all day long."

I coughed hard, choking on a huge gulp of beer. "Okay, I guess I asked for that. Well, I happen to agree with you, so we'd better finish up here so we can get our groove on." His eyes darkened as he signaled for the waiter.

The club was dark, only a few strobe lights illuminating the writhing male bodies. The rhythm of the bass reverberated through my whole body, making me want to let go and get lost in the music.

Twenty One Pilots' "Lane boy" blasted out, my favorite song to grind my way through with no problem. Dan still held my hand, allowing me to drag him into the throng. It didn't take long for him to get with it. With his hands on my hips, he moved to the beat. He was an amazing dancer, something I would never have expected from him. I soon let him take over. We danced and danced. I didn't know how many tracks had been played. We were lost in the music and the soft caresses we shared.

He pulled me up against his body and swung me around so my back was against his chest. I lifted my hands and hooked them behind his neck, letting my head drop back on his shoulder. Dan lowered his head and brushed openmouthed kisses on my skin. He was so hot. His hard dick pressed up to my butt. I hadn't realized how much I'd missed the soft touch of loving hands and the tantalizing nudges of a nice thick cock.

Memories of Archer filled my head, but that was all they were now. Memories, happy thoughts that deserved to be treasured. Dan ran his hands down my torso and rested them with his thumbs tucked just inside my front pockets. A true sign of ownership, of possession. It was a feeling I loved. I bumped my hips back against his groin and ground against him. His warm breath sizzled my skin as I rubbed over his dick.

"Fuck, Carter, the things I want to do to you." He scraped his teeth over my neck, then sucked on the tender skin. He was marking me, and I couldn't say I minded.

I twisted around again and, wrapping my arms around his neck, captured his mouth with mine and slipped my tongue through the small gap made by his sigh. Our hips still swayed to the music, but our mouths danced on their own rhythm. As I curled my tongue around his, I tasted the faint mint flavor from the candy after the pizza and beer, but it wasn't just his taste I couldn't get enough of. I held his head close to mine while his hands roamed down my back and cupped my ass cheeks, and he tugged me even closer to him.

Moaning, I pulled back. His irises dilated, losing the gleaming amber color, leaving his pupils as two small black discs, as his lust heightened.

"We need to get out of here," I groaned against his mouth.

We kissed the whole journey home. I hoped Dan had given the driver a decent tip to put up with us making out like teenagers.

When we got inside, Dan stepped back and gazed at me, waves of desire rolling off him. His tongue darted out and slid sensuously over his bottom lip. This was it.

Eighteen

Dan

"I may regret saying this, but I need to just clear this up in my head." Reaching out to him, I stepped back into his space. "Are you sure you want to do this? We can go slow if you're not ready yet."

"Daniel, I wouldn't be here if I didn't want this. I'm not going to turn you down. Let's just do what we feel is right. Because right now, I want to see you naked. I want to touch and taste you. I want to be here with you, doing this."

"Thank god. C'mon, let's get to my room. I want to peel you out of your clothes." I raced up the stairs, Carter hot on my heels. This was so much more than I'd imagined, and I wanted so much more from him. I needed to be inside him. He was perfect.

As soon as Carter had come in, I was transfixed, drinking in the sight of his slim body. His chest heaved with anticipation as he met my gaze head on. I took a step closer and grasped the hem of his shirt, then slowly peeled it up his body. The muscles I had only dreamed about emerged as I lifted the fabric higher.

"Damn, you're beautiful, Carter. Every inch of you is perfect." He raised his hands over his head, allowing me to pull his shirt off. As I dropped it to the floor, I kneeled and laid kisses over his chest and down to his abs. Each square inch of taut muscle got its share of adoration. I smiled against his stomach as he clenched when I dipped my tongue in his belly button.

Trailing my mouth from hip to hip, I reached up for his belt buckle and quickly unclasped it. I kept my mouth fixed to his skin. The rasp of his zipper being lowered filled the quiet room.

I raised my head. He was staring back at me, slack-jawed, eyes dark with pent-up raw need. His response to my quirked eyebrow was a subtle nod. His acquiescence spurred me on, and I hooked my fingers in his waistband and dragged the tight jeans down his thighs, leaving his snug black briefs in place. Carter took over, ripped his jeans down, and toed off his shoes. As he yanked the tight denim from his legs and feet, I stripped out of my clothes. In seconds, we were both standing in our briefs. Carter grabbed his junk through the fabric, and I had to hold back a moan.

Carter tugged me closer until our heated, eager bodies pressed together. His mouth was so close his warm breath ghosted my lips. I instinctively licked them, but before I could take it further, he stepped back until he bumped against the bed. As he sank down onto the mattress, I stayed between his parted legs. I was locked in the raw heat of his gaze, a feral desperate need I'd never thought I'd get to see from this amazing man, and now here he was, wanting me, waiting for me. He ran his hands slowly up my legs, making every hair on my body react to his touch as electricity pulsed like fire through my body, sparking every synapse inside me. I wanted to close my eyes and just feel, but his stare kept me fixed. His dark blue eyes were black now, shooting so much power I felt helpless. He licked over his lip, the sheen gleaming in the light from the hallway behind us.

Carter slid his fingers up the inside of my thighs, the touch light as a feather. I moaned as I pitched my hips forward. I wanted his mouth on me. I'd never needed anything more than I needed his hands, his mouth. Grazing over the fabric holding my painfully hard dick trapped, he reached the waistband and slowly lowered it. As the swollen, wet crown escaped from its confines, Carter only lowered the fabric enough to free my cock and balls.

"Watch." As if I could've looked away. His tongue darted out and captured the bead of moisture pearling at the slit.

The loudest groan escaped me as he licked me like a lollipop. He kept his eyes on mine as he traced the thick, throbbing vein with the flat of his tongue, then sucked the head into his scorching mouth. My hands found their way into his hair, and I held on for dear life as he took me deeper. This was a ride I wasn't sure I'd survive. My cockhead nudged the back of his throat. Then he pulled back, only to swallow me down on his next breath. He shoved my briefs down, letting them drop as they reached my knees. My legs buckled, but Carter's grip on my ass kept me upright as he worked on me. He continued to suck hard on the head, making me cry aloud. The sound of the slick, wet action and my unabashed panting filled the room. I couldn't hold back. My balls tightened. Carter noticed and snaked his hand between my legs and tugged on my balls, denying me any chance of release. I grunted but didn't complain too much. This man could do whatever the hell he wanted to me. Over and over, he took me to the edge with the best blow job I'd ever had. Even with his nose pressed hard on my skin, his eyes stayed fixed on mine. He tightened his hand on my sac again as he swallowed around me, my dick deep in his throat.

"Arggh. Carter, let me come. Fuck, I'm so close," I cried out as I squeezed my eyes shut and panted through my need.

Then his mouth was gone, and I whimpered at the loss. Opening my eyes again, I stared down at him. He'd removed his briefs, and I got my first glimpse of his cock. What a beautiful sight it was. Long and slim, just like he was. The rigid length stood proud from his body, the head deep red, glistening with the proof of his desperate need for me.

As I pushed him onto the bed, he scooted farther up and propped himself on bent arms. There was no hesitation or embarrassment in his eyes as I climbed up his body.

"Top or bottom," I murmured. Not that I gave a damn either way right now.

His molten eyes glazed over. "Bottom. I want you inside me. Take me, Dan. Fuck me. Own me." The hottest words ever.

I rifled in the drawer for the lube and a condom and threw them onto the bed next to us.

"God, I've dreamed of this moment. I've wanted to explore every inch of your sexy body, imagined my tongue sliding over every inch of you. I want to know every part of you, but that's going to have to wait.

Right now, I need to be inside you," I growled in his ear, then trailed my tongue over the shell and nipped the lobe. I loved how he was writhing beneath me as I sucked and bit his neck.

"Fuck, Dan. I need you. I need you now," he begged. His hands were feverishly roaming over my body as he clamored for me.

Kneeling up between his spread thighs, I grasped the underside and pushed his legs up to his chest. "Hold them, Carter."

He pulled on his legs, lifting his ass up higher to me, and I got to see his hole. Damn, I wasn't going to last when I got inside him. I grabbed a pillow and pushed it under his hips. With a shaky hand, I snatched up the bottle of lube, squeezed it, and generously coated my fingers, then dropped it again. God, I was nervous now. I needed to make it so good for him, to make sure he wanted me over and over. I looked back up at Carter. His face was flushed while sweat glistened on his skin.

"Please, Dan," he panted, giving me the go-ahead I needed. I rubbed my finger over his hole. He pushed down, and the tip slipped inside him. If I'd thought his mouth was hot, it was nothing to the feeling of his ass gripping my finger. As I worked it in and out a couple of times, he relaxed, and I added another, pumping him. His dick dripped precum over his stomach.

"More?" I asked as I nudged his hole with a third finger.

"Fuck, yeah." He wriggled his hips as I slipped the digit in. I was mesmerized by the sight of my fingers in his body, how eagerly he took me and wanted more.

After only a few more pumps and stretches, he was ready for me. I pulled my fingers out, and he whimpered. I tore the condom wrapper and quickly suited up and tipped more lube over the thin latex. As soon as I pressed against his pucker and slipped inside the first ring of muscles, he tensed up. I halted.

"Tell me when you're ready, baby," I whispered, and he smiled at me.

"You feel amazing and fucking huge." He chuckled, the action making me slip farther inside him. After another few seconds, he nodded. "I'm ready."

I pulled back slightly, then slid in fully, reveling in every ripple from his tight channel. As his muscles clenched and released, allowing me to bury myself to the hilt, I watched as Carter's eyes rolled back in his head. He groaned so sensuously and deeply the vibrations quivered over my dick, making my balls draw up again.

"More?" I asked as I pumped smoothly inside.

"Everything," he murmured back, giving me another glorious smile. My heart squeezed as I fell for him. I'd do anything and everything to make this man mine.

"Always." I pulled back and thrust deeper and deeper. Leaning over him, I captured his mouth and poured the depth of my emotions into him. When his legs wrapped around my ass, forcing me even deeper inside, I knew I wasn't going to last much longer.

"I can't hold on, Dan," he keened as he cupped his hands around my neck.

"Nor me. Let's do this together." I pulled out of his embrace and kneeled up again. "Stroke yourself, Carter," I ordered as I picked up speed. He did as I'd told him, his hand beating up and down his glorious cock, the tension in his body building. Fuck, I couldn't hold on. "Yes, baby, yes. Oh fuck, I'm coming."

As I stiffened and shot my load inside him, he coated his stomach with thick white ribbons. He came so hard his cum even hit my chest. I cried out and fired again. Carter let his legs drop as he threw his arm over his eyes. His chest rose and fell as he dragged deep gulps of air into his lungs. I'd never seen anything so beautiful.

I lowered myself and rolled off him. As my exhausted dick slid out, I dragged the condom off and dumped it into the trash can. Closing my eyes, I came down from the greatest high I'd ever experienced. When I turned my head, Carter was looking at me, his smile lazy and so hot. I leaned over and kissed him.

"You okay?" I murmured.

"Yeah, I am. I really am." He chuckled. Looking down at his chest and stomach, he laughed louder. "It looks like I needed that."

"Shower?"

"Yes, please, but only if you're coming too." He stroked his hand down my chest until he hit the sticky drops of his release. "Shit, you got it too."

After getting messy again in the shower, we cleaned up, and I waited hesitantly to see if Carter planned to leave. My stomach was in knots at the thought of him walking out. But when he climbed back into bed, my breath whooshed out of my body

"You okay with me staying?"

"I'd love for you to stay." I dropped my towel, clambered in next to him, and lay down. My heart beat faster when he snuggled into me and rested his head on my chest. As I carded my fingers through his damp hair, he drifted into sleep. It took me a while longer, not just because I was reliving every moment of this evening, but because I needed to make sure I kept hold of this amazing young man.

Carter rolled in his sleep and turned his back, allowing me to spoon up behind him. As he sighed, his hand tightened on mine, and he muttered, "good night" again.

Nineteen

Carter

I woke to a finger tracing patterns over my shoulder. Squirming, I opened my eyes and twisted around. Dan had his head propped up in his hand. He ducked his head and dropped a soft kiss on my mouth.

"Morning, baby," he whispered, and my stomach fluttered as the butterflies unfurled their wings. His amber eyes shone bright with happiness and a glint of mischief as he gave me a little half smile that showed off a dimple I'd never noticed before. The rough stubble on his face was new to me too, as he was always clean-shaven. I liked the early-morning Dan.

"Good morning," I murmured back and wrapped my hand around the back of his head. "I'll have another one if you don't mind." I pressed my mouth to his, and he quickly parted his lips to let me in. I softly moaned as he rolled me onto my back and deepened the kiss, sliding his body over mine. Without hesitation, I opened my legs to let him settle between them. As our dicks touched, another shameless mewl escaped me. Dan chuckled and flexed his hips into mine again.

He snaked his hand between us, grasped both of our dicks, and stroked them against each other. God, the feeling of our lengths rubbing up each other, with only our precum to lubricate the slide, made my eyes roll back into my head. It didn't take long before we were spewing our loads.

"You can't beat a bit of frottage first thing in the morning." Dan laughed. He surprised the hell out of me when he lifted his hand to his mouth and licked our combined cum off his fingers, then held out his index finger to me. Who was I to turn that down? As I flicked my tongue out, Dan groaned and attacked my mouth again. This guy was going to wreck me.

When we pulled apart, I looked around for a clock. "What time is it?" I didn't have anywhere to go, but I wanted to know how much time we had together.

"It's early, about eight. Do you have to leave?" His lips trailed tiny kisses up my neck, then reached my mouth. He kissed me with long lazy strokes of his tongue over mine.

I pulled back from his tempting mouth. "No, I'm good until this afternoon. Do you have to go to work?" I slid my tongue over his collarbone, reveling in the goose bumps that bloomed over his body.

"No, I'm free today. Shall we get breakfast?"

"I thought we'd just had it, or at least a protein shake." I winked as he laughed and pushed himself off me.

"Let's eat and then see what else we can get up to." His grin was contagious as he pulled me from the bed.

When I walked into the bar, it looked as if an intervention was about to take place. Kes, East, and Denver were here, as were Shelley and the new bartender, Paris.

"Hey, guys. What's up?" They wore all huge grins on their faces. "Why are you looking like goons?"

"We thought we'd come in and say hi. You know, just a catch-up." Kes's innocent expression didn't fool me for a second.

"Oh really, you just happened to drop by? Right, fine. I'll play along." I narrowed my eyes. I damn well knew why they were here. "How are you doing? What's new?"

Denver raised his eyebrow. Damn, I was wearing the same clothes as last night. Had he noticed? "Oh, we're all good, you know. Getting along with the joys of parenting. What about you? What's new with you?" His grin was devilish.

"I'm good. Nothing much to say. I'll just get to the office and start on the banking." I walked past, but East caught my arm and nudged the neckline of my shirt with his finger.

Scowling, I tugged away from him. "Fuck off, East."

"He's got a hickey." He smirked, and they all burst out laughing.

"Come on, Carter, spill the beans. What's going on with you and the hot lawyer?" Kes stopped laughing when I shot him a "back off" look.

But as the image of Dan and the amazing morning popped into my mind, I couldn't help grinning. "It's going well. That's all I'm going to say."

"Congratulations, Carter. Happiness looks good on you. And if it's Daniel who's making you happy, embrace it, buddy." Kes clapped me on the shoulder.

"Yeah, we're only messing with you. It's been great to see you smile more." Shelley hugged me and pecked my cheek.

The rest of the day dragged by while I kept watching the door. Dan had mentioned he'd try to come in, but he hadn't said when.

"Stop staring at the door. If he said he'll come, he will." Paris nudged me with his elbow.

"I'm not staring. I just glanced over when you happened to be looking at me," I grumbled.

"You keep telling yourself that." He bumped me again, a little harder this time. "It looks like your man's here."

I whipped my head around. There he was, my man—I gulped—striding toward me, his eyes on me and only me. His dirty-blond hair was in its rough-and-ready state that made me want to run my fingers through it. His amber eyes blazed with gold flashes. I drank in the fitted white T-shirt stretched tight over muscles I'd traced with my tongue. His well-worn blue jeans molded his long, strong legs.

His eyes flickered down to my mouth as I dampened my bottom lip. He was hot as hell.

"Hey, baby," he murmured.

"Hey, you," I whispered back as we both leaned over the polished wood bar. Our mouths touched, and I hummed against his soft but oh-so-firm lips. "I've missed you."

"I've missed you too."

When we pulled apart, the room had gone quiet, and everyone stared at us.

"Holy moly, you two are hot as hell." Shelley fanned her face. "I think they just got their Hollywood moment. That was straight out of the movies."

Not much later, I closed the bar. Paris had walked Shelley to her car, and Dan was waiting for me to finish locking up.

"Did you walk?" I asked.

"Yeah, I felt like having a beer or two while I gazed at you and thought about all the things I want to do to you when we get home." He had his arm wrapped around my waist with his thumb tucked into a belt hook as he told me more of his fantasies. Damn it. I was hard by the time we arrived at his place.

Twenty

Dan

These last couple of months—nearly three—I'd been with Carter had been the best I'd ever had. I was so close to telling him my feelings, that I'd fallen in love with him, but I still wasn't sure he was ready to hear it, even though I sensed he felt the same.

We'd spoken very little about his past. He'd told me his fiancé was killed in a car accident, but we didn't talk too much about it. I, for one, didn't want to talk about a man who had meant everything to him. Since Carter had turned up in Cooper's Ridge, I'd been watching him. The damaged man he had been then was nothing like the beautiful, funny, caring man he was now. And I wasn't going to remind him of that time again.

Even though he'd never so much as hinted at it, I could see how he felt about me, and not just when we made love. If he couldn't stay over, he'd leave me notes around the house that would make me smile. He remembered the things I liked, and he was a great cook. He'd told me that he'd had to learn, and instead of sticking to the basics, he'd dived in and learned how to do it properly.

I watched him now as he moved around my kitchen as if it were his own. He was comfortable here and knew his way around. So I let him get on with it and would deal with the clearing up afterward.

"What are you making tonight, baby?" I sat on one of the stools at the island, swirling the Pinot Noir around in my glass.

"Chicken Marsala. It shouldn't be much longer. How hungry are you?" He strutted toward me. I swung around on my seat and parted my legs so he could step between them.

"Hmm, that's a loaded question. What are you offering?" I tugged on his waist, pulling him closer as I waited for his mouth to touch mine. The taste of wine mixed with pure Carter made my head swim as I lazily stroked my tongue against his. I loved it when he slid his hands up my neck and into my hair, fisting it to the perfect level of pleasure and pain. I groaned as he devoured my mouth.

Releasing me from his clutches, he stepped back and wiped his thumb over his lip, a sight that was always so freaking sexy.

"I've made enough for you to freeze some for when your friend comes to visit. I know you'll eat pizza every night if I don't."

"We've talked about this, Carter. You don't have to stay away. I want you here. I want to show you off." I sighed. We'd had this discussion too many times for my liking.

"I will. I can't stay away from you for too long." He winked. "But your friend has had a shit time, and I'm sure he'd like some downtime with his best friend. He won't want me here while he's hurting and needs to talk it over with you."

"Dammit, Carter. I hate it when you make sense. Fine, but not too long. I don't want to sleep alone," I grumbled.

My best friend from college was coming to stay for a while. I'd offered him a partnership at my firm if he wanted or needed a change. He'd been in a horrific car accident that should've killed him, but he'd survived, only to find out his boyfriend had dumped him and run while he was still unconscious. He'd be here in a couple of days, so I'd better get my fill of Carter before he left me with my friend.

"You'd better be staying with me for the next couple of days, baby. Or I'll be tying you to the bed when you sleep." His eyes flared. Oh, he liked that idea. "Or maybe I'll just tie you to it tonight. What do you think?"

Carter flushed, and his eyes dilated as he nodded. "Fuck, yeah, you can tie me up anytime. I'd love that."

"That's good to know, baby. Good to know." I burst out laughing as he adjusted himself.

"Fuck off." He laughed. "Asshole."

"Yeah, baby, yours, all open and begging for me." Damn, now my dick was getting hard. "How long until dinner's ready?"

As we lay exhausted, breathless, and panting, I turned my head to him. It was now or never. His eyes met mine, the love blazing out of them.

"I love you, Carter. I know it's soon—"

He stopped me by placing his finger over my lips.

"I love you too, Dan, and it's not too soon. It's perfect."

Twenty One

Archer

"So what time does your flight get in? I'll come and pick you up."

"I've told you. I've got a rental car. I'll need some wheels when I'm with you. I'll call you when I land." A car horn honked. "Look, the cab's here. I gotta go. I'll see you in a few hours." Laughing, I cut him off. I walked out of the guest house Mason had kindly let me rent from him for the last couple of months.

The doctors had signed me off, and as long as I kept exercising and building up the strength in both legs, I was good to go. I'd accepted an extended holiday with my best friend, who was hoping I'd like the town so much that I would join his practice. Who knew? Maybe I would.

Before my accident, I'd always flown economy, refusing to pay extra, but this time I'd booked a first-class ticket. I still needed room to stretch out my leg. If I sat too long, it ached, and then I found myself limping when I walked again. I didn't want to look like I was an invalid anymore and had worked hard at the gym to improve my stance and gait.

The last nine months had been a living hell. I'd never thought I could lose a near-perfect life. I'd had a job I'd loved and excelled at, a home I'd been happy with, and then I'd found the perfect man. The age difference had never bothered me. Seven years was fine. I was only thirty-one, and Mallory always had seemed older than he really was. We just fit. It had worked. It had worked so damn well I still didn't understand why he'd left, and I guessed I never would. My family was the only fly in the ointment, but I'd shut down that part. My mother would get what she deserved in the end.

And now I was doing something for myself. Mason had told me I'd always have a job if I wanted one, and I hoped to go back, but not yet. A change of scenery was what I really needed right now, and I was excited about it.

When I collected my vehicle from the car rental, I laughed at the size of it. It was like a monster truck, but it had got a good-living-in-the-country feel about it. After setting up the GPS, I pulled out and headed off down the highway. Imagine Dragons were blaring out of the speakers, and I had a stupid smile on my face.

It took me just over an hour to drive into the town I hadn't visited since we were in college together. It had grown and prospered, with new houses and stores. The number of expensive cars driving past me showed there was still money to be made on ranches. As I turned into the street Dan lived on, I slowed down and checked the numbers. Soon, I pulled up into a driveway of a beautiful two-story house. I beeped the horn, then switched off the engine and climbed down. The front door opened, and my friend raced out.

"Hawkins, you fucker, look at you, standing on your own two feet. It's good to see you, man. It's good to know you're still living and breathing." He wrapped his arms around me and hugged hard, pounding his fist on my back. "You fucking scared me, Archer. Don't go getting nearly killed again, y'hear me?"

"Dan Mortimer, you ugly bastard. Get your hands off me, and let me breathe." My cheeks hurt from smiling so hard, and I was glad I wasn't the only one with a sheen in my eyes. "I promise no more fighting with trucks."

Dan chuckled. "Let's grab your bags and get inside. There's a beer with your name on it."

"I haven't brought too much. I wasn't sure how long you're prepared to put up with me. I'm not much fun lately."

"Dude, you can stay for as long as you want. I've got the room, and I think a bit of R and R is just what you need. I'm here if you want to talk about it, but I get it if you don't. Whatever you need, Archer. You know that."

"I do, and thank you. A beer sounds great. But can I take a shower first? Flying first class is good, but I've still got the whole airplane funk going on."

Dan grabbed my bag. "I'll show you to your room. It's got a bathroom attached."

"You've got a great place, Dan. You can't regret coming back here."

We were sitting on a gorgeous deck looking out over a huge backyard with a large pond and wooded area. The sun was setting, and the only other sounds were the cicadas chirping in the trees and the hiss of a beer bottle being uncapped.

"This is so the opposite of what I'm used to. I've never been anywhere so peaceful. You're a lucky man, Dan." I tipped my bottle at him as he stretched out on a lounger.

"I am, though it was tough at first. I had to deal with the death of my father and the expectancy of me stepping into his shoes. I never hated the thought of coming back. I just wasn't planning on it so soon after I qualified. But it's good here now. I'm happy." He waved his hand. "This place was a bargain, and I snapped it up. It had stood empty for a while. The old guy who lived here went into a nursing home after a stroke. After he died, his family just wanted to get rid of it. It needed to be gutted, but there's a great guy here who runs his own construction company, and he did all the work. I'll have to introduce you to him and his partners."

"Uh, partners? As in plural?"

He chuckled. "Oh yeah, and they're hot as hell. East is the construction guy. His boyfriend, Kes, owns a great bar on Main Street. They've been together for a few years now. In the beginning, it raised a few eyebrows, but then everyone got used to it. The fact that they didn't give a shit about what anyone thought helped, I think. Then a guy we all knew from school came back to live here, and after a couple of months, two became three. He's a hotshot surgeon and comes from a well-respected family. Again, a few of the oldies grumbled, but they ignored it, and it's great to see them all so happy. I envy them. I thought I'd be happily married by now, but the right guy has never come along. Until now."

"Wow. That's so cool. Lucky them." I looked over at Dan, who got a smirk on his face. "I know what you're thinking about, you dog."

He laughed hard and scrubbed his hand down his face. "I think that was one of the best nights ever. Something I've never repeated but wouldn't turn down again."

"I haven't thought about that in years, dammit." How could I have forgotten about the cute boy who'd tempted both Dan and me into his bed when we were together during college? Then Mallory's beautiful face filled my mind, and hurt and grief washed over me again.

"Yeah? Well, I have. When it's in your face, you tend to think about it. Not sure if Carter is up for that, though."

"So what's he like, your man? When do I get to meet him? I thought you were joined at the hip."

"He's being a stubborn ass and staying away so that we can spend some time together. He didn't want to tread on our time catching up and on me persuading you to stay and join me at work." Dan chuckled, but his eyes grew soft, the love he had for Carter pouring from him. "He's a good man. A keeper for sure."

"Yeah, I thought I had that, but it turned out he wasn't the man I thought he was." Pushing my hurt away again, I stood and stretched until the satisfying *pops* sounded. Dan was looking at me, or rather looking at my leg. After my shower, I'd put on loose-fitting sweat shorts. The scars running from my knee to almost my hip were still vivid and red. I wore support bandages on both ankles. They tended to ache and swell when I'd been on my feet too long. "Not a pretty sight, is it?" I said, my voice sounding hollow.

"Archer. I'm sorry. I didn't mean to look. You've been through so much. And I'm sorry I didn't visit. I was bogged down with a nightmare court case. But I realize I was wrong. I should've put you first. We've been friends, more than friends, for so long. I want to make that up to you. I'm fucking glad you're alive and here." Dan croaked out the last words as he rose to his feet, wrapped his arms around me, and held me tight. "It will right itself, Arch. I promise you. You'll get your happy ending."

I pulled away. "Yeah, I'm sure I'll have a long line of hot men wanting to love me." I snorted.

"Then you aren't seeing what I see. An amazing man who survived the most awful car accident. You've been through so much pain, and look at you. You're walking again. Your ankles must be more titanium than bone, and I can't imagine the hours of painful physical therapy you've endured. Archer, my man, you're an amazing, beautiful man. Any man should be honored to have you." Dan blushed as if he was embarrassed at his outburst.

"Would you?" I asked tentatively. It had been years since we were together, but we'd had a good time and ended it still being great friends.

"In a heartbeat, Archer. But I'm not the man you have in your heart."

"Thank you, and now you have a new man in your heart," I whispered and leaned forward to kiss his forehead. "I'm going to turn in. It's been a long day. You can show me the sights tomorrow."

"I'll do that. It will take about twenty minutes, but hey, why not?" He clapped me on the shoulder. "Sleep well, Archer. I'm happy you're here."

"Me too. Good night."

I woke up from the bright sunlight streaming through the curtains. A warm breeze washed over me as I tried to work out where I was. Birds twittered, and a dog barked, but nothing else broke the silence. I rarely had my windows open in my apartment, except the balcony doors. I didn't often hear birds singing, but the smell of coffee was something I was used to. I pushed myself upright and scanned around the room. Dan had done a great job of decorating it. The walls were a soft green, and the furniture in a distressed gray made it look elegant. The king-size bed was extremely comfortable, and sleep had come quickly last night. But now my stomach rumbled. I needed coffee and food. In that order.

After finishing in the bathroom, I washed my hands and studied myself in the mirror. The scars on my cheek and forehead were still fiery red, although the vitamin E cream I used was helping them to fade. I should probably shave but decided against it. I quite liked the stubble now. I was more tanned than I used to be after spending my time at Mason's place, and it suited me. I'd changed since the accident. Apart from the obvious pain of losing Mallory, I'd like to think I'd grown as a person. I'd had to toughen up and face all my challenges head on, and I'd won so far. Now I needed to get my heart and my head in the same place. Maybe it was time to believe Dan's words from last night.

As I walked downstairs, Dan was talking. Either he was on the phone, or he had a visitor. When I entered the kitchen, he was pacing the floor with his phone at his ear. He must've heard me, as he turned around and pointed at the coffeepot. I nodded and poured the hot, dark, and divine-smelling liquid into the two mugs on the counter.

"Yeah, baby. I miss you too....Yeah, he's good too. Just woken up, by the look of him. He's searching for the coffee....Yeah, Carter, I will....Call me later....I love you too." Dan ended the call and dropped the phone on the white marble breakfast bar. "Sorry about that."

"No worries. This is your place. You want anything in this?" I held up the mug.

"Nah, I'm good with this." He took it from me and put it next to his phone. "You hungry?"

"Yep, starved. Whatcha got?" I took a sip of coffee as he ambled to the huge black-lacquered fridge.

"I've got the lot."

Fifteen minutes later, we tucked into bacon, eggs, and waffles.

"Damn, that was good. I'm gonna need to exercise that off." Chuckling, I rubbed my stomach.

"How about we take a walk? I can show you around." Dan picked up the plates and put them in the dishwasher.

"Sounds good. How far are we talking about? Am I gonna need my cane?" My cheeks heated at the thought of him seeing me with a prop to help me.

"We'll do as much or as little as you can manage. It's getting cooler now, so we're not going to be ruled by the heat. But why don't you bring it with you, you know, just in case."

"You don't mind?"

"Mind what?" Confusion flashed over his face. "What, you with a cane? Of course not. Don't be dumb."

After thirty minutes of Dan pointing out everything new and where his friends lived, we walked into the town and strolled up Main Street. A lot of new businesses had settled here since the last time I was here.

"The tourist trade has taken off hugely, and many of the ranches offer hiking, horseback trekking, and hunting holidays and have had cabins built on their land. The guy, East, I told you about last night, has done most of them and has a large crew now. We really are a thriving town all year round because the skiing is great here too."

"It looks it too." I pointed up the street. "The Last Drop Inn, cool name. Is that the bar you were telling me about?"

"Yeah, that's Kes's place. Come on, he may be in. Carter is away in the city today speaking to a new supplier, so, unfortunately, you won't get to meet him." Dan slapped me on the back.

Inside, the bar was blessedly cool. More people seemed to have escaped the heat as every stool in front of the polished oak bar with brass rails was occupied. Prints of cool cars and iconic actors and actresses adorned the walls. The rich, brown leather booths looked cozy and inviting. In the back corner, a stage was set up. I guessed they had live music here too.

"This is a great place," I said as we made our way to the bar.

"You wanna grab a seat, Arch? I'll bring it over." Dan pointed over to one of the tables rather than a booth.

"Sure." At that moment, my ankle gave way, and I white-knuckled my cane to stop me from slipping. "Ow." I hobbled gracelessly to the table, pulled out the chair, and plonked down.

"You okay?" Dan asked as he placed two tall glasses of beer on the table, the drops of water already beading on the outside of the glasses.

"Yeah, maybe a bit too much walking. My ankle gave out."

"You gonna be okay to walk back? I can get us a ride from Kes." Worry lines creased Dan's forehead.

"Stop worrying, you old man. It happens sometimes. I'll be fine when I've sat for a while. This is a great place. I'm used to sports bars." It was better than the typical bar I'd go to with friends. Dan's eyebrows shot up under his hairline, questioning me. "Yeah, yeah, I know. I like sports, especially baseball. Those tight pants are hot. But the guys I work with are straight, so we got used to going there after work."

"Did you go there with your man?" Dan took a gulp of his beer and sighed. "That's good beer."

"Yeah, sometimes. He got along well with everyone. We liked to spend our time together. We'd hit the gay bars, have a few drinks, and dance. Damn, he was a good dancer. I guess he still is, but just not with me." A wave of longing and loneliness washed over me.

"Hey, I'm sorry. I shouldn't have brought it up. I won't again."

"No, no, it's okay. Look, I got used to the idea months ago, but it seems more real now than before. I guess it's because I'm getting my life together. But being here is good. It's new. I have no demons here. No one to constantly ask how I'm doing. Except you, you big girl." I nudged him as he picked up his glass, making him choke on his drink.

"Fine. I'll let you fall on your ass next time. Fucker," Dan muttered under his breath.

"This feels good. Thanks again, man." I grinned at him. "Is this where you met Carter? Where he kept turning you down?"

"Asshole. I only asked him out properly once, and he said yes. But dammit, I've been flirting since he showed up. About eight months ago now. He turned up on a hot black custom bike, and Kes gave him a job and the apartment upstairs. He was quiet and looked so broken down, but he's been happier lately. He got the manager's job and is simply a genuinely great guy. You'll like him too."

"Jeez, you've got it bad." I laughed, but it sounded strained, even to my own ears. I didn't really want to hear him talking about a guy he was in love with. It brought it all back to me. We finished our beer and decided not to have another, heading home instead. As we walked out, the scent of a familiar cologne—the same as Mallory used to wear—wafted in the air. I glanced behind me and just caught the back of a slim guy with dark wavy hair retreating through a door.

We lazed around for the rest of the day, lounging in the afternoon sun, then grilling steaks outside for our dinner. In short, a perfect day.

By ten, I was done for and needed to crash. Dan was almost asleep too. I'd forgotten how good looking he was. Why hadn't he been snapped up before? His new boyfriend was damn lucky to have him. Hell, I would've considered it again if he hadn't been taken.

Damn, I shouldn't have drunk that last beer. "Hey, Dan, I'm gonna hit the sack. You want me to lock up?"

"Nah, you go. I'll be right up. Night, Arch."

But sleep didn't come easily, although after the walking and the beers, I should've been knocked out. Eventually, I slid away under the blanket of sleep. I dreamed of Mallory, but a different Mallory. The same man but changed, so sad and lonely. I wanted to call out to him, but it had never worked in the previous dreams. Then the images morphed into something more, something so hot. Mallory was naked, and Dan and I were teasing and torturing his body to the greatest climax. I jerked awake, sweat soaking my body, with the biggest hard-on I'd had in months. Hell, since the last time I'd been inside Mallory.

I reached down and stroked myself, knowing there was no way I'd get back to sleep with this bastard. It took just a few strokes before a fountain of cum shot over my chest. I breathed hard, then chuckled as I looked down at the stripes of my release over my stomach and chest.

"Dammit," I whispered in the dark.

Twenty Two

Dan

I couldn't believe how easily Archer had settled into life here. We hadn't been out much. He was still in recuperation mode and spent a lot of time relaxing in the sunshine. I was getting used to the vivid scars on his body, and I admired his determination to regain full strength in his legs. Knowing his ankles had both been fractured and he had more metalwork holding him together, I didn't know how he managed to walk so well.

"Hey, what's got you all quiet and pensive? You okay?" Archer cocked his head to the side. "Am I outstaying my welcome?" He bumped his fist against my shoulder.

"What? God, no. It's great having you here. It's only been a week, so you're good for a while longer. I'll have to go to work after the weekend, though. You want to come with me, or are you happy hanging out here?" I stopped myself from running my eyes over his naked chest. He was still ripped, and his tan looked too damn good, although it didn't hide the scars on the side of his ribs where he'd had drains inserted to inflate his lung again.

"I'll stay here. I'm trying not to think about work yet. You've got a great setup here. I like the dynamics you've got going on there."

A couple of days ago, Archer had come with me into my office. I'd wanted to see how easy it would be for him to fit in here. I'd built up an excellent reputation and pulled in work from all the surrounding towns. There would be plenty for him to do if he decided to join me.

"I dreamed about you the other night, about us together." Archer's bright green eyes dilated as they roamed over my body.

"I guess I should tell you I've had a couple since you got here too." I perused his half-naked body.

"Yeah? Did yours involve a third? Mine did, but that might've been because we'd been reminiscing. I guess it was just an errant thought." A pale pink blush covered his neck and face.

"Who was the third?"

"Who do you reckon? He's always in my dreams, but this was the first time like that. The first time it was good."

"Yeah, well, in my dream, we did all the dirty with Carter." Smirking, I stepped closer to him.

His face looked as flushed as mine felt. His green eyes softened as his pupils narrowed. A slow, lazy smile spread over his face as he licked his lips as if he were tasting mine. I mirrored his action. A chuckle built in my chest

"I'm here for you. You're my best friend, Archer." I leaned in and pulled him against me. He ran his hands down my arms to clasp my hands.

"Daniel, I don't know what I'd do if you weren't my friend. You're stuck with me. Whatever happens, will happen, but I'm not looking too deeply into my life or too far ahead. I'm adjusting to a life I never thought I'd have, and being here with you is helping me. Thank you for being my friend." He pecked my mouth, then pulled away.

My cell phone rang, halting any further conversation.

"Hey, what's up?" I grinned when Archer rolled his eyes at my greeting. "Hold up. He's here. I'll ask him." I lowered my phone. "Kes wants to know if we'd like to go out tonight. Dinner, then a club. You wanna go?"

Archer hesitated, then nodded. "Yeah, sure. Sounds good."

"Kes, we're in....Yep, cool....See you there later. Thanks, man."

"You should call Carter and ask him to meet us after dinner. I would finally get to meet him, *and* you'd get your jollies with your man."

Archer winked at me. We'd just had a lazy lunch, and he was clearing away the remains of turkey club sandwiches. We seemed to have spilled mayo and mustard on every surface.

"You sure? I don't mind not seeing him tonight," I lied blatantly and laughed when he raised his eyebrow at me. "Yeah, yeah, all right. I'm missing him like crazy. I'll call him."

It turned out he was going out tonight with Paris, so he'd be at the club anyway. I took extra care getting ready. I wanted his jaw to drop when he saw me. Plus, I'd prepped everywhere else too. I wanted him in my bed and my body tonight. It had been too long.

"Is it a gay bar or a gay-friendly bar?" Archer's voice was calm, but his knee was bouncing. He was nervous but was playing it cool.

"It's a gay bar. You know the type. Lots of leather and bare chests, hips grinding, blow jobs in the bathroom." I burst out laughing at the look of abject horror on his face. "I'm messing with you, Arch. Relax. It's a gay bar but a good place to chill out. It's got a decent dance floor and plenty of eye candy, but it's not full of bare-chested alpha bear types. You'll like it, I promise." I rested my hand on his thigh to calm him.

"And the guys we're meeting are the three you talked about, right? And the bar owner is Kes?"

"Yep, and we're here now." I pulled up outside the restaurant. Denver's truck was parked a couple of cars ahead of mine. "The guys are already here, so let's hurry."

I laughed when Archer sighed. "I hate meeting new people. They always stare at the way I walk, and FYI, I'm not dancing."

"Oh, cheer up, you miserable asshole."

The restaurant was a great Italian one that did a mean lasagna. My stomach growled, and Archer laughed. Nudging Archer, I pointed to where my friends were seated.

"Damn, you're right. They're handsome men," Archer hissed at me.

After introductions, we sat and ordered. The conversation flowed easily. Not that I'd doubted Archer would get along with them. I'd been friends with East and Kes since high school, and it was great to meet up with Denver again as well. We hung out regularly, and I liked their company. Archer seemed relaxed with them too, another plus sign and a tick in the box to make him move here.

"Dan said you had an accident recently. You look like you recovered well?" Denver asked Archer. "I run the trauma unit over in Charlottetown."

"Yeah, it's been a rough few months. It was touch and go for a while, but I had a good orthopedic surgeon. He fixed me up. I'm very grateful for his hard work and determination. I broke my tib, fib, and talus. There's a heck of a lot of metalwork holding me together. I also broke my femur, which needed an external fixator. It's been a long road before I was able to walk this well. I had an amazing physical therapy team, and I'm good now. Plus, I broke my arm and wrist and had a collapsed lung, and I said good-bye to my spleen." My heart squeezed at how easily Archer shrugged off something that had almost killed him.

"Damn, that's seriously tough. Who was your bone man?"

"Alec Truman. He was amazing. Do you know him?" Archer replied.

The pause in the conversation was rife with tension. Denver swallowed hard, and Kes and East both took a hand in theirs. Then Denver smiled. "You did good. He's an excellent doctor. I know him and his dedication to getting everything perfect. I'm happy he was your physician."

"How long are you staying here, Archer? Hasn't Dan driven you crazy yet?" East changed the subject and lightened the mood.

"He's not too bad. I'm used to him. We were dorm mates and then shared a house. I can't believe it took me so long to come here to see him. But to answer your question, I'm not sure. I've taken a sabbatical from my job. Luckily, my bosses are great and understand my need for a change."

"I'm trying to persuade him to come and join me. *Soooo* the longer I can keep him, the better." I slapped Archer on the back.

"Are we ready to hit the club?" Kes clapped his hands. We'd just finished our coffees after a delicious dinner.

Ten minutes later, we walked into the club, and the sound of a heavy bass and the scent of hot male bodies hit me. My dick twitched in my pants. Was Carter here yet?

"Hey, Dan. If you want to find your man, that's cool. Get all your kissing over with before you find me," Archer shout-whispered over the noise.

"I think I will. Grab me a beer, and I'll be back in a few." I winked and headed off in search of my man. He was getting his groove on with Paris. I knew they were good friends and nothing else. I didn't feel jealous, apart from wanting him to grind against me.

I walked up behind him, wrapped my arms around his waist, and drew him close to my body. "Hey, baby, have you missed me?"

Carter twisted in my arms and lunged for my mouth, then delved his tongue into my mouth as he gripped my head, holding me still. As he pushed his hips forward, our dicks hardened. We both moaned and kept on kissing as if we were starving for each other, which I guessed we were.

Slowing the kissing down, I leaned back and stared into his lust-drunk eyes. His heavy lids were hooded over the black of his glazed pupils.

"Fuck, it's been too long, Dan. Do we have to stay long?" He pressed his forehead to mine and dropped more kisses on my lips.

"No, we can say hi to the guys. I want you to meet my friend. Then we can go." I kissed him again, then took his hand and led him back to the bar. Archer stood with his back to us, deep in conversation with Kes. I tapped him on the shoulder. As he turned, his face turned into a stone-cold mask. His jaw was tight, a muscle in his cheek twitching. I'd never seen such an angry look or stance on him.

"Archer, I'd like to introduce you to my man—"

"Mallory Halston," Archer spit out, his eyes blazing with fury.

Twenty Three

Carter

"Yes, fine." I finally gave in to Paris's demand to go to a club with him. He was a nice guy, but not my type, which was okay. He'd confessed I wasn't his either, but we got along well.

"Really? Yay. Awesome. That's great. We can go after work. It will be fun." Paris jumped up and hugged me.

"You ready to go, Car?" he asked, bouncing on his feet.

"Yep, come on. We'll go upstairs. You can shower and change if you want. I'm going to."

Paris had been here before for our Xbox marathons, after which he'd ended up crashing on the sofa. But there was nothing more between us, and I was grateful for a friend who didn't ask too many questions. He knew the diluted version of my background, and I had pictures of Archer in my apartment, which were bound to encourage questions.

"Go on. You take a shower first. I've got some leftover pizza if you want some. Oh, and Dan called. He'll be out tonight with his buddy and Kes and his men. We can meet up with them if that's okay." In the kitchen, I pulled the pizza box out of the fridge and put two slices in the microwave.

"I'm done." Paris walked out, and I had to admit he looked good. Black, skinny jeans, ripped at the knees, and a tight vintage Sex Pistols T-shirt, and worn-out Converse on his feet.

"You're gonna be every man's wet dream tonight, Paris." I laughed as he blushed.

"Fuck off. Now go get pretty. You'll want to look good for your man." He grabbed one of the pizza slices.

Fifteen minutes later, I was showered and dressed in clothes that were not far off what Paris was wearing: dark gray skinny jeans and a fitted black shirt with the Rolling Stones tongue on the front. I stepped into my high-top Converse and ran my hand through my hair. It was longer now than I used to keep it, but I liked it this way. As I put a black stud in my ear and a stud in my nose, the man looking back in the mirror was the new me, the me after Archer, and I liked it. I liked what Dan had brought out in me, and to be in love again was awesome.

"Come on, then, pretty boy. Let's go." I wrapped my arm around his shoulder. Where had the desire to be happy come from? Why did I care? For now, I was gonna just roll with it.

When we walked into the club, the place was already full. The beat of the music reverberated through my chest, reminding me of how much I loved dancing. The image of me grinding against Archer as he held my hips and whispered all the dirty things he would do to me when we got home popped into my mind. He'd never let me down and always taken me higher and higher every time he'd touched me. Now I got to do it with Dan, anytime we wanted.

I shook the thought away as we ambled over to the bar and waited for a bartender to take our order. The guys here were hot. It had a good vibe too. Once we'd gotten our beers, I checked out the men on the dance floor: a few leather harnesses and collars, but nothing too in your face. They would look but only touch if you invited them.

Imagine Dragons' "Thunder" came on. Paris grabbed my hand and dragged me into the clutch of heaving, swaying, and grinding hot male bodies. As I gyrated my hips, Paris placed his arms loosely over my shoulders. I grinned as we moved together to the rhythm of the music. Even though we weren't each other's type, it felt amazing to grind against him. I lifted my arms as I danced harder. Paris gripped my hips, and I threw my head back, belting out the words.

Then two arms wrapped around my waist, and I was pulled against a warm body. The musky scent of a familiar cologne tickled my nose. My man had found me. I quickly twisted in his arms and attacked his mouth. As soon as our tongues connected, desire rushed through me. I needed more. I plundered his mouth, twirling our tongues together, then sucking hard on it. We both groaned. My dick hardened and rubbed against his. We needed to get out of here, or I'd be dropping to my knees on the dance floor.

"Fuck, it's been too long, Dan. Do we have to stay long?" I panted as I rested my forehead against his.

"No, we can go say hi to the guys. I want you to meet my friend. Then we can go." His voice was equally breathless.

"Let's go, then." I followed Dan. My head still swimming from our kiss, I wasn't paying any attention to where he was going.

"Archer, I'd like to introduce you to my man," Dan said. The name of his friend hit me like a cannonball to my chest.

Archer...his eyes shooting flames of fury as he curled his lips. "It didn't take you long to move on, did it? I lie in a hospital waiting for you to come to me, and you fuck off out of my life." He sneered.

I stood frozen, unable to move a single muscle. Archer, in the flesh, not dead. How...how was that possible? My breath hitched as if he'd punched me in the chest and ripped out my heart. I jolted out of my stupor as he pushed me away and stormed past me.

My knees buckled, and only Dan's arm around my waist prevented me from falling.

"What's going on, Carter? How does he know you?" My heart broke at the confusion on his face. What could I do?

"He's your best friend? Archer Hawkins is your best friend? Jesus Christ." Freezing cold seeped into my bones. Archer was alive and well and so fucking angry, and I was in love with his best friend. Shit!

"We need to find him, Carter. Come on, baby, let's work this out." Dan's voice held an edge of panic, but I was so lost in the hows and whys, his words barely registered through the buzz in my head.

Twenty Four

Archer

The pain crossing his face confused me. It wasn't what I'd expected. It wasn't the look of a man who had chosen to walk away from me but a look of genuine distress and horror. I couldn't think anymore. I had to get away from him. With no thought of the men I'd come with, I rushed out of the club.

I leaned against the wall, pressing the balls of my thumbs hard against my eyes as I dragged deep, painful breaths into my burning lungs.

"Archer?" Dan spoke softly. "What's going on? How do you know him?"

"Because that's my Mallory, my boyfriend, who left me when I needed him the most." I ran my hands through my hair and tugged hard, welcoming the pain.

"Fuck." I couldn't stop the anguished cry from bursting from me. My chest heaved as the tears poured unchecked down my face.

"How can you not have known who he is? Dan, I talked about him all the time." I ignored the look of shock on his face.

"I had no idea, Arch. I promise you. Everyone here knows him as Carter. He's my boyfriend. I've talked about how much I love him, and he's been yours all along."

"He's not fucking mine anymore, though. He's yours. He loves you. You told me that. I can't deal with this." I looked past Dan. Mallory stood farther back, his arms wrapped tight around his body, tears streaming down his face. He looked so beautiful to me. He'd been in my dreams for so long, and now he stood before me, and I couldn't touch him.

All the anger left my body, and I slumped back against the wall. It felt like it was the only thing holding me up. "Dan, I'm sorry for yelling."

"We should go home." He walked back toward Mallory and held out his hand. The hesitation was clear in Mallory's eyes as they flickered between the two of us. He stepped tentatively to Dan and grasped his hand. I winced at the sight.

"We need to get home and talk about this," Dan said, his voice determined. "We need to know what happened and where we go from here."

Mallory sat in the front with Dan. I didn't pay any attention to my surroundings, dreading the upcoming conversation. Too soon, Dan pulled up in front of his house, the place I'd come to, to rebuild my life and start again.

When we got inside, Dan walked straight over to his liquor shelf and picked up a bottle of bourbon. He sloshed a couple of fingers of the amber liquid into three glasses, then handed me one, and Mallory the other. Taking only a sip of his own glass, Dan plopped down on the sofa.

Mallory sat next to Dan, looking at me like I were a ghost. What had she done to him? I had no doubt that my mother was behind all this.

"M-Mallory..." I croaked.

"You died," he stuttered, then clutched Dan's hand. Again, the way he turned to him was like a knife in my heart. I really had lost him.

"No, I didn't. I could've easily, but I made it. Just." My words dried up as I thought back to the pain.

"Archer, two policemen came to our apartment. They told me you died." The pain in his voice was palpable.

I sat on the other sofa, and unlike Dan, I took a huge gulp and shuddered as the fire hit my throat and stomach. Waiting for him to continue, I let my head fall back against the soft leather and closed my eyes for a second.

"I woke up five days after the accident. My mother told me you packed up and left me as soon as she told you." I sighed. "I hurt all over, but nothing was worse than the pain in my heart. I had a feeling my mother had done something, but I could never have imagined her telling you I died. I can't forgive her for that."

Dan narrowed his eyes, a frown creasing his forehead. I knew how analytical his mind was, and he was thinking hard.

"Carter turned up about eight or nine months ago. I remember Kes looking out for him from the start. He was a very different man than the one you see tonight. His eyes were clouded and dull. He was so thin. I reckon he was at least twenty pounds lighter. He stepped into the bar position well and would talk and joke with the customers, but there was never any joy in him when he was by himself." Dan paused and lifted Mallory's hand to his mouth and kissed the back softly.

"After a few months, maybe more like four, I saw a change in him. He filled out. He relaxed around people and would start a conversation rather than just answering. That's probably when I started flirting with him."

Mallory laughed. "You were a pain in my ass, baby. Always embarrassing me."

"He'd blush and shake his head when I asked him out. They were only flirty jokes, not a proper invitation. But whenever I did, I'd see the shutters come down, and he closed himself off. He never gave me a reason. He just said no. Kes guarded him, and so did Shelley. They were very protective of him. So I just had to be patient and keep encouraging him to take a chance."

"I'm really not that keen on how you made a play for my fiancé," I snapped at him. Mallory flinched as if I'd slapped him.

"I had to stop being your fiancé when your mother told me I was a lowlife and had fifteen minutes to get out of *her* apartment, not ours, before she'd have me arrested for trespassing. I grabbed the few things I could, told her to get fucked, and left."

"It's not her apartment, never has been. It's always been mine and then ours. Why didn't you go to the hospital? You were down as my next of kin." I jumped to my feet, the frustration and anger building inside me making me too tense to sit.

"I did. I fucking tried, but your mother had some huge motherfucker blocking me. She sneered and said it was just family allowed," Mallory cried out. Dan's hand on his arm stopped him from standing.

"Hey, come on. Cut it out, Archer. Calm down. This isn't what this is about. You two don't need to be hating each other right now. You need to find a way to talk to each other and figure out what the hell has happened. And most importantly, to find a way to move on from here, to move forward."

"What do you suggest? That we all become friends?" I spit at him. "I can't see that happening."

Mallory jerked to his feet and shot daggers at me. "You know, I've had enough of this shit." He looked down at Dan, and his gaze softened, shining with love. "I'm going home, okay?"

"No. No way." Dan stood and took his hand. "You aren't walking out of here, Carter. Not without me."

"Let's go, then," Mallory said without any further comment.

Dan glanced at me. "Think about it, Archer. Think about what you want. Think very carefully. We'll see you tomorrow."

I sat in silence as my best friend and the love of my life left the house.

Twenty Five

Carter

"What's going to happen, Dan? What the hell do we do now?" I paced the floor of my small living room.

"I don't know, baby. I'm as confused as you are. This is like something from a book or a film. It doesn't seem real." Dan picked up a picture of Archer and me, which was one of my favorites. We looked so happy and so in love. A flash of pain crossed Dan's face. I gently took the photo out of his hand and put it back on the shelf.

"I'm sorry, Dan. I feel that this is my fault. If I hadn't been so locked down in my grief, I would've mentioned his name, and we would've been able to work it out."

"I guess, but if you'd known he was alive, you wouldn't be with me. You would've gone back to him. We wouldn't be a 'we,' and as fucked up as this situation is, I love you, and I'm happy we got together."

"Oh, Dan, I love you too. But I don't know how I feel about Archer anymore. I'm happy he's alive, but I'm not the same man I was when we were together. And I'm sure he's changed too."

"Why did you change your name? If you'd kept Mallory, maybe I would've worked out that you were Archer's boyfriend. It's an unusual name, and given how unhappy you were, I could've put two and two together."

He shook his head sadly. "I changed it because I needed to be someone else. It's my middle name, so it was easy to do. See, it's still my fault."

"You can't blame yourself, Cart—" Dan took a deep breath. "Would you rather I called you Mallory?"

"No, I'm Carter now. I like it. It felt weird when Archer called me Mallory. It didn't feel like me." I leaned into him and sighed as Dan wrapped his arms around me.

"Let's go to bed, Carter. It'll all seem better in the morning. Well, maybe not, but at least we won't be as tired. You know, I can't believe I haven't been in here before."

"I never thought about it. We're always at your place. I like it there. There's so much space. This place is small and too close to work."

As we undressed and climbed into my queen-sized bed, I snuggled up to Dan and rested my head on his chest. I drifted off as Dan stroked up and down my back. A thought entered my mind.

"Dan, we need to go back to yours." I pushed myself up to look at him.

"What? Why?"

"What if he leaves? I mean, would you want to stay if you'd just seen your best friend leave with your ex-boyfriend? We need to sort this out. I don't think he should be by himself."

"You're right. Come on, let's go."

In record time, we were dressed and racing down the stairs. It would only take us ten minutes to get back to my place, but dread built up in my chest that we'd be too late and he had already left.

"Do you think he'll be there?" I asked Dan as we hurried back to the house.

"I do. He must've realized he shouldn't be driving after drinking this evening. I hope so anyway. C'mon."

I relaxed as his rental car came into sight, still sitting on Dan's driveway. Slowing down, Dan reached for my hand.

"Hopefully, he's gone to bed, and we can talk in the morning." Dan sighed.

The lights were still on in the front room, negating Dan's hope. As Dan put the key in the lock, the door swung open, and Archer stood with a bottle of scotch in his hand. He was swaying as he brought the bottle up to his lips.

"Whatcha doing back here? Haven't you rubbed my nose in it enough today?" Archer slurred.

"No, Archer. We came back because we didn't want you to be alone. I think we have got so much to talk about and deal with," I replied.

"Whatever." Archer stumbled back to the living room, where he collapsed down on the sofa.

"We should all get some sleep. It's late now. I don't think we can work out anything tonight. Archer, leave the scotch and get some sleep." Dan snatched the bottle from Archer's grip.

Archer glanced up at me, his eyes wet with tears. He looked so broken and lost I wanted to wrap my arms around him.

"Archer, please don't cry," I begged.

"I lost you, Mallory. I needed you so much, and you weren't there. You broke my heart. Now, just as I start to live again, I find you, and I've still lost you. I love you, and I can't have you." Tears streamed down his face, and I couldn't hold back and hugged him.

"Archer, I'm so sorry. I had no choice. I had no reason not to believe her. I should've questioned her, shouldn't have believed her. I lost you too, and now, like you, I've started to live again. I love you, but I love Dan now too." We held each other tightly. Tears trickled down my cheeks as I grieved for what we had lost.

Dan laid his hand on my back and rubbed circles over my spine, soothing me as I cried.

"I should've looked for you, should've called you. But most of all, I shouldn't have trusted my mother. I sensed she might've done something, but I just never thought she'd do something so abhorrent. I let you down, honey. I'm so sorry." His fingers tightened on my hips as he blamed himself.

"It's not your fault, Arch. I get that you're angry, and I understand why. Let's move on and see what we can do. I want you in my life, Archer. I hope you want me to be in yours." He nodded against my chest, and I couldn't stop myself from dropping a kiss on his hair. As I inhaled the oh-so-familiar scent of him, I sighed softly.

In what felt like slow motion, Archer lifted his head and pressed his mouth gently on mine. Dan gasped, but he kept his hand on my back, still stroking me. Was he okay with this? What was going on? Then Archer stepped back, away from me. His brilliant green eyes were glittering. Was it because of his tears or from the kiss?

"I'm going to bed," Archer spoke quietly. "Thank you, and yes, I want you in my life."

He sent Dan a sad smile. "You're a very lucky man, Dan. I hope you know that."

"I do, and I still want you here. I love you, Archer. You know that, right?" Dan pulled Archer in for a hug, and they held each other tightly for a few moments. Then Archer pulled free and walked out, leaving us in silence. His footsteps thudded heavily as he climbed the stairs.

Dan stretched his arms wide, and I stepped willingly into his embrace. "You let him kiss me," I whispered.

"I did. You both needed it. I love you, Carter. I want you to be happy, and I think seeing Archer again will make that happen." Dan kissed me, a long, slow burner of a kiss. Deep, lazy licks as his tongue caressed mine, and a low moan escaped me as I fisted his shirt.

"I want you, Dan. It's been too long. Take me to bed." I panted as he pulled away.

"Let's go."

The door to the guest room was closed, and I hoped Archer would sleep well, even with all the whiskey in his veins.

When we were in Dan's bedroom, Dan looked me up and down my body. My dick thickened, and I shivered at the hunger in his eyes.

"Strip for me, baby." His voice, low and husky, dripped with the promise of dirty sex. My insides clenched as he palmed his dick through the fabric of his slacks.

"Are you sure we should be doing this? Archer is just across the hallway. It feels weird."

Hurt flashed in his eyes. "You don't want to make love with me? We've been apart for over a week. I've missed you so much. Is he coming between us already?" The pain in his voice pierced my heart.

"No, Dan. He's not coming between us. I just think that if he hears us, it'll hurt him even more. He may leave us before we have a chance to talk."

"Carter, I want you. I want to make love to you. Please, baby, I need you," Dan pleaded, stroking down my face and neck, then resting his hand over my heart. I couldn't deny him something I wanted too.

I kicked off my Converse first, then slowly inched my shirt up my torso. I kept my eyes fixed on Dan, who licked his lower lip, then pulled it between his teeth. Leisurely I dragged the shirt over my head and threw it in the same direction as my shoes.

As I slid my hands over my chest, I paused to tug on my nipples. The sensations made me moan, and I pulled a bit harder. Leaving the reddened, pert nubs, I skimmed over my stomach, the muscles bunching under my touch. Dan was breathing hard now, his hands in fists at his side as he held himself back.

I traveled down the groove of my oblique muscles, dipped under the waistband of my jeans, and popped the button. I halted when he took a step toward me. Standing still again, Dan gazed, mesmerized, at my fingers, which slowly lowered the zipper. Then I pushed the denim down and over my ass.

Dan watched me silently as I stripped out of my clothes. His gaze roamed over my body. I loved how his eyes darkened and his breath quickened. He loved me, and I loved him, but my heart shifted and stuttered. Fuck, I still loved Archer too. What did this mean? This wasn't something that I could dismiss. That wouldn't be fair to me, Dan, and Archer. The coming days would be hard for all of us, but I knew it wasn't something I could run away from. I met Dan's gaze. His love for me was real, here and now. Just as his heart belonged to me.

"You're perfect, Carter." He yanked off his clothes and strode up to me. His expression was almost feral as he captured my lips with his. As he plundered my mouth, he trailed his hands over my chest and tweaked and teased my nipples. Groaning loudly, I squirmed, desperate for more.

Twenty Six

Archer

As I lay in my bed, I let my mind wander to what had just happened. I hadn't been able to stop myself from kissing him. I'd needed one taste of his lips. But now remorse gripped me. I still wanted him, and it was killing me all over again. When he'd hugged me, my heart had started beating again, pounding hard, calling out to him.

Then they came upstairs. Dan's room was at the back of the house, but the door opening and shutting firmly slammed through me. I squeezed my eyes tight as if by doing so I could erase the image of the two of them together. Concentrating on some deep, calming breaths, I tried to relax, but a loud moan flew from my lips. Oh god, no. I couldn't hear them making love. I couldn't bear it.

It went quiet again, but now the picture of all the things they could be doing was in my mind. My ears seemed to be on high alert, and as much as I wanted to block them out, I lay still, waiting for the moment they'd cry out their orgasms.

There. Mallory first, and my dick grew rock hard at his familiar grunts. Dan followed, his groan so guttural and passionate. I screwed my eyes tight shut, forcing back the pain. Tears escaped as my heart shattered again. I couldn't stay here. I couldn't do this.

The silence after their cries of pleasure was deafening, but with it, a calmness settled inside me. Something told me to hold tight, that Mallory didn't have a choice if I took myself out of the equation. I wouldn't try to win him back. That wasn't me. I didn't do shitty things like that. Then my dream and the three of us together popped into my head, something Dan had told me he'd dreamed about too. I never took much stock in my dreams, never had the desire to interpret and explain them. But what if they were a sign? What if they had a deeper meaning? Or was it just wishful thinking? Either way, Dan had been right. We did need to talk.

I wouldn't suggest it, but I wanted to be around them. Staying here might be a good idea after all.

Or was it? And who would be hurt the most? Yeah, that would be me again. Oh, fuck, what was I going to do?

Eventually, my eyelids grew heavy, and I slipped away in a dreamless sleep.

I woke up with the most god-awful splitting headache as if an ax was buried in my skull. My mouth felt like something crawled in there and died, and my eyes seemed to be glued shut. What the fuck had happened?

But then the memories came flooding back. Mallory was here. Mallory was Carter, and Mallory was dating my best friend. I pulled one of the pillows over my head and silently screamed into it.

I wanted to go home. Away. Anywhere but here. But I couldn't. I needed to see him. We needed to talk. Rats. I pulled the pillow away and blinked open my eyes. The sun shone brightly through a gap in the curtains, and I quickly turned my head away from the blinding rays. I grabbed my phone from the nightstand to see what time it was.

Eleven thirty. Wow, I never slept this long. Although it had probably been more an alcohol-induced coma. I never drank like I'd done last night, not since college, and now I remembered all too vividly why. I hated hangovers. They really knocked me on my ass. I dragged myself out of bed and stumbled to the bathroom. As I peed, the room swayed around me, and I had to rest one hand on the wall to keep me steady.

God, I needed a shower. The alcohol fumes wafting off me made me gag. I switched the water on and turned the heat up. Bracing myself on the wall, I closed my eyes and tipped my face up to the spray, letting the scalding water seep through my whiskey-soaked pores. Then I turned around and let the water pound over my neck and back. The tension in my muscles and bones eased under the soothing water. More memories of last night came back to me, the most vivid the sound of them fucking.

I slithered against the wall to the tiled floor, wrapped my arms around my bent legs, and dropped my head on my knees as I sobbed—deep, heartbreaking, wretched sobs. Pain sliced through my body. I loved him. I still really fucking loved him, and he didn't love me that way anymore. And it hurt. It hurt so damn much.

Eventually, the tears subsided. Shivers ran through me. I forced myself back up to my feet and turned off the now cold water, then grabbed a towel. With jerky movements, I scrubbed myself dry and staggered back to bed, where I burrowed under the duvet and let sleep take me away again. I didn't want to see them today. I needed to let my heart settle first before I could face them.

When I woke again, my headache had gone, but so had the sunlight. Shit, I'd slept all day. But what did it matter? I didn't have any plans, so why the hell not? My stomach rumbled loudly, protesting at the lack of food in it. Time to get up and get something to eat. Some grilled cheese sandwiches sounded heavenly right now.

I slung on some sweatpants and a T-shirt and made my way downstairs. I hoped Dan and Mallory would be out, but voices drifted my way from the kitchen. No such luck.

Twenty Seven

Dan

"Wow." I slid out of Carter and pulled off the condom, then swung my legs off the bed and got a cloth to clean him.

"How do you feel about getting tested? Is it too soon for us?" He took the cloth from me. "Here, gimme that. I'll do it."

"Really? Yeah, I want to, and I don't think it's too soon. We love each other. We're committed to each other, which leads me to ask you a question. Will you move in with me? I hate it when you're in your apartment. I want to wake up with you every day."

"Yes. Yes, I want to be here with you…" He glanced to the door. I knew he was thinking of Archer. "What about Archer?"

"That's up to you, baby." I lay back and pulled him against me. I loved the way he tangled his legs with mine. "Did you know we dated in college? For a while, actually."

"I did, but why did you break up? He never said."

"We were talking about it the other night, and we don't really know who decided to end it. Because of where we were planning to work when we left law school, we realized that neither of us was in a position to try a long-distance relationship. It seemed better to be friends than never see or speak to each other again if it had ended badly. I still love him, you know." I sighed and kissed the top of Carter's head.

"Yeah, I know. I do too. Is it going to be too difficult?"

"Would you consider him being a part of us?" I spoke cautiously, just testing the water.

"What? As a threesome? Wow, Daniel, that's a lot to think about. I doubt it's as easy as Kes, East, and Denver make it look." Carter studied my face, searching for something, or maybe he was getting pissed. "Is that why you want me to move in? So we're all together? Don't I satisfy you?"

"What? No, baby, you make me so complete. When we make love, it's everything I ever wanted. I want you to move in because I love you and want to be with you. Archer may still decide to leave or stay but find his own place. But I think he'd only be leaving because it would be too hard for him to be here without you. If you still love him and want him as much as you love and want me, maybe we should let him know." I trailed my hand lazily up and down his back while I let him think.

"Can you really see the three of us together? I mean, properly together, the whole sex thing?" Carter ran his fingers through the fine line of hair down to my dick.

"Yeah, I can. I had a dream about it last week, and dammit, Carter, it was so hot."

He shook his head, but it wasn't in admonishment, more that he couldn't believe I'd said it out loud. "We need to be sure. Just giving it a try wouldn't be fair to any of us. If we want to be committed to each other, we must trust we aren't just experimenting. I don't think it should be based on sex, simply because the thought of us in a ménage is hot. If we do this, it's because we love each other equally and we want a relationship, all of us together. Not just a third because you had a sexy dream."

"I know that, Carter. Do we discuss this with him? Or maybe we should hear what he has to say first. This could all be theoretical if he decides to leave."

"I think what's important is if you love both Archer and me enough to want us in your bed and your body."

"I don't want not to have him in my life. I love him, but I love you too, so much." Carter squirmed as I rimmed his tight hole. "Dammit, Daniel, pack it in."

"No, I want inside you again, right now."

"Jesus, Dan." He sighed as I dipped my finger inside him.

Reaching across to the drawer, I grabbed another condom. The lube was still in the bed somewhere. Good, Carter had found it. I suited up quickly and slid deep inside him. We both groaned loudly as I pounded into him. God, I couldn't wait to be free of the latex barrier and be bare inside him.

"Jesus, Dan. That was intense." Carter eased himself off me, and I slipped gracelessly out of him. We both wrinkled our noses. "Testing tomorrow!" Laughing, he grabbed the now cold, wet cloth and cleaned up his mess. He even disposed of the condom and washed me.

"I'm never letting you go, you know that, right?" I murmured.

"Good, because I'm not going anywhere."

The covers were tugged up over me, and sleep claimed me.

The alarm on the table next to my bed went off, and Carter groaned and put a pillow over his head. Chuckling, I pulled him into my body. "Not a morning person, are you, baby?"

"Not when I don't have to be, no. I'm not scheduled to work until later this afternoon, so I plan to sleep this morning," he mumbled but turned his head toward me, opening one eye to just a slit. "I'd be fine if you hadn't kept me up all night fucking my brains out. This is your fault."

"But, Carter, baby, you loved it." I grinned and kissed his pouting mouth. "I have to go to work today. Will you be all right here with Archer?"

He opened his eyes wider, and a frown wrinkled his brow. "I guess so. Maybe it would be good for us to talk, you know, clear the air a bit."

"I don't want you discussing what we talked about last night, not until we can all be together. You okay with that?"

"That's fine with me. It's going to be hard enough to ask him to be with both of us. Like hell am I doing that on my own." He sighed.

"What's going on in there, Carter?" I tapped his temple.

"Do you still want me to move in? And get tested?"

"Hell, yes to both of them. I'll make the appointment. We may be able to go at lunch. I'll see what I can do." I kissed him again. "Go back to sleep. I'll call you later. I love you."

"Love you too," he mumbled and drifted back to sleep.

Twenty Eight

Carter

It must have been an hour later when I woke up again, feeling a lot more human now. I thought back to everything that had gone down yesterday, and I still couldn't get my head around it. Archer being alive. Not just alive but sleeping down the hallway. Dan wanting to stop using condoms. Dan asking me to move in with him. Dan asking me to consider us having a three-way relationship. Jesus, what a mindfuck.

I got out of bed and hit the shower, my brain still full of all the things that could go wrong. Every scenario and disaster rushed through my head as I soaped my body, recognizing the ache in my well-used ass. That made me smile.

As I wandered down the hallway, Archer's door was closed. Did that mean he was still in there, or had he gotten up and gone downstairs? I was torn between wanting him to be awake and wanting to hide from him until Dan was home. At least I had to work this afternoon, so I could be out of here and back to my place after a coffee.

I sat, flipped my iPad open, and messed around on YouTube when the doorbell rang. I rolled my eyes. That could only be Kes, checking if I was okay. He still fussed over me, even though he was happy Dan and I were together. I tried to guess which of his lovers had come with him.

Bingo. Kes and Denver were bitching lightheartedly with each other. I knew they didn't mean it. I loved how they were always touching each other. Even now, Denver had his thumb through Kes's belt loop.

"Hey, guys, quit your moaning." I laughed. "What are you doing here?"

"You look better." Denver gave me a brilliant smile. "We went to your place, and well, Kes, wanted to check up on you."

"Come on in. I was just about to make coffee. You want some?" I let them pass and closed the door behind me.

"Has it sunk in yet, Carter? Can you believe what has happened?" Kes asked as he leaned against one of the kitchen cupboards. "Are you happy with him being here at Dan's?"

"Yeah, it has. His mother is behind it all, I guess. She's the one who made me leave." I grabbed three mugs out of the cupboard, put a pod in the fancy Keurig machine, and pressed Start. "I can't stop him from being here. He's Dan's best friend, and I'm not coming between them."

"He's a good guy, Carter. We really liked him when we met him last night. He's suffered some dreadful injuries, but he had a good surgeon." Denver looked at Kes, who squeezed his hand. "Actually, my ex had operated on him, so I know he'd gotten the best care."

"I know Archer's a good guy, Denver. I was engaged to him for a short time before...well, you know what happened." I handed over their coffees and sat at the island. "I'm glad you're here. I need your help."

Kes pulled out the stool next to me and sat himself down. "What's up?"

I let out a dry laugh. "Where do you want me to start? Okay, Dan asked me to move in with him last night, and I said yes. Before that, he asked if we could get tested so we don't have to keep using condoms. Again, I said yes. I hate those fuckers. I'm clean. I was clean when I was with Archer, and I haven't been near anyone else since. I'm happy to do it with Dan. I love him, and I want to be with him." I paused and took a deep breath.

"Go on, Carter, we're here for you. You're one of us. You're family." Kes placed his hand over mine and gave it a squeeze.

"Yeah, well, here's where it gets complicated because I thought Archer had died. I had to deal with the pain of losing him, not of falling out of love with him, which basically means I still love Archer too. It's a different love than the one I feel for Dan because I'm a different person than I was when I was with Archer, but it's there, and it's real. Dan knows this. He even asked me if I'd consider having Archer as well."

Their mouths fell open, and their eyes popped almost out of their sockets.

"And what did you say?" Denver was the first to gather himself.

"I said we should ask him. Guys, if his mother hadn't ruined our lives, I'd still be with him, even married to him by now. I'd picked up the marriage license the morning he died—of his accident, I mean. And the feelings I have for him are still real, but—and this is a big but—as I said, I love Dan too and don't want to compromise what we have now. What do you think I should do?"

"Carter, what do you want us to say? We can't make that decision for you. Only the three of you can. But if you love them both and you think they love you the same way, I'd say, what have you got to lose?"

A dry chuckle escaped me. "I could lose both of them. Even the thought of having Archer with me again excites me, but he may not feel the same way I do. Am I strong enough to accept it if he rejects me? Will Dan still want me to live with him if Archer turns us down?" I ran my hands through my hair and dragged them down my face. "I don't have a fucking clue?" I looked at Denver. "How did you know they were worth breaking your heart for? You'd just had a bad breakup, so what made you take the risk?"

"It took me a while, Carter. I didn't immediately jump into bed with them and think 'woohoo, I'm in love again.' I got to know them, just the same as when you started dating Dan. You must get to know each other as a new entity, a new unit. Don't just rush to have sex with them together. You and Archer have a lot to work through."

"I know, but where do I start? I have no doubt he's going to have masses of trust issues mixed in with some guilt."

Kes cocked his head. "His mother played both of you. Why should he feel guilty about it?"

"Think about it, Kes. I was told he had died, so I had no reason to call him. Dead men don't have cell phones. But he was told I left him, walked away without a backward glance, and yet he didn't try to call me. I mean, wouldn't you have tried at least once? Even if it was to tell me what a bastard I was, but he didn't. Not once. This could've all been cleared up five days after his accident when he woke up and banished his mother if he'd tried to call me."

"Do you blame him for that?" Kes asked gently.

"I don't know, maybe." I shrugged. "It's my fault too. If I'd used my first name, if I'd told Daniel that my boyfriend, Archer, had died, I could've had it cleared up. The whole situation is like a bad afternoon soap. No one believed it could really happen."

"This is why you need to reconnect before you can make any decisions. If I'm honest, I can see it working. I believe the three of you could be very happy. I just don't think it will be an overnight thing." Denver's sweet smile comforted me.

"Look, take a few days off work, starting today. Take it a day at a time and see what happens. As long as you're honest with each other from the start, you can only go forward." Kes placed his coffee cup in the sink, then turned to his lover. "Are you satisfied he's okay now?" He grinned.

"Hey. You got all stressed out, not me." Denver laughed and grabbed his hand. "Let's leave him alone now."

"Thanks, guys, for checking up on me and for your advice."

"Anytime, Carter, you know that. Just don't rush this. If it's worth having, it will happen." Kes gave me a peck on my cheek as he walked past me to the door.

After they'd gone, I tidied up the kitchen and put the used mugs in the dishwasher. The sound of a shower running drifted from upstairs, so Archer was still here and awake. He'd be down soon. The knots in my stomach cramped at just the thought of him and me together here.

My phone rang, and Dan's picture flashed up.

"Hey, baby. You okay?" he asked.

"Yeah, Kes and Denver were just here. Kes was worried about me, apparently." I chuckled. "Why did you call? Not that I mind, of course."

"Yeah, Kes is a good man. Did you talk about us?"

"I did. Do you mind?" I held my breath. Would he be mad I did?

"Of course not. He's your friend, and I'm sure he's got a lot of advice for you and me. We can talk about it tonight. I called to say we can get tested this afternoon. Can you make it over in about an hour?"

"I'm clean. I was tested when I was with Archer, and I haven't been with anyone else. I've still got the proof."

"Yeah, me too. I got checked before we got together. But we should still get tested. It's always been a part of my adult life. So will you be here in an hour?"

"Yes, I love you. I trust you, and fuck, I want you inside me with nothing between us."

"Carter, you can't say shit like that to me when I'm working. Look, I've got to get back to it. I'll see you in a bit. Love you."

"I love you too. See you later." I ended the call and listened for any movement upstairs. The shower was still running, and because I knew Archer, I knew he hated hangovers.

Soon, it went quiet, but Archer didn't come out of his room. I gave it thirty minutes, then decided to check in on him. I slowly pushed the door open. All I could see was a body-shaped bulge under the duvet, but not his head. He had to be cocooned in there. The thought made me smile. I'd seen him like that a few times before. I fought the desire to climb in bed with him and hold him tight.

Denying myself that right, I tiptoed out of the room, closed the door softly behind me, and walked back down. I cleared up the living room, then went to meet Dan.

"Hey," Dan greeted me as I dismounted my bike. "You look good in leather, babe." He slowly perused my body, his eyes like a caress.

"The gorgeous weather called for a bike ride. I hadn't ridden just for the sake of it in months. I'm going for a longer ride once we're done." I pressed a kiss to his lips.

"Ready?" he asked as he clasped my hand. I nodded, and together we entered the clinic.

As usual, it was done quickly, and now all we had to do was wait. Dan, in his desperate need, had organized that we would have the results by the end of the day. That was a perk of living in a quiet area. The clinics weren't swamped with work. I put on my jacket as we walked back outside. "I'll see you tonight." I kissed him gently. "I think we can celebrate tonight."

His amber eyes flashed gold as he pressed his mouth on mine again in a firm, possessive, and promising kiss that made my insides tighten with anticipation. "I can't wait. Ride safely, Carter."

I watched him walk away, heading back to his office. I put on my helmet, then swung my leg over my bike. As I fired up the engine, I was already smiling at the thought of riding for the fun of it.

This was what I needed to clear my head. I raced down the highway, not speeding so much but just enjoying the freedom. It would be good to reconnect with Archer again. I wanted to know everything that had happened to him, and I needed to tell him how my life had changed too. Hopefully, he was prepared to stay and try a life here. Cooper's Ridge was a good place. Being here without him had been so hard in the beginning, but not having any memories of us here had helped too in a way. Everything had been new. I'd been given a new start. I'd found myself again. I wanted him to do the same.

When I got home, he still wasn't up. I took another peek, and he was still burrowed in the bed covers. At least it wouldn't be long before Dan came home.

The minute Dan walked in, he dumped his briefcase by the door, removed his tie, and undid his top shirt buttons. He hadn't seen me yet, which gave me the chance to drink him in. His long legs clad in dark blue suit pants clinging to the rock-hard muscles of his thighs, which were strong enough to hold me up against the wall as he fucked me. The curve of his ass, firm and high, ready to be grabbed and bitten. Argh. I needed to stop. Just as I cupped my dick, trying to calm it down, he turned to me. He smirked and gave me a wink. The fucker, he knew I'd been watching.

"Hey, baby. Have you missed me?" He swaggered toward me, his eyes dark and heavy, full of promise.

"Hmm, not sure. Have you missed me?"

"Oh, Carter, you've been on my fucking mind. All. Day. Long." He lowered his head and grazed his mouth over mine, not giving me anywhere near what I wanted.

"What are you going to do about it?" I growled at him, then bit his lip.

He pulled back and grinned wickedly. "I'm sure I can think of something. Let me get changed."

"You need any help with that?"

"Definitely."

We raced up the stairs, scrabbling at our clothes as we went.

"Shower?" Dan asked, and I nodded, laughing as we tripped over ourselves in our haste to get in the bathroom. We were under the hot spray in less than a minute, Dan's firm body pressing me against the tiles, his erection growing as he rocked his hips to mine. "It all came back clear."

I nodded. We both knew we would be okay, but confirmation was a comfort.

Sated after mutual blow jobs, we were back in the kitchen, squabbling about what to make to eat. Dan touched me anytime he could, and I loved it.

"Have you seen Archer today? Did you manage to speak to him?" Dan kissed the back of my neck.

"No, he's been in bed all day."

"He's been sleeping all day? How do you know?"

"Because I looked in on him a couple of times. I was worried about him. Archer doesn't drink much, and I know how much he hates hangovers. I just wanted to make sure he was okay. I care about him. I care a lot."

At that moment, Archer walked in, looking like shit, and I knew exactly what he needed.

"Hey, guys."

"Archer, hi. How are you feeling?" Dan asked, his voice laced with concern.

Archer's face was pale, with dark rings under his eyes. "Pretty much as I look. Wrecked, ashamed, embarrassed. I'm sorry for my behavior last night. I shouldn't have gotten drunk."

"It was perfectly understandable, Arch. Yesterday was a clusterfuck of epic proportions. We're feeling a lot of those emotions too. C'mon, sit. I'll get you a coffee, and I'll make you a grilled cheese sandwich."

I set about making his favorite hangover food while Dan and he chatted. I didn't pay too much attention, but when I handed him his food, I instinctively dropped a kiss on his head. He froze under my touch. I glanced over at Dan, who gave me a nod. Showtime.

Archer picked up his grilled cheese. "Okay, guys, out with it."

Dan stood next to me and slung his arm casually over my shoulder, giving me the reassurance and strength I needed.

"We want you to stay. We want you to stay here. With us, the three of us together," I blurted out.

Dan groaned and shook his head. "Way to go, babe."

"You talk, then, Dan." I nudged him in the ribs.

"What Carter means is that we'd like you to think about staying and being with us, as in having a relationship with us. I know it's out of the blue, and maybe we've asked you way too early. Hell, you and Carter have only just found each other again."

The look on Archer's face was hard to decipher. Shock? Abhorrence? Bewilderment?

Twenty Nine

Archer

What the hell had they just said? They wanted me to stay and have a threesome with them? In what universe could this be real?

I watched as Dan kissed my fiancé, my ex-fiancé, and then smiled at me.

"We love you, Archer. And you've said you love us. What we want to know is if you love us enough to be with us? The whole nine yards." Mallory spoke quietly but honestly. I remembered every nuance in his tone and every one of his mannerisms. He had been my world, my everything. And now? Now he was Dan's world.

"Why?" It was the first question that popped into my head. "Why would you think this is a good idea, or is it your idea of a joke?"

Mallory—Carter—chewed on his lip as his face blanched. Dan tightened his grip on him, narrowing his eyes at me.

"Okay, I guess we got it wrong. I'm sorry, Archer. I thought this would be something good. We each love you. Carter has grieved for you for months, and he's still in love with you as much as he is with me. We thought you loved us too."

Carter had tears in his eyes, which he was trying to control and not let them fall. A stab of pain slashed my heart. I stretched my hand out to him but halted when he flinched. I'd hurt him. After all that had happened, I'd rejected him.

But was I really not even going to consider this? Did I want to be with them? Could I share myself with them? With all my scars, would Carter and Dan want me?

"I do, I do love you, but this is so…shit, so unexpected. I thought you were going to ask me to leave." I shook my head. I couldn't believe this. "You want us to be a threesome, or do you want me as a third? There's a huge difference." I wasn't prepared to even think about this as a third.

Carter sucked in a sharp breath. "How could you even think that? This isn't a game. I want you. I've missed you so fucking much. I want to try, but the decision is up to you."

"Dan? Why? Why not just keep him to yourself? He's perfect." I couldn't get my head around why he would want to share a man as perfect as Mallory—Carter.

"Because I love you too. I want you as much as I want Carter. We've both admitted to dreaming about it. Be honest, man, can you see us all hot and sweaty, teasing and tasting each other. Fucking each other? Because I can, and so can Carter. Christ, I'm getting hard now just talking about it. I want your ass, Arch, and I want your cock in mine. I want to watch you fuck Carter. I want to see him take you. I want the whole fucking thing."

I drew in a long breath. Goddamn, the picture Dan painted was hot. My dick twitched in my pants as it tried to overrule the logic in my head. "Carter, what do you think? You said you want me to be with you. Do you see us as a threesome? How do you expect this to happen, or how would you like it to happen?"

"Archer, I'm not going to rehash the past and what we suffered because you're here. I think shit like this happens for a reason. We were meant to be together again. We should never have been apart, and now we have the chance. Not just to recapture what we had but to take it further and expand it.

"I love Dan. He's let me remember what it's like to be in love again, the new kind of love where everything is fresh. We're learning so much about each other, and I think we'll have to go through the same thing. We have to get to know each other again. I want to know all about your accident. I want you to want to share everything with me again. And this is the important thing. I want to reacquaint myself with your divine body. I want us to grow and learn together, the three of us. I believe we have the chance of something very special, and that's because we're all in love with each other."

"Fuck. Carter, you've changed. You're a stronger, more mature man than you were nearly a year ago. We've all got a shit ton of stuff to talk about. Two days ago, I still believed you'd left me. I still tried to hate you. Finding you in love with another man is hard for me to take. I believe you when you say you're in love with me because of the way you look at me. It's the same as before. I don't know if us all being together will work, though. I need to think about this." I shook my head, unsure of what to do. "You see, my heart is saying yes, but my brain is telling me I'm the one who'll get hurt. And, Dan, we stopped being *in* love a long time ago. I believe you when you say you love me, but is it the right kind of love? What happens if you realize that it's not the passionate kind of love? That's easy to answer. I'll be the one who ends up alone."

Carter reached out to me, concern and need etched on his face. As his hand touched mine, the electricity zapped through me again, the same as it always had.

"Oh, Archer, don't you think I have the same worries? You and Dan have so much in common. You're the same age. You both have successful careers. Hell, you used to be together. Where do I fit in with all that?" He drew circles on the back of my hand with his fingers.

"You are and always have been a perfect fit for me, and I see it with you and Dan too."

"Then what's holding you back?" Dan asked me.

I sighed heavily. Weariness seeped deeply in my bones. "Self-preservation." They both flinched. "I'm going for a walk. Let me think about this, okay?"

"Okay," Dan murmured as he pulled the man I now had to think of as Carter against his chest. A spark of envy flashed through me as he kissed the top of his head. I wanted to be doing that.

Walking away from them was hard, but I needed to clear my head. The evening was warm. The moon was a sliver of silver in the violet sky. It was a clear, cloudless night, so unlike my head, which was a shitstorm of turmoil. The hangover I'd started the evening with had receded to a dull ache, leaving me with only the thoughts and images of Carter and Dan. I couldn't stop it switching back to Carter and me. Fuck, I wanted to call him Mallory. I wanted to snatch him and take him back home again. But he didn't want me; he wanted us both. Could I do that? My dream and the three of us together popped into my head. It had been incredibly hot, but it had been just a dream. It might not feel like that if we were together now. Or it might be even better. Kes and his boyfriends completed each other. How had they adapted and become a threesome?

My thoughts veered away from the sexual aspect of a threesome, and I imagined a more day-to-day life, and it seemed easy. I liked it here. I wanted to work with Dan as much as I wanted Mallory back in my bed. If I had to call him by his middle name to have that, then I'd do that. Now it came down to having to share not just him but also myself to have him back in my life. Could I do that?

I stopped walking and closed my eyes. How did I feel about Dan? Warmth spread through me as the image of his smile flashed behind my eyelids, the dimple in his left cheek. I used to kiss that dimple, making him laugh. How would it feel to slide into him again? I hadn't thought of it in years, but it got my dick twitching now. The sex between us had always been incredible, and I was sure now that we'd both gained a lot more experience, it would be out of this world. But it hadn't been only sex between us. We'd had a connection on a deeper level, similar in many ways, but our goals had been different. Choosing to stay friends rather than lovers had been hard, and we'd still ended back in bed a couple of times. Now his friendship meant everything to me. If this failed, then it would be a hundred times worse than our breakup in college.

The bottom line was did I want to take the risk? I didn't want to miss out on what could be the best thing that had ever happened to me. Getting my best friend and my lover back could only be positive. Maybe things did happen for a reason, and the reason was to get us all together.

Feeling lighter, my mind cleared, I walked back to the house. I followed the sounds of the TV playing to the lounge. Dan and Carter were lying together on the large sofa, Carter in front, cocooned by Dan's arms. They looked good together. Carter spied me first. He shifted out of Dan's arms and sat up. He regarded me with worry in his dark blue eyes. Dan rose to his feet and pulled Carter up with him.

My heart beat faster, and the butterflies in my stomach stirred. This was it.

"I can't turn away from you. Either of you, hell, both of you. Shit, I'm going to do this with you."

A broad smile spread across Carter's lips, his face flushing pink with happiness. Dan grinned and clutched Carter against his chest, kissing the top of his head.

I'd expected a twinge of envy, but nothing. Instead, warmth flowed through my body. "Hey, I want some of that too."

Carter pulled away from Dan and rushed to me. As he wrapped his arms around my waist, he buried his head into my neck, then kissed the soft spot under my ear. A burst of energy raced through my body as if I'd come alive again. He lifted his face up to mine, and I had to have his mouth. As our lips touched, Carter moaned loudly. I swallowed it down, then matched it with my own. Dan's arms came around me. Then hot kisses landed on my neck. Shudders racked my body.

Carter licked over the seam of my lips and, as I opened my mouth, dipped inside. As much as I wanted to taste him, I knew we had to pull back. Dan must've sensed it too because he stepped back, his arms dropping from my waist. Carter did the same, sighing, as he swiped his thumb across his plump lip.

"I think you two need to spend some time together." Dan held up his hand as I opened my mouth to protest. "I'll be at work the next couple of days, and that would be the perfect time for you to get to know each other again. I don't mean fuck. I mean get connected again."

"Hmm, really? No sex? Where's the fun in that?" Carter pouted.

"C'mon, Car, this whole 'get to know each other' was your idea." Dan sighed, pinching the bridge of his nose when Carter bit his neck.

"We all know each other. Maybe I was wrong," he teased, then popped a quick kiss on Dan's mouth.

When he did the same to me and gave me a wink to go with it, my heart skipped a beat. We were soon grinning like loons. Was it really going to be this simple? I couldn't remember being this happy, or I could, but that seemed to have been in a different life, the one I'd had with Mallory.

"When do you want me to start work, then, Dan?" It was time to change the subject. Otherwise we'd end up fucking each other after all.

The rest of the already late evening passed quickly. Carter lounged on the large sofa, regaling us with stories of the sometimes ridiculous things that went on at the bar.

"Do you think you'll stay there or look for something so you can use your degree?"

"What degree?" Dan swiveled his head to Carter. Obviously, he'd been unaware of his education. Carter flushed. Damn, if I'd known he'd never mentioned it, I wouldn't have said anything.

"I've got an engineering degree, top of the class." He chuckled drily. It hurt that he'd left all the opportunities behind. "And no, I haven't thought about it. I like what I'm doing now."

"But, Carter, why not?" Dan asked.

"Leave it, Dan. I'm not interested." The edge to his voice kept us both from responding but not from passing each other a worried glance, but Carter caught it. "I'm going to bed."

He had to walk between Dan and me to reach the door, and we both grabbed one of his hands.

"I'm sorry, Carter. I spoke out of turn. I didn't mean to upset you." I pushed myself up so I could hug him. He stood stiffly for a moment, then relaxed, his hand resting on my back. "I'm sorry, sugar." With a curt nod, he stepped out of my arms.

"Maybe we should all hit the sack?" Dan kissed Carter's temple. "I won't mention it again."

When we reached the top of the stairs, I walked toward my room.

"Where are you going?" Dan asked.

I shrugged. "Bed. I thought that was obvious."

"Nuh-uh, no way. You sleep with us now. If we're doing this, we're starting right now. We don't have to fuck, but we need to be together." Frowning, Carter beckoned me.

"You sure?" They both nodded. "Okay, I'll go change and join you."

I stripped off and stepped into a pair of loose sleep shorts. As I ran my fingers over the scars on my thigh, a wave of self-consciousness rolled over me all of a sudden. Dan had seen them, but Carter hadn't, and I really didn't want to put him off.

"Don't forget your toothbrush," Dan hollered after me. With a smile, I wandered into my bathroom.

The lights in their room had been lowered. Gratitude filled me. That must've been Dan's doing. He understood. I found them both in the attached bathroom in shorts, brushing their teeth. I snatched the toothpaste from the counter and copied them. The stupid grins were back again as we stared at each other in the mirror.

When we were done, I followed them back into the bedroom, where we stood awkwardly at the foot of the huge bed.

"Oh, for fuck's sake, get in." Muttering, Carter clambered in and lay down. I climbed in behind him while Dan sandwiched him from the other side, facing him.

I wanted to tuck Carter into my body, the way I'd always done before we were torn apart. When he stretched his arm back and tugged me closer, I did exactly as I wanted and curled myself around him. My lips found the back of his neck as if pulled by a magnet, and I kissed him softly.

"Night, honey," I whispered as I draped my hand around his waist and rested it on his stomach. Dan's hand lay on Carter's hip. This felt right. This was how it should be.

But why did they want me here? I didn't understand. I didn't know. But tonight, the act of lying with them, talking, laughing, and joking had made me feel more alive than I'd been since before the accident. Since I'd kissed Mallory good-bye and left for work. I had no fucking clue where tomorrow would take me. I simply hoped it would take me somewhere with them. As I buried my head into the pillow, the heat of my lovers' bodies warmed mine, and soon I slipped into sleep.

Movement around me and some quiet words being exchanged jostled me awake. Then it all went quiet again, and I fell back to sleep.

I woke up slowly, not wanting to leave the dream behind. The dream of Mallory being with me, loving me again. I'd had so many of them, but this one felt more real. As his hands stroked over my body, his mouth covered me in kisses. His tongue slid over my heated skin. So damn real, so damn heartbreakingly real.

I didn't want to open my eyes as his mouth moved down. His nose skimmed over my groin, ignoring my thick, throbbing, and achingly hard dick so close to his lips. Then his mouth was on my leg, sliding up and down my scars, nipping at the sensitive skin and dropping kisses as I trembled.

Wait. That wasn't right. Mallory didn't know about my scars. My eyes snapped open, and I looked around the unfamiliar room. Then Mallory's mouth curved up in a smile against my leg.

"Hmm, it took you long enough to wake up." He kissed my thigh again as he slid his long fingers up the inside of my sleep shorts, getting teasingly close to my junk.

"God, I thought it was a dream. Carter, should we be doing this?" I croaked out, emotion thick in my throat.

"Yeah, baby. I'm here, and I'm real, and I really fucking want you." His gravelly voice gave his need for me away.

"Really? Carter, are you sure?" *Please be sure. Please be sure.*

"I'm so damn sure." He dragged my shorts down my legs and swiped the flat of his tongue from my sac, up the length of my solid rod, then covered the crown with his hot, wet mouth.

I bucked my hips, thrusting deeper inside his mouth as I arched my back on the bed. "Fuuuck. Oh, god. I'd forgotten how much I love your mouth," I panted out, then clenched my teeth to stop myself from coming straight away. As he slurped up and down my length, the sound and feel of his mouth lavishing attention on me had me seeing stars. I was leaking into his mouth as he lapped at the slit. I opened my eyes and looked down. He gazed back, his dark blue irises shining like sapphires.

Trembling, I weaved my fingers into his long, dark hair and gripped him tightly, holding him but not guiding him. This was his show. I was just here for the ride. He gave me a wink, then bobbed up and down my length again, sucking harder and faster. The telltale tingle of my orgasm prickled in my spine, and I tugged on his hair.

"I'm gonna come, honey. God, you feel so good." I punched my hips up again as he sucked hard, his cheeks hollowing. The fire spread up my spine, forcing me up from the bed. As I flooded his mouth and throat, he swallowed everything I had to give. I collapsed back down while Carter licked gently over the ultrasensitive glans, making me twitch and squirm.

Climbing back up my body, Carter dropped kisses on my abs and chest, then plundered my mouth. I tasted myself on his tongue, but it was his flavor that broke through my defenses, emotions bubbling up, and a sob escaped.

He cupped my face in his palms, his eyes soft but determined. "Archer baby, don't cry. We're good. We're together. It's over. No more loneliness, just lots of love and joy from now on."

"I never thought I'd see you again. Even through all the pain and surgeries, nothing compared to losing you." Another sob slipped out, and he kissed my forehead, my eyebrows, and my eyelids, then continued down to my mouth.

"Tell me what happened. I want to know all of it not just your injuries but every part of your recovery. I hate that I wasn't there with you. I hate how we were torn apart." He ran his fingers over my rib cage. "What's this one from?" He shocked me by kissing it.

"My lung collapsed. They had to put a chest drain in to inflate it again. Twice. Plus, my spleen ruptured and had to be removed." I sighed as he traced over the scars on my skin.

He lulled me with his soft touch and kisses as he traveled over my body, running his mouth over my shoulder and down my left arm. "How about here?"

"Both bones in my lower arm and my wrist plus my collarbone." More kisses followed his touch.

He didn't stop peppering my skin with featherlight kisses, but as he moved down to my legs, I tensed. I was grateful when he chose the right leg first. Maybe he realized I'd be done for when he touched my left leg and thigh.

Sliding his fingers softly over my skin, he reached my ankle and kissed it, raising his eyes to mine, silently asking me the question.

"Broke bones in both ankles. This one was trapped under a foot pedal, and all three bones were broken. The other is about the same. There's a lot of metalwork in there holding them together. I wasn't sure if I'd ever walk again. They were so painful." Carter's chin wobbled as he swallowed hard to control his emotions.

"And here?" His voice quivered as if trying to hold back his tears.

"A broken femur. I had to have an external fixator to hold it all together. A lot of damaged muscle and tissue, but my recovery was hampered when an infection developed, and they had to open me up again to clean it all out and fit new metalwork." I kept my voice flat despite the pain coursing through me. Not physical but emotional. It hurt to rehash it all, the memories of lying there in the hospital, yearning for my man who didn't come. This was the hardest bit, but it would be the last time I needed to tell it. Hopefully, we could both move on together from this.

He buried his face in his hands for a few moments. Then he lifted his head, his eyes spewing fire. "I fucking hate your mother."

"Yeah, me too."

Thirty

Dan

Why was today going so slowly? I had so much work piled up, with court dates just around the corner, but all I could think about was what Archer and Carter might be getting up to. I'd said they should get to know each other again, take time to talk through their toughest memories. For them to understand what had happened that had kept them apart. But there was no way they would be able to keep their hands off each other, and I couldn't blame either of them. Hell, if I were there now, we'd be fucking, that was for sure.

At five thirty on the dot, I raced from the office. When I opened the door, silence greeted me. Maybe they'd gone back to Carter's. I walked through the kitchen and peered out into the garden.

Fuck.

Archer was lying on one of the loungers with Carter rocking his hips over and over. Archer had to be buried deep inside him. Carter's eyes were closed, his mouth a perfect *o*, his face blissed out as if he embraced all the feelings coursing through his body. Archer's hands rested on Carter's ass. He didn't seem to be controlling Carter's movement, stroking softly, caressing him as Carter continued to rock.

The two men I loved looked even more beautiful than I could ever have imagined. I took a step forward. My movement must've alerted Archer as he jerked his head toward me. Then a lazy smile spread across his face. So not what I'd expected, but then he moved. He lifted Carter a few inches and, with long, slow, and oh-so-deep thrusts, pushed his cock in and out of Carter's ass. My dick was rock hard in my pants. I rubbed my palm over it, hoping to calm it down, not to encourage it further. A damp patch appeared on my briefs as I started to leak. God, this was so hot.

Archer whispered something to Carter I couldn't hear. Carter nodded and wrapped his hand around his dick, then matched his strokes to Archer's movements. They were so in tune, even after all these months. Archer increased the tempo but still pulled the length of his cock all the way out of Carter's entrance before plunging back inside. No shallow thrusts to bring them both to a climax quicker. This was lovemaking at its finest. And instead of jealousy, which might've made sense, something else rolled through me, something warm and fuzzy and right. I tugged at my clothes. No way was I missing out on being a part of this, of them. In seconds, I was naked.

The late afternoon sunlight caught on the sleek sweat covering Carter's chest and back, giving him an otherworldly gleam. Archer pounded inside him hard, fast, and deep. His lips moved again, and Carter's eyes flew open, straight into mine. As our eyes locked, he stretched out his arm to me. Stepping closer, I tugged on my aching length. Carter wrapped his hand around it and took control, pumping me with long, firm strokes.

I leaned into him, wanting to get closer. "Suck me, baby. Get those plump lips around my cock."

Archer let go of Carter's ass and changed positions. Kneeling behind Carter now, Archer entered him again. I crouched in front of Carter, my dick in line with his mouth. On all fours, Carter looked so wanton, his eyes black with desire. He licked his lips, then parted them on a soft sigh. I slipped inside his hot, wet mouth and groaned as he sucked.

Archer held on to Carter's hips, keeping him still as he pumped his cock inside him. "I've never seen anything so fucking hot as this. Carter, you're divine. I worship you." His words were hushed as he panted, taking him deeper and deeper.

"I'm not going to last. Keep still, baby, let me do this." I stroked my hands through Carter's dark locks as I pushed into his mouth. I thrust farther into his throat, watching him the entire time. As he looked up at me, his lips tight around my length, his cheeks hollowing as he sucked, I was done for.

"Oh, baby, yeeees." I came hard as Carter sucked and swallowed, his eyes fixed on mine. When I had no more to give, I gently pulled out of his mouth and kissed him. "Your turn, baby."

With his arms wrapped around Carter's body, Archer pulled him upright, still plunging inside him as I kneeled and took Carter into my mouth. As soon as I closed my lips around his weeping cock, he trembled and quivered, and I knew he was going to come. Taking him deep, I swallowed around him. That was all it took before he bucked his hips and came, crying out loud as he filled my throat, then my mouth with his thick release. Archer groaned as he released inside Carter's body, thrusting erratically until he, too, was spent.

We collapsed down in a heap. Carter lay on my chest while Archer leaned over him, dragging huge lungsful of air in as he rested his forehead on Carter's shoulder.

Carter lifted his head and looked at me with heavy-lidded eyes, then gave me a heart-stopping smile.

"I love you, Dan. That was amazing." He kissed me softly, gently, and so sweetly. I fell even deeper in love with him.

"Carter, you have no idea about the depth of my love for you." I kissed his forehead. Then he groaned as Archer slipped from him.

"I'll get a cloth." Archer grinned at us both as he stepped around the lounger.

"I'd rather just shower." Carter pushed himself up from my body. "You two coming?"

"We're right behind you." Laughing, I gave his butt a swat.

After our shower, which involved much touching and kissing, we strolled into our room and got dressed.

"Have you brought your clothes in here yet, Arch?" I glanced over my shoulder as I tugged my boxer briefs up my legs.

"I'll do it tomorrow. Now I'll just grab something." He sauntered off to the guest room.

"Did you mind us being together without you?" Carter stepped up behind me and kissed my nape, then rested his chin on my shoulder.

"I was surprised," I answered honestly. "Was that the first time today?" My stomach clenched. Why did I have to ask that now?

"Yes, I know we agreed to wait and get to know each other again, but we ended up messing around a little bit this morning. Nothing more, I promise. Then we kind of had the idea for you to come home and find us, then join in. We all found kissing together last night sexy as hell, and we wanted to turn you on." Carter twisted me around so I was facing him. "Please tell me it was okay."

"I would've rather you waited until we were all together, but I'm not going to pretend that it wasn't amazing. We can work out what we want as we go along. I think as long as we continue to communicate, we'll be fine." I leaned in to kiss him while I gripped his hips.

"Mmm, I like this sort of communication." Carter's mouth was a hairbreadth from mine. He slipped his tongue between my lips, and soon, we were locked together, devouring, giving and taking, fastened at the hip and our hands tangling in each other's hair.

A chortle sounded, followed by a cough as Archer walked back in. "I was only gone a couple of minutes, and you two are at it again."

It had become easier after that, and I liked it. The three of us had settled, and any immediate concerns had dissipated. Now we were out in the garden, lounging around as darkness surrounded us, picking at the food Archer and Carter had prepared before we'd gotten all caught up.

My hand rested on Carter's thigh as he lay next to me. Archer slouched on the opposite chair, telling outrageous stories of our antics at college, trying to blame me for being the bad influence.

"Yeah, right. You go ahead and think that, but I remember the time you snuck in your politics lecturer's college and hid an open can of tuna just before spring break. The room had to be fumigated by the time the new term began." I shook my head. "You were the bad influence. I was just a country boy trying to get good grades."

Archer burst out laughing. "You were top of the class, you dork."

"What about you, baby? Did you have a good time at college?" I asked Carter.

"Um, not really. My folks kicked me out, cut off my allowance, and threw me out of my apartment halfway through my year. I had to provide for myself and apply for every student loan and grant I could get. I had to get a job, so it wasn't brilliant." He glanced across at Archer, who had a loving gaze fixed on my boyfriend. Fuck. Our boyfriend. "Then I bumped into Archer, literally, and my life turned around. I was happy again. I didn't hang around much with my peers because I got everything I wanted from Archer. He saved me, giving me time to work hard and graduate well. I was happy then."

"We were happy, weren't we?" Archer said.

"Yeah, we were very happy. We thought we had the world." Carter sighed.

"Have you two had any idea about what you want to do about what your mother did? Do you want to take any action?" I asked them.

Carter stayed silent, a frown marring his smooth forehead. We must've made him uncomfortable talking about our happy times. I pulled his face to mine and kissed him, then whispered, "You're here now. I've got you. We've got you." He relaxed and kissed me quickly again. I wrapped him in my arms, keeping him close against my body.

Archer was smiling again too; he was okay.

"Did you want to do something? You said you haven't spoken to your mother since the accident. Do you want to now?"

"I've had a couple of thoughts, ideas, really. I don't want to speak to her, but I think I might get a friend to do some poking around in her private life. If she could get police officers to approach you, I think she's got some secrets. My mother likes to be in control and will do anything to get it to the extent of playing some dirty little games. I want to find out what they are and bring her down." Archer's face was stony, his green eyes hard and determined.

"Who will you ask?"

"Lucas Davenport, Mason's cousin. He runs one of the country's top surveillance and security companies. If there's dirt, he'll find it."

"I've heard of him." Carter tensed in my arms. I could guess what he was thinking, and it hurt me.

"Don't look at me like that, please. I know what you're thinking, and the answer is because I'm a stubborn dick. I was hurting, and I was angry. I know how much I fucked up, okay?" Archer groaned.

"Okay, enough of the heavies. We're supposed to be excited about what's happening between us. I, for one, want a repeat of what went down earlier and maybe more," I joked, trying to break the tension.

"Then maybe we should go to bed?" Archer waggled his eyebrows, his eyes dark and hooded. Carter shifted and lifted his head. The hunger in his eyes had me hardening quickly.

"I think so too. Come on, baby." We all stood and walked inside.

Archer grinned and bolted up the stairs. Carter nudged me, and we raced up after him.

The only light came from the bedside lamps, leaving the room in a soft glow. Archer had dropped his shorts, and we both stared at his rock-hard dick.

"You'd better get naked quick." He fisted his cock and stroked himself from base to tip.

We'd never stripped faster.

Thirty One

Carter

It had been four days since Archer joined us, and for the first time, I woke up alone. The morning sun shone softly through a gap in the curtains, the light a gray shimmer. It was still early, and Dan wouldn't have left for work yet. I swung my legs over the edge of the bed, stood, and stretched until the tension eased with a satisfying *snap*. The muscles in my body were protesting, but it was a good feeling. I grabbed a pair of boxer shorts and headed to the bathroom. After I peed, I washed my hands and studied myself in the mirror. I stroked over the bite mark on my neck with my fingertip, then slid down to another on my chest just above my nipple. I smiled. The men were more alike than I'd thought, putting their mark on me. Last night had been so hot.

Both Dan and Archer were dressed in suits and looked so sexy. I let out a low whistle, and they turned in smooth synchronicity.

"I could say the same about you." Dan swaggered up to me, yanked me up to his hard body, and pressed his mouth hard to mine. Then he tugged my bottom lip between his teeth and gave me a nip. Wow, that was a welcome kiss I didn't mind getting every morning.

"Are you finally making it to the office, Arch?" I cocked my eyebrow as I walked into his arms and kissed him. Maybe a bit more gently than Dan had kissed me but just as sincere.

"Don't be cheeky, or I'll spank your ass," he fake-whispered in my ear. Dan chuckled behind me.

"Hey, no picking on me." I snickered as I grabbed his coffee mug from him and took a swig, then handed it back. "What's for breakfast?"

"You're too late. You'll have to get something after we've gone." Dan smirked but opened the oven and brought out a plate of bacon and pancakes for me.

"Oh, this is why I love you." I picked up a piece of bacon with my fingers. They both took a seat and snatched at my food. "Hey."

"What are you going to do today, baby? Will you be okay with us both gone?"

I rolled my eyes. "Yeah, I'm sure I'll manage. I have so far." I snorted. "Seriously, though, I'm going back to work for a few hours. Then I'm going to grab some boxes and pack up my apartment."

"Shall we meet you there for lunch?" Archer asked, but I wrinkled my nose at him and shook my head.

"Nah, I'm gonna be busy. I'm sure your partner may have plenty of work for you." I grinned at Dan, who smiled back. "Can I borrow your truck? Then I can bring my stuff over." I tried to ignore Archer's disappointment, but he wasn't going to let it go.

"Don't you want your boss to know about us?"

"Don't be stupid, Archer. I don't care about that. I just believe we should get into a work routine, and I'd like to catch up with Paris if I can. I haven't seen him since the club. I owe him an explanation," I explained, but he was still scowling. I shot Dan a "help me" look.

"C'mon, Archer, let him get on with packing up. I'm sure he'll make it up to you tonight." Dan nudged him with his elbow. "We do have a shit ton of work to go through. I guess we'll be working through lunch."

"Fine, but we'll be seen together this weekend, the three of us." He huffed and pouted, and as much as I wanted to laugh, I knew he was serious. He didn't want to hide us.

"Absolutely. I promise, Archer. I love you, and I'm proud of us." I kissed him, a long, slow, lazy kiss, and he moaned softly in return. "Now you've got my dick hard. I'd better deal with that when you've gone."

Dan laughed and gripped the back of my neck, then leaned in. "You keep your hands away from your dick, baby. Consider it your punishment for turning up in just your underwear," he growled.

"I hate you," I muttered.

"No, you don't. You love us." Chuckling, Archer nuzzled my neck.

"Yeah, I do. Go on. Get to work, you fuckers." I was trying to be stern, but I was laughing too much.

"Bye, baby. Call me if you need me." Dan gave me a quick kiss and hurried after Archer.

Surprising even myself, I did as I was told and left my dick alone. I cleaned up the kitchen, then headed out to the bar.

Kes was wiping the bar but raised his arm and hollered, "He's back. Woohoo. Good to see you, Carter."

Heat flooded my cheeks as everyone in the bar turned to me. The locals all cheered and clapped, whereas the tourists looked bewildered at the scene.

"Yeah, great. Thanks for that, Kester." I used his full name, but he only laughed harder. On my way back to the office, I passed Shelley, who gave me a peck on my cheek and patted my arm. Kes followed me, and as I stepped into the office, I understood why. Denver had their newly adopted little girl with him. A broad smile broke out on his face while the little girl clapped her hands and waved at me.

"It's good to see you, Carter, and looking so damn good too. How are you?" Denver studied me, then gave me a one-armed hug.

"I'm good. Still can't believe it, but damn, I'd forgotten what it feels like to breathe properly. Things are good." I hung my messenger bag on the hook at the door and ran my hands through my scruffy hair.

"Are you moving in with Dan?" Kes asked with a twinkle in his eyes.

"I am. I'm gonna grab some boxes and pack up my stuff. I can't thank you enough for what you did for me. You helped me when I didn't know which way to turn or where to go. I don't know what I would've done without you guys."

"It was meant to be, Carter. You needed to be here for when Archer reached out to his friend. You can't mess with fate." Kes clapped him on his back. "Just like Denver needed to come home to find his forever with us."

"So how are things? Are you in a triad now?" Denver lifted his brow.

I nodded. "It's early days, but it's good. Dan has finally convinced Archer to go to work, so I think he's happy."

The phone rang, and Kes leaned across the desk to answer it. I didn't pay any attention to the conversation until he said my name.

"Hold on. He's here. I can ask him." Kes looked at me. "Paris is going through some shit at home. Can you take his shift tonight?"

"Of course, no worries."

Kes went back to talking to Paris. I knew his father wasn't happy with Paris's sexuality and they'd plenty of arguments about it. I hoped my friend was all right.

"What's going on?" I asked Kes when he ended the call. "Is it his dad again?"

"You know about it?" Kes's eyes widened.

"Of course, I do. Paris is my friend. He's crashed on my couch enough when his father's been drinking and gotten too happy with his fists."

"Damn, I didn't realize it had gotten that bad. He says he's going to have to move out, which may mean moving away."

"Why doesn't he move into my place? I was planning to leave the furniture I'd bought, as I've got nowhere to put it. It's only cheap stuff, but it's good." Letting Paris have my place gave me a good feeling.

"That's a great idea. Why don't you call him, Carter? I think he could use a friend today. You don't have to be here now if you're working tonight. Call him and bring him here."

"Yeah, I need to call Dan too." Would Archer and Dan be okay with me working tonight at such short notice? But why shouldn't they? This was my job. I didn't need their consent.

"Okay, do you want me to grab some boxes from the store cupboard?"

"That would be great."

Kes and Denver left me in the office. I dragged my cell from my pocket and called Dan.

"Hey, baby. How are you doing?" he answered, and my heart swelled at the endearment.

"I'm good. There's been a change of plans, though. I'm gonna be working tonight. Paris's father is giving him a hard time again, so I'm working his shift. I'm going to offer him my apartment too. I'll be packing up my stuff and, if he wants my place, help him move in. It's gonna be a long day. If I don't get it all done, I'll crash here tonight. Just giving you the heads-up now."

"Hold on a sec."

Muttered voices sounded in the background, and then Dan came back.

"Okay, Carter. Archer's here, and you're on speakerphone. We're alone."

"Carter, I don't think so. Dan and I will be there and wait for you. There's no way you're going back to sleeping alone," he growled.

Dan spoke up. "You're coming back here tonight, Carter. I don't care what time it is."

I pinched the bridge of my nose. What was it with these guys? Did they think they could make the decisions for me? I took a deep breath to stop myself from giving them a piece of my mind. That would have to wait.

"You're being crazy, both of you. It could be three a.m. before I finish. You don't get to tell me what to do, Dan. It's not your call. I'm sorry. I'm busy now. I'll talk to you later." I ended the call before either of them could answer. The next call was much more pleasant. Paris was stoked at the thought of taking over my place. "I've got the truck today. Grab your stuff, and I'll come get you. Text me when you're ready."

"I will, Carter. Thanks, man. You're my savior."

"No worries. I'll see you soon."

I spend the next couple of hours boxing up my stuff and giving the place a good clean. Both Dan and Archer called me, but I let them both go to voicemail. I wasn't interested in hearing them beat their chests and order me around.

Just as I was done, Paris messaged me he was ready, and I headed out to get him. When I reached his house, he was standing on the porch with a couple of duffel bags and a few boxes. He'd wrapped his arms around himself as if he was only just holding it together. He had a black eye, and bruises bloomed on his chin and cheekbone.

"C'mon, dude, let's get you settled. You'll like it there, and hey, it's rent-free. I'm leaving all my furniture. Let me know what else you need, and we can get it for you."

"Thanks, Carter. The cops came around last night. It got as bad as it could. It's not fair to my mom to be stuck in the middle. She's not happy about me leaving, but she knows my dad is getting worse." He shuffled his feet, not looking at me. There was more than having the cops paying a visit. Aah.

"Was it Conn?"

Two red spots appeared on his pale cheeks. "Yeah, it was. Pretty embarrassing for me too."

I'd noticed Paris had a crush on our local detective, but as far as I knew, he'd never acted on it. The next few hours we sorted out his stuff in the apartment. Then we loaded my boxes into the back of the truck.

"Have the night off, Paris. You need to get your head straight. Enjoy the quiet here, and get yourself settled. I'm downstairs if you need me." I gave him a hug and kissed his forehead.

"Thanks, Carter. I owe you, man." His voice was thick with tears.

"No, you don't. Just pay it forward when you can. This place is a good place to heal. You'll be fine."

I headed downstairs for my shift. Dan and Archer hadn't called me again, which was supposed to feel good, but sometimes the silence could be worse. What were they plotting?

We were a couple of hours away from closing. It had been busy, but I'd managed to fill Shelley in on Paris, and her mothering instinct kicked into overdrive. She was already making a list of things she could help him with.

"He'll be fine, Shell. Stop clucking over him." I nudged her playfully.

"What can I get you?" I asked the guy in front of me. I hadn't seen him before. He gave me the once-over and smiled, but it didn't reach his eyes. He was dressed expensively and immaculately in black pants and a light-blue shirt. Not a hair out of place, and considering it was nearly eleven o'clock, I would've expected a more relaxed dress code, but his dark red tie was still in place.

"Hmm, now there's a loaded question." His perusing gaze made my skin crawl.

"To drink, sir. What would you like?" I stayed polite but took a small step back.

"I'll take a single malt scotch. Make it a double."

Turning my back, I picked the most expensive scotch we had and poured him his measure.

"Twenty-six dollars, please."

He offered me a hundred-dollar bill. "Why don't you join me?"

"I'm good, thank you." Out of the corner of my eye, I caught Shelley's subtle lift of her chin. "Excuse me. Enjoy your drink."

When I walked up to her, she frowned at me. "Do you know that guy?" she asked.

"Never seen him before. Why?" Without looking back over my shoulder, I knew he was still watching me. His eyes boring into my back made my skin prickle.

"He asked for you by name two nights ago. He wasn't here yesterday, though."

I tried to ignore him and continued to serve the other customers with a happy smile and a few words, but I remained aware of his presence. He never ordered another drink or spoke again, but he unnerved me.

Who the hell was he?

Thirty Two

Archer

"Did he just hang up on us?" I looked at Dan, who was looking as pissed as I felt.

"He did. What was that all about?"

"I'd forgotten about his stubborn streak. He was like this before. He would never let me help him. We had so many arguments about money and how he wouldn't take any from me. I paid off his student loans for him when he graduated, but I don't even think he knows. Then I got into the accident, and well, you know what happened. At least he had money in his account when my mother ruined our lives."

"Am I treading on your toes, Archer? I feel like I'm the third wheel. You know so much about him, and we're still in the learning phase." Dan pinned me with a sober gaze. What did he mean?

"What? God, no. Mallo—I mean Carter—loves you. I can see it. I should be the one to worry. Does he want me out of duty? Does he feel he should stay with me?"

"I doubt that. As you said, Carter's stubborn, and he gets what he wants. He loves you, Archer. It's written all over his face. I'd given up on loving you. I thought we'd lost any chance of that when we split up. Then you met Carter. But I do love you. You coming back to me brought that fact home loud and clear. All my feelings for you returned in a flash. I want this to work. I know it'll be so good."

"I guess it's up to him. As always, that man has me wrapped around his little finger. We're good together, Dan, but I think if he had to choose now, he'd choose you. And as much as it would kill me, I'd walk away. I wouldn't fight for him. That's not fair to him or you. I had my chance with him."

"Why are we even talking about this? Carter hasn't said he's not happy. In fact, I think having you back has completed him. You've healed him, and that works for me. I get a much happier man. We'll give him a while to cool down and then call him. Now let's get some work done."

I strolled back to my office, where I browsed through the files Dan had shared with me and chose one to start on. After an hour, I picked up my phone and called Carter, but the little shit had turned on his voicemail. I smiled. Just the thought of apologizing to him made me hard.

My phone rang, and without looking at the caller ID, I growled, "You ready to get your ass spanked tonight, baby?"

"Hey, you're not really my type, but I'll pass the message on to my wife." The caller chuckled.

Heat flooded my cheeks, and I checked the screen. It was a good thing Lucas Davenport hadn't FaceTimed me.

"Sorry, man. I was expecting someone else." I laughed loudly, then got my head in the game. "Thanks for returning my call. I've got a job for you if you've got a space for me."

"Tell me more," he replied.

The next thirty minutes, I filled him in on my accident, what had gone down after, and what my mother had done to Mallory.

"Shit, Archer, I wish you'd asked me to do this nine months ago. I could've had him back with you in days."

"I fucking know that now, asshole," I muttered. "Mason offered, but I was too mad to deal at the time. I was a dick. Both Carter, as he's now called, and Dan have told me plenty of times. Can you help, though? That bitch had to have a hold on someone to pull the tricks she did. I don't care what it costs. I want her brought down. How many other lives has she wrecked?"

"I'm on it. Do you want updates or just facts when I have them? She really is a bitch, isn't she?" Lucas chuckled drily.

"She might be my mother, but she's the lowest kind of human, Lucas. Let me know when you've got something, but I don't want to be directly involved with bringing her down. I'm not doing her courtside shows. Let me know so we can put the facts in the hands of the right people to end her."

"Consider it done, Archer. It's good to know you're happy again. Please put my cousin out of his misery and call him." Lucas ended the call.

Relief flooded me, and I felt lighter, as if a weight had been lifted from me. Finally, I'd set the wheels in motion to what I should've done months ago: take her down.

I gave calling Carter another try, but it went straight to voicemail again. He might've given us the finger, but he was a good man, helping his friend. I tuned him out for the rest of the day and only saw Dan a few times when he popped his head around the door to ask me how I was getting on.

So it was a surprise when he walked in with his briefcase in his hand.

"You ready to get outta here?" he asked as I looked up from a file two inches thick.

"Is it time already? Hell, yeah, let's go." I shut down my computer and locked the files in the tall wooden cabinet behind me.

"Did you get hold of Carter?" I walked up to him and dropped a kiss on his mouth.

"No, the little shit didn't answer me." He frowned. "Did you?"

"No, but I figured he was helping his friend and would've focused on him."

"I guess. He and Paris are good friends. I know a bit more than you, though, about why he's helping him."

"You gonna share?"

"Yeah, Conn Martinez called me. He's a cop and a good friend." He slapped my chest. "Don't look at me like that. He's just a friend. Anyway, they got a call last night, and Paris's father decided to try to beat the gay out of Paris. The boy got away before his father could hurt him too badly, but he's gonna have a hard time today. Carter's a good man. He'll make sure Paris is okay."

"Are we going over there tonight?" We reached his car, and I climbed into the sleek leather seat and relaxed.

"Too fucking right. Carter's going to be in our bed tonight. And I'm looking forward to reminding him of how much he likes it there."

"I like the sound of that. Hell, I'm horny as fuck. How long do we have to wait until we can get him?" It was only partially a joke. I couldn't wait to see him and get my hands on him.

"Did you get in contact with your surveillance guy?" Dan asked as he drove us home.

"Yeah, he's going to look into it. I told him I don't need updates but only want to know when he's done. Then we can hand what he's dug up over to the authorities. I know she's hiding something. Sorry if I sound cruel, her being my mother, but she's a cold-hearted, calculating bitch."

"Well, let's hope it doesn't take him long. For all we know, she's been aware of where Carter is, and has the whole time. Now that you're here too, she might get pissed enough to act on it."

"I never thought of that. Do you think he's safe?" Cold sweat broke out over my body at the thought of her harming him, physically this time. She'd never lift one of her own hands against him, but she had plenty of people who would be more than willing to do it for her.

"I don't think we should mention this to him, but maybe you need to call your friend again. Of course I could be completely wrong, but if she hates him that much, maybe she's capable of hurting him."

"It's as if you've read my mind. I'll call him when we get home. Dammit, why won't she just leave me the fuck alone?" I could be wrong about her, but I doubted it.

By the time Dan had come back downstairs from his shower, I'd spoken to Lucas again, and he'd said they'd already managed to get into a private bank account and a personal email account. I was impressed at the speed he worked. I guessed that was what made him one of the best.

While I brought Dan up to date, he grabbed us both a beer from the fridge and cooked dinner. Just a simple steak, baked potatoes, and a salad.

"Did he tell you if he's found anything?" Dan asked as he sliced the tomatoes.

"No, but he thought watching out for Carter was a good idea, so maybe he has. I hate keeping this from Carter, but if it turns out to be unnecessary, why worry him too?"

"I agree. We have to carry on as normal and let him get back to being Carter again."

Would he still be pissed at us?

Thirty Three

Dan

As soon as we walked in, I zeroed in on Carter behind the bar. For a minute, he faltered, then continued wiping the bar top, his brows knitted, his mouth a hard line.

"What are you doing here?" he asked in a less-than-friendly tone.

"After you hung up on us and refused to answer our calls, we decided we needed to come and remind you of what you'll be missing at home."

"You shouldn't have bothered. I've got the truck. I can make my own way back when I'm done." Despite his harsh words, he uncapped two bottles of beer and shoved them at us with two glasses.

Shelley walked over, a huge grin on her face. "Ahh, boys, are you missing your man?" I chuckled back at her, but Archer choked on his beer, only just managing not to spit it all over me.

"Oh, boys." She smirked. "I watched what went down with Kes and his men. Don't play innocent with me." She wagged her finger at us but gave us a wink.

This lightened the mood between us, and heat rose in my neck and face.

"Shelley, please, for the love of god, pack it in," Carter pleaded, but I couldn't help laughing hard.

"You can pack it in too, or you won't be getting anything from me tonight." Carter tried to act stern, but he couldn't fool me. He'd forgiven us.

Shelley faux-whispered in his ear, "Which one were you talking to, sugar lips?"

It was a fair assumption. Carter begged her to stop embarrassing him and berated Archer for encouraging her.

We quietly chatted while Carter worked through his shift, but soon it was time for him to close down for the night. The patrons grumbled lightheartedly that it was too early, but they left with promises to come back soon. Only one guy dragged his feet. At the door, he turned and nodded at Carter, shooting him a smug smile. The weird interaction put me on edge. Carter followed him with his eyes as the man disappeared through the door and walked past the windows.

"You okay, baby?" I didn't like the frown on his face. Something was off. Carter broke his gaze away from the window and plastered a smile on his face, but it wasn't a genuine one.

"Yeah, sorry. I'm good." Shelley had locked the door and walked back to the hallway at the side, a broom in her hand.

"Hey, Shelley. Give me that. I'll do that for you. Let me walk you to your car." I took the broom from her and leaned it against the bar. She gave me a look I couldn't decipher, but I ignored it and strolled with her to the parking lot.

"Thank you, Dan. It looks like you've got a lot going on there, sweetie. Be careful. They have a past to deal with." She stroked her hand down the side of my face, her eyes full of concern.

"I know, Shell, and thank you for caring. We're just getting to know each other again." I kept my voice low. I loved Shelley. I'd known her all my life, and she had a heart of pure gold.

"That's not what it looks like, Dan. It looks like you've fallen hook, line, and sinker for them both."

"I'll be careful, I promise." I kissed her cheek and waited for her to get in the car, start the engine, and back out of the space.

As I came back inside, Archer had Carter in a tight embrace and was kissing him so damn hard my dick swelled.

"Okay, lover boys. Pack it in. It's time to go home." I clapped my hands, and they lazily pulled apart. Archer ran his thumb over Carter's swollen lips and smiled so tenderly I felt the tug on my heart. Archer strode up to me and kissed me, slipping his tongue between my parted lips. Out of the corner of my eye, I caught Carter with his gaze locked on us, rubbing his hand over the bulge in his pants.

I let Archer control the kiss, but then another set of hands landed on my hips. Panting, I broke away and swiveled around to Carter. Archer grasped his wrist and tugged, bringing him to stand between us. He kissed me, then Carter, who sighed softly.

"You ready to go home, baby?" Archer asked him.

"I'm ready for all of us to be together," Carter whispered. "I'm sorry I was a dick this morning. Don't gang up on me, please. We need to be equal and respect each other."

"I know. I'm sorry too." Archer kissed him again.

"I need to close down the office. It'll only take me a few minutes. Can you sweep in here?"

"I'll do that," I told him. Carter rushed to the office. "Is he serious?" I asked Archer as he followed him with his gaze.

"I don't think he wouldn't have said it if he didn't mean it. We must've really pushed him today."

We then swept the floor and wiped down the tables. Between the two of us, we made quick work of the mundane tasks, but it felt like a lifetime before Carter came out of the office and switched the last lights off.

"I'm ready." His voice was low and gravelly, sounding as if he really was ready.

During the drive home, we didn't speak. Archer seemed lost in his thoughts, and I had my eyes more on the rearview mirror, watching Carter following in the truck, than on the road.

I pulled up on the driveway, switched off the engine, and waited for Carter to park alongside me. "Come on, let's go in."

Before Archer could respond, I'd rounded the car, opened his door, and held my hand out for him. Without any hesitation, he grasped it.

In three long strides, Carter stood in front of me. His mouth hit mine as he reached around and grabbed my ass. As he plunged his tongue into my mouth, he squeezed my cheeks hard, dragging my hips up to his. As quickly as he'd attacked me, he pulled back, his blue eyes turned black with lust.

"We need to get upstairs and get naked, like now," he growled at me, then turned to Archer. "Let's go."

I liked this side of Carter. Not that I wanted to keep pissing him off. But seeing him take charge was hot as hell. "Yes, sir." I gave him a quick salute.

Grinning, Carter gave Archer a nudge, making him dart up the stairs, then hot on his heels, followed him, managing to give his ass a swat when he reached him. I climbed up at a more sedate pace, shaking my head at their antics.

Carter had wasted no time and had already pulled off his shirt, which now lay in a puddle on the floor. As he tugged at his belt, releasing the buckle, Archer watched him with hooded eyes for a couple of seconds, then yanked his T-shirt up over his head and toed off his shoes. His jeans were next, leaving him in just a pair of tight black briefs.

"Fuck," I whispered and stripped quickly. In no time, we were all standing in just our underwear. Both men's erections peeked out from their waistbands. I rubbed my hand over my hard dick.

Carter dropped to his knees and peeled down Archer's briefs, exposing his rigid cock, then took it into his mouth. His cheeks hollowed as he sucked on just the head. Archer let out a guttural groan. I stepped out of my boxer briefs, tilted Archer's head to the side, and slipped my tongue between his lips.

Then Carter wrapped his hand firmly around my dick and pumped it.

My breath hitched as his hot, wet mouth closed around my dick.

Thirty Four

Carter

His dick was divine. I closed my lips around the swollen crown and flicked my tongue over the slit, tasting a burst of his precum. Humming, I took him deeper and glanced up. Archer was watching me as he stroked my hair, gripping and tugging on the strands. He held my head still as Dan pumped his hips, pushing his length deeper into my mouth.

"Oh, god, you look amazing. Fuck, I love you. Take him deep, baby," Archer crooned at me, then loosened his grasp on my hair as I swallowed around Dan's cock. His deep groans turned me on even more. My nose hit his smooth groin. I loved his shaved cock and balls. I sucked and licked and lapped as I circled his base to keep him from coming. After a few minutes, I pulled back and turned to do the same to Archer. Swapping between the two of them felt so empowering. I reveled in their moans getting louder and their movements more erratic.

"Fuck, you need to stop. I'm gonna come," Dan said as I swallowed him again.

"We need to get on the bed." I scrambled to my feet and kissed both men on the mouth. "Come on."

Archer ran his hands over my chest and plucked at my nipples, teasing them into hard peaks. He covered one with his mouth, flicking it rapidly, then biting down. The sharp pain traveled straight to my dick, making it weep precum, as he relentlessly tortured the tight bud.

"Arghh, god, that feels good." When Dan sucked on the other one, the tingles and prickles intensified. Hands slipped under the waistband of my briefs, cupping my ass, then pushing them down my legs.

We stumbled back and collapsed onto the bed in a heap of arms and legs. I burst out laughing. "I would've thought we'd be better at this threesome malarkey by now. We're not very graceful at this yet."

"Oh, Carter, baby, we can practice this every fucking day." Dan laughed and kissed my neck.

Archer untangled his legs and pulled me up to the middle of the bed, then kissed me again. Dan roamed his hands up my legs, followed by his mouth, leaving a trail of long, wet kisses in his wake. The sensation of having so many hands stroking my body drove me higher and higher. Something I hoped I'd never get used to. As Archer traveled down my body, his teeth scraped over my abs, making me writhe as he got closer to my dick.

"Oh god, feels so good," I panted. "Please, oh god, please."

"What, baby, what do you want?" Archer's hot breath ghosted over my skin. "Tell us what you need."

"More, I need more. Your mouth on me. Suck me, Archer. I need your mouth on my dick before I come," I begged, and I didn't care. My dick was pouring a steady, slick stream of precum onto my stomach. I was so close. As Archer lapped down my whole length, I cried out, but it was the feeling of Dan's mouth on my heavy sac that had me screaming. He swirled his tongue around my balls, then sucked them into his mouth. I bucked up my hips and arched off the bed.

Archer lifted off my dick and fisted it, pumping it hard. "I want to see Dan bury his cock deep in your ass, Carter. Do you want that? Do you want his big, fat dick inside you?" His eyes bored into mine as Dan tilted my ass and slid his tongue over my taint and down the crease to my hole. He licked a long stripe over my needy star.

"Fuck. Yesyesyes," I cried out as Dan's tongue speared my pucker. He spread my cheeks, opening me up to him. As he spit on my hole, Archer sucked me again. I couldn't bear it any longer. I grabbed my legs and pulled them up to my chest.

"Oh, baby, you look so beautiful." Archer moved up. "I love you so much. You look amazing with his tongue in your ass."

Dan pierced me again, then added a finger. As he stretched me, ready to take him, the burn was exquisite, pain mixed with pleasure. Then two fingers were in my passage. He pumped them in and out, scissoring as he went. He licked down my taint and dipped into my ass as he spread me with his fingers. Then he slid farther up my crease just to come back and repeat the action. His fingers slipped out, and I groaned at the empty feeling. His tongue took their place and stabbed inside my hole. I'd never been eaten out like this before, and I writhed and squirmed, needing more. I darted my eyes to Archer, who was stroking his dick as he stared at my ass. He must've sensed me looking at him because he bent to kiss me.

"You're the sexiest motherfucker alive. I love you."

"I'm ready, Dan," I cried out, then moaned as he pulled his tongue out of me, only to replace it with his fingers. The torture continued as my dick leaked, dripping precum onto my stomach.

"You're so fucking sexy, Carter." Dan took the bottle of lube from Archer I hadn't even noticed him getting. The cool liquid dribbled down over my balls to my pucker. Dan shoved two fingers back inside me as he lubed up his dick.

He pulled his fingers out, then pressed the head of his dick up to my hole. Dan had taken hold of my legs and spread them up straight. As he slid all the way in, I let out a groan so deep it seemed to come from my toes.

"God, you're so tight. I fucking love your ass." Dan held still, his cock throbbing inside me, his balls resting on my ass.

Archer kneeled by my head. "You look so beautiful." He bent down and kissed me hard, but it was his dick I wanted in my mouth. I reached out to grab him, but he had other ideas and swung his leg over my face so he was facing Dan. I opened my mouth and let him feed me his dick. As Dan pumped in and out of me, I sucked Archer's cock in sync with Dan's movements. Dan leaned in and kissed Archer. It was perfect, the three of us each pleasuring each other.

This felt unreal yet so absolute. This was how it was always going to be. The heat of Dan's cock brushing against the bundle of highly charged nerves in my ass sent bolts of lightning through my body. His hands gripped my ankles tight as he pulled his solid shaft to the muscled ring of my entrance. The rim of his crown slipped free, only to plunge back inside. I muttered a cry of sheer ball-aching pleasure around Archer's cock, which trembled in my mouth. The *slick-slick-slick* of Dan's cock sliding in and out as it glided through my lube-coated channel mixed with the moans of both men. I closed my eyes, letting the heightened sensations of touch, taste, sound, and smell wash over me. I wouldn't last much longer. Archer leaned over me and took my dick into his mouth. Dan thrust faster and harder. My legs trembled, and my stomach quivered as my climax built.

"Christ, I'm not going to last," Dan cried out. "Come, baby. Come for me." His hips hammered like pistons, making the head of his cock pound my prostate. Each punch sent a tsunami of pleasure through my body.

Archer pulled off my cock and kneeled next to me again. I tried to reach his cock, but he was already jacking himself while he fisted me with his other hand. The telltale tingles crept up my spine, and I stiffened, then erupted. I cried out their names as my cum fired from my cock. My ass clamped hard around Dan as he filled my ass, the white-hot heat of his release scorching my insides.

As the white ribbons of my cum painted my stomach, Archer came too, covering my chest with his hot spunk, grunting our names. We lay still, panting hard. Dan trailed his fingers through the ropes of our combined cum. He lifted them to my mouth, painting my lips with the salty-sweet mixture. He did the same to Archer and himself. Then we kissed.

Three mouths joined together, each of us tasting each other, moaning at the flavors. Dan shifted away, and his dick slipped out of my ass, the slick slipperiness of his cum dripping out of me.

Lazy fingers caressed my rib cage as I lay back, my chest still heaving. Archer leaned over me and dipped his tongue inside my mouth, then slid languidly over mine. Shivers sparked over my body, and my dick gave a little twitch but stayed limp and spent.

Dan chuckled from the other side of me. "I thought you were going to get hard again there, baby." He nudged Archer and took my mouth.

"I'm sure we could go another round in a few. I'd love to be in your ass, Dan, while Carter's in mine."

"Fuck," I groaned, and my dick did plump up at the image Archer's words conjured up.

"Let's get cleaned up." Dan moved off the bed and sauntered to the bathroom. The water gushed as he turned on the shower.

"You must've had a premonition you'd need a shower this large, Dan." I stepped into the huge glass-walled enclosure. A bench was built in the back wall, with shelves and nooks for soaps and shampoo bottles. "We could easily get another three men in here."

I laughed when both of my lovers growled. "Calm down, tigers. I have no plans of letting anyone else touch either of you or me."

"I think we're doing well enough with the three of us." Archer kissed me softly. "We still have so much to learn. I'm sorry we hurt you today, Carter. I'll do my best to let you be the person you are now. I'm loving the new Carter. As much as I hate the reason why we got separated, I'm so happy to be back here with both of you."

"This is meant to be, Archer. I love having you back in my life. I don't want us to be apart again. You need to be here with Dan and me." I pecked his lips as Dan crowded behind me. The water pounded down on our heads as we kissed, the three of us together, just how it was meant to be.

As the water turned cold, we broke apart and washed up. And soon, we were back in bed, me lying between them, wrapped in the arms of my lovers.

Thirty Five

Archer

"How was last night for you, babe?" I reached past Dan to grab the coffee mugs, managing to snag a kiss on his lips as I did.

"Really? You have to ask that? Archer, last night was the best we've had so far. Every touch and sigh are imprinted on my heart. It was amazing." He kissed me this time.

"Do you think we're topping too much? I know Mall...fuck, Carter likes to top, but..."

"Hey, I don't give a shit who tops or bottoms. Jeez, Archer. Last night was amazing, but if you're worried about not getting your ass tapped, I'll do it tonight." Carter swanned past us in just his boxer briefs. He seemed to make a habit of not dressing at breakfast.

"I love your choice of clothing for breakfast, honey. It fills my mind with wicked thoughts." I let him kiss me as he walked up to Dan.

"And, Archer, I know you think of me as Mallory. I get that it feels weird for you, but Carter fits me now." He gave me a sneaky look and smirked. "Although you called Mallory out last night when you came all over me."

"Did I? I'm sorry."

"I'm pretty sure I'll cope."

He turned to Dan, who had his arm wrapped around him now. "Did you notice or mind when he called out Mallory?"

"Carter, my love, I don't care what you're called as long as you're happy with it. I love you, and so does Archer." Dan put a finger under Carter's chin and kissed him. It was a slow, burning kiss. After a moment, I chuckled, and that broke them apart. I guessed I'd have to get used to it.

"Dan, sweetheart. I think you're getting him too excited, especially as we're about to leave." I grinned and looked down at Carter's very prominent erection in his boxers.

"Crap, you did this to me yesterday, Archer. Go on, go to work. The pair of you are nothing but trouble. I'll see you tonight." He shook his head and made his way past us.

"Hey, where are you going?" I tried to catch his arm, but he swiveled out of reach. "I was only messing with you, baby."

"Oh, I know that, Arch. Just think while you two are at your desks, I'll be lounging in bed with my hand around my cock." He swaggered away from us with a cocky grin and a wink over his shoulder.

"What are you working today, baby?" Dan asked.

"Two until ten. I'm going to see Paris first, though. I'll see you here tonight. Love you," he called as he climbed the stairs back to bed.

"Love you too," we yelled back, then headed out to work.

"Shall we go for a beer?" I asked Dan as we walked out of the office. "It's been a long day."

"You mean, you want to see our man?" Dan clapped me on the back. "C'mon, let's go."

It was busy in the bar with white-collar workers who had the same idea as us: chill out with a cold beer to decompress after being stuck in an office all day. Carter gave us a wide grin, his dark blue eyes sparkling.

It was time to claim him. I nudged Dan forward, and we made our way to the bar. "Hey, sugar, have you missed us?" I leaned across the polished mahogany bar and captured his mouth with mine.

Dan caught on and did the same. A chuckle rose up. Kes was looking at the three of us, a knowing smirk on his face.

"Yeah, I have." He sighed, smiling shyly, a faint blush on his cheeks. "You want a beer?"

"Please." I scanned around the bar. We got a few raised eyebrows, but most people didn't pay us any attention. A poster on the back wall promoting an open mic night caught my eye. "Are you playing?" I turned back to Carter.

"Um, that would be a huge no." The expression on his face was one of utter horror.

"You play?" Dan looked surprised. "What do you play? You've never mentioned it."

"He plays piano, and he's amazing at it. Why do you look so horrified? You love playing." I didn't understand his aversion.

"I haven't in a long while. Anyway, we don't have a piano here. It's mainly just acoustic guitar. A few bring other instruments." Carter walked away to serve someone, adequately ending the conversation.

"You know so much more about him. I wonder if he'd ever have told me that. How good is he?"

"Hey, c'mon, you're the one who gave him back his happiness. He would've told you when he was ready. And he's really good."

"Why don't we ask Kes to get a piano here? I bet he'll be up for it. Denver plays guitar here regularly. Maybe Carter could join in." Dan's eyes lit up.

"Yeah, let's ask."

Together we walked to the back, where Dan knocked on the open office door. Kes looked up from his computer and waved us in.

"Hey, guys, come in. Is everything okay? Is Carter okay?" A worried look spread over his face.

"Yeah, everything is good, but it's something to do with him." Dan gave him a small wave and continued. "Did you know he plays piano? And apparently very well."

"No, I didn't. I wonder why he's never mentioned it. We have one at home now. Denver plays too. He prefers his guitar but messes around with it with Ellie. Come to think of it, I've seen Carter eye it up a couple of times."

"Yeah? Well, we'd like him to play at the open mic night. Maybe not the next one, but soon. Maybe if you had a piano here, we could coax him out of his shell again. He really is that good. You wouldn't want to miss it," I tell him, hoping to persuade him.

"It's funny you bring this up now. Someone wanted to play on the open mic night but couldn't bring a keyboard with him. So I've already arranged for one coming tomorrow." Kes leaned back in his chair. "I want to start organizing a gig night where we have a different group or artist get the chance to play a full set. Having some of the instruments here would help. I'm not going to ask him to play, though, guys. This has to be up to him." Kes's eyes darted between us. "Can I be frank with you?"

"Sure." Where was he going with this?

"Okay, you both seem to have a dominant side, but be careful not to overwhelm him. He's not as much of a pushover as you think he is. Let him be him, the man you both love. Don't try to mold him into something that you, Archer, used to know, and, Dan, something you want him to be. Let him love you the way he wants to. He isn't a third. Don't make him feel like one."

My stomach knotted, and my muscles tightened. Why did he think he knew Carter better than I did? I'd been engaged to him. I was ready to bite back, but Dan must've recognized the tension building up in me and ran his hand down my spine, relaxing me again.

"You have nothing to worry about, Kes. Carter is most definitely holding his own." Dan chuckled.

"That's all I needed to know. As for the piano, I'm sure he'll find his way back to it."

"C'mon, babe. Let's get back to our drinks. Thanks, oh, and, Kes, this has to come from you."

"Sure thing. Anytime."

As we walked back through to the bar, Carter bumped into us both. He narrowed his eyes, but a small grin hid under his scowl.

"What are you two doing back here? You'd better not have been meddling."

"I don't know what you're talking about. We just wanted to say hi to Kes." I bit the corner of my lip to stop myself from grinning.

"You want to be on my shit list, Hawkins?" Carter quipped back, his eyebrow cocked.

"Hmm, that depends on what you're gonna do to me?" I laughed.

"Archer, baby, I can think of a lot of things I could do." He smiled wolfishly.

"I'll look forward to every single one of them." I leaned over and murmured in his ear, "Especially if it has something to do with your cock and my ass."

"You bet. Now get back out there. This is a staff-only area." He slapped my ass.

We didn't stay long after that, just enough to finish our beer. Dan gave Carter a kiss good-bye as I paid for our beers.

At the door, I stepped aside to let a man through. He gave me a penetrating, dark look, then thanked me. It was a fleeting moment, but it made me uneasy.

"Do you know him?" Dan asked as he glanced back over his shoulder at the stranger. "The look he gave you was really weird."

"He was here the other night, watching both me and Carter." I looked through the window. The man now stood at the bar, his eyes on our man. "Do you think Carter's okay?"

"Do you want to stay?"

"No, it's probably nothing. He doesn't work the late shift, and he has the truck again. I'm not going to baby him. He's a grown man."

"Yeah, the guy may have been having a bad day."

"Yeah, you're probably right. C'mon, I'm ready to shower and change into some sweats."

As soon as we got inside, I headed upstairs while Dan wandered into the kitchen, talking about finding us something to eat. I stripped off and stepped into the shower, tipping my head back under the water. The image of Carter and the stranger filled my mind. What was it about him that had set off the alarm bells? He'd given off a strange vibe as he'd thanked me. Something wasn't right, but I couldn't put my finger on what.

Should I tell Carter about the guy tonight? Why was that even a question? I couldn't mollycoddle him, and besides, we promised each other to communicate. Feeling slightly better when I finished, I switched off the shower, grabbed a towel, and dried my legs. Looking down at my scars still shocked me and gave me an uncomfortable feeling. Not so much about the ugly crisscross patterns—I wasn't that vain—but about how it had happened. Even after all this time, anger surged inside me at the hurt and pain my mother had caused us both. The possibility that she could still be a threat to us made me worry and seethe in equal measure.

I dragged my sweats up my legs and went back downstairs. Dan had taken off his jacket and tie and rolled up his shirt sleeves to the elbow. He was stirring something that smelled delicious. I came up behind him and kissed the back of his neck.

"You want me to take over so you can take a shower?" I murmured.

"Nah, I normally wait for Carter to get home when he's on this shift. We shower together." Dan twisted his head around, his lips puckered, but I stepped back.

"What?" Dan put down his wooden spoon. "Why are you looking at me like that?"

"Why didn't you tell me?"

"What? I didn't think about it. What difference does it make?" Dan frowned, confusion written all over his face.

"I would've waited and showered with you both." A wave of jealousy washed over me. This was something they did, something private I didn't know about. They had a routine. They had the relationship I used to have. I ran trembling hands through my still-damp hair, trying to calm down.

"Hey, Archer, baby, I'm sorry. There's no law to say you can't have another one." He winked and moved to kiss me, but I took a step back again. I was being a dick, but I couldn't help myself. "What's going on, Arch? Why are you acting like this? It's just a shower."

"It's more than that, Daniel. It's the life you two have, that you're building together. That used to be mine." I sighed and walked over to the fridge. I needed a beer.

"You sound like you're jealous. You know that's crazy, right? I love you. Carter loves you. So why does one shower bother you?" Dan turned the heat down on the stove and grabbed a beer from the fridge for himself. "Don't you think I have worries about you two and the past you shared? I've got more reason to be jealous than you, but this isn't a competition about who knows Carter best. We both know him, but I know a very different version of the man you know."

"How would you know? You didn't know him then." God, the petulance in my voice was grating, even to my own ears. Dan rolled his eyes. Yeah, it had gotten to him too.

"Are you seriously turning this into a pissing contest, Archer? Just listen to yourself."

He crossed his arms over his chest and pinned me with a glare, his eyes penetrating, searching for an explanation.

I shook my head, trying to clear it and finding a reason for my shitty reaction.

"Yeah, I know. I'm a dick. I'm stressed as hell. This situation with my mother is getting to me. Just the thought she might be after him still drives me crazy. One minute, I'm thinking I need to go back home and confront her. The next, I want never to see her again, to let Lucas do his job. I'm shit-scared that Carter will get hurt." Running my hands through my hair again, I sighed, relieved to get it off my chest.

"Oh, baby, you know, she may not be doing any of this. She may have walked away like you told her to. I am seriously against you going back and seeking her out. She'll hurt you, Archer. Let Lucas do what you're paying him to do. If she's hiding something, has any dirt on her, he'll find it. She's got to have some shit sticking to her somewhere."

When Dan walked toward me, I leaned back against the counter and let him step between my parted legs. He draped his arms over my shoulders and pressed his hips up to mine. A small smile crept over his rugged, handsome face.

"It'll be okay. You know that, don't you? We don't put up with any shit, Archer. We'll face any problem, and we will face it together, the three of us. We're a team, baby. Don't lose focus of that. We're in this together." He touched his lips to mine. I relaxed into him as his tongue drifted over the seam of my lips, nudging for entrance.

As the tips of our tongues met, Dan knitted his fingers into my hair and gripped tightly as he deepened the kiss. He explored my mouth, lazily caressing the roof of my mouth, then sucking on my tongue. I dug my fingers into his hips as I ground up against him, our dicks growing harder with every bump.

A beeping sound broke us apart. Dan unlocked his fingers and dragged them out of my hair.

"What was that?" I asked, still half-dazed from the scorching kiss.

"The oven. Dinner's ready."

As he took care of the food, I pulled myself together. I was here, and I was loved.

But the niggle hadn't disappeared. Did I want Carter to myself?

We ate and laughed and chilled out until Carter walked in the door. We took a shower—my second of the night.

Thirty Six

Carter

I stopped in the doorway of the bar and scowled at the stage area in the corner. A fucking piano. I knew it. I knew they wouldn't leave it alone. The problem was the flare of excitement that flashed through me at the sight of the baby grand in gleaming black-lacquered wood.

When I caught movement on the other side of the room, I swiveled around. Kes stood watching me. I tipped my head in the direction of the corner. "What's with the piano?"

"Thought it would look good here. Someone wants to play on the mic night and couldn't bring theirs. Den likes to play sometimes too. Why? You play?"

"I used to, but not anymore." I shrugged and sauntered to the office, Kes following me.

"Why not?" God, he wasn't going to let this go.

"I dunno, just stopped wanting to." I hang my coat on the hook at the door. "You want me to go to the bank for you? We need to get change as well as bank yesterday's takings."

"No, I'm going to do it, then head home again. East's there with Phoebe. God knows what trouble they'll get into. He's a bigger baby than she is." Kes beamed at the thought of his lover and their child. Would I ever want children? No, not yet at least. I was still trying to get my head around having two boyfriends.

"Have a fun afternoon while I slave away here." I laughed as he grabbed the bag with the money in it.

"I'll be back with your change before you open." He waved and walked out.

I sat behind the desk and clicked on the order form on the computer, but Kes had done it all. If I'd known, I wouldn't have come in this early. Leaning back in the chair, I propped my hands behind my head and daydreamed about my two men.

A loud bump from upstairs, followed by a clatter, disrupted the peace and quiet. Was Paris okay? What if it was his dad? I jumped up and raced to his apartment.

"Paris," I called out as I knocked hard on the door. "Paris, you okay?"

Muffled voices drifted through the door. Then it opened. Paris was standing in his jeans that weren't done up all the way, his chest bare.

"Are you okay? I heard a crash when I was in the office. Christ, Par, what the hell?" I took in the multicolored bruises mapping his chest and abs. These were much darker than the couple on his face, but he didn't seem injured anywhere, no blood I could see. And his hair was mussed up like he…Oh, he wasn't alone.

"Huh? What? Oh, yeah, I'm okay. Sorry to worry you." He glanced over his shoulder, a blush spreading over his pale cheeks. Oh yes, he had definitely someone with him.

"Paris, I'm sorry. I thought maybe your dad had shown up. My bad." I backed away, shaking my head, but a laugh broke out. "I'm sorry to have interrupted you. You'd better get back to him, whoever he is." I gave him a wink.

"Fucker." Paris grinned and shut the door.

I went back down to the bar, where the first thing I saw was that damn piano. The tightness in my chest built again. The memories of playing for Archer flooded my mind. After I'd played for him, he would make love to me, sometimes on the thick rug by the piano; other times he'd carry me to our bed. For that reason alone, I couldn't play for Dan. It wasn't fair to him or me.

Not when I was wondering if I'd made the right decision. Not when I was so confused. But when Archer had called me Mallory as he climaxed, I'd been back with him in our apartment. Even with Dan with us, I'd felt separate.

I couldn't believe this was happening to me. Two men loved me. I loved them both too. I stared again at the piece of wood in the corner. Maybe I needed to make memories for the three of us. I weaved my way through the tables and lifted the cover, then lightly stroked the keys. Not enough to make them press down and emit a sound but enough to make my heart race again.

I pulled out the stool and sat. My heart pounded in my chest, and sweat broke out on my top lip. Gingerly, I placed my fingers on the keys.

Closing my eyes, I let my fingers play their own tune, the room around me fading. I took a deep breath in and hummed to myself as Halsey's "Eyes Closed" burst to life in my mind. I sang along quietly to the music that poured from my fingers. I'd never let myself think too much about the lyrics because I loved Halsey's voice, but the chorus hit me hard in the chest.

Lyrics I'd tried not to relate to Dan and Archer because I'd never felt that way. But maybe it was me who was different. I didn't even think I was replacing Archer with someone new. He was a new Archer. He looked the same, felt the same, but he'd changed. Just as much as I had. We weren't the lovers now we had been several months ago. But were we doing this to find our old selves again? In which case, where did Dan come into this? I couldn't hurt him. I wouldn't hurt him. God, my head was spinning from all the confusing thoughts tumbling over each other.

I really didn't need to be thinking this sort of crap. My voice hitched, but I carried on singing, managing to voice my pain and fear. The worry I had for keeping both Dan and Archer, for them to understand how broken I was.

I stopped singing but continued playing, keeping the music in my head. As the song came to an end, I let my hands fall off the keys, closed the lid, then rested my arms across it and dropped my head on them with a soft thud.

Something had been going on between them last night, something they'd said to each other. I didn't know what, but the air had been rife with the tension between them. We hadn't made love. Archer had spooned me, his arms around me, while Dan had faced me, both whispering soft words of love. But had they aimed those at each other or only me? What the hell was going on between us? Were we falling apart already?

I sensed movement to the side of me. Lifting my head, I wiped the stray tears from my face. Kes stepped toward me, his eyes clouded with worry.

"What's going on, Carter?" He laid his hand on my shoulder. "I'm not gonna lie and say you weren't amazing, but the song? The lyrics? Damn, they were powerful. You can talk to me if you need to. I won't judge, you know that. I sure as hell won't share it with anyone else."

"I don't know what I'm doing." The words flew out of my mouth before my brain had caught up and I could tell him I was fine. I clenched my eyes shut against the tears that threatened to fall again.

"With your men? Is it not what you expected? Not what you want?" Kes pulled a chair over to me and sat. He waited patiently as I was trying to think of the right words.

"I love them. I really do, but it's different. Sometimes I feel we're together because neither of them will give me up." I dragged a deep breath in my lungs, embracing the pain as my lungs inflated too hard. "Fuck," I gasped and shook my head. "I didn't mean to say that."

"Are you sure?" Kes raised his eyebrows. "Or you didn't mean to say it aloud?"

"I don't know. Something happened last night before I got home. I don't know what, and they didn't say. It just felt different."

"Carter, without thinking about it, who do you want to be with?"

"Dan." My heart skipped a beat. Where had that answer come from?

"You look surprised, Carter. Did that come as a shock?"

"Yeah, I guess. It's because we just got serious. We told each other we were in love, and it's true. Dan helped me find who I am after Archer died. I like the Carter I am now, and I love living here, working here. This is a great place to be. I just...it's difficult to explain." I paused and looked around the empty bar, trying to gather my thoughts. "Hell, I want the silly part of just falling in love, the parts where you learn so much about each other. When all you do is talk in the dark in the middle of the night. The chance to make our story, to find the things we love doing together."

"Do you think you've lost that because of Archer?"

"Yeah, I mean the shock of finding him alive and that he's Dan's best friend floored me. The stark reality of him standing in front of me blew me away. I couldn't believe it. Then my heart connected back with his, but...it's not that it didn't feel right. It simply felt different. I love him, but I'm not the man I was when we were together, and neither is he."

Kes rubbed his hand over my arm. "You're allowed to feel like this, Carter. You have a right to decide who you share your love as well as your body with."

"Yeah, that's where it gets more complicated because the sex is amazing, like out-of-this-world fantastic. But I'm afraid we've jumped in too fast and it'll burn out. Or they'll decide it doesn't work and want to end it. What do I do if they ask me to choose? Or what if I'm not what they want after all? And they want each other again? Where do I fit in? They're both lawyers, and I'm running your bar."

"You know that doesn't matter. You're great at your job, Carter."

"I know, and I didn't mean to offend you. I love it here and am proud of what I've achieved. It's just...I'm confused."

"I can see that. So tell me about this." He waved at the piano. "Why the aversion? And why that song?"

"The piano? That's easy. It reminds me too much of what I had. What I lost. We were engaged. Did you know that? I got the marriage license the day he died."

"Oh, Carter, that's tough."

"Yeah, I know. And now he's calling me Mallory again, although not all the time. What if he's just looking for a way back to what we were? That wouldn't be fair to the three of us."

"You're going to have to talk to them. They want you to play, you know that, right? Maybe it would be a good way to open the discussion. Denver managed to reach us through his music. He's a little shit sometimes." Kes smiled, his eyes soft with the love he had for his partner.

"Am I being silly about this? Could I be reading too much into a situation that isn't there? Dammit, Kes, I'm so confused."

"I think you're like Denver. You bottle it all up inside you until you find a way to vent. I think music is the key for both of you. Look, open mic night's tomorrow. There will be a space for you if you want it. It's that simple. Please don't keep this inside you for too long. It's not good for you, nor is it fair to the men who love you. Even though you're struggling and have your doubts, don't ever forget how much they love you."

"I know. Thanks, Kes." I gave him a smile as I pushed myself from the piano stool.

"Anytime, Carter. You're family. I've told you that." He squeezed my shoulder, then walked out the front door.

By the time I opened the door, I'd pushed the dark thoughts away and just put it down to melancholy after seeing the piano. Paris breezed in, looking very content and, if I wasn't mistaken, with a hickey on his neck. It didn't look like a bruise his father had given him, but I wasn't going to tease him with it. He'd share when he was ready.

I was busy serving lunches to two women when Dan and Archer walked in and made their way to the bar. They both looked so damn hot in their suits. Archer winked at me while Dan seemed to eye-fuck me as a long, lazy smile spread over his face.

"Oh my, I wouldn't kick him outta my bed," one of the women said to her friend. "Or his friend. Jeez, the men in this town are hot."

I snickered as I placed the tray on the table. They both blushed when they realized I'd heard.

"You wanna share your digits with me, sugar?" Her friend was the first to recover. "We could meet up later."

"Sorry, we're not allowed to give out our numbers." I gave them both a polite smile. So not sorry. "Enjoy your meal."

"He's so cute," she whispered loudly as I walked away. I couldn't contain my grin.

"Hey, baby," Dan said as I joined them at the bar. "Do you mind us having lunch here?" He ran his hand down my back and let it rest at the base of my spine. "I think your admirer is disappointed now," he whispered huskily in my ear, then dropped a kiss on my neck.

"She said she wouldn't kick you out of her bed. So it's you she's after." I pinched his ass. Laughing, I dodged his hand and jogged back behind the bar.

Archer watched me with a wry smile. "You must leave a trail of broken hearts behind you, sugar." He slicked his bottom lip with the tip of his tongue, then leaned over to peck my mouth.

"Stop embarrassing me. Go and sit. I'll bring you some drinks over. What do you want?"

"We'd better stick to soft drinks. I'll have a mineral water, and I guess you know what Dan drinks."

"I'll bring them to you." I shooed him away.

Paris stepped up behind. "Go have lunch with them if you want. I can hold it down here. You only ever see them in here when you're working. Enjoy their company for an hour."

"You sure?" I liked the idea of this.

"Yep, go on. I'll bring you a platter of club sandwiches." Paris sauntered off to the kitchen, and I wandered over to my men with three drinks instead of two.

Thirty Seven

Dan

"Hey! Are you joining us?" I beamed a happy smile and moved out of the booth so Carter could slide in and sit between the two of us.

"I should probably sit on the outside in case Paris needs me." Carter shot a glance to the bar, but Paris waved his hands to make him sit.

"It's good to have this time with you, honey." Archer draped his arm across the back of the seating and pulled Carter in for a hug.

"Paris is going to bring us over some sandwiches, but if it gets busy, I'll have to go back to work." Carter settled in his seat, relaxing a little. "It seems strange from this side of the bar. I'm not normally here during the day unless I'm working."

"You do an amazing job, baby." I took his hand in mine and kissed the knuckles.

"You don't mind that this is what I do?" he asked quietly, a frown creasing his forehead.

"Of course not. Why should that matter? It suits you." I wiggled my eyebrows. "Besides, we wouldn't be together if you hadn't worked here."

"Are you not happy here, Carter? Do *you* feel you should be working someplace else, using your degree?" Archer asked him.

"Nope, I love it here. I just wondered you might be embarrassed to have me working at a bar."

"What's going on then? Why are you doubting yourself?" Archer shot Carter a concerned look.

"Archer, don't worry. It was just an errant thought. And you two are on my shit list. What were you doing telling Kes you want me to play tomorrow night?" He tried to glower, but a smile broke free, so I knew he wasn't too mad at us.

"Oh, he told you that, did he? Well, you should be playing. You're amazing." Archer had the decency to look a little bit guilty.

Their gazes locked, showing their closeness and something more. Shared memories of the naughty kind if the sparkle in their eyes was anything to go by. They tore their gazes away from each other, neither wanting to laugh first. Just then the door flew open, and about ten people crowded in, filling the room with chatter.

"I guess that's my cue to get back to work." Carter nudged my leg to get me to move out of the way.

"Come back once you've served them." I squeezed his hand as he shuffled past the table. "Please, baby."

"I'll see how long it takes. Your lunch won't be long." He dropped a kiss on my mouth, then repeated his action on Archer, unaware or uncaring if anyone watched.

"We're lucky bastards, you know that, right?" I said to Archer as I looked over my shoulder. Carter was laughing with the new customers. As if he sensed us watching him, he glanced up and gave us a little wave.

"Yeah, we are. I find it hard to believe most days. It's surreal, something that should never have happened. In this enormous country, my fiancé ends up in the same town as my best friend. Soap operas make this stuff up."

Paris strolled over with a platter of sandwiches and chips. "Here you go, guys. Dig in. I'll send Carter back over to you as soon as I can, I promise."

"I agree." I took a sip of my water. "I could never have thought of this. I knew that when I first set eyes on Carter he was important. That I needed to have him in my life. Now I know why. It was for us to connect again too. We needed him as the catalyst or as the pivotal link to bring our lives back together the way they should be. I'm happier than I could ever have imagined."

"Me too. All I want now is to end things with my mother. I want to know she can't hurt people anymore and wreck innocent people's lives just because she doesn't like them. Like the way she hurt Carter."

Archer picked up one of the sandwiches, almost squashing it, he gripped so hard. His eyes darted around the room. Why was he so tense all of a sudden? Then it hit. He was looking for any bad guy who could be out to hurt Carter. My heart eased as I understood his stress. But why was he worried now after Carter had been here for nearly a year and hadn't had any trouble? Was Archer the catalyst? Was he the one who could tip his mother over the edge of reason? We had some serious talking to do when we got home together tonight.

I grasped his hand. "Listen to me, Archer. We're supposed to be together and have a happy ending. So stop looking for trouble, babe. We're in this together. Here comes Carter."

"Sorry about that. I should be home by seven, seven thirty. We'll have the evening together." Carter shuffled in next to me, grabbed a sandwich, and bit down.

"God, I needed that," he mumbled with his mouthful. "Sorry, I was so hungry." He settled back on the bench, munching on some of the chips.

"We didn't ask Kes to get a piano, you know?" Archer grinned at Carter, who just shook his head.

"I know, but you're both a pair of sneaky shits who still pestered him to get me to play." He pointed at both of us. "I'm watching you two. There will be consequences if you keep this up."

"I like the sound of that." I nudged him with my shoulder.

"Yeah, I thought you might."

Having lunch with Carter had been a good idea. Some of the awkward tension between us had dissipated, and we were all on the same page again. Warm tingles flooded through me. We were gonna be all right. Even Archer's chuckle sounded different, more at ease. A glance at the clock on the wall told me our hour was up.

"Come on, Arch. We need to get back to work."

"Yeah, me too." Carter stood, and we followed him across the bar. Carter walked with us to the door, then quickly and far too briefly kissed us good-bye. "I'll see you guys tonight."

As we walked back to the office, Archer shot me a sideways glance. "We're gonna be okay, you think?"

"Yeah, baby. I really do." I took his hand and gave it a squeeze.

We had the TV on, but I didn't think either of us had been paying it any attention. We were just happy to laze around, happy to be together.

The front door opened, and seconds later, Carter walked in. He took one look at us, and an enormous grin spread over his face. We were both still in our suits, although we'd lost our ties and the top buttons on our shirts.

"Not showered yet, then, boys?" He waggled his eyebrows, then turned on his heel and headed for the stairs.

"I thought we'd wait for you. Do you want anything to eat?" Archer called after him.

"No, I'm good, but I am horny. So let's go. We're going to suck and fuck," Carter yelled back.

I let out a whoop of laughter and sprinted after my man. "Come on, Archer. You really wanna feed him when he's talking that dirty?"

"Fuck, no." Archer followed me, almost knocking me off the stairs in his haste to get to Carter.

When we reached our bedroom, Carter's clothes were strewn all over the floor, and the shower was running. I stripped in record time and walked into the bathroom, then stopped in my tracks. Archer bumped into me and groaned.

Carter stood facing us, his legs apart and his head tipped back, the water pounding down his chest, his cock in his fist. He jacked himself off lazily with long, deep strokes. His mouth was slack, his features relaxed. With his other hand, he drew circles over his body, tracing the outline of his taut muscles until he cupped his sac and rolled his balls between his fingers.

My eyes fixed on his body, I took a step forward and another. When I reached him, my hand followed his and traveled over the hard muscles of his chest.

"You're a fucking god, Carter. I worship you." As he slowly opened his eyes, they were dark with lust. I leaned in to capture his mouth.

Archer moved to the side of our beautiful man and placed his hand over Carter's as he continued to stroke himself.

"My turn, my love," Archer murmured into Carter's neck and kissed him on the tender spot under his ear, his hand pumping up and down the length of Carter's rigid shaft.

I stepped behind Carter and ran my hands down the length of his spine, splayed out over his hips, skimmed over his buttocks, and kneaded the firm rounded cheeks. He trembled as Archer kneeled in front of him and took him into his mouth.

"You look beautiful, baby, so hot," I crooned as I snaked my finger between his cheeks, heading for his pucker, and circled over and around his hole.

Carter let his head fall back on my shoulder. "Take me to bed," he moaned.

Archer let his mouth slip from Carter's dick and stood. I switched off the shower while Archer grabbed a towel and rubbed it slowly over Carter's chest. With another, I dried his back, then chucked the towel into the laundry hamper and took Carter's hand.

Archer climbed in first and lay down with his head at the foot of the bed.

"I want my cock in your mouth while I suck you, baby."

Carter's eyes lit up, and he quickly clambered over Archer. Soon they were locked in the perfect sixty-nine position, Carter's ass dangling before me like two ripe peaches I couldn't wait to bite into. I shuffled behind him, spread his cheeks wide, and swiped my tongue up his taint and over his hole. Taking my time, I licked over and around the tight pucker. At the same time, I tortured and teased him with my finger. As I pressed gently over the muscle, he pushed back, letting me slip inside him. I fucked him with my finger and tongue until he tensed up, the telltale sign his orgasm was imminent, so I backed off and withdrew my finger.

Carter lifted his head from Archer's cock. With his lips dark red and swollen and his brilliant blue eyes black with lust, he looked more beautiful than ever. He studied me, then licked over his lip oh-so-slowly. "Fuck me, Dan. Fuck me now."

No way in hell was I going to turn that down, so I scrabbled for the lube, squirted some of the gel onto my cock, and tipped it over his hole. I pressed my finger back inside him as I stroked the lube over my cock with my other hand. With my eyes glued to him, I nudged my swollen head against him and pushed inside. First past the ring of muscle, then holding still until he relaxed.

"Suck him, Carter. Make him come as I fuck you," I growled.

As he dipped back over Archer's cock, I thrust all the way in, gripping his hips tightly. Archer had let go of Carter's dick and was now sucking on his balls.

"Harder, Dan. Fuck him harder." Archer shifted away and twisted around so he was lying down with his back on the pillows. Carter took Archer back into his mouth as I pounded Carter from behind.

God, this was heaven. It wouldn't take me long to come. Angling my hips, I pegged his prostate. Over and over, I glided the head of my dick over his swollen gland. Judging by the grunts and groans, Archer was about to blow too. Easing back, I let him take control. Not seconds later, Carter stilled and, with a hoarse cry, poured his release into Archer's mouth. Carter slumped down, wiped his mouth with the back of his hand, and kissed Archer.

I pulled out of Carter, flipped him over, and plunged back inside him. More slowly now, I rocked deeply into his hot, tight channel. Every tremor and shudder reverberated through me as his climax built up again. I didn't think I'd be able to last much longer.

"Stroke him, Arch. Let's make him come together."

Archer grasped Carter's dick, matching his strokes with my movements as we took him higher and higher. His eyes rolled back in his head, and with a deep guttural moan breaking free, Carter came. Ribbons of thick, white cum pelted from his cock. As he fired out, his ass clenched me so tightly I exploded. I flooded him as he milked me dry.

I collapsed over him and covered his face with kisses. "I love you, Carter Halston," I whispered as I hovered my mouth over his lips.

Archer's hand landed on my back as he leaned over to kiss both of us. "That was incredible, just amazing."

Carter smiled, a lazy, satisfied smile. "Yeah, it was. We needed that."

Thirty Eight

Archer

I lay back with my eyes closed and let the endorphins racing through my body subside. The bed shifted as Dan pulled away from Carter. His footsteps padded across the floor, and then the water rushed.

"Are you okay, Arch? You feeling all right?" Carter's voice was soft as he shuffled to lie beside me.

Opening my eyes, I turned my head. The man I'd lost and the man who had replaced him was studying me with concern etched on his face. I lifted my hand and ran my fingers over his stubbled cheek.

"Now? Now I feel blissed out. I feel loved and happy." I twisted on the bed so I could face him.

Dan walked back in with a wet cloth. "Here you go, baby." He smoothed the warm cloth over Carter's stomach and chest, then lower to clean up the lube and the rest of the mess we'd made.

Carter squirmed and wriggled away. "Stop. That tickles."

"Maybe you shouldn't have made such a mess?" I leaned over and captured his mouth, pouring all my feelings into this kiss. I needed him to understand just how much I loved him.

And I needed this moment with just him, my Mallory, my Carter. As I stroked my tongue over his, I shifted so I lay over him. Propped up on my forearms, I tangled my hands lightly in his long, dark locks. He spread his legs, allowing me to slot between them. His cock twitched and swelled as I rubbed mine along his length.

Carter traced his fingertips softly up and down my back and over my ribs, sending shivers through my skin and making goose bumps pebble on my skin. Our tongues continued to dance languidly. There was no rush, no urgency. Just me pouring my bliss into a single kiss. As Carter writhed beneath me, I swallowed his moans down with my own.

Pulling back, I blinked my eyes open and gazed down at Carter. His lips were dark pink and kiss bruised, shining with the slickness from my tongue. "This is how you make me feel, Mallory," I whispered his name against his mouth. "This is how much I love you."

"Take me, Archer. Take me back." As he opened his legs wider, I bent my knees and easily steered my dick down to his hole and nudged my way inside him. His muscles rippled around me as I gently pushed, savoring the slickness inside his channel. I couldn't hold back the deep groan building in my chest as I kissed him.

With hardly a movement, just a flex of my hips, I pumped slowly but steadily. It wouldn't take either of us long to reach our climax. As he tangled his tongue with mine, shivers ran through him. Then without any stimulation, his cum burst between us. He shuddered through his orgasm, tightening around my shaft. As explosive as my last orgasm was so gently I filled him with my hot release now.

I gazed down at my man, whose eyes shimmered with unshed tears.

"I love you, Archer. Fuck, I've missed you." A tear escaped and ran down the side of his face. I caught it with my mouth, kissing his anguish away.

As I lifted myself and pulled out of his body, a moan filled the room. I swiveled my head around. Dan. I'd totally forgotten about him.

"Wow, that was something else." His eyes flashed at me as he dropped his hand with his cell in it.

"Did you just film us?" I asked.

"Umm, yeah." Dan smiled, but his voice held an edge I didn't like.

Had we upset him? Had we been too intimate without him? Carter shifted underneath me. Even though I'd taken my weight off his body, we were still touching, and the cum on his abs cooled to a gross stickiness.

"I need a shower. This isn't a great feeling." Laughing, Carter wriggled until I rolled off him with a theatrical sigh. "Come on. We could all do with one."

We both clambered off the messy bed and stumbled to the bathroom. Carter took Dan's hand.

"Come on, babe. I need you to scrub my back."

"Yeah, give me a minute, and I'll be with you. I'm gonna clean the bed." Dan gave Carter a sweet but brief kiss but pulled his hand free.

Carter shot me a questioning gaze to which I shrugged.

With the shower running and the room steaming up, we both stepped under the multijets. The water cascaded over us like heavy rain beating against our skin.

"Is he okay?" I asked Carter.

"I don't know. He said he liked what he saw, didn't he? But he does seem tense." Carter chewed on his bottom lip. "Let's get cleaned."

He lathered up his body and sluiced away the sticky remnants of our lovemaking. As he tipped his head under the spray, I grabbed his shampoo, then washed his hair. Running my fingers through the wet locks, I scraped my fingernails over his scalp. With gentle movements, I rinsed the bubbles away, tracing their course down his back and over his ass. I dipped my middle finger down the crack of his ass and licked over his pucker, but I had no intention to take it further. He'd taken enough there today, but he wriggled and laughed.

"Fuck off. My ass is out of bounds." He pushed at me, but I grabbed his hand and wrestled him down to the floor. We were both laughing hard as we goofed around when a shadow loomed over us.

Dan was watching us with an expression devoid of any emotion, although the skin around his eyes was stretched tight. Before we could say anything, he bolted out of the bathroom.

"Shit." I jumped up, but my foot slipped on the wet floor. I fell back down, and white-hot pain pierced through my ankle. "Fuck." My foot was throbbing and swelling rapidly. Damn, damn, double damn.

"Archer. Don't move." Carter darted past me, grabbed a towel, then called out for Dan.

Another agonizing flare shot through me, and nausea welled up. Luckily, my stomach was empty, so I didn't have anything to threw up. It didn't look good, and it felt even worse. Gritting my teeth, I pushed myself to a sitting position, using the shower wall to hold me up. I pulled another towel from the rail and tried to stand, but I didn't have enough strength in my left leg to support me.

Carter came racing back into the bathroom with his phone stuck to his ear. "Yes. Just get here."

Chucking his phone onto the vanity counter, he rushed back over and threw his arm around me. "We need to get your foot elevated."

With his arm supporting me, I managed to scramble up and stumble to the bed, where I flopped down. "Who were you talking to?" I clenched my teeth against another burning twitch. "Where's Dan?"

"I don't know. I couldn't find him." He gathered all the pillows and, after gingerly lifting my foot, shoved them underneath.

"Can you grab me some boxers? And who's coming?"

"Denver. He'll be here any minute." Carter raised the injured leg and gently slid a pair of boxers up over the ankle. He waited until I'd put my other foot through the other hole, then shimmied them up my legs and, as I propped myself up on my arms, over my ass. His touch was so tender and careful as he concentrated on not jiggling me around.

"Don't bite your lip, hon." I teased his bottom lip from his teeth. Tears swam in his eyes. "Hey, what's up?" I stroked my hand down his face and cupped his chin.

"This is my fault. I shouldn't have messed around with you in the shower. I should've been more careful." The tears fell then, and I leaned forward and kissed them away. He trembled under my touch.

"Honey, this could've happened at any time. I could slip when I'm in the shower alone. At least you were here to help me." I kissed him again until someone yelled from downstairs.

"That will be Denver. I'll go get him." Carter sniffed and wiped his face.

"Carter, put some pants on, please." I looked pointedly at the towel still wrapped around his hips.

A blush staining his neck, he snatched his shorts from the chair and pulled them up his legs, then raced off down the stairs.

Voices drifted from downstairs, and it seemed that not only Carter and Denver came up the stairs. Damn. This wasn't how I wanted to see my new friends again. Well, there was nothing I could do about it now.

Denver rushed into the bedroom, his face serious and in total doctor's mode.

"Hey, Archer. Let me have a look." Denver's hands were cool and firm as he gently touched my swollen ankle, testing down my foot, checking the pulse point and the feeling I had, making me wriggle my toes. "I think you've just sprained it, Archer. It may be a matter of just resting it, but because of all the metalwork in there, I'm not prepared to risk it. I won't know until it's been X-rayed. On a scale of one to ten, ten being the highest, what's your pain level now?"

"It's fine. I've had worse. I'm okay." But the sweat spreading over my body as he carried on with his examination belied my words.

"I can give you something if you'd like. You don't need to be brave." Denver gave me a sympathetic and understanding smile.

I looked past him to where Carter was chewing on his lip again. "Carter, babe. Come here. I need you."

He hurried to me and carefully curled up against me, making sure not to jostle my leg. "I'm sorry, Archer. I really am." He turned his head into my shoulder and sobbed in my arms. His hand snaked over my chest and wrapped around my neck. I kissed his forehead over and over, murmuring soothing words in his ear.

"It's not your fault, honey. Please don't cry. It hurts me to see you so upset," I whispered to him. "It's gonna be all right, I promise."

Denver was quietly talking on his cell phone, probably arranging transport to the hospital for me. I really didn't want to go through it all again. But at least I'd have Carter and Dan with me this time.

East had followed his boyfriend upstairs but was hovering in the doorway. I motioned for him to come in.

"How're you doing?" he asked gently.

I chuckled and gave him a wry smile. "I've been better. Can you call Daniel? He seems to have disappeared, and we're not sure where he is. I don't want Carter to be alone if I have to have surgery again."

"I'll get on it. Any idea where he could've gone?" East pulled out his phone and scrolled through his contact list. I shook my head. "Okay, leave it with me." East put his phone up to his ear, moving out of earshot.

Ten minutes later, the paramedics arrived and, after conferring with Denver, strapped me on a gurney, and I was on my way to the hospital. There was still no sign of Dan, and I was getting seriously pissed at him.

"Where the hell could he have gone?" I whispered to Carter.

"I don't know, but I'm coming with you. East says he'll keep trying his cell and will have a look around too. I'm more worried about you, baby." He leaned in to kiss me, brushing my hair from my forehead. He'd already fussed about getting me into a sweatshirt.

The only reason he was getting away with riding in the ambulance with me was that Denver had insisted on it. He would follow us in his car. He must've realized how important it was to both of us not to be apart this time I was taken to a medical facility. The memories from my accident were still vivid scars on both of our hearts.

Thirty Nine

Dan

My head was in a complete mindfuck; watching the two men I loved together as if there was nobody else in the world was fucking hot. The simplicity of it had me growing hard again. I grabbed my cell phone and turned on the camera. But as I recorded them, their interaction morphed into something so much more. Archer called Carter Mallory, and my head and my heart hurt as if a thousand shards of glass speared through the center of my chest. I knew it would never be me, not when Carter finally made his choice. This was too intimate. This was private. This was them going back to the start.

When I walked in, Archer was washing Carter's hair, his hands all over him. Then Carter pushed at him, which resulted in a playful wrestling match. The sight of so much intimacy, seeing how happy and comfortable they were with each other, made me realize they didn't need me. They'd always have each other. They knew so much of each other's life that I'd always be the third. Sure, they were up for us being a threesome, but they didn't need me to make them happy, to complete them. Not like I needed them.

I pivoted on my heels and darted from the bathroom, grabbed my keys and cell phone from the bowl on the table at the front door, and rushed out. I was out of the house and in my car before I'd even had time to think. As soon as I'd fumbled the key in the ignition, I put the car in reverse and backed out of the driveway.

I had no idea what to think or where to go, so I headed to the office. It was the weekend, and no one would be there, which would give me a chance to work out what the hell to do. Just as I pulled up in my space and switched off the ignition, my phone rang. Carter's number came up, but I couldn't talk to him right now. One word from him would have me racing back to him and into the confusion in my head. I let his call go to voicemail and got out of the car. Pain prickled through my feet, and I plopped back down in my seat. My mind had been so focused on having something that wasn't mine to have I'd forgotten to put on shoes.

I slapped my hand on the steering wheel, then laid my head on it, clenching my eyes tight against the gathering tears. Coming here had been the worst idea ever. My office wasn't the place to think things through. When I came back to work on Monday, it would be the only thing I'd be able to think about. I straightened, staring unseeingly through the windshield. Where could I go? I needed to get out of here before someone called the cops about a lunatic who was crying in his car. I snapped my fingers. The cabin at the lake. That would be the perfect place to drown in sorrow and think about what to do next.

My chest tightened at the thought of them again. Decision made, I drove away. My phone kept going off with messages and voicemails, but I ignored them. Happy, long-forgotten memories chased away the distressing images from earlier. I'd loved spending long summer days during the school break at our cabin, messing around, fishing, and kayaking. Then drinking and making out as we'd gotten older. My sisters had brought boyfriends just as many times as I had. I had gotten my first kiss here and my first blow job, but no way had I ever wanted to know if they did too. Gah, no.

My parents had insisted my sisters and I have a key. I'd wanted to decline, had shrugged it off as not having enough free time to come here when deep down I hadn't wanted to stay without the family. But now I couldn't be more grateful to be able to unlock the cabin and walk inside. Even though my parents hadn't come here as often as they used to and my mother even less since my father's death, she always took care to keep it clean and stocked. I felt guilty for not calling her. I'd been selfishly holed up with Carter and Archer. Maybe now that I'd probably lost them, I'd stay for a while. I filled the old-fashioned coffee maker with water, dumped coffee in the filter, and switched it on. As the coffee percolated, I stared out the window, keeping my mind blank, not dwelling on my emotions of less than an hour ago. Not yet anyway. With two insulated mugs of coffee in hand—I so didn't want to get up for a second one—I made my way down to the jetty sticking out twenty feet into the water. I sat down, placed the mugs next to me, and let my feet dangle above the water, which gently lapped against the wooden poles. The soft breeze cooled my warm cheeks. I leaned back on my hands and stared at the brightly shining stars in the clear dark night, letting them calm and soothe me. Now I was ready to think about what to do next.

I was a problem solver, always had been, so I set about sorting my emotions and actions into the appropriate compartments in my head, ready to work out how to fix each one. The saddest thought was I could gather them all up in one fell swoop and just stop this...whatever this was, with them right now. Walk away and let them keep their forever to themselves. So if that was the easiest way, why did it hurt so goddamn much? My chest clenched as if a huge hand had grasped my heart and squeezed, making it hard to breathe.

Because I still fucking wanted them. That was why.

Okay, the next option was to accept being a third and only be invited to be with them when they wanted a touch of something more. I disregarded this one straight away. My heart was too invested in this, in them, to let that happen. I owed it to myself to find myself a forever man, one who made me feel as happy as they were. One who made me cry and laugh in equal measure. I'd found that when Carter came into my life. I wanted it again. I wanted him.

I bolted upright and slapped my hand over my mouth. I'd had that a long time ago with Archer, even though I'd been too young, too naïve, too stubborn maybe to see it then. But I loved Archer just as much as I loved Carter.

That was it. I loved them both, and I wanted them both. And they'd said they wanted me. After all, being in a threesome had been my fucking idea in the first place. I jumped to my feet. I needed to talk to them about how I felt. Right now. They had to be worried about me, going crazy even, trying to find me. Oh, fuck. What had I done?

As I strode back to the cabin, a truck drove up and stopped next to mine. What was he doing here?

"Hey, East, what's up?"

"What's up? What's fucking up? You disappearing, that's what's up. For fuck's sake, get a move on. You need to get to the hospital." East's eyes were blazing.

"What? How? Who's hurt?" I couldn't believe this. I'd been ignoring my calls, being too busy in my own pity party. God, what had I done?

"Archer slipped in the shower and screwed up his ankle again. Well, Denver thinks it might be just a sprain. He called the EMTs, who have transported him to Charlottetown for X-rays."

"Oh, Christ. I've seriously fucked up. I can't believe I've been so selfish." I fisted my hair and tugged hard, holding back a scream.

"C'mon, Dan, let's go." He opened the driver's door of my car. "We can talk more on the way, but FYI, both were asking for you. Right up to the ambulance taking them away."

"Oh, fuck."

East pulled out onto the road and maneuvered my BMW skillfully through the local traffic. He cast me the odd glance but didn't say anything until we were on the highway as I chewed on the skin by my thumbnail.

"You wanna talk about it? I reckon you've got loads of questions racing through your head, and I'm guessing they are all about three-way relationships and how they work for me and mine. You wanna share some of them?"

"I don't have a clue where to start." I slammed my fist against my thigh, still so angry at myself for the way I'd behaved. "I can't believe I ignored the calls and messages. I just panicked over something and fled. I'm a dick. They're gonna be so mad."

"Don't worry about that. I don't think they will be, but you may have some groveling to do when you see them. Carter was frightened, and he needed you. If you're going to be a part of a threesome, you need to man up and take what you want." East shook his head. "Do you think Denver knew what to do or how to act? Hell no. He ran off a few times before he finally got the message into his thick skull that we loved him equally. He doubted himself every step of the way for weeks."

I raised my eyebrows. "Really? From what we all saw, he was always very open with you both and never shied away from being with you." I paused. "I'm so jealous of that," I muttered.

"No. It wasn't like that at all. Look, can I ask you a question?"

I nodded. What could it be? East was good at drawing things out of me I had no intention of sharing.

"Are you jealous of them when they're together?"

"Not really. I wasn't until I saw them together. Just the two of them and then in the shower just before I fled. They were so happy and comfortable with each other. They were goofing around, wrestling on the floor, and laughing so hard. I was jealous. I thought they'd never need me because they have so much with each other. After what his mother did to them, I'm wondering if they need more time together alone. It comes down to the fact that they don't need me to make them happy, but I do need them to make *me* happy."

"But they both needed and wanted you this evening. They were both worried and concerned about where you'd gone. They need you now. They want you with them. That should answer your question."

"Yeah, it does. But I think I may have blown it now, don't you?" I buried my face in my hands.

"Oh, c'mon, Dan. They're not going to think anything like that. They want you there, and if Archer has to have surgery again, Carter will need someone to hold him through it all. He never got the chance to be there for his man last time, so he's going to need your help to get him, get them both through this."

"I fucking hope so."

"Daniel, my man, I know so. Trust me, I've seen the look in their eyes before, in the eyes of my men. Trust them and, for fuck's sake, trust yourself." East pulled into the hospital grounds and stopped in front of the ER.

"East, I-I mean...thank you, I appreciate it."

"Whatever, man. Just get your ass in there and find your men. I'll park and come find you in a few. I need to check in with Kes. He's with Phoebe."

I squared my shoulders to get a grip on myself, then jumped out of the car and sprinted through the doors, looking for my young lover.

"Dan! Oh, thank god you're here." Carter ran toward me and slung his arms around me. He buried his head in the crook of my neck. "I'm so scared. I don't know what's going on. Denver said he'd come and tell me, us. But it's been ages, and I haven't heard anything."

"It's okay, baby. Come on, let's sit. You can tell me everything." I kissed the top of his head, and he tilted his face up to mine.

"Where were you? Where did you go?" Tears pooled in his eyes, and I leaned down instinctively to kiss them away.

"I'll tell you in a minute. Fill me in, Carter, please."

He relaxed into me again as I wrapped my arm around his waist and walked him to the seating area. Tremors ran through his body as he clung to me. I found a wide chair and dropped down into it. Carter sat on my knee and curled himself into me.

"When you ran out, he stood too quickly and slipped. His ankle gave way. I should've remembered. I shouldn't have been goofing around and especially not on wet tiles. It's my fault he's hurt. I called, but you didn't answer. Why not?" His dark blue eyes bored into mine.

I cringed under his penetrating and accusing gaze. I balled my hands into fists, anger at myself and guilt coursing through me.

"Oh god, this is all my fault, not yours, baby. I came into the bathroom and saw you both, but I couldn't handle it. Watching you make love with him freaked me out. It was so beautiful and deep, and I wondered if we'd ever made love like that. I doubted what we have, and then the way you were both laughing cut right through me. It made me think you don't need me to make you happy. It's so obvious you're deeply in love with each other. That you'll be happy with or without me. I ran, baby. I'm sorry."

"Why? Why...How could you think that after what we've said? You said you wanted it all? We may not have been together as long I was with Archer, but that doesn't mean I love you less. You made me whole again. I love you, Daniel. I want it all with you. Have you changed your mind?" Carter pulled away, his expression cautious.

"I just don't understand why you would want me when you and Archer have so much together. It doesn't make sense to me. I want you both so much, but I don't trust myself to be enough for you, to make a difference to your already amazing relationship. I'm so sorry, Carter. I'm doubting myself. I'm worried you don't want me anymore."

"I'll always want you, Dan. I don't think I would've chosen Archer over you. I want what we have—a new start. I think that's what we're getting with Archer. Neither of us is the person we were so many months ago."

We sat quietly, locked in our own thoughts.

Forty

Carter

"How did you meet him?" Dan asked me.

"Hasn't he told you?"

"Only a little bit. He found it too difficult to talk about you."

"We bumped into each other, literally, nearly knocked each other on our asses. I'd had to move into a dorm and find a job to pay my way through school. I was rushing to the coffee shop I worked at. I was nearly always running late. Archer was a customer, and he asked me out every day for two weeks before I gave in. He was a pain in my ass. I only agreed just to get him to leave me alone to work." Warmth spread through me at the memory.

"That doesn't surprise me. He's a tenacious bastard. When he sets his mind to something, he doesn't let go. So it must've gone well, that first date?"

I snickered. "Uh, no, he was an ass at the end. I wanted nothing to do with him and walked away. Fortunately, that just upped his game, and he waited for me at the back of the coffee shop. He was there when I left in the evening. Our man's quite a stalker. After that, it was on. It took him a while to get me to move in, and we had a huge row about him not letting me pay my way. The lawyer in him came out, and he had a counterpoint for every one of my arguments. In the end, I gave in and let him be in charge."

"What's wrong with his mother? Why did she take an instant dislike to you? Did you ever find out?" Dan ran his hand softly up and down my back the whole time we talked. It felt so good and so right my skin hummed.

"She's such a bitch. She wouldn't even look at me. She doesn't like my father, but she must pretend to." I shrugged. "He's huge in commerce and doesn't need or want her patronage, even though they move in the same social circles. Maybe that's why. But her hatred for me? I think it's more to do with not wanting her precious reputation damaged by having an out and proud gay son. Which makes no sense, since Archer has never hidden who or what he is. She just expects him to marry a nice girl and fuck men on the side. Cheating and lying his whole life isn't something he'd ever entertain, nor would he let a woman go through marriage based on lies and deceit. Archer is a good man, and he doesn't deserve her as a mother." I relaxed into Dan and closed my eyes.

"Thank you, Carter," he whispered and kissed the top of my head.

"What for?"

"For loving me, for sharing yourself with Archer and me. The list is endless, baby. You have no idea how much your touch, your faith, means to me. I'm so sorry I let you both down this evening."

As Denver walked over to us, we turned our attention to him.

"Hey, guys. Dan, it's great to see East found you. Carter, how are you doing?" Denver's smile gave me confidence.

"How's Archer? Tell me, Denver. How bad is it?" I spoke quietly, but even I could hear the strain in my voice.

"He's okay, Carter. His ankle is going to be fine. It's just a sprain. We're going to strap it up, and he'll have to wear a support boot for a week or two, but he'll be okay. My ex did a good job fixing him up, and it's held well. I'll take you through now."

"Oh, thank you, Denver. Thank you so much for being there for us." I jumped off Dan's knee and hugged my friend. "I'm so happy you were able to help us so quickly."

When I let go of Denver, I turned back to Dan, taken aback by the chagrin written all over his face. "C'mon, Dan."

Still, he was hesitating.

"Daniel. Are you in or out?" I barked at him, breaking through his reverie.

"I'm in," he said, determination in his voice. I grabbed his hand and dropped a sweet kiss on his mouth.

"Never make me doubt you again," I murmured against his lips.

"I won't, I promise," he whispered back.

We followed Denver through a set of doors. He pulled back a curtain. Archer was sitting up but had his eyes closed. He looked so handsome. It made my heart ache.

"Hey, baby." I picked up his hand and held it between both of mine. He blinked open his eyes, then tried to focus on me. By his dilated pupils, it was clear he'd been given pain meds. "Dan's here." I leaned over and pecked him on his mouth.

Dan walked to the other side of the bed and copied my action with Archer's other hand. "I'm so sorry, Arch. I hate myself right now."

Dan lifted Archer's hand to his mouth and kissed across his knuckles.

"Not your fault, Dan. Could've happened at any time. Happy to see you here. I'm feeling stupid. I should've been more careful."

"Just rest. The sooner we'll have you home with us."

Forty One

Archer

"Good, I've spent far too many hours in hospitals." I cringed at the thought of having to be here any longer than necessary.

"The nurse will be here to strap your ankle and fit the boot. I'll get the paperwork ready for you to be discharged." Denver tapped the bed.

"Thank you so much, Denver. I'm sorry to have wrecked your evening."

"It's no problem. It's what friends do." He waggled his eyebrows. "And I believe there's a dinner invitation in the offering?"

"Absolutely, just name the day, and we'd love to have you over," Dan spoke up. "I want a pool in the yard, and I've heard your guy is the best around."

"He really is the best. In fact, I'm going to find him." The curtain was shoved aside, and a nurse walked in with a black brace. "I'll get the paperwork done. See you soon, guys. Be careful."

It took another thirty minutes before I was released and I shuffled out with crutches. Again. At least I knew how to use them properly. Carter and Dan walked on either side of me but didn't offer me any support. I was guessing the scowl and snarl I'd given them when they both jumped toward me when I stood was enough to hold them back.

The drive back was quiet, both Dan and Carter lost in their thoughts, and I wasn't inclined to break the silence. I felt I'd caused a rift between us but had no idea how to fix it. I clunked my head back against the headrest and closed my eyes, letting the quiet hum of the engine lull me to sleep.

As a car door closed behind me, I woke up with a jolt. Carter and Dan talked to each other outside of the vehicle. Dan bent his head down to Carter and dropped a sweet but chaste kiss on his lips. Carter had linked hands with Dan, but both of their faces were solemn. Dan said something else, and Carter nodded. A small smile curled around his lips.

I pulled the handle and opened the door, pushing it wide so I could swing my body around. First, I propped my crutches against the car. Then I placed one hand on the window frame, the other on the back of my seat, and stood. At least I tried to. The car was too low for me to get a decent grip to push myself up. Carter took a step toward me, his hand outstretched, then stopped. I understood. I was going to have to suck it up and ask for some help.

"Any chance of a helping hand?" I called out. They both lurched forward with grins on their smart-assed faces. "Yeah, yeah. I know." I grinned back. "Fuckers."

After a light dinner, we'd taken up residence in the back garden, enjoying a soft drink and chatting about anything and everything except the elephant in the room. As the sun went down, the tension between us built, and an awkward silence descended. It was time to speak about what the hell had happened this evening with Dan. I sat up straighter. Carter had always been good at reading my body language, and with a nod, he got up and went back inside.

"You gonna tell me what went down with you, Dan?" I chugged the last of my soda and put the glass on the ground next to my lounger.

"I was a dick, that's all. I've sorted it out, and it won't happen again," he replied, his tone flat, not meeting my eyes.

"Not really enough information there, babe," I growled.

He jerked his head back to me. "Look, I got jealous of you two when you were making love and then again when you were fooling around in the shower, and I bolted. I feel like a prick and don't want to talk about it." A frown marred his smooth forehead.

"Does Carter know?"

"Yes, and he put me right. I'm sorry, Archer."

I raised an eyebrow at him. "Not good enough."

"Fine. I want this between us, but I'm worried I'm not going to be enough for you. That you don't need me as much as I need you. I can see me with you until I'm old and gray, but I'm not convinced you see that with me. That was why I ran off this evening." Dan let out a long sigh and stared back down at the garden.

"Then I guess we'll have to prove it to you, won't we?" I held out my hand, and when he caught it, slight tremors tickled my fingers.

Carter returned and darted his gaze between us. "Is everything okay?"

"Yeah, I'm just trying to let Dan know we're here for the long haul."

"Good. I want to go to bed, and I want us to be together and happy. And most of all, I want this shitty fucking night to be over." With that, he turned on his heel and marched back inside.

"Shit. Now he's mad. He's right. Let's go and write this evening off." Dan helped me get to my feet and handed me my crutches. "Come here, baby." I gathered him close and pressed my lips firmly to his. "No more doubting us. Let's just grow into this together."

Dan nodded and let me step through the doors so he could lock up for the night. I hobbled up the stairs to our room.

"At least the bed got clean sheets before all this happened. Otherwise we'd have to sleep in the guest room." Carter snorted. Dan swatted his ass in response.

"I can't believe this went down this evening. Thank god Denver was home tonight. We really do owe them dinner," Dan murmured and ran a hand down my back, sending shivers all over me.

"Let's get into bed." Carter stripped off his shorts and T-shirt.

"I don't think I'll be up for much with my foot all strapped up," I grumbled and let them undress me.

"I'm sure we can come up with something," Carter muttered as he kneeled in front of me, his mouth against my abs. He slid my shorts down my legs as he planted kisses farther down my body.

As I tipped my head back, another set of hands roamed over my body, gliding down over my ass, squeezing my cheeks hard, and pulling them apart.

"I think you need to lie down now, baby," Carter purred.

Forty Two

Carter

I lay on my stomach with my head on Archer's chest while Dan ran his hands up and down my spine. The featherlight touches made me purr with contentment. Archer had been home for a week now, and I'd never been so happy. His foot was on the mend. He just had to heal and get some physical therapy. According to him, he was a pro at this, so we were letting him do what he thought was best.

"I don't want to go to work." I moaned as Dan's hand traveled down to my ass, stroking over each cheek.

"You don't have to be there for a while, honey. Just relax here with us." Archer carded his fingers through my hair. My dick throbbed, trapped between the sheet and my stomach.

"I need to cover Shelley's shift. She's got a doctor's appointment, and it's the only day they could see her." I tried to move, but Dan now had his mouth on my ass, leaving wet kisses as he traversed the curves. "No. Let me up." Laughing, I wriggled my way out of their clutches.

"Oh, baby, you know you want to." Dan snickered and rolled over to show me his hard dick.

"Of course, I do, but I have to get to work. I'll take a rain check and let you two play." I headed to the bathroom and switched the water on.

After a too-short shower, I was dry and dressed. Leaning over the bed, I kissed Archer and then Dan. "Call me later if you feel up to it, Arch. Dan, don't let him overdo it."

Fifteen minutes later, I unlocked the door to the bar and let myself into the silence, reveling in the calm before the storm. I loved the quiet times as much as the heady rush of the manic hours, the ones where I was rushed off my feet and never felt like I'd be able to take a load off again.

The bar looked good. Paris and Hunter, our newest bartender, had stocked up well last night, cleaned behind the bar, and piled the chairs on top of the tables. The cleaner would be here in an hour to get the floors mopped. We'd found it easier to get someone in early in the morning rather than the guys closing doing it. As I walked around to check everything, warmth spread through me. I loved this bar. To me, it was more than just a place to work. It had become a home. And Kes, East, and Denver had become my family, my brothers. Every day I thanked my lucky stars for Kes offering me a job and a home at a time I needed them most in the world. That was something I'd never be able to thank them enough for. Maybe one day I could pay it forward. I often forgot the life I'd planned to have, the life I'd expected with Archer. I'd studied to be an engineer. That was all I'd ever wanted to be, but not anymore. Nope, now I was the manager of a cool bar and the boyfriend of two amazing men, and I wouldn't change it for the world.

I got busy in the office, going through the paperwork. All the mundane stuff Kes loathed but I got a kick out of sorting. The clatter of chairs being moved around pulled me out of my work. Wow, I'd spent more time in here than I'd realized. It was almost time to open the bar.

"Hey, Cart. How's it going?" Kes walked in and dropped his leather jacket on the desk.

"Good, it's good. I wasn't expecting to see you here today. Did your boyfriends kicked you out?" I chuckled.

"Nothing of the sort. I just thought I'd show my face. I haven't seen you for a while. How's your man?"

"Archer's good. Moaning about being bored, so I think Dan is going to get him to work this week. His ankle is doing well, thanks."

"We're looking forward to coming over for dinner."

"Yeah, me too. Dan's good in the kitchen." And that wasn't the only thing he was good at.

"Are you feeling happier than when we spoke last week? You seem a lot more content."

"Was it only a week ago? It seems longer. Yeah, I'm much better. I hadn't realized Dan and Archer had the same worries as I did. We've learned to communicate better. It's early days, but it feels good. We've all stopped trying to prove ourselves so much and learned to just be." I scrubbed the back of my neck. I still had a load of work to do.

"Do you want me to stay for a while? I've got a couple of hours free. East is working, and Denver has taken Phoebe over to his folks' place."

"Yeah, that would be great. Just do what you want."

Kes ended up staying for most of the day. A group of women had come in, taking up three tables, and wanted to have a long, lazy lunch. They were loud and flirty but fun.

At five, Paris showed up for his shift and weaved through the still busy room toward the bar. "You should've called me, Car."

"Nah, Kes was here. It was fine."

"Okay. I'll just put my jacket away and grab my apron. Back in a sec."

I turned to the next customer with a smile, but it dropped. Damn, the smartly dressed man stood in front of me. Although his mouth was curled in a broad smile, his eyes were cold and calculating as he gave me the once-over.

"Hello again, Carter. I haven't seen you in a few days." His voice was low and off-key. What a creep. Coldness seeped in my veins. I hated the way he spoke my name, almost lasciviously.

"I had a few days off. What can I get you?" I just want him served and away from me.

"I'll take a scotch again. Will you join me this time?" His steel-gray eyes bored into mine.

"Thanks, but no drinking on the job, I'm afraid." I mustered up all my politeness.

"Shame. Maybe on one of your days off? Would you like to come on a date with me?" Again with the staring.

"Um, thanks for the offer, but I'm in a relationship. Let me get your drink." I turned away before he had a chance to reply.

"With the two gentlemen I saw you with before?"

He was seriously giving off some freaky stalker vibes. I pushed his glass across the bar, making sure there was no physical contact. He picked up his drink and sauntered over to the table in the corner, the same one he'd sat at the last time.

"Is he causing trouble?" Paris asked, worry etched on his face. "He's asked for you a couple of times. I don't like him."

"No, I have no idea who he is, but he seems to know me. He's just asked me out on a date."

"Yeah, he's a creepy dude, for sure."

Creepy guy had another couple of drinks, but every time Paris took his order, and he left me alone. Thankfully, my shift was nearly over. As I wiped down the counter, a shiver ran down my spine. Yep, creepy guy was back, again with his oily, snaky smile on his face.

"Let me know your answer. My number's inside." He slid an envelope over the bar, then tapped it twice. "I'll be waiting for your call."

I glanced down but didn't pick it up. My name was typed in large print on the expensive-looking paper.

"I'm not interested in anything you have to offer. Please take it away with you." I pushed the envelope back to him, but he ignored it.

"We'll see, Mallory Halston. We'll see." He walked away, leaving me staring at his back.

My blood froze inside me, and my stomach clenched. He knew who I was. How? Why?

Paris laid a hand on my arm. "Car, what the hell's going on? Who's that dude?"

"I have no idea, but he knows me. He's given me this." I pointed at the envelope like it was a bomb about to explode.

"You gonna open it?" Paris looked as freaked out as me.

"I don't know. What would you do? Shit. I don't know what to do."

"Take it home, show it to your men. That way you can decide together. I'd take it to Co—" Two red spots bloomed on his cheeks.

"You and Conn, eh? Nice one, Par. Go for it. He's a good guy."

"You don't think I'm too young for him?"

"Hey, of course not. You're twenty-one, Paris, and if you work well together, it's right. Age is just a number. Be happy with him, Par. You deserve someone good."

"And there's no way my dad will try anything with a cop." He snorted, and I chuckled too.

I snatched up the envelope, folded it in half, and shoved it into my back pocket. I'd see what Dan and Archer thought.

Thirty minutes later, we were closing the doors behind the last customer. After locking the door, I cashed up while Paris and Hunter cleaned. It didn't take us long before we were ready to go.

"See you later, guys." I waved as I climbed into Archer's new truck. He'd finally taken the rental back and bought one for himself. I smiled as Hunter slung his arm over Paris's shoulder. Hmm, was there more to their friendship? No, Paris had said he was with Conn. Not everyone is looking for a threesome. They're just friends.

As I pulled up into the driveway, the house was shrouded in darkness. They'd only left the porch light on. They'd have gone to bed, and I couldn't blame them. It was getting close to one a.m.

I locked up behind me and quietly climbed the stairs. My men were fast asleep, Dan's head resting on Archer's chest and his hand around Archer's waist. I needed a shower but didn't want to wake them, so I went to the main bathroom. After a quick washup, I tiptoed back in and slid in next to Dan.

"Hey, baby. You okay?" Archer whispered.

"Yeah, sorry if I woke you."

"I wasn't really asleep. Kinda waiting for you to get back."

"Get some rest, Arch." Sleep was pulling at me already. "Love you," I mumbled.

Forty Three

Archer

"I need to talk to you, guys." Carter stood on the other side of the kitchen island as Dan and I made breakfast.

He was flicking an envelope over and over, his fingers nimble but shaking slightly. Uh-oh, him chewing on his lip wasn't a good sign. He was stressed about this, whatever it was.

"What's that?" I pointed at the envelope in his hand.

"The past few weeks, a guy has shown up in the bar a few times and, when I'm not on shift, always asks about me. He"—Carter pinched the bridge of his nose—"I don't know. He makes me feel uncomfortable. He acts so overfamiliar, you know."

I went rigid, fisting my hands at my sides. How dare anyone scare my man?

"What does this asshole look like?" Dan's eyes had turned to slits. "I bet it was that dick we saw the other night."

"Has Kes CCTV installed in the bar?" I rounded the island, my hand outstretched for the envelope. "I'll take that, babe."

"Of course he has. Do you want to take a look?" Carter held on to the envelope as if reluctant to hand it over. "I don't want to know what's in here. You see, he called me Mallory Halston. He knows me from before."

"Damn. We need to go over the video from last night. C'mon, let's go," I barked.

"No, not yet."

I scowled at him and opened my mouth, but he shut me up with a glare.

"I want coffee and food before we go anywhere. He's not going anywhere. He's waiting for my call. He asked me out on a date too." Carter winced and accepted the mug of coffee from Dan.

"He'd better fucking not have," I snarled. "Let me see the envelope, Carter. Please."

"No." He glanced at Dan, who shook his head at me, then pecked Carter's mouth. Carter leaned into Dan's body and wrapped an arm around his waist.

"Why not? Why show it to us if you don't want us to see it."

"Because, Archer, we don't have secrets. We never have, and I'm not starting now. Plus, I'm not sure I'm going to open it. I don't want anything to do with someone from my past, someone who used my old name as a warning. I don't need anyone from the past back in my life. I have you two, and I have my friends, and that's all I want and need." He smiled again and held out his hand.

More relaxed now, I kissed on his upturned face, his mouth soft and willing.

"Okay, but we're going to find out who this fucker is. The rest is up to you. What do you say to handing this over to Lucas to follow up? He'll alert us to any danger." Carter frowned. "Don't look at me like that, Carter. I'll keep you safe, and if he has anything to do with my mother, it might be more sinister than a check for 50K."

"Fine, we'll find out who he is and if he has anything to do with that woman." He shuddered.

"You know, we could find that out by just opening the envelope, baby." Dan ran his hand up and down Carter's back.

"Look, let me eat before I have to make any more decisions."

"Then sit, and I'll make breakfast." I poured the eggs into a skillet and stirred as Dan and Carter took a seat at the kitchen island. Dan said something I couldn't hear above the sizzle of the eggs, but it was okay.

Like Carter had said, we didn't have any secrets, but we were entitled to be private with each other. Minutes later, I piled scrambled eggs on top of hot, buttered toast, added some bacon to the side, and slid it over the counter in front of Carter.

Groaning, he picked up his fork and dug in. "This is perfect. Thanks, love." He winked, then threatened to stab Dan's hand with his fork as he reached for some bacon. "Mine."

I grinned. His eyes latched onto mine and softened as if he remembered it too. "Archer would try that all the time too, and it never worked."

We chatted about more mundane subjects while Carter ate and tried to figure out when was the best time to invite Denver and the others over for dinner.

"We need to work around his hospital shifts. We can ask Kes to check with Denver. I know he's strict about his hours now that he has his daughter to look after, but Kes knows exactly when he's home." Carter placed his fork down. "Thanks, Dan, that was delicious. Just what I needed. Shall we go? I'll give Kes a call to let him know we're on our way."

"Do we have to do that, Carter? Can't we keep it to ourselves?" I rolled a few crumbs back and forth over the counter.

"No, Arch," Dan answered for him. "Think about it. Kes owns the bar. Someone, a stranger, is harassing his bar manager. He needs to know what's going on in his business, and we need his permission to look through his CCTV recordings. Besides, Kes would want to keep Carter safe. He's like family to him."

"You're right. A fine lawyer I am. I hadn't thought it through. I just want any decision we make or Carter chooses to be what we want, not because of some unknown, unnamed man. I don't like being kept in the dark."

Carter closed the dishwasher. "Let's go."

Dan drove as I sat next to Carter with my hand resting on his thigh as he talked to Kes.

"Yeah, he's been in a few times. Shelley told me he's asked for me." Carter went quiet as he listened to Kes. "No, you don't need to do that....Yes, they are....Oh, okay. See you in a few....Yeah, bye, Kes."

"What's he saying?" Dan asked.

"He's going to meet us at the bar. He wants to see the recordings for himself." Carter sighed and leaned his head back.

I gave his thigh a squeeze. "It'll be okay, honey. We've got you. Whatever and whoever this is, we've got you."

"I know." His voice was quiet, subdued, and I hated it when he crawled back into his shell. He had to be riddled with confusion and uncertainty now. The confidence he'd found here made me proud. Would he have had it if we'd stayed together all through the accident, or would we have been the same people we were before? We'd never know the answer. What was done was done.

And what was in the letter? Carter constantly folded and unfolded the envelope. I still knew him so well. He was warring with himself, but I had to respect his decision and let him open it in his own time.

Dan pulled up outside the bar, switched off the engine, and sat back, waiting for Carter to make a move. We sat silently for only a couple of minutes. Then he shook out his shoulders and grasped the handle.

"Let's get this shit over with. I want to spend the day naked with you two without some asshat's words hanging over us." He jumped down from the cab, strode over to the door, unlocked it, and stepped inside.

Dan took hold of my hand and helped me out of the truck. I'd ditched my crutches two days before as my ankle had gotten so much better. I could walk again without them, but the cab was too high to climb out comfortably. I didn't want to take the risk of another mishap. With a tight smile, his eyes on our lover walking away, he closed the door. "This is going to be okay. It may take a little while and cause a few headaches, but he's our man, and we fight alongside him."

"I know, but my gut is telling me this is my mother's doing." I cast my eyes up and down the high street. It was a busy morning, so the chance of spotting the guy I'd seen all those nights ago was nonexistent, but still, I took in my surroundings.

I shut the door behind us, making sure it was locked. Kes would use his own keys when he got here. Without customers, the bar looked strangely empty and silent, our footsteps loud on the wooden floor. Carter was already on the computer in the office, his fingers flying over the keys as he stared at the screen. Paying us no mind, he kept his eyes fixed on the screen as we stepped behind him and, each of us resting a hand on his shoulders, leaned forward. I couldn't keep up with the speed he ran through the video from last night's CCTV. The timer raced away in the top corner of the screen, but Carter ignored it, focused as he was to spot the creepy guy.

I pulled my cell out of my pocket and called Lucas.

"Hey, dude, how's it going?...Look, I'm going to be sending you a visual of a guy. He approached Carter....Yeah, Mallory. He goes by Carter now." Carter tensed under my hand. I gave his shoulder a squeeze, and he relaxed again. "He handed him an envelope and said he'd be waiting for a reply. The fucker also had the nerve to ask him out on a date."

Dan growled next to me, making me chuckle. "Yeah, that's Dan. He's about as happy as I am." The screen stopped racing and came to a stop with the image of the guy we'd seen in the bar. The bastard had something on Carter, and he knew we were all together. No wonder he looked so smug. I hated bastards who thought they had one up on me.

"We've got a visual, Luc. You ready for me to send it over?"

"Sure, Arch. I'll get on it and send it over to Ben. It won't take us long. You wanna stay on the line, or can I call you back?" Lucas asked.

Just then, Kes walked in with both of his boyfriends. There was a moment of bro-hugs, and then Kes stepped up next to Carter.

"Call me back, Luc. Carter's family has turned up....Yeah, he has good people here....Gimme a couple of minutes, and you'll have it."

Kes was bent over next to Carter and whispered into his ear. Everything inside me wanted to shout out that it was me he should be talking to, but I shoved it down and let them finish.

"This is him, Arch. I guess you want to send it over to your guy?" My heart broke at the haunted look in his eyes. At home, he seemed relaxed and easy, but now he was so tense and unhappy my strength crumbled.

"Oh, Carter, hon. It'll be okay, I promise." I brushed my hand through the hair at his nape.

He turned to me, his smile achingly sad. "I know that, Arch. I just hate this is here. Whatever this is, I know the three of us can deal with it."

I took a screenshot of the image on the screen and sent it to Lucas. He pinged back that he'd received it and would be in touch. Leaning back on the desk, I took in the people around us. Paris had joined us and, to my surprise, Conn Martinez. I'd only spoken to him a couple of times, and I liked him. I didn't know he was with Paris, but they looked good together. These weren't a couple of men, of friends. They were a family, the family Mallory had made when he became Carter. These men were good people. They were his people, and I liked it.

"What next then? How do you want to proceed when we find out who he is, Carter?" Dan was still holding on to Carter's shoulder, his fingers trailing a soft pattern over the exposed skin at the juncture of his neck and shoulder.

"I guess I should read whatever is in this envelope." Carter sighed heavily.

"Why don't we just call him and get him to come here? All this seems very cloak and dagger when a simple call could have it all over with?" Paris looked at me bewildered.

"I want to see if my mother has anything to do with this guy before we speak to him. I've already got Lucas investigating her. I feel she's a threat to Carter and could be out to harm him," I explained.

My phone rang, making us all jump. Carter paled. "It's okay, honey." I answered the call. "Lucas, what have you got?"

"The guy's name is Leon Dukas. He's a lawyer, and it seems he's working for Carter's brother, Roman."

"What? Why is he contacting Carter? He hasn't seen him for years....Hold on, Luc. Let me tell Carter." I lowered my phone. "Carter, he's a lawyer, and he's working for you brother, Roman. Do you want to talk to Lucas?"

Carter's eyes sprang wide, and a sheen of tears built up, but he nodded. I handed him the phone and, with my other hand, reached out for Dan, whose face was as white as a sheet. He walked into my arms, tremors shaking his body.

Forty Four

Dan

Now there was another part of Carter's life I knew nothing about. I couldn't help thinking that this was because we'd fallen straight into this relationship with Archer. This was what Carter had been talking about when he said we'd missed out on all the "getting to know you" talks we would've had if it had just been the two of us. Like the piano and his degree in engineering. I had no idea. Would Carter have ever talked about his family or told me Archer's name? Or had he closed the door to his past? I felt totally out of my depth here. Carter had a brother? I'd never known. Hell, I didn't know *him*. As I glanced at Archer, he opened his arms, and I stepped into his embrace.

"I didn't know. I know so little about him. I feel so useless," I murmured into Archer's ear as he held me against him.

"I know, baby. I felt the same when I met him again. I look around this room and see so many people who know the new him. People who care for him, and I feel like the odd one out. But we'll get through this together. We're a family, and we can learn together," Archer spoke quietly, then brushed his mouth across mine. "Okay?"

I swallowed. "Yeah, okay." I leaned my back against his chest and watched Carter as he talked to Lucas.

It seemed like everyone in the room was holding their breaths. Carter said good-bye and handed the phone back to Archer. Tears had gathered in his eyes again as he shook his head as if trying to clear his mind, then picked up the envelope.

"Carter, baby. Are you sure?" I held out my hand, and to my relief, he grasped it.

"Yeah, it's from my brother. I need to know what's going on." Carter slipped his finger under the edge of the envelope and slid it across the top, opening it raggedly. With a deep breath, he pulled out a sheet of paper, unfolded it, and started to read.

"It's my father." Carter gasped, his hands shaking as his eyes flew across the paper. "He has cancer and is dying. Roman wants me to go home and see him. He says he's been asking for me." He slapped his hand over his mouth, tears dripping down his face. "Roman says he misses me and wants to reconnect."

"Carter, what do you want to do? Can you really see yourself back there?" Archer kneeled in front of Carter and gripped his trembling hands. "What do you think?"

"I don't know. Why did he go to all this trouble? If he knew I was here, why didn't he just come to see me? Hell, I haven't seen or spoken to my family for, what, over three years now?" He wiped the tears from his cheek with jerky movements. "What does my father want to do? I can't imagine him apologizing. He's never been sorry for anything he's done." Carter ran his hand through his hair and stared back down at the letter. "I can't think straight. This is crazy."

Carter jumped to his feet, but with the room so full of people, there wasn't anywhere he could go, and he bounced on his heels, hands balled in fists. "I don't trust my father a fucking inch, so he's suddenly got a conscience? I doubt that."

"Maybe you should think about it for a few days. Does he say it's urgent? How long does he say your father has left?" Archer stepped in front of Carter. "Carter, look at me."

He waited until Carter lifted his head. "We'll come with you. You don't need to do this alone." He pulled him into a hug and held him until Carter relaxed against him and wrapped his arms around him too.

Feet shuffled, and a throat cleared. I jerked my head around. I'd been so focused on Carter I'd forgotten about our friends. Still, their silent support meant the world, and I gave them a grateful nod. They didn't need any words—they understood—and they filed out of the room, giving us the privacy we needed. The door shut softly behind Kes.

"Carter, baby. Come here." I opened my arms wide, and he rushed to me. His head rested on my chest as I stroked his back, soothing him the best I could. "Archer's right. We'll come with you. You never have to do anything alone anymore. We love you, baby."

His shoulders shook as he cried. Finally, the heart-wrenching sobs subsided, and he lifted his head, his eyes red and puffy. "I've missed my brother and sister so much. I've thought of them so often. I was told never to contact them again, that I was disgusting, an aberration, and I'd twist them into my own evil ways."

"Carter, you're an amazing man. A strong, brave, intelligent man, and it's your father who's sick and twisted. Your siblings should be proud to have you as their brother, and I'm sure if you get to meet them again, you'll rekindle your love and friendship."

Archer had stepped up behind Carter so that he was sandwiched between us. "Why don't we arrange a meeting with this Dukas dude? We can have it in the office so it's an official meeting and find out more. I'm just as intrigued as you to find out why they chose this clandestine way of reaching out to you. What do you say?"

Sniffing and wiping his nose with the back of his hand, Carter nodded. "Yeah, I think that's a good idea. I'm not sure what I want to do yet. This has come as a complete surprise. I really was expecting some shit blackmail from your mother." Carter let out a dry chuckle. "I think I would've preferred that. At least we could throw the big guns at her and tell her to get fucked."

We all chuckled at this, and Carter relaxed. He looked around the room and sighed. "Where did everyone go?"

"They realized it was a private moment and we were better off alone. I'm sure you'll want to call Kes later."

"You're not working today, are you, Car?" Archer asked, and relief spread across his face when our boyfriend shook his head. "Good, let's go back home. We could all use a rest."

"Yeah, I could go along with that." Carter looked drained, and I was guessing he'd be asleep as soon as his head hit the pillow. "What about this?" He picked up the letter.

"I'll call Dukas, and the rest is up to you when and if you're ready," I told him.

I tipped his chin up and pecked his lips. He slipped his tongue into my mouth and stroked against mine, then broke away, pulled Archer's face to his, and kissed him with as much fervor as he had me.

"Let's go, baby. We'll take care of you." I scraped my teeth up his neck as he panted into Archer's mouth.

"I need you. I need you both so much." His moan hit my heart and my groin equally.

In the time we'd been in the office, the bar had opened its doors, and already every table was occupied. As we weaved through the customers, Paris walked up to Carter and hugged him. Carter reciprocated, bunching his fists in Paris's shirt. I was happy Carter had such a good friend in Paris. When they separated, Paris whispered in his ear and stroked his cheek in a sweet gesture of friendship.

I got behind the wheel, while Archer sat in the back with Carter. He held him close against his side, and Carter rested his head on his shoulder with his eyes closed. Not ten minutes later, I pulled up into the driveway.

Inside, we led our weary lover upstairs and into our bedroom. "Get undressed, babe. Then you can get into bed."

"You coming, too?" His voice was muffled as he pulled his T-shirt over his head, kicking off his shoes at the same time.

"Yes, baby, of course." I shed my clothes as Archer did the same.

We climbed in together and cocooned Carter between us, his head on my chest, Archer's body pressing against his back. I stroked through Carter's hair while Archer brushed along his ribs down to his hip, soothing him as he shut down and settled into sleep.

Archer frowned, his gaze clouded with worry. "What should we do?"

"Nothing yet. He needs us here. The lawyer can wait. I'm so mad at him. He should've come clean straight away, not playing games with Carter and, sure as shit, not asking him out on a date," I hissed.

"Yeah. Let's give him an hour to sleep. Then we'll give the asshole a call." Archer snuggled into Carter and closed his eyes, and soon he was asleep too.

I found it harder to relax, my brain racing at the discovery of his family. Of course I knew he had to have one, but he'd never mentioned them. I was positive we would've shared more about ourselves had it just been me and him for longer. This had rattled me. I wanted to know more. I wanted to know everything. With a sigh, I slipped out of bed. Carter stirred but didn't wake, turning his body into Archer's instead. I put on some sweats and a T-shirt and padded downstairs. Carter had placed the envelope and the business card on the console inside the door. Leaving the letter—that wasn't mine to read—I picked up the card and headed down to my office.

"Dukas," a deep voice answered my call.

"My name is Daniel Mortimer. You've overstepped the mark, Dukas. Be in my office in an hour."

Forty Five

Carter

    I woke up alone. The sun had moved, giving off a late-afternoon glow across the room. I couldn't believe I'd slept for so long. Then everything came rushing back. Roman. My heart squeezed as I thought of my younger brother. What was he doing now? He should be finished with college soon, if he hadn't already. Did he work with my father? Did he share the same opinion of me? I doubted the latter, or why else would he want to reconnect? And why in such a shady way, such an unorthodox way? Was the overly confident and brash lawyer testing me? Or was he just a dick?

    The house seemed unusually quiet. I would've thought I could hear at least one of them. I got dressed and went downstairs, where my eyes fell on my brother's letter. I needed to read it again. Picking it up, I walked into an empty kitchen. Had they already gone to see douchebag Dukas? I should be pissed that they met with him without me, but I didn't care if I never saw him again. He was a creep.

    After grabbing a bottle of water out of the fridge, I headed out into the garden and sat in one of the loungers. The quiet tranquility settled over me, soothed me. Now that I was calmer, I could pay more attention to my brother's words. Taking a deep breath, I opened the letter.

Mallory,

God, I hope this gets to you. I can't believe it's been so long since I've seen you, spoken to you, asked you for advice, and hugged you.

I don't know where to start. Maybe I should just say I'm sorry. I'm sorry for so much.

I'm sorry I sat at the dinner table like a mute and didn't stand up for you.

I'm sorry I didn't look out for you after our father threw you out.

I'm sorry I've never said I'm sorry.

But now I'm sorry for why I'm contacting you. I don't expect an answer. Hell, I don't know if you'll ever read this, but I have to try to reach out to you.

Father's dying. He has lung cancer, and after two attempts of chemotherapy and radiation, the doctors say there's nothing more they can do. His stubbornness is matched by his irascibility. Recently, though, he's started to talk about you, about how wrong he's been. How he should never have banished you. His words, not mine. About how he'd like to see you again. Mother is as much use in this as you can expect. Pippa is no help at all. She hasn't coped well with family life for a long time now. She's busy with school, and I try to keep things neutral.

I don't expect you to come. Like I said, I'm not expecting to find you, but if you can find it in your heart to reach out to me, that would be great. Even if you tell me to fuck off, I'll understand. I wish I could have a few moments to tell you how proud I am of you. You stood up for yourself. You were proud to be a gay man. I love you, my brother.

Ro
Xxx

PS: This is my cell number (241) 567-4973.

For the second time today, I wiped the tears from my face, then dug into my pocket. Dammit, where was my phone? I needed to call him before I was too chickenshit. I raced upstairs, snatched my phone from the drawer, and dialed the number. I held my breath as it rang, once, twice.

"Hello?"

"Ro?" The word came out strangled in my throat as tears pooled in my eyes. I'd thought I'd have been all cried out, but hearing my brother opened the floodgates again.

"Mallory, is that you?" Roman answered, his voice deeper than I remembered. A male voice murmured in the background, and my brother shushed it.

"Yeah, it's me." All I got was a heavy silence down the line. Just as I was about to hang up, he spoke again.

"Oh, god, thank you. Thank you for calling me. Christ, Ry, I've missed you." He sighed and sniffed back a sob.

"Yeah, me too, Ro. Me too. How bad is it?" My brother filled me in on all the details. Even between his sobs and brave words of telling me he was coping, it was clear how much he needed me.

"Ro...Ro...Ro! Stop talking. I'm on my way." I couldn't believe I'd just said that, but this was family. This was my brother.

"Oh, thank god. Thank you, Mallory, thank you," he cried.

"It'll take me a day or so, but I'm on my way."

"I'll send the jet," he blurted out. I chuckled. Old habits die hard.

"No, I'm okay. I'll be with you soon. I'll be in touch." I pressed the End Call button and scrubbed the back of my neck. What would be the easiest and fastest way? Should I get a rental car? No, I shook my head. I'd take my bike.

I pulled my large backpack out of the cupboard in the walk-in closet and stuffed some clothes in it. From the bathroom, I added toiletries. I glanced around the room, making sure I had everything I needed for the journey.

When I got downstairs, I found a notepad in Dan's office and left them a note.

I've gone home to sort this mess out. My brother needs me.

    I won't be long, and I promise I'll be okay. I promise to come back.

I love you both

Xxxx

Next, I sent a message to Kes.
I've gone home, Kes.
I'm sorry to leave you like this.
I need to get closure.
Thank you for everything.
See you soon.
Carter
Xx

I climbed on my bike, started the engine, and rode away from the town I now called home.

Forty Six

Archer

When I woke up, I felt calmer and more relaxed. How long had I slept? I checked my watch. Thirty minutes. Not too bad. The side where Dan had lain was cold, but Carter was still sleeping soundly. I eased myself away from him, being careful not to disturb him, but he burrowed deeper in the duvet. Good. Sleep was the best thing for him right now.

I got dressed and went in search of Dan. As I'd expected, he was sitting at his desk. He'd been too wired to sleep and needed action more than rest in these kinds of situations. His geeky black-framed glasses on his nose made him look fucking hot as he stared at his computer screen.

"Whatcha doing?" I carded my hand through his messy hair.

"I'm looking up this Dukas dude. We've got a meeting with him in thirty minutes. I want to know what he's been playing at. He should've handed that letter over to Carter as soon as he met him." Dan pounded the keyboard.

"Then let's go. Carter's still asleep. If we hurry, we can be back before he wakes. You can fill me in on the way."

"I need to change. I can't wear sweats." Dan laughed, but rather than heading upstairs, he wandered off to the laundry room. As he picked a pair of jeans from the pile of clean clothes and pulled the soft denim up over his bare ass, I let out a low whistle.

"Commando? I like it." I smirked and ran my hand over the firm swell of his ass.

We got into Dan's car and quickly made our way through the town to his office. "Tell me more, Dan."

"His company is sound, and he's the head with two partners. They've been practicing as long as we have with a good reputation. He's mainly a corporate lawyer. Halston Commerce is his main contract, but he has other companies on the books. Why would he have behaved the way he has? It doesn't make sense, and I want to get to the bottom of this."

"I agree. He's a shifty bastard for sure."

When we stepped into our office, we had ten minutes to spare before Dukas was due to arrive. We sat together and studied his profile again. At the exact appointment time, the buzzer rang, and I walked to the door.

The same smug look he had in the bar crossed over his face. Stepping aside, I let him in.

"Good afternoon, Mr. Hawkins, Mr. Mortimer. I'm Leon Dukas." He offered his hand, and we shook firmly.

"Take a seat, Mr. Dukas." I gestured to the sole chair in front of the desk.

"Please, call me Leon," he smarmed.

God, what a creep, but I plastered on a smile.

"I think you need to explain yourself, Dukas." Dan skipped any pleasantries.

"Why? What business is it of yours? I had my instructions from my client, and I acted them out accordingly. I had to be sure I was actually speaking to Mr. Mallory Halston. My client had given me a visual, but you have to agree Mr. Halston looks different from how he did over three years ago. Add to that the fact that he no longer calls himself Mallory. I had to confirm he was who I believed him to be."

"You have to admit it was underhanded, asking members of staff about him. Why didn't you introduce yourself and hand over the letter immediately?" I couldn't believe how cocky this guy was. Maybe I had to remind him of who I'd been working with for the last five years. "Do you feel that asking him out on a date was appropriate?" I snapped.

"I admit I overstepped the mark there, but he's an attractive man. I couldn't resist. I had my suspicions the three of you were together, but if not, why shouldn't I take a chance? It's unusual to find two sets of threesomes living so closely together, even more so in such a conservative small town. Tell me. Do you share?"

"Shut the fuck up, Dukas. I mean it, not one more word about our private life," I growled.

"I'll take that as a no. Pity." He smirked again. "Let's get to the point of this pissing contest. Is he going to answer the letter, or am I going home empty-handed, so to speak?"

"Carter hasn't decided yet, and trust me, he'll never be traveling anywhere with you." I glanced at Dan, who gave me a subtle nod. "We're done here. You've handed over your letter. Your job here is done. I suggest you leave quickly. This is a small town that looks after its own. Carter is one of them, and you aren't welcome here."

"My instructions from my client are to wait until I hear from Mr. Halston."

"Then I'll pass my instructions to my lawyer regarding your harassment of my partner. Mason Reynolds will be quick to act and have a restraining order against you in no time. You won't be able to talk to him about pissing contests."

He blanched at the name Mason Reynolds. Such was his power. I didn't even try to hide my grin.

Dan narrowed his eyes at Dukas. There was more he wanted to say—I knew him too well— but he kept it to himself for now. "I'll show you out. I hope we don't have to meet again."

Before Dukas walked out the door, he turned. "Well played, Hawkins. You're most definitely your mother's son."

Dan locked the door behind Dukas and let out a sigh. "Jezus, what an asshole."

"I'm nothing like my fucking mother. That dickhead better stay out of my way."

"No, babe, you're not. He just didn't like your threat of Mason." Dan walked over and wrapped his arms around my neck. Leaning in, he captured my mouth and kissed me, then bit on my bottom lip, tugging it between his teeth.

I groaned as he released it, only to thrust my tongue into his mouth. Grabbing his hips and pressing my groin up to him, I rubbed my hard-on against his through the fabric of our jeans.

"Come on, let's take this home. Carter should be awake by now." I panted as I broke away.

We got back to the house, which was still quiet. We kissed and stumbled our way upstairs, heading straight to our bedroom. I let go of Dan so I could take my clothes off.

"Carter's not here." Dan looked around as if he was expecting to find Carter hiding somewhere.

Striding out of the room, I called out to him, then raced downstairs. I checked the kitchen and the garden, but both were empty. As I walked back into the hallway, Dan stood with a sheet of paper in his hand, and I knew what Carter had done. I didn't need Dan to tell me.

"He's gone home, hasn't he?" My voice was bland and monotone. I already missed him.

"Yeah, he says he needs to sort this mess out and that his brother needs him. He loves us and will be back soon."

"Fuck! I knew he'd do this. Why couldn't he have waited for us? We would've gone with him." I hated this, hated him leaving again.

"He needs to do this, needs to settle things with his father. And we have to let him do this. I don't expect him to stay silent. We can talk through Skype or FaceTime."

"How do you know this?" How could he be so calm yet so sure?

"Because he left the letter from his brother for us to read. I can totally see why he needs to do this. We are his, Archer. He won't ever forget that. Because of the love we share, he feels confident enough to go to his parents. He knows he's good enough. Good enough for anything, and he needs to tell his father this." His face was etched with pain at the loss of his love but strong and proud of the man he loved. "Okay?"

"Okay. I hate it, but okay. I'm sure he'll call us later, but I'm going to leave him a message. He needs to know we understand and love him and that we're only a call away." I rubbed my chest as if that would scrub away the hurt of losing my lover.

I was going to be a wreck the whole time he was gone, but deep down, I was so proud of him. I opened my arms, and Dan stepped into them. We stood quietly, clinging to each other, holding on tight.

Forty Seven

Carter

The nap this afternoon had done me a world of good. I was rested, calmer, and could ride for a long stretch. As I embraced the open road, my head cleared even further. I'd expected a cacophony of voices, of doubts and regrets, but all I felt was certainty and confidence. Yes, it was as if I'd left a piece of me behind, but I was coming back, back to two men who meant more to me than words could say. It was nothing like the last time I'd mounted my bike and ridden away. This time I knew where I was going and what I was coming back to.

After several hours on the road, my stomach growled, and my arms and legs ached. Time to find a place to stop for the night. I passed the seedy motels and kept riding until I found a decent hotel with a diner alongside it.

The receptionist handed me my keycard with a smile. "Have a good stay, Mr. Halston."

"Thanks." I strolled to the room, unlocked the door, and dumped my bag onto the bed. I'd made good time, and if I got up early, I could be back at my parents' place by lunchtime. I pulled my leathers off and went into the bathroom for a quick shower before heading back out for food.

Here Without You

The diner was busy, but as it was just me, I got a seat quickly and accepted the offer of coffee. I pulled my phone out of my pocket. Archer would've messaged me. Maybe Dan too. I just hoped they'd understand. My frown turned to a smile as I read Archer's message.

Honey,
I love you. Please be careful.
I get why you need to do this, but it doesn't mean I wish we hadn't gone together.
Call us when you can, and don't be away too long.
My heart won't take it.

Xxxx

The next was from Dan.
Baby,

I love you.
Take the time you need.
Your brother loves you, but not as much as me ;) That's not possible.
We'll be here for you.

Xxx

The pretty young waitress came back with coffee, and I ordered a burger and fries. My stomach rumbled again, making her laugh.

"I'll rush the order through for you, honey." With a wink, she sashayed away.

As she'd promised, only minutes later, she brought a loaded plate over. I groaned at the sight and dug in. My phone vibrated on the table next to my plate, and another text came through. Swiping my finger over the screen, I opened it up. This time it was from my brother.

Mallory,
I can't wait to see you again.
I'm hoping you'll stay with me at my place.
I have someone I want you to meet.
I'll be with Dad tomorrow, so come straight to

the house.
Roman
X

After finishing my meal, I declined another coffee and strolled back to my room. With slow movements, I undressed, clambered into the large and comfortable bed, and closed my eyes. Was it a good idea what I was about to do? The images of the last time I'd seen my father flashed through my mind. Was I strong enough to this alone? Why had I fled the house? I was a damn fool. I should've asked Dan and Archer to come with me. I grabbed my phone and called Dan. My heart raced as I waited for him to answer.

"Hey, baby, you okay?" Dan's voice blew over me like a warm breeze.

"Yeah, well, maybe...fuck, I hope so. Am I making a mistake, Dan?"

"Baby, you're on speaker. Archer's here. Talk to us, Carter."

"Hey, Carter, honey. You need us with you?" As always, Archer came straight to the point, and it soothed me, strange as it might sound. He was just so...Archer.

"No, yes, I don't know. I-I'm just fucking scared, scared of what I'll see, scared he isn't really sorry. And I'm dreading meeting my mother. She let him send me away. She turned her back on me. What if she still feels like that?"

"Carter, listen to me. The second you feel they think like that, you turn and walk away. You have us. We're your family. You have Kes and his family. You have your friends. Friends who will never turn their backs on you. You are loved. You're loved for who you are and by so many people. You hear me?" Dan spoke firmly, but it was so heartfelt I could breathe again.

"Yeah, I hear you. Thanks, Dan. I needed that."

"Carter, I've told Lucas you're on your way there. If you have any trouble, you call him. He'll be straight to you," Archer told me.

"Thank you, Arch." I yawned. "Sorry, I'm gonna crash. I'll call you tomorrow. Love you," I mumbled.

"We love you too. Night, babe," they both said at the same time. I ended the call and let sleep take me under.

I turned the bike in through gates I'd never wanted to see again and drove slowly up the long asphalt driveway to my parents' home. The ride over this morning had been uneventful but long, and I'd be happy to get off my bike. It had been a long time since I'd ridden this much, and my back and legs ached.

After I switched the engine off and removed my helmet, I scrubbed my hands through my hair and shook it out. To my right, the front door opened. I held my breath. Then he was there. Roman, my brother. He was much bigger now, grown and filled out, with a lot of muscle under his well-fitting T-shirt. He smiled, but it was tentative, the set of his jaw tense. Of course he'd be feeling as nervous and awkward as I was.

I swung my leg over my bike, straightened my aching back, then took the first step forward. As soon as I did, he rushed up to me and threw himself at me. With his arms around me, he hugged me tight. Shudders shook his body, and I held him just as hard.

"Christ, I've missed you." Roman stepped back, using the heels of his hands to wipe away the tears streaming down his face. "Come inside. You can get out of your leathers and get a coffee."

I studied him for a second longer, then smiled. "You grew up good, Ro." I nudged him with my shoulder. "Not so much of a shrimp anymore." He chuckled at the name I'd tease him with.

"Yeah, I guess I had to." Sadness clouded his eyes. "We can catch up later at my place. You ready to do this?"

"Nowhere fucking near ready, but I'm here now, so let's get on with it."

Roman lifted the backpack from my shoulders. When I went to take it from him, he shook his head. "I've got it."

The solid oak door never seemed larger and more unwelcome, and I stepped reluctantly over the threshold, my heart beating wildly in my chest. My brother laid his hand on my shoulder, reassuring me.

"It's just us here." He waved at my leather bike pants. "You want to get changed?"

"I only need to strip these off. I've got jeans in my bag." I slid the zipper down and shrugged out of the soft leather.

"I guess you want to know what happened?" Roman asked as we sat opposite each other at the kitchen table.

"What, with Dad?" I raised an eyebrow. "I'm guessing he knew he was ill and decided to do fuck about it until it was too late."

"Well, yeah, that's about it, but I meant after you left." He frowned, his jaw tight again.

"I didn't leave. He threw me out. And no, I really don't give a shit about what happened here. It was bad for me, and that's painful enough to think about." I didn't take my eyes from his, and I kept my voice low and level. "It's done, Roman. It's in the past. Leave it there."

"I will, for now. Let me tell you about him." Roman filled me in about my father's treatment, how much pain he was in, and how it was regulated. "He sleeps a lot now, but he's due to wake up soon. The afternoon is the best time to catch him at his most lucid."

"Why now, Ro? Is this so he doesn't die with a dirty conscience? That he'll get his place in heaven? I don't think he has a right to atonement. Right now, I'm thinking karma's a bitch for him."

"I know. Trust me, Ry, I know." He held my gaze, unblinking. Then a flicker.

"You're gay," I blurted, then burst out laughing. Roman didn't join in, and I sobered up quickly, but I couldn't help the bitterness in my voice. "And yet you're still here." I shook my head and pushed myself upright. It had been wrong to come here. God, I needed to go home.

"Yeah, I'm still here. I only told him a few months back, and by then, he was already ill. I have a boyfriend. We met in college, and while I've never been in the closet so much, I just chose not to tell him. And I'm guessing Dad chose to ignore it. I wasn't brave like you, Mallory. I wanted to work with Dad. I wanted to be a part of his company, so we just played the denial game. I hated it. Marcus, my boyfriend, nearly left me over it, but I did what I had to do. Look, can we talk about this again tonight? Dad will be awake now. If you're ready, that is."

"I guess I have to be. I'm here now." My head was spinning. Roman was right, though. We had time later to talk it through.

We walked together down the long hallway toward Dad's office.

I stopped my brother with a hand on his arm. "Why the office? He's ill, for fuck's sake."

"He wanted to stay in his office. We've turned it into a bedroom for him." Ro shrugged, gripped the door handle, but didn't open it. "Do you want to do this by yourself?"

"Bro, I don't want to do this at all," I answered gruffly, then gave him a small smile. "C'mon, let's see how it goes."

My heart skipped a beat. The man I'd hated for so long now seemed to have disappeared, and here, in his place, was half a man. He was so small and fragile looking. Where was the domineering tyrant I'd grown up with? His skin was so pale it was translucent as it stretched over his bones. It looked like brittle paper, easily torn and crumpled.

"Dad, you awake? You have a visitor." Roman's voice was clear. I'd expected hushed whispers, but he talked in a normal tone.

"Hey, Dad," I said as loudly as I could through the tourniquet around my throat. His eyes flew open, and he stared at me, his gaze more vulnerable and softer than I'd ever seen. Gone was the accusing and hard-as-flint look. Instead, tears swelled and spilled over before I could even blink. His lips trembled as he tried to find his words.

"M-Mallory?" He cleared his throat. "Oh, Mallory, my son, you're here." He reached out a shaky hand, and I stumbled toward him. "I'm sorry. I'm so very sorry."

"Yeah, I'm sure you are," I blurted out. I sat in the chair next to him, and he clasped my hand in his, his grip tighter than I'd thought he'd be capable of. "But you know what? It's okay." I wasn't going to let him get away with what he'd done, but now wasn't the right time. We'd definitely be talking about it again.

"No, it's not, son. Don't forgive me that easily. I don't deserve it. I was wrong and so very cruel," he gasped, then coughed so heavily his chest rattled. Oh god, was this normal? My breath hitched, and I turned to Roman to check if this was okay, but I was alone.

"What do you need, Dad? Would you like some water?" On his desk stood a cup with a straw sticking up from the lid.

"A whiskey would be good if you can sneak one in for me." He chuckled ruefully

"Yeah, that's not gonna happen." I shook my head and held the cup up to his mouth, and he sucked weakly on the straw.

"Thank you for coming, Mallory. Thank you for letting me see you again before this bastard disease carries me off." His eyes fell closed, and he leaned back on the pillows. I placed the cup back on the table and rested back in the chair.

Silence descended in the room, but it wasn't a heavy or awkward silence. It was calm, sedate; he seemed peaceful. I thought he'd gone back to sleep, but then he spoke again. "Are you happy, Mallory? Did you find a good man to love you?"

"I was, and then it all fell apart. I picked myself up and started again. I seem to have had to do that a lot." He opened his eyes again, sorrow pouring from them. "But I'm in a good place now with good people around me. I'm happy. I'm very happy."

It went quiet again.

"I-I thought you were with the Hawkins boy," my dad said.

"Yes, I was. We were together for nearly two years. How did you know that?" Just how much did he know about my life after he'd thrown me out? Not that it was important anymore. "He asked me to marry him the day I graduated." I loved that this chapter no longer caused me pain, that I had him back in my life.

"So why didn't you marry him?"

"Um, it's complicated." I really didn't want to get into this now.

"I'm sure I'll keep up. It's my body that's dying, not my brain."

I looked at him. A sliver of the man who'd raised me came back, but now I didn't mind his no-nonsense attitude. "Yeah, he was in a really bad car accident."

"Well, that's not a reason to end an engagement. So are you going to tell me what really happened?"

"His mother told me he had died. She sent some cops to our apartment. Then I was banned from the hospital. She turned up at the apartment later and told me to get out. That's what happened. The woman always hated me being with Archer. She got her own way in the end."

A hard bark of bitter laughter broke free from my father. How could he laugh at my pain?

"I'm glad you find it funny. It nearly killed me. The grief, the pain of losing him made me want to be dead too. Nothing hurt as much as losing him. Not even you hurt me as much as that bitch did. Look, this is tough for me to talk about. I'm still pissed at you. You kept track of me, yet you didn't reach out again. Maybe you wanted to watch me struggle, to get to see me drown myself in debt and having to work an almost full-time job just to be able to eat. Did you get a kick out of that? Of knowing that you were responsible for my struggles, that it would teach me a lesson. That I deserved it all simply because I was gay."

"I don't have an easy answer to that, Mallory. I don't know why I wanted to know what you were doing with your life. And I hadn't watched you. You were right. I let you go and didn't care what happened to you. Then I stumbled upon a photograph of you at a charity ball. Archer Hawkins was holding your hand. The smiles on both of your faces showed how in love you were. And you didn't care who knew. It was a look I'd never seen on your face before, and I was ashamed of myself for not knowing who you were anymore. I thought about contacting you again. I wanted to, but I decided you were better off without me. You'd proved that you could live and grow without me. I was proud of you but ashamed of myself. That shame kept me watching you from afar. But no, son, that's not why I was laughing. I can't imagine how dreadful and painful that was for you. I laughed because nothing Valerie Hawkins does surprises me. That woman has no heart in her body. She's a wicked and selfish woman."

"I thought you must've known each other. She guessed I was your son when I first met her." There was a story here, one I wasn't sure I wanted to know.

"Unfortunately, I know her very well. What else happened, son? What else went on?" He sounded angry, but he was also struggling to breathe properly.

"Not enough for you to tire yourself over. Maybe we can talk more later or tomorrow?" I patted his hand. The seed of forgiving him had been planted, and maybe it would bloom into full-on forgiveness, but that would take time. And even then, I might always keep a little resentment toward him, but I'd do my best not to let it overgrow my feelings.

"Yes, Mallory." His eyes shone. "I can't believe you came back, thank you." He lifted my hand and placed a kiss on the back of it.

"I'm gonna go find Roman. I'll be staying at his place. We've got a lot of catching up to do." His gesture of happiness at seeing me was messing with my head.

"You do that. He's missed you so much. I hate that I forced you apart. I guess I'm paying for my sins now." He gasped in a breath and broke out in a violent coughing fit.

"Don't talk like that, Dad. I'm here now, and I'm not going anywhere."

The door behind me opened, and I jerked my head around. My brother dropped his gaze to my father's hand holding mine, then quirked an eyebrow at me.

"He's getting tired again, Ro. I think he's had enough excitement for today." When I turned back to my dad, I smirked. He was snoring softly.

"Yeah, he doesn't stay awake very long. Do you want to hang around here, or shall we head out?"

"Will he be okay by himself?" Why was I worried about him now? He'd never cared about me. But his frailty still called out to me. I wasn't a cruel man. I'd seen enough of that to last me a lifetime, and this man had caused much of it. Yet I couldn't find it in me to strike back. All the things I'd thought of saying to him if I'd ever get the chance dissipated. It didn't matter anymore. I'd come here for me as much I had for Roman. The chance of closure was here, right now, in front of me.

"Yes, his nurse is here now. He won't be alone, Ry. The nurse will call me if something happens. C'mon, you look beat."

I let go of Dad's hand and laid it gently on the blanket. Gingerly, I rose to my feet, the crick in my spine shooting stabs of pain through my body. The tension from over nine hours on my bike plus the mental overload caught up with me. I was suddenly exhausted.

Together we walked out of the room and down the stairs.

"I've put your bike in the garage. I thought I'd drive you to my place. You've probably had enough of concentrating on the road."

"Yeah, that's great. I could use a shower." I gave him a sly look. "And a beer wouldn't go amiss either."

"Mallory, there will be a meal, a beer, and a bed with your name on it when we get home. It's not far. Grab your bag, and we can go."

When we walked through the kitchen and into the four-car garage, I grinned. My brother had always had a passion for cars, and in the middle sat a shiny Shelby Mustang. "I can guess which is yours."

"Yeah, I love my car. What car have you got?" Roman asked.

"I don't have one. I just use my bike. Dan has a BMW, and Archer has a fuck-off-sized Ford pickup. Seriously, you could live in that truck. It's huge." Oops. I'd mentioned both Dan and Archer, but my brother didn't blink an eye. Still, I didn't look at Roman as I dumped my bag into the trunk and sat next to him. "I need to call them when we get to your place. They'll be worried about me."

"Yeah, no problem. Take all the time you want. You wanna tell me about your life now? What do you do? Did you finish college?"

"Yeah, I finished top of my class. It was hard work to begin with. I had nowhere to live and no money to buy anything." I ignored my brother's sharp intake of breath. "I got a room in a dorm and then maxed myself out in student loans and grants. I got a small scholarship too. I found a job, and I met Archer, and everything got better after that. For a while anyway…"

"You must be very proud of yourself, bro. I feel like a fake and a fraud now. I've taken everything that's been handed to me. Yes, I had to work hard through college, but I didn't have to juggle a job and money worries to get good grades. I had it easy."

It took us fifteen more minutes to reach Roman's place. He parked in an underground parking garage from where we took the elevator to his apartment. I chuckled when he pressed the button for his floor.

"What, no penthouse and a private code for the ride up to your floor?" I cocked my eyebrow.

"What? No. We've got a good-sized place, but I'm not a penthouse type of guy."

"I used to be. Archer had, well, he still has, one of those apartments."

The ping signaled our floor, and the doors slid open, letting us out. We walked a short way down the corridor to his door.

"Hey, Marcus?" Roman called out as we entered. Photographs of all sizes in black and white frames covered the walls of the large hallway. I followed my brother into the spacious living area. "Come on in, Ry. Meet the man who keeps me in my place."

A tall, broad, and incredibly handsome man walked toward me, his dark eyes twinkling and his mouth curled up in a welcoming smile.

"Mallory, it's wonderful to meet you. Roman has spoken about you so much. It's good to see you two together again."

"Marcus, it's great to meet you too." I held out my hand for him, but he dragged me into a big bear hug.

"Okay, Marc, let him go." Chuckling, Roman pulled me back. "I'll show you to your room. You can shower and call your men before we eat."

He led me back into the hallway and pushed open a door on the left-hand side. The walls of the good-sized room were painted a soft gray, which complimented the navy-blue-and-white bedding of the large bed. Just like in the hallway and living room, photographs covered the walls and surfaces.

"Marcus is a photographer, so we have masses of pictures everywhere," Roman said as I studied the ones on the dresser.

"They're really good. He's very talented." I grinned when I held up one of my brother pulling a goofy face. Just then, my cell phone rang, and I almost dropped the picture. "I'd better get that. I should've called by now. They'll be pissed at me."

"I'll leave you to it. There's no rush."

I grabbed my phone and answered. "Hey, Archer."

"Hi, honey, how are you doing? We've been worried," he asked quietly, but his voice was clipped.

"Are you together?"

"Yeah, you're on speaker," Dan answered. "Please tell us how it went. Did you meet your brother?"

"Sorry, it's been a crazy day. Yes, I met Roman, and it's, hell, it's amazing to see him again. We've just gotten back to his place. He guessed I wouldn't want to stay at the house. And I've met his boyfriend, Marcus."

The phone went quiet, so quiet I pulled the phone away from my ear to look at the screen, but I hadn't lost the connection.

"Your brother's gay?" Archer's voice was dangerously soft, the telltale sign of his anger simmering just under the surface. Dan shushed him.

"Carter, how do you feel about that?" Thank god for Dan being the calm one.

"It was a shock for sure, but hell, not much I can say, really. He chose never to confront our father with it, and my father chose to ignore it. Maybe that's what I should've done." I let out a dry laugh.

"No fucking way. You could never have lived your life as a secret. We wouldn't have met if you hadn't come out to your family," Archer snapped.

"Archer, calm down. It doesn't matter. It was years ago, and I have you now. I have both of you for reasons I could've lived without, but we make our own journeys, and I chose to be honest to myself. I don't regret it, and I doubt my brother would choose to do it differently."

"What about your father, Car? Did you see him today?" Dan asked gently.

"Yeah, yeah, I did. It's not looking good for him. It was difficult. He cried when he saw me and wouldn't let go of my hand. He just kept saying he was sorry. It was hard for me, but dammit, I needed to hear that."

"Oh baby, that's so good. I'm happy for you. What about your mom?" Archer sounded less tense now. I appreciated his protectiveness, but sometimes he tended to overdo it, and I was happy he was back to his normal warm self

"You know, he never mentioned her, and neither did my brother. When we left, Roman said dad's nurse was there, not that my mom was. Weird. I'll have to ask him. Anyway, what have you been up to?" I pinched the bridge of my nose. A headache was brewing. Time to talk about something else, something that didn't make me tense.

"East came over, and we've agreed on a swimming pool, so he's going to start on that. Apart from that, not a lot. We went to work and then had a beer at the bar. Kes and the rest send their love and warn you not to stay away too long."

"Yeah, about that. I don't know how long he's got left. I'll talk more to Roman about it tonight and make a decision then. I really don't want to be away from you, but I might need to be here a little longer."

"You want us to fly up on Friday? We can do that," Dan said.

"Yeah, maybe. Let me see how the next couple of days go. I might be needing you both by then."

"Just say the word, Carter, and we're with you." Dan chuckled. "Does your brother know you have two boyfriends?"

I laughed. "He probably has figured it out by now. I let a couple of things slip. I might've mentioned both your cars and that you'd be worried about me. I'll tell him all about you tonight." I sighed. "I'd better go. I need a shower, and they're waiting for me so we can eat."

"Okay, call us anytime, day or night. We can be with you in a couple of hours if you need us," Dan pleaded.

"I will. I love you."

"We love you too. Night, hon," they said together.

After rushing through a shower, I toweled off, pulled on clean jeans and a Henley, and hurried to my brother and his boyfriend.

Forty Eight

Carter

"Two? Wow. I'm impressed." Marcus grinned unabashedly. "I have my hands full with just him." Then he blushed as if he realized how that sounded. Roman and I just laughed louder.

"It's early days for us, and it isn't easy. There's a lot of history between us that has made it hard at times, but we're learning to talk more. Plus, the whole name thing didn't make it easy."

"What name thing?" Roman asked as he lifted his wine glass.

"That's what made the whole situation such a mess. I go by Carter now, not Mallory. I needed the change when I was forced away. It felt easier for me to start over. If I had stayed as Mallory, Dan would maybe have remembered me from when Archer and I were together."

"Why would Dan know to connect you and Archer together?" Marcus frowned. This was confusing as it was without factoring in the two bottles of wine we'd gone through over dinner.

"Because Dan and Archer are best friends. Hell, they dated through college." I sighed. God, this sounded bad.

"Fuck!" they both said, then burst out laughing.

"It's like daytime TV." Roman wiped his eyes, then stopped laughing when I hadn't joined in.

"Yeah, grieving for your fiancé, being banished from your home for the second time, and running scared, only to hope you've found someone good to take the pain away, made me think that too. I'm gonna crash." I got to my feet. "Thanks for dinner, Marcus."

Before I'd made it to the door, Roman was by my side. "I'm sorry, Mallory. I didn't mean to hurt you or belittle what you went through."

"It's okay. Thanks for letting me stay here." It really wasn't, but what else could I say without getting angry. It seemed I wasn't as ready to forgive everyone in my family as I'd thought. Exhaustion took over, and as soon as my head hit the pillow, I was asleep.

When I woke up the next morning, a flicker of panic coursed through me. This wasn't my bed, comfortable sure, but not mine. Where were Dan and Archer? Whose bed was it? I shoved the duvet from over my head and blinked my surroundings into focus. Oh yeah, Roman's place. Fuck, I had to go back to see my dad again. My stomach clenched. The adrenaline running through my body yesterday had burned out, and I was left with the hollow feeling of hurt or that I was about to get hurt again. He was going to die, and after what Roman had told me last night, I guessed it was going to be soon. As in, damn soon.

His cryptic comment on Valerie Hawkins came back to mind. Would he be able to talk about her again today? He might know something I could tell Archer. Something he could use against her.

I didn't bother with a shower and pulled on my jeans and the same Henley from last night, then followed the tantalizing smell of coffee to the kitchen. When I stepped in, Roman looked at me, chagrin still all over his face, and as he opened his mouth to speak, I held up my hand, stopping him.

"Stop shitting bricks, Ro. I'm not angry at you. It was a fair comment to make. It's fine. You've always been a dick. I should've remembered." I slapped his shoulder as Marcus laughed.

"Coffee?" he offered.

"Please." I leaned back against the door frame and accepted the proffered mug. "Ro, where's Mom? Shouldn't she be helping with Dad?"

The two men shared a glance.

"Mom left Dad last year. She just said she'd had enough and walked out. The divorce papers came through not long after, and he signed them and hasn't mentioned her since. She got the New York apartment and the house in Aspen, but nothing else."

"She didn't get in touch when he became ill?" They both looked at me as if I'd missed something. Then it clicked. "He already was ill. That fucking bitch."

"Yep." Roman shrugged. "You ready?"

"Yeah, I guess. What about Pippa? You said something about school?"

"Yeah, she went with Mom. C'mon, I'll tell you the rest on the way. Bye, hon." He kissed Marcus, and we took the elevator down to the parking garage. "Are your guys okay with you being here? I was surprised when you said you'd be coming on your own."

"I, um, left them a note." I scrubbed the back of my neck as he laughed.

"Are they giving you grief?" I shook my head. "I wasn't surprised it took you so long to answer the letter, but I'd just about given up on you getting in touch."

"What do you mean? I only got the letter the night before. Your lawyer gave it to me when I was at work."

Roman white-knuckled the steering wheel. "What? Not that I don't believe you because of course I do, but I hired Dukas weeks ago. Why did it take him so long? You need to tell me what happened, Ry. Or do you want me to call you Carter? I don't mind."

"Nah, let's not confuse Dad with that. He's got enough to deal with. I still can't get over Mom. I thought she'd be ready to get her hands on all his money."

"She knew she wasn't getting any. I guess she thought at least she'd get the houses by divorcing him. Anyway, fuck her. Tell me what went on with the letter."

For the rest of the ride, I filled him in, but he still shook his head. "He told me he'd done it when he first got there and was waiting for your reply."

"Well, he didn't, and I guess that after I turned his offer of a date down, he thought he might as well hand it over." I snickered. "And I think Archer and Dan had gone to see him when I was on my way here, which is why I couldn't tell them. Maybe you need to call him back before they rip him apart."

"Oh, I'll be calling him all right," he snarled.

As soon as we walked in the door, we met Dad's nurse, a good-looking fortysomething guy with warm eyes. "Hey, guys." He held his hand out. "You must be Mallory. He's been talking about you. He seems happy to have you back here. Roman, he wants you to get the large black leather wallet from his bedroom. He said you can't miss it. It's folder-sized. He's restless this morning. I'm guessing it's important for him to speak to you, but don't let him tire himself out. He's really not doing all that great anymore. I'm going to speak to his doctor and bring him up to date, but I don't think you have many days left with him."

"Thanks, Rudy. We'll see you this afternoon," Roman said with a grim look on his face.

"Yeah, be kind to one another." He smiled and stepped out the door.

"You want coffee before you go see him?" Roman asked, but I shook my head.

"What's in the wallet?" I asked him. What was so important that my father had to have it now?

Roman shook his head. "No idea. You go in. I'll get it."

I tapped on the door but didn't wait for him to reply.

"Hey, Pops." My kid name for him came out of nowhere, but his eyes lit up.

"Hey, son. Good to see you again. Where's your no-good brother?"

"He's gone to get the wallet you asked for."

"Ah, that's good. Now listen to me, Mallory. I know I don't deserve you coming to see me, and after I tell you this, you may not come back again. I wouldn't blame you." He pinned me with a fierce gaze, his eyes glittering with grim determination.

I gave him what I hoped was an equally stern look. "I have something to say too." I took a deep breath. "I forgive you for what you did. We both know how wrong it was, but I'm okay. I have a good life, friends I consider my family, and I'm loved and love back." I laid my hand on his, his fingers trembling under my touch, then let it drop.

"Thank you, son. I hope you still feel the same way after I've told you everything."

He sighed as Roman walked in with the wallet. "Where do you want this, Dad?"

"Give it to Mallory. Can you get some coffee or something, Ro? I'd like some time with Mallory alone, please."

"Uh? Yeah, okay, sure." Roman frowned. I shrugged, having no more idea than he did.

When the door closed behind Roman, my dad reached for my hand again.

"Listen, Mallory. I want to tell you something I wanted to keep from you, but you have a right to know. My actions may have caused you a great deal of harm and hurt."

"Dad, what do you mean?"

He squeezed my hand. "Don't interrupt me. Let me say my piece, and if you've any questions, everything I know is in that wallet. I'm sure you and your man, Archer, will know what to do with it."

I squirmed uncomfortably under his gaze.

"Valerie Hawkins hates you because she hates me. She and I had an affair a long time ago, from before you were born. It lasted a long while, five years or so. I know how wrong it was, and the only excuse I have is that I was young and easily tempted. She was so beautiful. Your mother knew and didn't care as long as she had me. But when Valerie began to make demands about divorces and us marrying, I ended it. But as you've learned, she is a vindictive woman and doesn't like to lose. I think she took my dismissing her out on you. When you showed up on the arm of her son, she knew she'd found the opportunity to hurt me, but even more so you. She contacted me, threatening to tell you about me. I told her you wouldn't care about my opinion. So that stopped that plan of hers. It took the worst kind of accident to really get her revenge. If she couldn't keep her son, you sure as hell weren't going to have him."

I gaped at him, not sure what I was hearing. Was she really that much of a bitch? Oh, hell yeah, she was. Then another thought crossed my mind, one that made me sick. Archer!

"Dad, for the love of god, please tell me Archer isn't your child." The coffee sloshed around in my stomach, getting ready to make its appearance.

"What? Good god, no. She already had him before she sank her talons into me." He sounded as horrified as I was.

"Thank fuck for that," I murmured, then burst out laughing. "Damn, Pops, I almost brought up my breakfast."

"Anyway, Mallory. I'm so sorry I was the cause she hates you, but please make good use of what's in there. It's all documented, and my lawyer has copies, but every bit of it is true. I hope it brings you and Archer some peace of mind."

"Okay, you gonna say any more than that?"

"No. Go and get your brother. We can talk for a few more minutes. Then I'm going to close my eyes for a while."

He patted my hand as I stood up. Smiling, I brushed the hair from his forehead, the skin clammy and damp under my fingertips.

When I entered the kitchen, Roman was raiding the fridge, probably looking for something more than the toast he'd had at home.

"Come on, he says he's got a few more minutes left in him."

I let Roman sit closest to him this time and tried to keep my eyes from straying to the wallet on the table. We talked quietly about something to do with work and moved on to stuff that had happened when we were kids. We joked and laughed for a while, and then my father's eyes drooped, and he fell asleep midsentence.

Neither of us was ready to leave him. I told Roman what my father had said about Archer's mother.

"That bitch had better watch her back," he grumbled.

My father slept for the rest of the day, but it seemed more than that. It felt like he was losing consciousness, drifting in and out of a deep sleep. Sometimes he recognized us; other times he was confused as to who we were. When Rudy came back for his night shift, we'd already decided to stay here for the night. Roman called Marcus to let him know about our plans. He offered to come over, but Roman declined. We both knew our father wasn't going to last much longer, and we prepared ourselves for a vigil through the night.

At least we were able to sit in comfortable chairs rather than stiff hospital chairs, which raised the question of why my father was at home and not in the hospital.

Roman laughed. "He was adamant he wanted to die at home. He said he wouldn't take his last breath in a place that smells of illness and disease, where you don't get a decent night's sleep because someone keeps waking you up to check if you're still alive."

"Sounds like Dad." I chuckled and took his hand in mine. My stomach gave a twinge. What if I hadn't been here when he took his last breath? What if we hadn't been able to make the rift between us disappear? It had been almost too little, too late, but I was grateful for the time I had with him now.

"Did he ever mention me after he threw me out?" I didn't know why this was important to me.

"Not for a long time. Then I caught him browsing through the photographs of you. He looked so lost. I asked him, and he told me that sometimes, in the blink of an eye, you make the worst decision of your life. When I tried to push for more, he'd already shut down, and the subject was closed. I'm sorry I didn't look for you. It was very selfish of me. When I realized I was gay, I balked from telling him. I took the coward's way out and left for college with my mouth firmly closed. I wasn't in denial, but I wasn't as strong as you. I couldn't own up and be proud. I wouldn't have known where to start surviving without the financial support, not like you did. I admire you so much. I'm so proud you're my brother. I'm not sure I deserve to be yours."

"Don't think like that. You did what was best for you. You're here now, and that means everything. You could've taken his money and left with Mom."

"I could never have done that. I owe him everything. He has given me the chance to be successful, to be good at my job. It's not the money I earn or the luxuries I can have. It's the pride he has for me. I can never pay him back for that. I want him to know I love him and he's not alone."

"Is that why you reached out to me? How did you find me?"

"I needed to have you with me because I wasn't strong enough to do this alone. I put your picture on social media, asking if anyone had seen you or knew you. A woman contacted me and said she'd seen you working in a bar when she was on vacation. As soon as she gave me an address, I sent Dukas to hand you the letter."

"He's a dick. You know that, right?" I sighed. What had Dan and Archer said to him?

"Yes, and he's been reprimanded and has lost his contract with us."

We sat silently, each holding our father's hands. Rudy came in and checked his blood pressure and heartbeat. He sent us a sad smile when he left us alone again.

My eyelids grew heavy, and I shifted in my chair, trying to stay awake. Roman was asleep, his head resting on his arms on the bed. I watched them both sleep, a sense of calm washing over me. I'd been right to come. I settled back down in the chair and closed my eyes for a moment.

Dad coughing in his sleep startled me awake. Beside me, Roman stretched his arms over his head. I straightened from my slouched position, wincing at the pain in my back and shoulders, and smoothed the hair from Dad's forehead. He calmed again, but soon another coughing fit had him struggling for breath. When he was quiet again, he gazed at us both, his eyes as clear as always, a sweet smile on his lips. "My boys, you make me proud."

Then the light faded from his eyes as he slipped away.

"Oh, no. Dad, no!"

Forty Nine

Dan

"Archer, calm down." I placed my hands on his shoulders and turned him around to face me. "He'll come home."

"Yeah, you sure about that? I'm not. His father died three weeks ago. The funeral was ages ago, and we haven't heard shit from him for days. Lucas isn't fucking helping. He just said to leave him alone, that he's with his brother. If I don't hear from him by tonight, I'm going there and dragging him home." He sagged against me. "I can't go on without him for much longer. We've been apart because of my shitty mother. Now his shitty father has done the same thing."

"Archer, stop being a dick. His father died because he had lung cancer. Your mother forced you apart by lying and cheating and acting despicably. Now come on, we promised Kes we'd show up for Denver's gig tonight." I kissed him softly, then held him close and deepened the kiss. I fisted my hands in his hair as he groaned into my mouth. I poured all my feelings for him into this kiss. I knew how stressed he was because I was too, but one of us had to keep some modicum of reason, or we'd both be going batshit crazy. Sex had all but been forgotten. We'd had a couple of nights we'd both needed it, but without Carter, it wasn't the same. We missed him too much.

Breaking apart, I wiped my thumb over his swollen lower lip, then kissed him chastely one more time.

Smiling, he smacked my ass. "Come on. We'd best be going." Like it had been him nagging me all afternoon.

The bar was packed, but Kes had told us he'd be keeping a booth for us. Both Kes and East were working, but they'd join us when Denver started to play. Paris waved at us and pointed us to the corner. We waved back and squeezed through the throng. Paris whispered something to Shelley, then nodded over to us. I caught their badly hidden smiles.

Hunter dropped two bottles of beer on the table, then disappeared again quickly. We sat and talked for a few minutes until Kes stopped at our booth.

"Hey, guys. Glad you could make it. It's crazy in here tonight. I'll be with you soon. East isn't any use behind the bar, so I'll send him over with a couple more beers. He always gets twitchy when Den's playing." Clapping Archer on the shoulder, he wandered off again.

East slipped in beside Archer just as Denver took a seat on his stool and picked up his guitar from the stand next to him. In mere seconds, the whole place went quiet. As the first tones floated in the air, I scanned around the room. Everyone was captivated by Denver's music, but no one more than Kes. He leaned against the pumps, his eyes fixed on his lover. No one dared order a drink while Denver was playing. I didn't even pay attention to the music. I was so transfixed on Kes and the love that poured from him. Christ, I missed Carter. We were getting there. We all were on our way to having what Kes had with his men. The three of us together. But now, as much as I'd castigated Archer over his doubts, I was having them myself.

The lights switched off, darkness shrouding the bar. People were talking in hushed voices, and chairs scraped over the floor. Denver started to play. It was a faster tempo than his usual set and familiar, although I couldn't put my finger on it. But, as always, he was rocking it. Then the tones of another instrument joined the guitar—a piano. Archer let out a moan and jumped to his feet, rocking the table. We still couldn't see anything, but now I recognized the melody of Tom Petty's "American Girl." Then a voice started to sing, and fuck, I'd know that voice anywhere. Carter, it was Carter playing. I clung to Archer's hand as I stood next to him as our man sang not about an American girl but an American boy. The song, usually so fast and hard, with a heavy drumbeat, had been slowed down to a romantic love song. Denver stopped playing and let Carter continue to stun the whole bar.

For the first time in weeks, my heart beat properly again. I'd missed him so much. Archer sniffed as tears rolled down his face. This version wasn't new to him; he'd heard it played before. We held on to each other as Carter sang and played so brilliantly. The lights had gone back on, although still dimmed, but they allowed me to see him. He was nervous. He had his eyes either lowered to his hands or clenched shut. As he came to the end of the song, I expected him to stop, but even as the clapping and the cheers continued, he started another.

One he had on his iPod, and one of the few I'd heard him singing along to: X Ambassadors' "Unsteady." I held back a sob this time because I was feeling more than a little unsteady myself. Denver joined him, and they sang beautifully together. Had they practiced this? If so, when had the little shit gotten back here? I snorted. As if I could be mad at him? I might be pissed at Kes for keeping this from us, though. I sought him out. He was as emotional as both Archer and me, so maybe I'd let him off the hook.

When the song finished, Denver stood and held out his hand for Carter. The bar went crazy—whistling, stamping, and hollering. Paris was crying in the arms of Conn, who had the hugest grin on his face. Standing next to him were two men I didn't know, but one of them had to be Carter's brother; he looked just like him, only a few years younger. They were clapping and cheering along with the rest of the crowd. Finally, it quieted down, and Carter stood still, staring at us, his face tense and his eyes wide as he waited for our reactions.

I grasped Archer's hand and dragged him up onstage. I stopped in front of Carter and lifted my hand to his face.

"Good to see you again, baby." I pulled him against me as Archer wrapped himself around Carter. We stood for a few moments, reveling in each other's presence, the audience forgotten. Then Archer broke away and kissed Carter so tenderly.

"God, I've missed you two." Carter sighed. "I've missed you so fucking much. Do you forgive me?"

"What for?" Archer asked.

"Everything, leaving you behind, not letting you come to visit. Not telling you I was coming home. This little stunt." He shot us a sheepish glance, but a playful glint sparkled in his eye.

"You know what? I think you're good. As long as you're back for good, I'm happy. I'm so fucking happy," Archer said and then pounced on him, his mouth devouring Carter's. After a minute, he pulled back and kissed me with the same fervor, then pushed my face against Carter's.

As soon as my mouth touched Carter's, I moaned. I got lost in his taste and his scent, and I couldn't stop my hands from roaming over his body.

"We need to go, like right now. C'mon, I need you in our bed."

"But my brother..." Carter stammered.

"Your brother will understand." I took his hand and led him through the parting crowd. Kes, his arms around Denver and East, gave me a watery smile as we walked out of the bar.

Carter sat between the two of us in the front of Archer's truck. I was still holding his trembling hand while Archer rested his hand on Carter's thigh, the other on the steering wheel. No one spoke, but a sweet calmness surrounded us. Carter cleared his throat, and the quiet was broken.

"When did you get home?" Archer asked, his voice tense.

"This afternoon. I wanted to surprise you. Was I wrong?" Carter sounded wary.

"No, honey. I've missed you, and I need you. I hate that you went somewhere else before seeing us, but to hear you play again was something special. Thank you."

"It's been a really hard time. I'll tell you everything tomorrow. Right now, I need you. I need you to reclaim again." Carter's words came out as a plea that shot straight to my dick.

"We can do that, Car. We need you just as much," I whispered in his ear.

Archer pulled up into the driveway and killed the engine. When he turned to Carter, his emerald-green eyes were dark and hooded, desire blazing from them.

"Let's go," Archer growled in a low and husky voice full of dark promise.

We all but raced up the stairs. Archer made it to the bedroom first and ripped his shirt off his body, then his pants and underwear. We were not far behind, but then we stood there in the middle of the bedroom, awkwardly gazing at each other.

"This feels like the first time. Why am I nervous?" Carter sighed.

"Because you've changed." I cupped his face. "Your life has shifted again. You've found your family and then lost a part of it. You're bound to feel different. It's not a bad thing, baby. I changed after my father died. I became a stronger man. You have too."

Archer moved in behind Carter and placed his hands softly on his shoulders, then slid them lazily down his arms. He traced his fingers over Carter's inner arms as he worked his way back up. Carter let his head drop back on Archer's shoulder. A deep shudder ricocheted through his body. I stepped in front of him and smoothed my hands over his collarbone and down his chest. His nipples hardened under my fleeting touch, but I carried on caressing his torso and glided my fingers over his heaving chest and down to his six-pack, which flexed and contracted as I left featherlight strokes.

Archer followed my pattern over Carter's back until our hands met at his hips. I slipped mine behind him and grasped his butt cheeks while Archer reached forward and traced the groove of his oblique muscles. Carter panted, moaning heavily. I grazed my mouth over the flushed, heated skin, where goose bumps bloomed under my tongue. Sweat broke over him as he rocked himself between us. Carter was struggling now as his senses overloaded.

"What do you want, Carter? Tell me where you want me," I crooned to him and flicked the tip of my tongue over his pebbled nipple.

"I need your mouth on me. Take me deep. I need it, need you," he keened.

Archer shifted us over to the bed—Carter too far gone now to do anything other than shuffle along—and laid Carter down. I dropped long, wet kisses over his body and let the heat of my breath wash over his beautiful cock. I wanted nothing more than to capture the thread of precum that hung down, pooling on his stomach, but I needed him desperate. Archer had claimed his mouth. With his hands in Carter's hair, he poured his everything into his kiss. Carter writhed and squirmed. I licked down the crease between his thigh and groin, then slipped between his parted legs. As I nudged his tight sac, he punched his hips up, crying out, begging for more.

It was time. I lapped over his sac, making him roar again and thrust against me, then slid my tongue up the length of his dick. I didn't think he'd ever been this hard before. He wouldn't last long.

Archer had captured one nipple with his teeth, and his fingers plucked and teased the other. Carter fisted the sheet, panting. When Archer tilted his face, I winked at him, then took the swollen head of Carter's dick into my mouth. Sucking hard, I twirled my tongue over and over the satin-smooth skin, drinking down the burst of liquid weeping from him. I gently scraped my teeth over his frenulum, which made him thrust up into my mouth. I drew him in deeper so that he nudged the back of my throat, then pulled off him, only to blow cool air over the head.

"Fuckfuckfuck. Don't stop. I'm close. I'm so close," Carter mewled, his eyes screwed tight shut, his neck long as he tipped his head back. The tendons were taut, and his Adam's apple bobbed as he swallowed hard.

"Not yet, baby. I'm gonna be inside you when you come. When you give it all to Archer." Archer scooted away from Carter, opened the drawer of the nightstand, and took out the lube, which he handed over to me.

"Take him, Daniel. Bring him back to us," he said softly and kissed Carter again.

Kneeling up, I pushed Carter's legs up, opening him up to me. "Hold your legs, my love." Carter wrapped his hands around his thighs and pulled them up to his chest.

My mouth watered at the sight of his tight hole exposed to me. I needed to taste him before I entered him. I swiped my tongue over his hole, drenching it, then teasing the oh-so-sensitive ring of nerve endings. He relaxed, which allowed me to dip the tip of my tongue inside, stabbing in and out as he squirmed. His legs shook as he held them tight to his chest. I drew back, cracked the lid, and poured the cool gel onto my fingers. The next moment I was back at his ring, and as I slipped my tongue inside, I added my middle finger. Fucking him with my tongue and finger made my dick so hard. I had to be inside him before I exploded. I let my fingers take over, and soon he was riding three fingers, grinding down hard, greedy for me. I pulled my fingers out and quickly coated my cock with lube. With his hole still open for me, I plunged all the way in.

We both cried aloud. Carter let go of his legs and wrapped them around my waist, holding me still inside him. But I pulled back, leaving just the head of my cock inside him, then thrust hard again. Archer had Carter's length in his fist, and we worked in synch, his strokes matching my thrusts.

"I'm gonna come. I can't hold on," Carter cried.

"Hold on, baby. Wait for me. We can come together," I moaned. I wouldn't last too much longer. His ass squeezed me tight as he tried to stave off his orgasm. I pulled out, ignoring his anguish, and flipped him over onto his hands and knees. With one powerful thrust, I sank deep inside him again. I wanted Archer's mouth on Carter's dick, so I pulled him upright against my chest. I kept rocking in and out of his hot channel. "Take him, Archer. I won't last much longer."

Archer lay beneath him, and I lowered him back down. With his head between Carter's legs, Archer swallowed Carter's cock. With my hands on his hips now, I picked up speed and fucked him harder and faster than I'd ever had before. My spine tingled as my thigh muscles tensed.

"Now, Carter. Come now," I cried out as my orgasm fired from me. A second later, he came, and his muscles clamped around my ass, holding me in a viselike grip. Archer sucked him harder as he took every drop of his release. Carter's muscles relaxed, allowing me to slide out of him and collapse next to Archer, my head near his dick. His balls were high and tight in his body, ready to blow. I lifted my face and licked his length.

As Carter pulled his softening dick out of Archer's mouth, he fell to the other side of Archer's body. I expected him to add his mouth to mine, but he didn't. Instead, pushing me gently away, Carter swung his leg over Archer's waist and grabbed his dick, then slowly sank down on him.

The noise from Archer as Carter slid down his rock-hard length made my dick twitch again. I shifted between Archer's legs and spread them while I wet the fingers of my other hand and slipped them into his asshole. As Carter rode Archer, I fucked his ass with my fingers. I curled them and swiped over his sweet spot. Archer bucked up his hips violently as I relentlessly tortured his prostate.

"Fuck!" he yelled, then stilled. His ass clamped on my fingers as he came, pouring himself inside our lover.

Carter collapsed on top of Archer, his shoulders shaking. I pulled out of and away from Archer and swung my legs out of bed. Archer wrapped his arms around Carter, whispering sweet words of love to him.

Letting them have their moment, I ambled to the bathroom and started the shower. We needed more than a warm cloth to clean with. When I walked back in, the two men I loved more than anything in the world were sitting up, Carter in Archer's lap with his legs wrapped around his waist.

Carter gave me a wobbly smile, his eyes wet with tears, and held out his hand to me.

"I love you, Dan. I love you so fucking much." He hiccuped, which made me smile.

"I love you more, baby." I hugged him and kissed the top of his head. "You ready to stand? We should clean up."

"Yeah, I'm okay, although I might have a gallon of cum in my ass." Laughing, he wiggled on Archer's lap.

"Hey, don't dump it on me, Halston." Archer slapped his ass, and suddenly the mood was so much lighter.

As Carter stepped under the hot spray, I grabbed the sponge and his shower gel and washed his body. He squirmed as I ran my soapy hands down the crack of his ass, and I squeezed a cheek. "Stay still. You said it yourself you were leaking."

"Eww, you're gross. You know that, right?" He wrinkled his nose, but he laughed.

"Head back, hon." Archer kissed his neck, then washed his hair.

"I've missed this," I said quietly as I finished washing him. "These little moments. I've missed them." I took Carter's mouth, kissing him soundly, then turned my attention to Archer. "I feel whole again. Do you?"

Archer nodded, swallowing hard, and kissed me. "Yeah, I love you, Dan. I couldn't have gotten through this without you."

"Come on. It's happy time. We're together again." Carter slung his arms around our shoulders. "Let's get back into bed. I want to tell you what happened."

Fifty

Archer

Oh, god, the feeling as Carter slid down my cock was sublime. The heat of his ass mixed with the slickness from Dan's orgasm almost had me shooting my load before he'd fully gone down on me. I'd wanted to rip him away from the stage the moment I'd heard the first bar of "American Girl," or "Boy," as he'd always sung when we lived together.

I'd had to let Dan take charge when we got into the bedroom, or I would've pinned Carter down and fucked him hard, not caring how he felt. I'd just needed to be inside him. But Dan's way had been the right way. I'd never expected the earth-shattering, heart-stopping, mind-altering connection I felt from both of them. If I'd ever doubted we were supposed to be together as a threesome, that moment had cleared my doubts.

Now, as we lay together, in a quickly changed bed, under crisp sheets, I was ready to hear Carter's news. "You gonna keep us guessing, hon?" I joked with him as he was sandwiched between us.

"I'm trying to find the right words. My father and I made peace with each other. It was easier than I thought it would be. He admitted his mistake. I realized I've moved on, grown up. I've lived through pain and emotions so much worse than my father's rejection. The, what was it, ten-hour ride back? That gave me a lot of time to think about myself. Who I was. Who I was when I was alone. Who I was when I was with my buddies at work. Who I was when I was with the men who have become my family. But mostly who I was when I was with you.

"When I stood in front of, first my brother and then my father, I realized I'm still Mallory Halston. A good man, a man worthy of the love of the people who surround me every day and a man who loves and is loved. So I forgave him. It was worth it to see the love shine from his eyes again. We talked, we joked, and then the day he died, he gave me, gave us"—Carter looked at me—"the chance of freedom, of clear consciences, and a brighter future. For that, I am grateful."

Dan spoke up, and his words sounded forced, painful. "You said you're Mallory Halston, not Carter, but Mallory. Have I lost the man I fell in love with?"

"Oh, Daniel, no. No way. I'm the man you helped me become, the man who took a deep breath of fresh air in and cast out the bad, all because of you. I love you, Daniel. Call me Carter. That's who I am to you. But I just feel the man I used to be has finally caught up with the new man I've become. Don't ever doubt my love for you. You're the catalyst, the man who brought the three of us back together."

"What do we call you now, honey? It's going to confuse a hell of a lot of people that your name's Mallory, not Carter."

"I want to still be Carter. I don't feel like I've lost the part of me that was Mallory anymore if that makes sense to you. I'm just happy *I* know who I am."

"What was the freedom your father promised you?" I tried to take in everything he'd said, making sure I didn't focus on just his epiphany.

"Well, that's something I'll be able to fill you in with soon." He smiled and leaned across to peck my lips.

"Nuh-uh, that's not going to work, Carter, and you know it." I was happy he'd chosen to still be the new version of him.

"It'll all become clear soon, like, really soon." He grinned. The little shit knew I wasn't going to stop.

"Mallory Carter Halston, quit your shit and talk," I snarled.

He glanced at Dan for reassurance, but Dan shrugged. "Babe, if you want to sleep tonight, you need to spill."

"Fine." He sighed and turned to me. "I'll tell you one thing, but the rest has to wait. Okay?"

I nodded.

"Well, it seems my father and your mother had an affair. It started before I was born and lasted about five years or so. And before you look at me all horrified, you aren't my half brother. You'd been born before they started their relationship. Part of your mother's hatred of me may be because my father refused to leave my mother and marry her. After she threatened to expose him, he reminded her she had more to lose. A woman never comes out well from an extramarital affair. Would her career survive the scandal? So she left him alone, but as you know, your mother doesn't forgive and forget. That's why she hates me so much."

"Wow. My poor father. He doesn't deserve this any more than we do." Suddenly, not speaking to him for so long hurt. I needed to contact him again, see if we could repair our relationship.

"That's all fine and dandy, Carter, but where does our future happiness come into this?" Dan asked.

"Well, you see, my father kept a dossier on Valerie Hawkins's antics and behaviors in her personal life but, more importantly, in her work and her rise through the ranks. He handed this to me just before he died, telling me to do the right thing for me and you, Archer. Something to settle the score and to give us peace and satisfaction."

"What have you done with the information, honey?" I dreaded to think who he might've handed it over to.

"Oh, ease up, tiger. I gave it to Lucas. He'll be in touch." Carter's smile morphed into a smirk.

"Oh, Carter, sugar, you're in so much trouble." I dove on him as he shrieked with laughter, which soon turned to moans as the three of us took pleasure from each other again.

This time it was my turn to have my ass filled, and dammit, I didn't think I'd ever felt happier.

As we settled again, Carter said in a sleep-laden voice, "Love you both so very much."

He was asleep before either of us could answer him.

"Really? What time?....Okay, yep. Sure, yes, I'll tell him. Thank you, Lucas....Okay, I'm sure he'll call you....Yep, bye."

The name Lucas woke me up more than Carter talking. Shifting onto my side, I looked up at him. He was sitting up, but the call must've woken him because his cheeks wore creases from his pillow, and his hair was all mussed up. He had never looked more gorgeous.

"What's going on, Car? Where's Dan?" I pushed myself up and pecked a kiss on his mouth.

"He's gone to make coffee. It looks like everything's going or has gone down. Where's your iPad?"

"It's downstairs. Carter, what's going on? You're freaking me out."

"Put the TV on and get the news channel up. You're *so* gonna want to see this."

Dan walked into the room, carrying a tray with three coffees. "What's going on?"

"That's what I'm trying to work out." I took a cup from him and handed it to Carter, then grabbed one for myself, which I almost dropped again as I stared at the TV. Or more at the ticker that was running along the bottom of the screen.

Supreme Court Judge Valerie Hawkins arrested on charges of blackmail and extortion. Press conference at 10:00 a.m.

Carter had a smug smile on his face. "You did this?" I asked him.

"Well, theoretically, my father did it. He was planning to do this himself, but his illness got in the way. He left instructions with his attorney, so it would've gone to the police after he died. I think he wanted to do this for me, for us. When I handed the dossier over to Lucas, he took care of the rest."

"This is huge. I need to call my father. Is he involved, do you know?"

"I don't know, Arch. I'm sorry. Maybe you should call Mason."

What should I do? I'd always known my mother was a bitch, but I'd never expected it to be this bad. "Did you read it? The dossier, did you read it?"

"Of course, I did." He was really grinning now.

"Then tell me."

And so he did. My mother had accepted money for both putting and keeping people in and out of jail. She'd bribed and blackmailed a large number of individuals, including police officers, lawyers, and other judges. I couldn't believe the depths she'd gone to, to rise above others.

"How has nobody come forward before? This really doesn't make sense. Hell, I'm not surprised after what she did to us. That's probably how she got the cops to tell you I'd died. Shit. I can't take it."

At ten o'clock, we watched the press conference. The chief of police explained the charges and the ongoing investigation. Then my mother's attorney read out a statement, refuting the charges and proclaiming a witch hunt against her. He said she was ready to fight to prove her innocence.

We all laughed aloud at this. I couldn't believe the bullshit this guy was talking. Then another statement was read, this time by my father's lawyer. I clutched Carter's hand. Dan sat next to me, his arm around my waist, holding me against him. I felt safe between them, cocooned in the bed, and held tight as I watched my family fall apart. Not that there was any love lost between her and me, but I'd pushed my father away because of her.

This statement was perfunctory, issued from my father's home in Florida. Huh? "When did he move there?"

His lawyer said Mr. Hawkins had no involvement with his ex-wife and no knowledge of any charges against her.

"When did he divorce my mother?"

The screen flicked back to the anchorman. I'd had enough. I snatched up the remote, switched the TV off, and flopped back down in the bed. Burrowing deep in the covers, I tried to block out all the sights and sounds around me, but the voices in my head shouted for attention. How did I turn them off?

My cell phone rang, but I ignored it. I didn't want to speak to anyone. Dan was talking, but with the covers over my head, I couldn't hear the words.

"Archer, it's Mason. He needs to talk to you." Dan pulled back the duvet.

"No, not now. I'll talk to him later," I mumbled.

"Best to do it now, Arch."

The next thing I knew, Carter was under the covers with me. He cupped my face, worry lines marring his forehead.

"I fucked this up, didn't I? I should've told you, warned you what was happening. I'm sorry, Arch. I thought I was doing the right thing. Lucas told me you didn't want the ins and outs of it, that you simply wanted her brought down."

"No, honey, it's not you. I promise you. It's just overwhelming. I think the biggest shock is my father. If he divorced her, why didn't he contact me? I refused to see him after he wouldn't tell me what she'd done. But after getting divorced, he could've reached out."

"Maybe he wasn't sure how you would take it. You'd banished them both. I doubt if he thought you'd welcome him with open arms."

Damn, I hated that all made sense. It was my fault we'd stopped speaking. "Fuck." I threw back the duvet, then pushed myself up to a sitting position and ran my hands through my hair. "Okay, it's time for action."

Fifty One

Archer

"I need to see my brother. He's at Kes's place, but I'd like him to stay here if you don't mind." We'd made it out of bed and were making breakfast.

"Of course. I can't wait to meet him. He looks like you. Not as gorgeous, obviously, but there was a definite similarity." Dan ran his hand down my back, and I leaned into him, cherishing his touch.

"Do you wanna call him and invite him over for brunch?" Archer asked.

"Yeah, but I'm sure Kes and his guys will come too. You'd better make more pancakes, Dan." I swatted his backside, then grabbed my cell.

Twenty minutes later, the room was full of people, laughing and kidding around as if they'd known each other for years. Warmth flowed through me. My family, not all by blood but certainly all by heart. And one of them who held half of my heart walked over, a huge smile on his face.

"You look happy." Dan dropped a kiss on my mouth.

"I am. This is more than I ever imagined. When I moved here, I was so lost and broken, but the people I met helped me heal. I made friends, who became more to me. They became my family. Then you came along, always flirting, making me feel something again." I cupped his face in my hands. "You gave me a chance to be happy again. I love you, Dan. I don't think you realize just how much."

"Trust me, I do. The faith you had in me, the trust you gave me, made me fall in love with you. I love seeing you so happy with Archer and me. And now with your brother. It's wonderful to see *and* be a part of."

As if he sensed we were talking about him, Roman glanced up. He excused himself from the conversation with Denver and East, sauntered over, and slung his arm over my shoulder.

"Have you told them yet?" he asked me.

"No, and I don't see what difference it would make if they knew. Leave it, Ro."

Dan arched his eyebrows. "What? What haven't you told us?"

"Nothing, it's not important." I shot daggers at my brother, but he laughed, a smug expression on his face.

"Yeah, not important." He snorted. "Leave everything to the two of us. You're looking at the Forbes 30 Under 30 list headliners."

Dan's eyes widened, and he swallowed hard, pink tinging his cheeks.

"Nice one, asshole." I pushed past my brother, who at least had the decency to look uncomfortable. "That wasn't your news to share."

"Carter—" Dan started.

"I thought you were going by Mallory again?" Roman still hadn't put a lock on his damn mouth.

"Oh, for fuck's sake, Roman. Please stop talking. I don't mind Dan calling me that. It's who I am to him," I snapped, my voice louder than I'd intended.

Archer jerked his head in our direction, his eyes darting between the three of us. I shook my head, but it was too late. He reached us in four large strides.

"What is it? Carter, you look like death warmed over. What's going on?" Archer frowned at my brother. It seemed he hadn't forgiven him yet. He still had issues with Roman's choice of lawyer and the way he'd behaved toward me.

"Nothing. Roman was shooting his mouth off. He's always done it." I tried to lighten the mood, even though Archer didn't buy it, and Dan still looked like he was going to be sick.

"We'll talk about this later. C'mon, let's take this party outside." Archer took my hand and led me through the packed kitchen.

Everyone followed our lead, and we were all enjoying the still warm weather. Soon, the temperatures would drop, and snow would fall, covering the mountains around us in a white blanket. The ski vacations would start, which meant the bar would have an influx of tourists.

Archer kept hold of my hand while Dan had his arm around my waist. Neither of them showed any sign of letting me go. Roman had found his way back to Marcus after a mouthed apology. He knew he'd fucked up.

After another hour, the guys made a noise about getting back to pick up Phoebe from Denver's mother.

Kes made his way over to me. "It really is good to have you back. Will you be coming back to work?"

My mouth dropped open. Was he for real? "Um, yes, I'd loved to. Never in a million years did I expect you to keep a place for me. I don't have to be the manager again. I let you down. A couple of calls while I was away wasn't good enough. I'm sorry, Kes."

"Carter...or is it Mallory now?"

"I don't mind. Whatever you want." I wrapped my arms around my waist, something I hadn't needed to do for a long while now.

"Okay, Carter. I haven't given your job to anyone else. I consider you my friend. It was understandable that you needed to be away, to take some time off to get your thoughts sorted. I want you to run my bar, but I don't know if you'd want that too. You've had some massive changes in your life. I don't want you to feel you have to come back."

"Roman told you, didn't he?" I shook my head. The little fucker.

"Yeah, but it was more about him and how he felt about it. He's a lot younger than you and not just in age but in experience as well. He didn't have to grow up fast and learn to live in the real world. He hasn't felt the pain and grief you have. I know his father, the man he had a good relationship with, has just died, but that's not the same as losing the love of your life. Be patient with him. He doesn't know how to do this with you any more than you do. It's only money, Carter. It doesn't have to mean anything if you don't want it to."

"I guess so." I scratched the back of my neck as I worked through what he'd just said. "But to get back to the point, when do you want me back at work?"

"Tomorrow's fine. Just pick up your normal hours unless you'd like to lose some of your late nights. Paris is happy to work more shifts. I think he could use the money."

"I'll talk to him and see what he wants to do. I'll see you tomorrow, then. And thank you for yesterday. It was perfect."

"You were amazing. The stage is yours whenever you want it." He chuckled as East wrapped his arm around my waist and kissed my cheek.

"Hey. Keep your hands and lips off my man," Dan shouted and yanked me out of East's clutches, laughing, and hugged me close to his body. I didn't think I'd ever seen him this happy, and warmth filled my heart.

The three of us stood in our doorway, waving our friends goodbye. Roman and Marcus were still here but had decided not to stay. They understood the stress Archer was under. Roman had apologized to Archer and Dan for being so flippant earlier.

"You want to talk, or are we good?" I whispered into Archer's neck as he pulled me close to him.

"Carter, hon, we are so good. Is the money your father left you going to make a difference?"

I shook my head, unable to answer him. Mainly because I was angry with my father that he'd thought leaving me half of his fortune would. But after our private conversations, I knew it wasn't his way of apologizing. He'd never changed his will, so I would've gotten it anyway.

What I would do with it, though, I had no idea. I didn't need private jets and holiday islands. I wasn't saying they wouldn't be good, but not what I was looking for in my life.

"Then nothing changes. Things are going to be weird enough with all the shit going on in my family without adding yours to the mix."

"I guess so. Enough thinking about that. We need to clear up the kitchen."

But we entered a clean kitchen. My brother and Marcus had loaded the glasses and plates into the dishwasher, put the leftovers Saran wrapped in the fridge, and even wiped down the counter and kitchen island.

"Whoa. Thanks, guys." Dan patted them both on their backs. "Awesome job."

"We're gonna head off. Marcus has an idea for a shoot he wants to scope out." Roman nudged his boyfriend. "He never stops working. We'll be around for a couple more days, but then I need to get back to work."

"You got somewhere to stay?" I was feeling guilty about them not staying here.

"Yeah, we got a cabin down by the lake. Denver arranged it for us." He put a hand on my arm. "I'm sorry I was a dick. I shouldn't have done that."

"Hey, no sweat. I would've told them, but with all the crap from Archer's mom, I decided now wasn't the time." I pulled him in for a hug, which he reciprocated fiercely.

Then they were gone, and the kitchen was empty, even my men had disappeared. I wandered off in search of Dan and Archer and found them in the living room, where they were watching the news on the TV. His mother was still the hot topic. The debating had started over how someone in a position of such authority had managed to get away with this for so long.

"How bad is it?" I sat next to Archer.

"About as bad as it can be. More and more people have come forward, all citing her for blackmail. Some incriminating themselves in the process, but it seems they might be striking a deal with the police. Not so much an amnesty, but only time will tell what happens to them. The police are asking people to come forward with any evidence, and it's pouring in. She doesn't have a leg to stand on here. The case will go to trial, but it will take months. There's no way they'll let her slip through on a technicality."

Fifty Two

Six months later

Archer

"Are you ready?" Carter asked, even though it was a pointless question, and he was simply looking for something to say. I loved him for it.

"No, not in any way, but I have to do this. This is closure." I ran my hands through my hair for the thousandth time, then smoothed it back down again. Smiling, Carter ruffled it again.

"You look so much better with it all messy, babe. And it'll irritate your mother even more." He gave me a wink and a peck on the cheek. "It'll all be over soon."

For the last two weeks, we'd been coming to the courthouse every day, hearing the full extent of her deception and the extreme lengths she'd gone to, to secure her position, but today was it. The jury had made its decision. The members had been deliberating for over thirty hours now, which I guessed was only fair. To give her legal team credit, they'd put up a good fight, feeding confusion and lies to the jury. In my eyes, there was only one way the verdict could go, though.

A knock sounded on the door, and a clerk of the court called us. We were only in the gallery, but as we were family, we'd been given a private room.

Dan took my hand. "Let's go." He kissed Carter's forehead. "It'll be okay."

Then another man stepped up next to me—my father. "Come on, son. It'll be over within just minutes."

Getting the call from my dad had been a surprise, even though I would've sought him out if he hadn't. Dan and Carter had understood my need to meet him alone. It had been a bittersweet reunion. I'd worried it would be awkward, but I hadn't needed to. My father had embraced me, apologizing over and over for allowing her to control our lives. When I'd told him I was with Carter again, he'd beamed, which had quickly turned to amazement when I'd added that Dan was also our boyfriend. After a cough and a splutter, he'd accepted it, happy to know I'd found the loves of my life.

Now he was a welcome part of my family and had visited a few times in the six months running up to this day. Dan and Carter loved him as much as I did.

We filed back into the courtroom. All eyes were on us as we took our seats, hushed voices rolling through the room. Valerie Hawkins sat between her lawyers, their heads together as they whispered. My eyes kept drifting to my mother. How in heaven's name could we share the same DNA? As if she sensed my staring at her, she turned and met my gaze. I held my chin up, upholding the strength and stoicism I'd managed to maintain through the whole trial. Then I lifted Carter's hand, which was clasped tightly in mine, and kissed the back, proving to her that nothing she'd done had kept us apart. The look of disgust and hatred etched over her stony face had me smiling.

Her lawyer whispered something to her as he narrowed his eyes at us, then faced the front again.

As the judge entered the courtroom, we rose, as ordered, then sat silently again. The clerk went through all the protocols. Then the lead juror stood to read out the verdict. I held my breath.

"Guilty."

The air whooshed out, and I slumped back in my chair and buried my face in my hands. The "guilty" for every count of the long list of charges barely registered as I sobbed out my relief.

My father laid a hand on my shoulder and squeezed, giving me the affirmation I needed to believe that it was well and truly over.

"You okay, Arch?" Carter asked, worry lacing his voice.

Lifting my head, I smiled a smile I hadn't found inside me for a long time now—relieved, strong. Unable to hold back my chuckle, I shook my head in wonder, then pulled my dad into a firm embrace. His shoulders were shaking; he had to be filled with the same emotions as I was. As we broke apart, we both had to wipe our eyes.

I turned back to Carter. "Yeah, I'm good. I'm real good." Then I kissed him long and hard.

Flickering candles cast dancing shadows on the walls. As Dan kissed Carter, a sheen of sweat covering their bodies, I couldn't hold back the groan building in my chest. Carter leaned over me, his huge, blown pupils hiding his dark blue irises, his kiss-swollen lips close to mine.

But instead of kissing me, he scooted farther down and licked the crease at the top of my thighs. He traveled up over my body, nipping and biting at my taut skin. Dan followed his lead and tongued my nipple, capturing it between his teeth. He tugged hard, and I arched off the bed. They kept torturing me, biting, licking, sucking, marking me, leaving purple bruises on my skin. Carter reached my chin and scraped his teeth over the stubble, then licked over my lips. I opened for him eagerly. He dipped his tongue inside and flicked against the roof of my mouth. Moaning hard, I thrashed on the bed.

"Carter, hon, please, god. Please get inside me." My hands were fixed above my head, tied to the headboard by a black silk ribbon.

"No, not yet, baby. You're not ready yet." He grinned, then kissed me again, trailing his mouth down my neck to my chest. Dan shifted back down my body, and while my kiss-fogged brain tried to decipher all the feelings coursing through my body, he took the swollen head of my iron-hard dick into his mouth.

"Arrrgh," I cried out as he slid up and down my length. The heat of his mouth as he hollowed his cheeks swallowed me deep into his throat. "No, no. I'm gonna come. Fuck."

Dan popped off my dick and licked down to my balls. He sucked on one, then the other, while he circled my tight pucker with his finger. Christ, I wanted something inside me.

"Please, baby, please. I need you," I keened.

Carter stopped teasing my nipples and moved down the bed. Sliding between my legs, he pushed them up, making me bend my knees. I put my feet flat on the bed, spread wide, exposing my hole. His eyes locked on me.

"You ready now?" he asked, his voice so fucking deep and husky. A burst of precum dripped onto my stomach. As he coated his finger and then his cock, I wiggled my ass. I loved having him inside me. He stroked my hole with two slippery fingers, then pushed one in, pumping in and out. Two or three times before a second finger glided in, the twist and stretch of them relaxing my muscles. I was ready for him, but he added a third. I writhed, squirmed, panted, and cursed him until they slipped out, leaving me empty and bereft.

With the head of his cock pressed against my entrance, he lifted my legs and hooked my feet up on his shoulders. In one long stroke, he entered me, then held still while I adjusted. When I nodded, he went to town. This was what I needed, what I'd been craving. Someone to take me higher, away from all the crap that had happened.

Carter picked up speed as Dan wrapped his hand around my dick, working me at the same pace. I wasn't going to last. The thought hadn't even fully formed before fireworks exploded behind my eyelids, and I erupted. Fuck, it felt good. Streams of my release pelted my stomach. Spent, I opened my eyes. Dan was fisting himself, the tendons in his neck tight as he cried out my name and came. He painted my chest with thick ribbons of cum that mixed with my own.

Carter pounded in me, then went rigid. He pulled out and bombarded me with his cum, over my groin and my chest. A few drops hitting my chin and lip I licked up hungrily. He slumped over me, panting hard. I let my legs fall to the bed as he leaned down and cleaned me, lapping through the mixture of our spunk. When he reached my face, he wiped my chin clean, then pushed his tongue in my mouth. I sucked hard, tasting the flavor of all three of us.

Sitting back on his heels, he burst out laughing. "Fuck. Archer, I needed that as much as you did." Dan joined in as he traced his fingers through the mess on my chest.

"Is someone gonna untie me? I really need a shower." I arched an eyebrow at Dan.

"Yeah, okay. I thought about leaving you like that. I like submissive Archer." He smirked but untied the ribbon. "We might have to keep these, though." He winked.

Carter gently took each arm and massaged the muscles, making me feel cherished.

After a calm shower in which we did nothing but share a few kisses and get ourselves cleaned, we were back in bed. Carter lay with his head on my chest while I was resting in the crook of Dan's shoulder.

Today, I'd been back in the courtroom. My mother got sentenced to a minimum of thirty-five years in prison. The judge didn't waste any time condemning her and ordering her incarceration. I'd needed to see her one more time, and Dan and Carter had understood my need to do this alone, so it was just my father and me in the gallery this time. She stood in front of the judge, a man she had probably socialized with many times, and looked him straight in the eye. Only when he delivered her sentence did her shoulders droop. As the bailiff escorted her out of the room, she turned to us. There was no remorse or apology anywhere in her face or demeanor. Then she was gone. And I'd never see her again. When I'd gotten home, Dan and Carter had been waiting for me, ready to take care of me, and now I was lying in the afterglow.

"It's been more than a year, you know," Carter said quietly. "Since the accident. It was over a year ago. Our lives changed irrevocably, all because of the hatred of one woman. I can't believe how little she cared, how she only ever thought of herself. We lost each other at a time that should've been so special."

"But she didn't win, Carter. We made it. We found each other and more. We have Dan with us too. I've never been happier."

"I know. I wish neither of us had had to go through the pain and grief. She broke me, Archer. She stood in front of me and lied, with no remorse. She told me you were dead and that I had to go. She told you, while you lay in a hospital bed, that I had left you. We'd be married by now, Archer."

"I found our marriage license. I still have it in my wallet," I murmured and kissed his temple.

"So I've been thinking." Carter pushed himself up to a sitting position. "I know we can't get married, the three of us, I mean. But I want us to show our commitment to each other."

Dan and I shifted until we were both sitting up as well. Carter bit his lip, his signature gesture how nervous he was, and I knew what he was going to say.

"Dan, you brought me back to life. In a time when I thought I had nothing to live for, you showed me how to love again. Archer, I thought I'd lost you. I grieved for you. My heart broke for you. Then you came back again. You didn't run from us. Instead, you embraced us and made us whole. So to both of you, I'm asking if you will marry me. I want to show the world who we are. I want us to have a commitment ceremony." Carter took a deep breath and, with his hands twisting the sheet over his lap, looked at us, love shining in his eyes.

"Mallory Carter Halston, I want nothing more than to spend the rest of my life with you. I love you so much. Yes, I will marry you." Dan's voice was shaky as he tangled his fingers in Carter's hair and pressed his mouth to his in a chaste but oh-so-powerful kiss.

Breaking apart, Carter turned to me. His eyes were blazing, the look so potent I gasped. "Carter, we've already chosen to be together forever. This time it seems so much more. I want you and Dan to be with me for as long as I'm still breathing. Yes, I will be proud to stand with you and commit to being together."

"Thank fuck for that because I've done something." Carter blushed, then scooted across the bed and opened the drawer of the nightstand. He took out something I couldn't see. He sat back on his haunches and uncurled his hand.

Three pale blue velvet bags, each tied with a different color ribbon—one gold, one emerald green, and the third a deep sapphire blue. He dropped the gold one in Dan's trembling hand, then gave me the green one and held on to the blue one himself.

"One for each of us," Carter murmured. His body buzzed with nervous exhilaration. "Open them."

My fingers were shaking so much I struggled to undo the bow, but then the ribbon slipped free, and I tipped the bag over in my other hand.

Out fell a heavy platinum ring with in the center a row of three emeralds, so beautifully crafted yet still so masculine. The ring was stunning in its simplicity. I lifted my head at Carter and opened my mouth, but words failed me. Instead, I glanced at Daniel, who had his fingers clenched tightly around the ring, tears falling down his handsome face.

"I chose the gemstones for the color of our eyes, and the inscription inside is the same for all of us." Carter bit his lip again. "Have I got it wrong?" He held out his hand—sapphires for him—as Dan did the same and showed us his amber stones.

I twisted the ring so I could read the inside. "Here With You–Forever." I couldn't hold back anymore. I grabbed Dan and Carter by their hands and dragged them against me. We collapsed back on the bed, and I buried my head in Carter's chest. "You sure know how to make a bad day good. Hell, it's perfect. I love you."

"So we gonna do this?" Carter asked as he held out his ring to me. Then he took Dan's from him. "Give him yours, Arch. We'll put them on each other's fingers at the same time."

We scrabbled back upright again, sat in a triangle, and with shaky hands and huge grins, pushed the rings down the fingers of our forever lovers.

Flopping backward, Carter covered his eyes with his arm, his shoulders shaking. Was he crying? No, the sounds he made were not from crying but from laughing. Deep belly laughs that had him doubling up.

"Baby?" Dan asked when Carter calmed down.

"This wasn't supposed to go like this. I had it all planned. You know, beautiful location, good food, and wine. Definitely with clothes on. This isn't a story we'll share with our kids." Then he dove on us again.

Fifty Three

Dan

It seemed that when Carter decided to do something, he did it quickly. The confidence he had in himself and us left me breathless. He really had found himself again, and making peace with his father had given him his identity back as well as his brother.

For the last four weeks, his focus had been on our commitment ceremony. Finding the perfect location had proved difficult and frustrating. Nothing was right for his very fussy taste, and sitting here now at the end of the day, with a cold beer, Archer and I watched him stomp around the garden.

"Why is it so difficult? We live in one of the most stunning parts of the country, but nothing is right." His hands were in his hair, making it even messier than usual.

"Carter, the last three places were beautiful. You may be looking for something that isn't here." I chuckled when he scowled at me.

"Don't be ridiculous. Of course, the right place is out there," he snapped.

"Okay, honey, tell us what you want. What do you see when you visualize it?" Archer said in a soothing tone.

"I want somewhere simple. I want trees and a large open grass area, and there must be a lake or a pond. Something that would make for a great backdrop but not take away from what we're doing. Big enough to hold a marquee for the reception but still with plenty of outside space." He sighed.

I looked at him pointedly, and he just glared back with his hands on his hips. "What? Why are you looking at me like that?"

"Because, my love, you've just described exactly where you're standing. You just pictured our garden."

He spun around, his arms wide as if embracing the large backyard, with the trees in the background surrounding the freshwater pond.

"Fuck." He turned back to me, his eyes wide. "How did I not see this? Can we have it here?" His face lit up, making my heart beat faster.

"Why are you even asking? This is your home. Do you still think of it as mine?" I frowned. "Carter, you've lived here for nearly a year now."

"Of course, I think of it as home. I was simply questioning if it's feasible. I wasn't asking for permission."

"Then yes, we should have it here. Archer, what do you say?"

"It's perfect, but even though we love it here, do you want to live here forever? Is it going to be big enough for us to raise a family? I was an only child and don't want that for us. I want a horde of kids. If we get married here, we may not ever want to move."

"That's easy. We can rebuild here if we need to. I don't think we'll be rushing into having a family. We have so much to do together, so many places to see. We won't need to worry about the house yet," Carter replied.

"How long do you want to wait?" Archer asked, his voice clipped.

Carter shrugged. "I don't know. I hadn't really thought about it too much. Maybe two or three years."

"Archer, shall we leave this conversation for another time? Let's get back to whether having the ceremony here is something we all want."

"Yes, I think it's perfect, and I know Carter will make it an amazing day for us." Archer looked up at Carter, who was chewing on his bottom lip. "Hey, sugar, come here." He stood and strode to his fiancé. "I'm sorry. We have plenty of time for a family. I'm excited for what the future holds, and children are a part of that. I love you two, and that's what we should be focusing on now."

Carter leaned into Archer's embrace and lifted his face for a kiss. It was a sweet moment I captured on my phone. When they separated, they were both smiling again.

Pocketing my phone, I joined them. "Shall we take a walk around?"

We spend the next hour coming up with ideas, laughing at the outlandish ones Carter had discovered on the Internet. By the time the darkness had closed in, we'd come up with a plan. Now it was time to make it happen.

"Who's going to be your best man?" I asked Carter as we lay in bed.

"I don't know who to ask. I want Kes because he's done so much for me, but I don't know if that will upset Roman."

"You should go with your heart, not with your conscience. If you want Kes, then have him. Roman is back in your life, and it's working well, but I doubt he'll expect you to ask him to be your best man. He'll be thrilled to be included in any way you'll have him." I kissed the top of his head as he rested between my legs, his back against my chest.

Archer lifted his head from the pillow beside us. "I'd go with your heart on this one, honey. Kes will be honored to stand beside you."

"Who are you having, Archer?" Carter asked as he twisted the beautiful ring around on his finger.

"Mason Reynolds. He's not only my old boss, but he's also a good friend. He helped me through so much when I was recovering and let me stay at his place when I couldn't bring myself to stay in our old apartment."

"I always liked Mason. I'll be excited to see him again." Carter stroked his hand down Archer's face softly. "I hate it I wasn't there to help you."

"Everything happens for a reason, and look where we are now. My mother's gone from our lives forever, and we're together despite her." Archer turned his face into Carter's hand and kissed his palm. "Who will you ask, Dan?"

"Conn. We've been friends for a long time."

"Just friends?" Carter smirked.

"Yes, just friends." I slapped him lightly on his arm. "That's all it's been for a long time now. He's a good guy."

Carter nudged me right back. "Yeah, he is. He's been good to Paris. I don't know how serious they are, but they seem happy together."

Archer yawned and pulled the covers up higher, hinting us he needed to sleep. "I've got a full day of meetings tomorrow."

"I've got a wedding to plan." Carter shifted down between us. He kissed Archer, then me.

Fifty Four

Carter

It was all done. After six weeks of planning and organizing, we were ready. The backyard had been transformed into the venue I'd wanted and imagined. By the edge of the water, we'd had a platform with an arbor built. Hundreds of tiny white lights meandered down the path, entwined with jasmine that filled the heat of the evening with its heady fragrance. Rows of chairs covered in midnight-blue fabric with a silver silk bow stood ready for our guests. We'd invited over one hundred people to witness us take our vows.

The marquee was perfect. The finest bone china plates and crystal glasses were laid out on the tables that were decorated with white roses and calla lilies mixed with tall candles. All I needed now was for Dan and Archer to be here. They'd left for the airport this afternoon to collect more of our guests and hadn't seen the final results yet. I was nervous and excited in equal measure. This time tomorrow, we'd be married. Not in the eyes of the law, but our commitment to each other was strong and true and, for me, till death do us part.

Someone walked up behind me. "This is breathtaking, Ry, so perfect. I know who I'll come to when it's my turn." Roman threw his arm casually over my shoulder. "I'm so happy for you, bro."

"I can't believe it's going to happen. I never thought I'd find love again."

"I admit to being surprised and skeptical when you first told me, but after seeing the three of you together, I can see how well you work together, that you've got it right."

"I sure hope so. This cost me a damn fortune." I laughed and took one more look around, then went back inside. The guys would be back anytime now.

"It's good you have a fortune, then." My brother clapped me on the back, chuckling.

It was another fifteen minutes before the cars pulled up in the driveway. Doors slammed, and bursts of laughter drifted to me as I opened the front door.

"Hey," I greeted as Archer grabbed two pieces of luggage from the back of the truck. "You want some help there?" I stepped down from the porch.

"How are you doing, Mallory, or should I call you Carter?" Mason pulled me into one of his bone-crushing hugs. He was six and a half feet and swamped me.

"Mason, it's good to see you. I'm good. Nervous, but I'm good."

"You look good. You've both had such a tough time. It's good to see you happy again."

Dan came around from his car. He'd collected Archer's dad, and both of them had their arms full of bags and suitcases.

"Let's all get inside."

Mason walked behind me, holding his wife's hand. Lucas followed with his wife, Tamsin. These guys looked like they'd just walked off the runway; they were so beautiful. But more importantly, they were some of the kindest and most grounded people I knew.

With all the noise of about five different conversations, I sneaked out of the room to the kitchen, where I made drinks for everyone. Archer and Dan joined me not long after and sandwiched me between them, their mouths finding my mouth and neck. I moaned and melted against them as they deepened their kisses. When we broke apart, my head was spinning, and my legs had gone wobbly.

"Is it ready?" Dan murmured, his mouth still hovering over mine.

"Can we see?" Archer whispered in my ear as he held my hips against his groin.

"It is, and it's amazing." I grabbed their hands and led them out into the garden.

"Wow." Dan stopped walking and stared in awe at my dream.

The night had closed in. The fairy lights shone and twinkled in the garden while on the water, several solar lights floated. This was exactly how I'd wanted them to see it. The ceremony was going to take place at dusk, when the lights would stand out against the darkening sky. I'd bought oil burner lights for tomorrow, but I didn't want to light them tonight and have to refill them again.

The soft electric lights in the marquee highlighted the crystal glass on the tables. To me, it looked perfect, but now it was up to the other grooms to cast their opinions.

Archer stood still, dumbstruck. "Talk to me, Arch. Is it what you wanted?" I spoke quietly, watching his expression.

"I-I don't know what to say. Carter, this is beyond anything I could've envisioned." He tore his gaze away from the garden and took my hands in his, then lifted them to his mouth and kissed them one at a time. Tears glistened, brightening his eyes. As he blinked, a tear broke free and slipped gracefully down his cheek. I tenderly wiped it away with my thumb. "It's perfect, so perfect. I wish we were doing this now."

Dan was as emotional as Archer. The tick in his jaw flickered as he brought himself back under control. "You're a genius, Carter. You've achieved something magical. I can't wait for tomorrow."

Now that I had my men's approval, it was time to relax with our friends and family. When we'd been outside, Kes, East, and Denver had turned up with boxes of pizza. The jokes and laughter took away any nerves trying to creep up on me.

At about ten thirty, our guests started to leave. Archer's dad, my brother, and Marcus were staying with us. Dan's mother and his siblings were all here too. They were staying with friends, catching up with people they hadn't seen for a long time. The others had booked rooms at one of the hotels in town.

Finally, the house was quiet, and we could go to bed.

The house was a hive of activity as more and more guests arrived. With the local catering company, I'd organized an afternoon buffet. Tables had been set up, giving everyone somewhere to sit and eat. Waiters wandered around with mimosas balanced on silver trays. It was going very smoothly.

"I can't believe you've done all this." Archer stood next to me, looking out the bedroom window at our guests below. From this angle, we could spy on them undetected. "It would've been a few friends and some steaks on the grill if you'd left it up to me."

"Is it too much?" Suddenly, I was worried I'd gone too far.

"Fuck, no, this is amazing. I can't wait to be down there." He wrapped his arm around me and pulled me close. "I love you so damn much. This is the beginning of a new chapter in our lives."

As his lips touched mine, I lifted my hands and grasped his head, tangling my fingers in his hair. I moaned as he lazily slid his tongue across the seam of my lips, parting them gently. Our tongues met and slowly stroked against each other while Archer caressed down my back and grabbed my ass. I pushed my hips into him, bumping the solid length of his erection.

"I want you," I murmured against his lips.

"We can't. We said we'd wait until tonight," Archer whispered back.

I ground against him. "I can't wait."

"What are you two up to?" Dan's voice made us break apart.

"Carter's misbehaving." Archer chuckled. "He doesn't want to wait until tonight."

"Aww, poor baby." Dan crowded me from behind, pressing me into Archer. "I promise it'll be worth the wait." He bit on my earlobe, giving it a firm tug, then stepped away. "We need to get showered and dressed. It's nearly time."

"Really?" My heartbeat sped up in double time. "Christ, are we really going to do this?"

Smiling, Archer and Dan each took one of my hands. Dan spoke first. "We are, my love. And if I remember correctly, you asked us. This was your idea, and look what you've achieved." He pointed out to the garden, where the tables had been cleared, but the number of guests seemed to have doubled.

I took a deep breath. "I know. It's just nerves. I'll be fine. Who's going first in the shower?"

"Since when are we taking separate showers?" Archer looked at me, confused.

"Because, Arch, if I get in there with you and we're naked, trust me, there will be fucking." I bumped him with my hip and stepped past him. "I'll go first."

I got the water running, then stripped out of my shorts and pulled off my T-shirt. Stepping under the hot water, I tipped my head back and let the hot water sluice away the stress of the day. I'd keep my vows simple. I only wanted to tell them how much I loved them and that this was forever.

I squeezed a dollop of shampoo into my hand and lathered up my head. Another pair of hands massaging my scalp startled me so much I wobbled on my legs, and I slapped a hand on the tiled wall to keep me from falling.

"You're not supposed to be here," I muttered belligerently. "You said no fucking."

"I'm not fucking you. I'm washing your hair." Archer chortled.

"I hate you. You know that, right?" I snapped at him, but he only laughed harder.

"I know, honey. That's why there are over a hundred people down there waiting for us. They're eager to hear you tell me just how much you hate me." He kissed my shoulder, then tipped my head back under the water.

After my hair was free of soap and bubbles, Archer picked up his body wash.

"C'mon, Car, hurry up."

"Asshole," I grumbled.

"Yeah, and it's yours tonight."

"Too fucking right." I finished washing, grabbed a towel, and dried off. I'd chosen midnight-blue suits for the three of us to wear, with pale-gray shirts and silver-gray ties.

Dan sat on the edge of the bed. The heat in his eyes left me breathless.

"Do you have any fucking idea how much I love you, how much I want to worship you? You're the most amazing man I know."

"I love you too, Dan. You are my world." I brushed my lips over his. "Go take a shower. We've got a wedding to go to."

Thirty minutes later, we were all ready. The knock on the door saved us from an awkward and nervous silence. Our three best men stood in the doorway, each holding two glasses of champagne.

"Don't you three look good." Kes lifted a glass in salute.

"Here, take one of these." Mason handed Archer and me a glass while Conn gave one to Dan. "I'd like to say something if I may?" Mason looked at the three of us as we stood close together. "Archer, you've been my friend for many years now. I've been with you through the hardest times, and now I get to see you at the happiest moment of your life. You've found your soulmates. Having Carter back with you is so wonderful, and to then find love with Dan makes your life complete. I wish you a long and happy life together."

"Okay, let's do this." Kes clapped his hands. "Come on, Carter, let's go." I walked out with him first, followed by Dan and Conn, then Archer and Mason.

The timing couldn't have been better. The sun was just setting, painting the sky in hues of orange and red. The night jasmine gave off their delicious fragrance while the lights were sparkling like fairy stars. We'd chosen "This Is It" by Scott McCreery to walk down the path.

By the time I reached the platform by the lake, butterflies were dancing around in my stomach, and my heart beat as fast as the rhythm of the song. I was so ready for this now. I felt rather than saw Archer and Dan step up next to me. Finally, I turned to our officiate and curled my lips in a smile. Denver gave me a huge grin, and I thought back to how we'd decided he would do this.

"Look, it's not difficult. You just have to stand there and pretend you know what you're doing." I sighed.

We sat in Kes's backyard. Ellie and her friends raced around the garden with Missy, Denver's dog. East tried to get them to keep the noise down, but it really wasn't working.

"You know you can do this." I gave Paris my best puppy dog eyes. "Please?"

"I can't, Car. I love you, dude, but seriously, I've seen your guest list. I can't speak in front of that many people." He looked so apologetic I almost forgave him.

"Who's gonna do this for me, then?" I slapped my hands on my thighs.

"I'll do it."

I looked at Denver with wide eyes. "Really? You'd do this for us?"

"Yeah, why not? I give speeches all the time." He shushed Kes. "I mean, at work, I have to do loads of presentations. I'll just pretend it's as interesting as they are."

"Oh, fuck you." I threw a beer cap at him. "But thanks, Den. That's really cool of you."

"Carter, you're family. It's what we do." He gave me a wink. "And I get a chance to embarrass you in a speech."

And now we were here, standing in front of our family and friends.

"Ladies and gentlemen, please take your seats." Denver's voice traveled over the chatter from our guests. "Thank you. Now I guess you all know why we're dressed up in our finery at the end of a long Saturday. And that's to witness the vows of the three men standing, nervously shaking and about to do a runner, in front of me."

Denver was perfect. I couldn't believe how good he was at settling my nerves.

"So the guys have decided to say a few words to each other. Before we start with Dan, I'm going to do the whole official part and ask if there's anyone here who knows of any lawful impediment as to why these men can't join to speak now or forever hold their peace."

Nervous titter rolled through the rows. As if someone might speak up.

"No? Then over to you, Dan." Denver grinned and stepped back.

Dan took Denver's place and faced us and the audience. He straightened his already immaculate tie, then wiped his hands down his pants. I'd never seen him so nervous. He took a long look at Archer and me and pulled his shoulders back. He was ready.

"You know, I never thought I'd find the day I'd be standing here pledging my love to someone I love with every fragment of my heart. So to be here with two men—and believe me, I pinch myself every morning to believe it's true—has my heart beating fast." He took a deep breath. "Carter, you entered my life as a broken man, a man I wanted to take care of. I wanted to take away your pain, but you're as stubborn as a mule and as difficult to capture. Somehow you let me. You showed your true colors, and my god, how they shine. You let me in, you shared yourself, and you let me love you. For that, I'll be forever grateful, and I will spend every day showing you how much I love you.

"Archer, my best friend, my first lover. The man I owe so much of my confidence to. You came back into my life at a time I didn't realize was so pivotal to all of us. To find out that you and Carter..." He chuckled at this. "Hell, where do I start? Let's just say it got complicated. But then the storm passed, and I suddenly had two men I couldn't live without. Two men I'd do anything for. Two men I wanted to be tied to for the rest of my life. That's why we're here today. Carter, Archer, you're my life. You are my everything. I love you."

Dan stepped back, and I didn't think there was a dry eye in the house. Archer was up next. I regretted saying I'd go last.

"Okay, I'm not sure what to say now. I'm the new boy in town, but not to both Daniel and Carter. We've known each other for a very long time. I knew Carter was the man for me the first time he crashed into me. I just had to find a way to make sure he knew it too. He was a slippery little sucker to begin with. Every time I thought we'd made progress, he would scarper again." A few chuckles rose. Fleetingly, Archer's eyes drifted to the audience, then landed back on me. "I got him, though, but not for long. We both experienced pain and grief in the months that followed, and meeting again wasn't the movie-style reunion you'd think. It was, in fact, as much of a car crash as the one that separated us in the first place." Archer stretched his hand out to me. "I learned I wasn't prepared to let him go again. I found myself with the first man I loved and the last man I had loved, and I was sensible enough to realize that life doesn't throw second chances around. I grabbed it, and I'm never going to let go."

Archer looked at Dan with stars in his eyes. "Dan, my first love, choosing friendship over trying to work a long-distance relationship was one of the best things we've done. Today being the other best thing, but I think our time apart made us good, kind men, hardworking and determined. Things we needed to learn to be the men Carter deserved, both separately and together. Now I don't ever have to live without you. Carter, Dan, you are the men who make my heart beat, the men who give me a reason to be a good man, one worthy of you. I love you."

Oh god, it was my turn. With a smile, Denver gestured to the space in front of him and everyone I knew. I looked past the men I was committing myself to and spoke to my father, telling him all the reasons why I should be with these men.

"I guess I should've thought harder about marrying two lawyers. I'm not sure I can match their speeches, but I'll give it a go. A few years ago, I lost everything when I came out to my family. I had to become a different person. I had to toughen up and trust myself. When I was beginning to stand on my own two feet, I met Archer, but he tried his hardest to sweep me off them again. For a while, he did. We lived a perfect life. We had everything because we had each other. Then life changed, and I lost everything again." I didn't dare look Archer in the eyes because I'd break down. "I found myself in a strange town with no reason to stay except the deep feeling this was a good place. Here, I found a new family, a group of people so real and true it felt like home. I also met a very handsome, very persistent, and very sexy lawyer named Dan." The guests laughed, and I turned to Dan. Bad move. Tears were shining in his eyes. "It was my good friend, Shelley, who told me he was a good guy and I could trust him. So I did, and he is. Dan's one of the world's good people, someone who will always have my back, and it didn't take him long to have my heart too. But then Archer came back, and boy, did he upset the applecart. I'm going to keep this short because you know what happened next, and that's why we're standing here today. Because I love these men. I want to spend the rest of my life with them and grow old with them. I love you."

Denver coughed. "Okay, I think we've cried enough, so I'll just do the formalities. Daniel, do you take Archer and Carter to be your wedded husbands, to have and to hold, from this day forward, for better, for worse, for richer, for poorer, in sickness and in health, until death do you part?"

"I do." Daniel's voice was firm and strong.

As Denver repeated the same words to Archer, my body thrummed as he replied, "I do."

Denver turned to me with a twinkle in his eyes. "You want me to repeat them?"

Grinning, I shook my head and clasped the hand of my almost husbands. "I, Mallory Carter Halston, take thee, Archer Lawrence Hawkins and Daniel David Mortimer, to be my husbands. I promise to love you, care for you, and keep you, in sickness and in health, for as long as we shall live."

"I think it's fair enough to say I can now pronounce you husbands. You may now kiss." Denver moved back as we stepped up to each other, and with our hands wrapped around each other's waists, we kissed. Our three mouths joined together in perfect harmony.

The gentle laughter from the seats behind us made us separate far sooner than we wanted to, but we could wait for now. We had Dan's cabin down by the lake for tonight, and we had forever.

Epilogue

Two years later

Carter

As Archer and Dan walked through the door, the butterflies in my stomach danced and twirled, as they did every time I saw my men. I was thankful for them every day. We had done so many things, traveled to so many amazing places in the last two years, but today was the biggest adventure of them all.

"Hey, baby." Archer dropped a deep kiss on my expectant mouth, moaning when I flicked my tongue over his bottom lip. "Hmmm, have you missed us?"

"Maybe." I sighed.

"My turn." Dan pulled me against his firm chest and claimed my mouth.

We pulled apart, and I led them into the kitchen, where I'd laid out two gift bags on the table. They were hard to miss, but I didn't say anything, and neither did they, although they eyed them as if they were bombs ready to explode. I wanted to laugh, but then my mind drifted back to how we got to this in the first place.

"I want a baby," Archer spoke quietly in the darkness.

"I know you do," I whispered back. I'd been waiting for this conversation. In fact, I'd discussed it with Dan after Kes and his husbands had a baby. We knew we'd made him wait this long while our lives had changed.

"I think it's time too," Dan said.

"Really?" Archer's voice was filled with hope.

"Yes, I saw the way you looked at Kes's new baby. You wanted to snatch him and run." I laughed.

"I wasn't that bad. Okay, maybe I was."

"Do you want a baby or a child? Are we looking for adoption or surrogacy?" I knew what I preferred, but this was Archer's choice.

"I want a baby. I want one we've made." He sounded so excited.

"Then let's do it. We've been selfish enough, Arch, and you've let me do my thing and change my life. I want to do this with you both." My decision to open and run a shelter for LGBTQ teenagers had taken up much of our time. But now that I had all my qualifications and was doing something I loved, it was Archer's turn to get his dream.

"I'll ask Kes for the list of surrogates they had. They had a tough time choosing because they were all great," Archer said. "And, Carter, you haven't been selfish. You did what you needed to do, and it was the right thing. I'm proud of what you've achieved."

It took us six weeks to find our surrogate. We interviewed six women, but the last woman on the list was perfect. Penny was twenty-eight and already had two children of her own. She'd never done this before but had been through the relevant counseling to allow her to make this decision.

The entire process had been quick and easy on our part, but Penny had had to have injections to stimulate her ovaries. Then the doctors had fertilized three eggs, each with our semen. We wouldn't know who the father was, but at least it would be one of us. I really hoped it would be Archer's child. This morning, Penny had called me and confirmed her pregnancy.

A hand landed on my shoulder, pulling me out of my thoughts.

"Are you all right? You were miles away," Archer asked, his voice laced with concern.

"Yeah, I'm more than all right. I've got a surprise for you."

They each picked up one of the bags.

"Do I really want to know what's in here?" Dan asked cautiously.

"Oh, I think you do."

Archer opened his and pulled out a pair of the tiniest socks ever. Next came a onesie that said "I love my daddies."

"We're having a baby?" he asked, his eyes shimmering with tears.

I shook my head. "Nope, we're not having *a* baby."

"Then what's all this for?" He darted his eyes from the onesie in his hand to Dan, who was holding a similar little sleepsuit. "We're having two babies?"

With a roar, he pulled us both in for a hug. "Thank you, Carter, thank you so much," he hiccuped, crying and laughing at the same time.

Here Without You

Three more years on

Archer

I was watching Nixon and Amalie shriek with laughter as their big brother, Cole, chased them around the yard. Their chubby little legs worked hard to keep away from the fourteen-year-old boy who loved them with everything he had.

Cole was Carter's son. A year ago, he'd turned up at the center. Beaten up by his father after being caught kissing another boy, he'd made it to the shelter by hitching a ride. Denver helped at the center and ran a weekly clinic there, but Cole had been in such a bad way, he'd come in to check his injuries. Luckily, he'd gotten away without any broken bones, but his ribs had been badly bruised and painful for a long time.

Carter had known he had to make Cole's life better. He hadn't known what it was about him over the other kids he'd helped, but he'd just felt it. So Cole had become one of us, and he was an amazing kid. Our family was now complete.

Laughter drifted up from behind me, and I turned. Carter and Dan stepped through the kitchen doors.

"Oh, it's all right for some, lazing in the garden all afternoon while the rest of us slave away." Dan chuckled and leaned over the back of the lounger to kiss me.

"I'll make it up to you later," I whispered against his mouth.

"You'd better." He nipped my lip.

Carter sat next to me, stroking my bare arm. "How's your day been?"

"The usual domestic bliss of being a house husband. I've stopped Amalie from trying to water the keyboard in your office because someone didn't lock the door." I scowled at him. "I've done the laundry and cleaned up after the terrible twins, and now I'm letting Cole exhaust them so they go to sleep early and through the night." I gave him a wink.

His eyes dilated as he bit on his bottom lip. "I like the sound of that," he said, his voice husky.

"I thought you might."

My life didn't get better than this.

The End

About JJ Harper

You will normally find her in the living room—typing away—with her wayward puppy, Siddiqi. As a hopeless romantic, JJ dives into her stories, always falling in love with her men, making sure they get the happy-ever-after they deserve, even if they do have to work hard for it.

JJ lives in a small, very quiet, village in Lincolnshire, UK, with her husband and dogs, and spends all daydreaming up stories full of really hot men.

If you like the book, please leave a short review. It really makes a difference to indie authors, and it makes JJ smile.

You can get more information about upcoming releases from JJ on her website: www.jjharper-author.com
or sign up for her newsletter
and in her reader group
Follow
Twitter
Instagram
BookBub

JJ Harper

More by JJ Harper

The Reunion Trilogy

Reunion
Reunited
Elysium
Reunion the Complete Series

The Troy Duology

Troy Into the Light
Troy Out of the Dark
Narrow Margins

Cooper's Ridge Series

Denver's Calling
Here Without You

Standalones

Here Without You

Reckless Behavior
Square One
Trulli, Madly, Deeply (Destination Daddies)

The Redemption Series

Home to You
Family Ties
A Safe heart
A New Chapter

HeavyLoad! Series

My Kind of Man
Your Kind of Man
His Kind of Man
Our Kind of Man
Not Your Boy

BAR 28

Gus
Sawyer
Leo
Beck (coming soon)

Wild Oak Series

Awakening
Reckoning (Coming soon)

Always Series

JJ Harper

Anything, Anytime
Everything, Always

The Finding Me Series (M/F)

Rising Up
My Turn
Missing Pieces
Set to Fall

Printed in Great Britain
by Amazon